The Girl Who Rocked Stars

Daniel Basil Lyle

LylePublishing

Sulphur, Oklahoma

The Girl Who Rocked Stars

Copyright © 2018 by Daniel Basil Lyle

ISBN 978-0-9985937-1-5

Published by LylePublishing
505 W. 12th Street, Sulphur, OK 73086
(www.LylePublishing.com)

Printed by CreateSpace, an Amazon.com company. Available from Amazon.com and other retail outlets. Also available as an ebook on Kindle and other devices.

LCED08082019

DISCLAIMER and FORWARD

Although this book draws heavily from some of the author's own experiences, all characters are fictitious. Though based in actual events, the words and actions of historical figures presented in this story are fictionalized. This book is a sequel to "*The Girl Who Wrangled Asteroids*," beginning where that book left off.

Chapter 1

<u>**ALBUM SIX, WORLD TOUR**</u>

__Soothe my soul__, oh blessed savior
When my way grows dark and cold
When I'm hurt and can't keep going
Lift my feet and make me whole...

One more step oh Lord, I ask
Keep me on the noble path
I am slow and tired and weary
Oh, give me strength to believe!

Recharge my spirit with kindness
Help me see past Negatives
Put my hands to work in actions
Grasping, using Positives...

One more step oh Lord, I ask
Keep me on the noble path
I am slow and tired and weary
Oh, give me strength to believe!

The Suzette Anthology, Lyrics #1

If you're reading this, I'm dead.

I wanted my life to be a fairy tale. It was. But it didn't end up as I or anyone else expected...

—I made everything a stinking mess!

I'm including this document with my will, instructing my attorney to have it decoded (I'll explain later) and released to the world following my execution. You deserve to know why I did what I did, since what I did directly affected your life and health. Why I couldn't tell you this story earlier or use it in my defense at my trial will become obvious.

Yes, this is both my official autobiography and final confession.

I admit to what I consider my biggest crime: causing *music* to *vanish* from the world!

I'm sorry! And for all the rest, well...you'll just have to decide for yourself. But there's nothing I can do now except accept my punishment. What's done is done.

So why should you want to hear my story?

I guess it depends on what *you* want...right?

Well, what the hell *do* you exactly want?

Ok. If you ever wanted to know the intimate, juicy life details of a world-famous pop Superstar, I'm gonna let it all hang out. My story has it all: *sex, drugs, intrigue, mystery, time-travel, space aliens,* and lots of *hardcore rock & roll!* Hey! I'm not proud of my wild behavior, but if laying out all the gory details gets you to read this, then fine. But I'm actually not writing this for you. Neither am I making excuses, trying to convince you I'm some noble artist fighting for her craft against the norms of society. I'm making this confession totally selfishly. I just need to clear my conscience...and maybe in the process find out what the hell *I* truly want.

God, I'm a mess...

Yes, I know I'm rambling. I'll get to the "juicy" story in a sec'. Writing this introduction is a bitch. I'm trying to get my head on straight, to give you the whole, ugly truth!

Not that it matters much. In the end, we're all royally screwed, aren't we?

You see—as I type on this old laptop my lawyer brought me—I'm sitting here in a maximum security cell on death row. I'm (impatiently) waiting to be marched in front of an old-fashioned firing squad. Why not the more "humane" lethal injection? Well, my crimes were so outrageous, so beyond anything previously committed in the history of mankind, the public (you) demanded I be riddled with bullets.

I'm not bitter! Please forgive me—if not my crimes then for my bad writing. I'm under a lot of pressure here, time-constraints and such.

Also, I admit I'm a little short-tempered. My sentence should be carried out any day now. I just want to get it over with. Hopefully I'll have time to finish this testament. If not, then screw it.

My guards have been decent to me, though they've no reason to be civil. They haven't interfered with my frantic typing, nor restricted my lawyer's access. I guess it's just their professional pride in doing a good job no matter who they're guarding. It's obvious from their expressions that they hate me as much as anyone else. They'll be glad to get rid of my sorry ass.

Plus, the State will be relieved I finally absolved them of any guilt in the terrible things that happened to our world. I'm sure that's why they allowed me the laptop and aren't interfering with my writing. My confession will confirm that I—and only I—am to blame. I'm sure that will help quell the world-wide riots still threatening to topple local governments [they don't allow me Internet connection, but my lawyer tells me what's happening out there]. So I'm confident the authorities will not suppress this "gorography" (gory biography, hah!) but allow my story to see the light of day.

I suppose a few people—maybe even you—might feel a tiny bit of sympathy for me. But don't let it bother you. I don't need your pity.

Yes, there have been a few half-hearted attempts to get stays of my execution, but those didn't come from me. I'm not fighting my sentence. The stays are just automatic parts of our "humane" system to go the "extra mile" to not execute innocent people. Well, that certainly doesn't apply to me. I freely admit to "crimes against humanity." Yes, I did it all! I *ripped apart* the fabric of society, *condemned* billions to a drab and weary existence, directly *injured* millions in the savage riots, and—worst of all—directly and brutally *killed* people I loved the most.

Even sweet Scotty, who stood by me to the very end, I *stabbed* in his back...

Sorry, I had to pause for a fit of crying. I'm back in control now, back to telling my story.

Oh, you think you remember it all, do you? I should just get on to telling you the juicy stuff? Sorry, I was just summarizing for any kids in the far future that might get curious about me and read this "swan song" of a disgraced, dethroned teenaged Diva. But there's a lot more to my sad odyssey than the official newscasts revealed.

You probably saw my televised trial. I sat there stoically at the defendant table, saying nothing. I didn't even reply to questions from the Judge, earning numerous "contempt of court" penalties added onto my sentence [not that they mattered much; dead can't be deader]. I maintained a stoic silence, a blank look fixed upon my pretty little face.

Yes, you thought I was a cold-blooded killer, untouched by her proven atrocities, right? Actually, my uncaring attitude was the only defense left to me. It was a wall I put up against the *naked hatred* radiated at me from everyone in the court. After all, I was obviously guilty. If I'd opened my mouth to say anything...well, then instead of my just being sentenced to death, I'd have been *torn apart* right there on the spot! My public defender did her best, of course, but all she could claim was insanity. She was right. I *was* driven mad by what happened. But, still, that's no excuse for what I did.

Denying humanity a "quantum leap" in its evolution was debatable as to its criminality.

But t*aking music out of the world, forever,* was unforgiveable!

Look, let me make it plain—I'm *not* asking for your forgiveness. I deserve to die. I'm breaking my silence at this late date to put on the record the extreme *extenuating circumstances.* You can still hate me! Christ, even *I* hate me. But now, maybe, you'll join those who feel just the tiniest, wee bit of *understanding.*

After all, like any true artist, I'm only an extension of *you.* I spent my short life thrashing about trying to find what I wanted. Little did I know when I seemingly had it in my hands I'd piss it all away. Yep, I had what everyone thinks they want: *fame, fortune,* and *power!* But I wanted even more. This is the story of my search for that mysterious missing factor.

So, we're back to the start of my thesis: What do *you* want?

At the core of your being, do you *also* lust for fame, fortune, and power? Well, I'm going to show you what happens when you get it all.

Or is your deepest motivation—right this very moment—just to hear and see me *suffer?*

If so, you're going to get it. But surely *revenge* is a stunted objective, isn't it? Well, maybe not for you...but for me it sucks

Wow, that's a sobering thought, huh? Maybe it'll make you pause and take a glance at what I'm writing, correct? Then again maybe my "preaching" will just make you slam this book shut. But if you can't share in the blame at least a little bit—as a likewise fallible human— then to *bloody hell* with you! Go on and mindlessly bumble through life: eating, excreting, and screwing without regard to the wider Universe around you! Go on then! Live your "unexamined" life until you trip and fall into your own open grave! Go on and just be a smart animal! Or, open your mind just a crack and let me in to...

Oh, Jesus Christ—did I really write all of that trash? I'm so sorry! I guess the pressure's getting to me. I didn't mean to go "philosophical" on you. That's not like me. In my career I tried to *entertain* people, not trap or confuse them.

I won't blame you if you delete this e-book, or toss the print version into the trash...

[I had to take another break. My hands were shaking so bad I couldn't continue typing. I'm composed now, determined to accomplish this last task.]

What, still here after my little rant? Alright then, let's get on with it. Let's go back to the very beginning, when my golden life started falling to pieces...

You see, the very first time I felt like *quitting* and walking away for good was midway through my "*Suzette Kingly's Album Six World Tour.*"

I'd been discouraged before, of course (what musician isn't?) but nothing like this. This was bone-crushing. And I should have done it! I should have just said: "*Screw* it all, screw *you*, and screw the *horse* you rode in on!"...and then just walked away! But I couldn't. Why?— because I was a God-damned *coward*.

And even more than allowing my juvenile fears to control me, I was an *addict*—not yet to drugs but to *fame, power*, and (above all)

money. And although staying was causing me ever-escalating pain, the *agony* of abandoning my "goodies" would have been far greater.

Yep, Jesus nailed it, didn't he? *"The root of all evil is the love of money."* I started out like most musicians: a starving artist doing the craft for its beauty and power to move people. But in the end I sold my soul to the Devil for a measly little bowl of stew.

[That's a Bible story, by the way. Look it up.]

Well then, the *Hollywood* "bowl" meal was rather substantial, *hah!* ...but all the rest was ephemeral: substantial today and vanished tomorrow.

If I'd just accepted my fate, then none of the terrible things that subsequently happened would have occurred. Sure, I'd still be vilified and hated, but at least the world would be intact.

[Alright then, girl, stop whining! Jesus Christ, I've got to get this moaning and groaning under control. I can't have my legacy be crying like a little bitch. I have to stand up for myself!]

You want to hear what *really* happened, right—not just the official version? Ok, then, let's get back to my story...

As I just mentioned, we were at the *Hollywood Bowl* for a run of ten performances. But I literally knew in my guts I couldn't make it through even one more performance, let alone ten. I had already figuratively climbed Mount Everest, made it to the peak, started back down, tripped, fell, and discovered myself dangling above a 10,000-foot drop. Without the strength to climb back up the rope there was but one option: let loose and fall.

I could have walked away right then, saving myself, you, and the world from incredible disaster. Instead, I started on an odyssey that would take me into the *past*, the *future*, and even to *other worlds*. Yes, I know that may sound like a wonderful "science-fiction" movie. And, yes, you're gonna have your mind blown when you hear all the details. But because of what I did on that epic journey, my wonderful, beautiful *music* wound up doing the exact *opposite* to what I intended: *crippling* society and *killing* those I loved the most.

[Jesus Christ—there I go complaining again. I'm sorry about that. But it feels so good to finally let it all out.]

It began that very evening.

Of course I didn't know about the world-shaking consequences facing me as I *collapsed* while gowning up for yet another grueling performance.

"I can't do it tonight," I whispered, physically unable to rise up out of the make-up chair.

"Would some water help you, Ms. Kingly?" a young aid asked me, holding out a glass. I didn't recognize her. She must be new. She was a perky sort with her face half-hidden under a big baseball hat, wearing dark eyeglasses.

I was trembling, nauseous, and feverish.

"No!" I snapped at her, batting the glass to the side.

It fell and shattered into a thousand pieces.

"You know I only drink bottled water!" I yelled to no one in particular. "Now there's broken glass all over the floor," I moaned.

The petite girl looked like she was going to melt into the floor, trembling with fear.

"Oh...I'm sorry," I gulped, embarrassed at my uncharacteristic rudeness. My vision was blurring. I was having trouble breathing, raggedly gasping for air.

"No problem, Ms. Kingly," she said, backing off. "I'll get a dustpan to clean up the glass shards and find you some..."

To make matters even worse, I cut loose a prolonged, noisy *fart*.

Brrrrrrrrrpppppppppptoooooooeeeeeee...

"Oh, honey, that was a bad one," my long-time makeup artist, Eun Jung gasped, wrinkling his nose in disgust.

He was a slender, elegant man of Korean ancestry, now with bags under his slanted eyes. His brown-gray hair was fashionably wavy on the top of his head, shaved on the sides. He'd been with me from the start and knew all my quirks. He was dressed in a blue silk shirt and velvety purple pantaloons.

"Sorry," I whispered, squirming uncomfortably. "I couldn't help it."

"Is your IBS acting up again?" he asked me kindly.

"No...it's the flu or something...I'm sick."

"Oh, girl, it's your IBS. You know your 'irritable bowel syndrome' makes you miserable, especially when you're all agitated before a performance. When that new girl gets back, drink a full bottle of water.

You're dehydrated. Your poor intestines are all clogged up. You'll be ok onstage if you can just hold in those awful farts. Those are *lethal.*"

"No...it's more than just my IBS."

Even fingering my *lucky charm marbles* I always carried in my innermost pocket didn't help me. I still felt awful. Yes, I knew my stress went right to my guts, causing me painful bloating, diarrhea, constipation, and gas—separately or all together.

But it was even worse than that. I felt like I'd been run over by a truck.

My makeup and initial costuming were complete. A *bright blond bushy wig* sat solidly on my plastered-down bald cap. My face was painted *porcelain white*, my lips stained *ruby red*, my forehead adorned with *rubbery fake eyebrows*, and my *black eyelashes* pasted so far out on my eyelids it was hard to see past them.

My opening getup was complete. I was transformed from a nineteen year old, blond, every-day girl into a sexy, teenaged *Alice-in-Wonderland* character. I had on black striped leggings up to my calves, a very short blue dress down to the bottom of my butt, frilly lace white panties clearly visible at my crotch, puffy transparent sleeves, and a blue apron hanging from my neck festooned with big sparkling jewels.

It was the first costume of *nine* that would occur throughout the concert. Just making the changes on cue was a brutal physical chore, not even counting the dance numbers and constant, fervent singing. How could I do all that if I couldn't even get out of the makeup chair?

I slumped down face-first on the table, one arm sweeping the jars and brushes off the side onto the floor.

As they "clanked" and "cracked," Eun gasped but didn't admonish me. He knew me better than I knew me. Normally he would have protested at my "acting out," but not tonight. Instead he frantically phoned for my manager.

—who came storming into the room, a scowl on her dark-skinned face.

I wearily looked up at her.

"I've...had...it," I gasped. "Honestly, Darlene...I can't do it anymore."

The young aid returned, tentatively holding out a plastic bottle of water. I grimaced, waving her away. She stood discretely in a corner, awaiting further directions.

"Sure you can, Suzette," Darlene insisted, her intense black eyes drilling into my own. Then she fanned a hand in front of her nose. "Oh, God—what's that smell?"

"I farted," I admitted, my voice trembling. "I'm sick."

She was an older, white-haired, buzz-cut African-American woman who took no nonsense from anyone. She was a hard-hitting professional. She had already handled a number of "superstars' in her long career before she took me on. Though she treated me respectfully, she had a domineering attitude that always intimidated me. She was famous for wringing millions from her Talent then casting them aside when their popularity dipped. That hadn't happened to me...yet. Hooking up with her had been the lucky break of my life, propelling me to world-wide stardom. Presently I was the *most famous, richest teen Superstar* on the entire planet! But I knew at nineteen I was getting a bit "long-in-the-tooth." Unless I kept Darlene happy, my career could take an instant tumble.

"I've got a fever," I moaned.

"But the doc gave you stronger meds today, right?"

"It's just antibiotics and anti-inflammatories."

"There's an old saying, kid. You know it as well as me: '*The show must go on!*'"

"Not if I'm dead," I peevishly whispered.

"Look, Suzette," she sighed, sitting down next to me, "we're sold out tonight. This is the first performance of our *Album Six World Tour* that really counts, here in America. There are *18,000* of your fans out there. You can't let them down! They've got all your recordings. But to get them to buy even more, they need to hear you *live!*"

I was beyond tired. I was thoroughly exhausted. It wasn't just my IBS or whatever bug I'd caught. We'd already toured through all the major countries of Europe. Before that we'd spent two months in Asia. At first it was like any of my previous, shorter tours—a real "high" to get out and perform my new album for hordes of adoring fans. But now my performances (for the first time ever) had devolved into just a "job": slogging through the same words and dance-numbers over and over and over. Maybe it was the extended length of this tour. Previously, they'd gone no longer than three months, tops. This one was scheduled for a full *nine* months. After the first three months it became incredibly boring. Then it became drudgery. And finally, at six months, it became torture.

"To hell with their needs," I whispered, "You'll just have to cancel."

I laid my painted head down in the middle of the scattered makeup tins. "Tell them I'm sick. I *am* bloody well sick!"

I wasn't just making excuses. My statement was true. I *had* been fighting the flu for a couple weeks, doggedly taking antihistamines and decongestants while struggling to keep my voice from crumbling. But by then I should have started getting better. Instead I was getting worse. A doctor had just prescribed me broad-spectrum antibiotics on top of my anti-inflammatories. He said I had pneumonia. He ordered me to take a hiatus, do nothing for a month, allowing my body to heal. Of course I couldn't do that. I had obligations. I was *booked*, damn it! I *was* determined to "soldier" through...but there's a limit as to what flesh and blood can endure. I had my *own* needs.

"Come on, Suzette—you were alright the last couple days. The rehearsal this afternoon went ok, didn't it?" Darlene needled me.

"Yes," I reluctantly admitted.

We'd started setting up three days ago at the Hollywood Bowl. I was excited to be back for the last segment of our World Tour in the good old U.S.A., especially at such an iconic venue. It was nestled in a natural hillside concave located in the Hollywood Hills outside Los Angeles, California. It was a historic site, dating from 1919. A giant half-shell covered the huge stage, in front of which were arrayed many tiers of ascending seats. Large fixed screens, "Jumbotrons", were located to each side of the shell. They provided close-ups of the performers, who'd otherwise be tiny when viewed from most of the seats. Another set of giant screens further back assured that even the most distant fans could see everything. The design of the enclosed half-shell plus the natural acoustics of the concave hillside provided spectacular resonance and amplification.

Many famous groups had performed there. Normally I'd be humbled and honored to be included in that august group. But now it was just a gigantic, painful chore.

Forcing myself out of my sickbed I'd overseen installation of all the props, mechanisms, instruments, electronics, pyrotechnics, and high-wire cables. Then we rehearsed selected bits, insuring that all the musicians and performers knew their cues and marks on the (to us) new stage. It went well. I felt good, performing well even though I was juiced to my gills on antihistamines and decongestants. But then as evening set in and our opening night performance loomed I crashed. That was when my assistants called in a physician to examine me, discovering the surging pneumonia. But despite his orders I was determined to keep on, at all costs.

But I'd hit a wall. To quote the Bible, "The spirit is willing but the flesh is weak."

Yet Darlene was unconvinced. Was she right? Was I just making excuses?

"So what's the problem? You've done this hundreds of times before."

"Ok..."

I took a deep breath, tried to stand up, then collapsed back down. My legs just wouldn't hold me up. I endured a fit of coughing before getting my breathing under control. Then I just *wheezed* as I tried to speak.

If I couldn't even talk, how could anyone expect me to sing for two hours straight?

Darlene seemed to finally realize I wasn't joking or exaggerating.

"Look, just get through tonight, Suzette...here, take this. It'll perk you up."

She put a little blue pill in my hand.

Then she motioned to the nervously standing aid who handed her the plastic bottle of water. Darlene twisted open the cap and sat the bottle on the table in front of my nose.

Hah! Just like Alice. One pill made her big. The other pill made her small. Which one was this?

"What's in it?" I suspiciously asked, not wanting to enflame my guts further with either water or some suspicious pill.

"It's just a harmless stimulant...no worse than caffeine. I take them all the time myself. I've a tough job also, Suzette. This tour's way bigger, in every way, than anything I've ever attempted before. You're not the only person in the troupe hanging on by a thread. I'm just as tired as you."

"I've already drunk a ton of coffee today and..."

"This is much better. It'll give you strength to..."

"You know I hate pills," I rudely interrupted her.

"You took what the doc gave you, right? These are no different than..."

"Bull crap! This is *drugs!*"

She sighed deeply, putting a firm hand on my trembling shoulder. For a woman in her sixties he could be tender when needed. Since my Mom—despite my generous financial support of her pet projects—refused to accompany my tours or even attend any of my concerts, Darlene had taken on the role of a mother-figure. I was trying hard not to cry in relief at her unexpected kind gesture. I wasn't a kid anymore. I'd just turned nineteen. I'd just gotten my GRD after five years of "home schooling" all done in my "spare time" on the road. I'd finally gotten past the hell of high school classes. I was an adult!

But I felt just like a guilty little kid trying to get out of taking a tough test at school because I "didn't feel well."

"Look, if you make it through tonight we can cancel the next performance," Darlene's sharp voice penetrated the haze around me. "I promise you'll get a break."

"Hah...you've said that before, but..."

"You know our financial situation, Suzette. This is the 'break-even' point. After tonight it's all profit. It's cost us a fortune to put on this world-class tour. And tonight we're also paying for a *full orchestra* to back us up. Having to refund the gate tickets could throw us into bankruptcy. I won't be able to meet the payroll. And that's not even mentioning the *IMAX filming* being done tonight for a feature-length 3D documentary and a virtual reality game that..."

"I know! I know!"

"There's a lot on the line tonight, is what I'm saying," Arlene relentlessly continued. "To put on this giant tour, every asset we've got had to be leveraged—including your own personal wealth."

Hauling dozens of large trailer-equivalents of props, electronics, and instruments around the world was a mammoth undertaking. Plus there were the salaries of hundreds of roadies and extras, plus dozens of key performers...

—and my *personal assets?* That shocked me. Sure, Darlene slid a lot of contracts and agreements and bills under my nose to sign, without time for me to read them. I just had to trust her. But I never thought that my hard-won millions, properties, and holdings might be on the line.

I suddenly realized I should have diversified more, put pots of money aside for the inevitable "rainy day." If I'd kept back only a fraction of what I'd donated to charitable causes I'd be set for life. Even my own ungrateful mother got *millions* from me while I was now apparently facing financial ruin!

I suddenly realized that the present situation was not just embarrassing, but *desperate.*

It wasn't just the audience's needs or the backer's needs. *My* needs were in jeopardy too!

"And it's not just our present and future revenues," the hard-voiced woman relentlessly continued. "Like I said, your *fans* are out there waiting for you. You're onstage in twenty minutes. For God's sake, Suzette—you *can't* let them down! Don't you love them?"

Ah, man, that was hitting below the belt. She knew how I luxuriated in their adoration. They were the best "drug" of all, which I craved more than anything.

"I don't want to let anyone down, but..." I peevishly tried to argue.

"Look, just try the pill, Suzette. I swear it won't hurt you. If it doesn't perk you up in the next couple minutes, then I'll personally go onstage and announce that you collapsed. Maybe we won't get lynched or bankrupted if they think you're dying and..."

"Well..."

She let me think about it for a moment. Then she pointedly lifted up and thumped down the bottle of water on the tabletop.

"Look, you need some hydration whether you take more 'medication' or not. We can't have you farting onstage! The mikes will pick it up and the family audience out there will hear it as the ultimate insult!"

"Right...of course I'd never want that to happen. Thanks, Darlene," I gasped, again tearing up. In my ragged condition the smallest kindness had me teetering on the edge of a complete breakdown.

"Just try the pill, Suzy. Just this once! Look, I've got to go see about the pyros. There's some last minute problem with the local inspectors and police. I'll see you out there...or not! Whatever you decide, you know I'll handle it. I'm here for you, kid—you're number one."

Nice pep talk. But it fell short. I knew she'd drop me without hesitation if the receipts from my current album took a nosedive. But for the moment, out of necessity, she was on my side.

"The pyros are...?"

"Don't worry about it!"

"But...police? Is there some problem with the crowd?"

"It's nothing! I've got to go."

I blearily watched her race out of the room. Time was short. She was right. I had to make a decision. Terrible pressures were forcing me out onto the stage—obligations to my colleagues, my fans, and my own finances. For God's sake, I was no longer a solo writer-musician living in a one-room studio apartment. I had a mansion, a private jet, and a yacht to finance. I had household servants to pay. Plus I also had expensive bodyguards, chauffeurs, cooks, sea captains, accountants, publicists, editors, recording studios, collaborators, and *on and on and on!*

Yes, I was no longer a singer/songwriter—I was a franchise.

And now the Tour finally had momentum. All our routines and stage-mechanisms had been "stress-tested" throughout Asia and Europe. The remaining three months of the tour, all located in the continental U.S.A., without the huge costs of traveling out-of-country or rejiggering the now-optimized sets, would be hugely profitable. Plus Darlene was right. I couldn't let my fans down. But...even beyond my physical limitations there was a line beyond which I'd *sworn* I wouldn't go.

I was determined to *not* become just another drug-addicted has-been once-great performer.

But...

Just take the little pill! It'll be just this one time. After all, this is an emergency!—I sternly ordered myself.

But I knew better. I'd promised my mother years ago I wouldn't become one of those drug-addicted Divas spiraling down into their own personal hells. I wasn't going to end up like my heroine, Janis Joplin, dead at age 27 from a heroin overdose. I was going to be one of those rare superstars that "made" it, sustainably drifting along on a cloud of pure creativity, *wahoo!* But being a pop Icon meant a lot more than just strumming chords in a nightclub belting out my teen-age-angst tunes. It required brutal, mind-numbing, "W-O-R-K" *work!*

To stay on top meant juggling heavy responsibilities: running a mega-business, managing a troupe of unruly characters, performing a "circus act" night after night, and still finding time to write new stuff. Discovering the next "catch" that kept one's music on the "cutting edge" instead of sliding into the oblivion of recently recorded, forgotten history was itself a mind-numbing chore.

"What do you think, Eun?" I asked my old friend, woozily lifting my head up from the tabletop.

He shrugged. He was gruff as a bulldog. But he'd always given me good advice whenever needed.

"It's probably just Amphetamine, dearie," his deep voice penetrated my throbbing skull, "but you never know unless it comes direct from a pharmacy. You're always taking a chance when you consume street-swag, no matter who gives it to you."

"So it's 'meth'?"

"No, honey," Eun sighed, speaking slowly as if to a little child. "If Darlene takes them they're probably just plain amphetamines. She's right. They increase your ability to focus while juicing you up metabolically. They're often prescribed for ADHD or weight loss and..."

"Do you take them?"

"Huh...what haven't I taken? I did do some meth when I was younger. It almost killed me. It's a more potent form of regular amphetamine."

"Will I get addicted?"

"Just one pill, probably not, but..."

"Damn it!" I grimaced, impulsively tossing the blue pill in my mouth and gulping it down with half the bottle of water.

I lapsed into yet another coughing fit as the pill cut across my enflamed throat. I nearly vomited it back up.

"You ok, honey?" he asked, concerned.

But somehow I kept it down, sipping studiously at the remaining water in the plastic bottle. I didn't expect much from the pill. That was the first time I ever did any "drugs" other than occasionally required flu or cold medications. I expected the worse. So I was totally shocked to find it was *heavenly*.

Chapter 2

THE LAST CONCERT

My puppy is my pal
My kitty is my Queen
My doggy makes me happy
My cat lets me please her
So why do I love them both
Instead of one or the other
You want to know the truth?
I'm a panther raised by wolves!

Or (hee hee)...
My puppy is my pal
He's not a big fat cow
My kitty is my Queen
She's skinny as a dream
My doggy makes me happy
My cat lets me please her
So why do I love them both
Instead of one or the other?
It's a fun-ny mys-ter-y!
The Suzette Anthology, Lyrics 2

"SUZ...*ETTE!* SUZ...*ETTE!* SUZ...*ETTE!*" the thundering chant *vibrated* the closed-in walls surrounding me.

I was wobbly standing upright in a small, enclosed lift located beneath the stage of the Hollywood Bowl. In seconds I'd be hoisted up to dramatically emerge into an elaborate mushroom jungle. The au-

17

dience was restless. The opening band had already departed the stage. I was ten minutes behind schedule, still trying to recover from my prior collapse. It was now or never to start the concert-proper.

"You ready?" Sam Greene, my overweight stage manager nervously asked, looking very worried. He was a long time veteran of mammoth road productions and was well aware of the pressure that Stars endured. It was no secret to the roadies that I was sick and getting weaker each performance.

He was frowning, one chubby hand scratching his stubbly chin while the other caressed a big red button that would launch the lift upward.

I swallowed, closed my eyes, opened them wide so I could see past the bush of fake eye lashes, slowly shifted up the edges of my mouth, dropped my lower lip, and planted a big "stage smile" on my painted face.

"Let's do it," I nodded, holding the garish grin in place.

Yes, it was a remarkable act of courage in my weakened state to attempt the two hour, physically grueling performance. But I wasn't near as brave as I made myself out to be. Truthfully, I was riding an amphetamine *high:* alert, energetic, enthusiastic, and happy. Yes, I was still feverish, clogged up, and in pain...but all that retreated from me. It was like I'd leapt upward from a muddy swamp into the beautiful blue sky! Sure, the ground was still there beneath me, but for the moment I was floating on fluffy clouds.

Maybe it was because I'd never taken drugs before. But the feeling of well-being and boundless energy was amazing. If I'd known little blue pills could do this for me I would have been taking them before every concert.

I tightly clutched the black mike in my hand, flipping the bottom switch to "on." A green, blinking light appeared on its side, telling me it was live.

—and of course there was the *natural adrenaline rush* I always got before going onstage. Hearing the roar of the crowd alone was almost better than any drug. Despite my prior funk, once I got out there I knew I'd be ok.

"Alright, then, I'm counting down, Ms. Kingly," Sam gruffly informed me, fingering his mike so the other performers were in sync with the launch. "Alice is *up*—in *five... four... three... two...*"

I bent my knees as I was *launched* skyward, emerging into the giant, multi-colored mushroom forest. My rock band, *Strinjet*, blasted out the opening chords as a *bright white searchlight* caught me in midair. I fell into the arms of my scantily clad male dancers.

"*Daddy's home!*" I belted out the first words to my opening song.

The audience of 18,000 fans *erupted* at the sight of my Alice-In-Wonderland character landing then striding out onto the runway that protruded from the huge stage. The giant mushrooms behind me swayed back and forth erotically. The male dancers all bowed down to me...

"DADDY'S HOME!" the audience roared back at me, drowning out my amplified words.

Yes, I knew it didn't make any sense. But emotionally I was connecting with my grade-school-to-high-school aged fans, mostly young girls. My character embodied the virginal, innocent, little-girl, runaway Alice surrounded by sweating male hunks and phallic giant mushrooms. It set all their little hearts to swooning and their crotches to creaming. I always felt a bit guilty playing on their hormonally induced emotions, but by *Album Six* I considered that to be my main job. I was no longer just a sweet voice on a heart-gripping album mirroring their teenaged angst. I'd become, for better or worse, the physical embodiment of their romantic and erotic dreams.

"*You're my love, you're my angel...*"

"YOU'RE MY LOVE, YOU'RE MY ANGEL..." the crowd roared back into the inserted pause of my adaptation of Shep & The Limelite's classic "doo wop" 1961 song "Daddy's Home."

I and my dancers swayed and ran, zipping in and out of the white stalks of the looming mushrooms.

"*You're the girl of my dreams...*"

"YOU'RE THE GIRL OF MY DREAMS..."

Fireworks blasted overhead as I now walked slowly back to the runway, soulfully launching into my own inserted lyrics of a sad, plain, unappreciated girl waiting on her "soulmate" to magically appear.

Hah. Fat chance...

I'd started out just like them, you see. Actually, I *was* them. I was the nerdy little girl playing ancient *doo wop* songs and swooning to their magical lyrics. I was the grade school "good" girl who regularly attended church, said her prayers, and read the Bible. I was the sweet soprano singing with her parents and little brother in their own gospel band. But we were actually good! We did gigs all around the local area. We even put out a couple Christian-rock records that did well on the Gospel charts. And, like all young girls, I yearned for romance beyond a pat on the head from a platonic Jesus.

And then...it happened. A terrible tragedy hit my family.

Not able to stand the pain, at age sixteen I ran away to Nashville, determined to become a country-western star. I lied about my age, waited on tables in the day, while strumming my guitar at night in whatever open-mike slots I could find.

Barely legal for consensual sex, with a strong church upbringing, and an unrealistic sense of my own inflated worth, I had trouble getting boyfriends. I had a few I liked. But as soon as they tried to get into my pants I moved on. Sure, I knew I was being weird. Everyone else around me was cohabitating with their boy-or-girlfriends, whether of "legal" age or not. But I had those same damn illusions of finding my "soulmate." I thought I needed a lifelong lover who would truly "understand" and support me.

Hah. The guys I dealt with at the restaurants and bars couldn't see beyond the end of their dicks. All they wanted was a warm vessel to receive their sperm before compliantly hopping up to get them another fresh beer. I just wasn't attracted to that type of person. I was looking for a kindhearted, long-thinking, compassionate fellow *successful* artist.

Yep, a "super-sugar-daddy"!

My point is I knew all about the dreams and fantasies of my mostly young-girl audience. I lived them out, as did thousands of other would-be teen stars who barely surviving waiting tables while scribbling down whiney tunes destined to go nowhere. Likewise, I'd been going nowhere fast, though the local drunks I performed for on "open-mike" nights seemed to like me a lot. I guess alcohol makes any cute girl's wailings attractive. But, amazingly, Darlene happened to see me at a club, steered me to an innovative record producer, helped me put out my first album, super-charged my online social platform—and it was nothing but *up* from there! I put out a frenetic two albums a year, each more successful than the last.

My first three albums were true creative genius. After that, though, the quality went down. But who the hell cared as long as each one sold in the tens of millions? By my *Album Six* World Tour I'd fallen back to reviving ancient "doo wop" classics. Surprisingly, the critics still acclaimed my genius: lauding me for "infusing new life into a forgotten genre." In reality I was grasping for straws, my creative muse fast fading.

And I was nostalgic for my Gospel roots. The first songs I'd written, after all, were about Jesus and God. Now I was onstage singing love songs to simulated giant penises. The superficial emotions were similar, but their impact was profoundly different. My stage show skewered the groins of my feverish fans. My first songs, however, had penetrated their very souls.

My guitar skills weren't the best, but serviceable. After the first number concluded, I "magically" shed my Alice garb and became a black-clad alley cat. I was breathing hard but still on an amazing high. The amphetamine plus adrenalin mix was doing its job. Grabbing up my signature *red electric guitar* I ripped off a series of squealing riffs that had the audience jumping up and down and screaming in ecstasy. Flipping the guitar to my dancers I grabbed up a white mike and launched into *"The Boy's In Love With You."* It was a pure fantasy rock ballad tuned to each squawking girl's personal heart strings.

Once again the standing-room-only audience of now nearly 20,000 fans who'd crowded into the Hollywood Bowl all sang along with me...

"HE WANTS ME AND HE NEEDS ME!"

It was one of those moments of amazing synchronicity, where the artist and the fans merge into a mutually self-perpetuating *superbeast:* the crowd feeding on the incredible harmony, beat, and amplification while the artist takes in their energy and returns it ten-fold greater. It was magic!

"...BUT HE MAKES MY HEART BLEED..."

Yet despite the incredible synergy it induced, I hated those lyrics. They were too simple and blatant. But that's what I'd been reduced to writing because of my success. My earlier poetry was daring, extreme, and shocking. The poetic rhymes were unexpected, stealthy. These words were exploitive, derivative, in simple patterns, and easy to parrot. My first albums were works of art. The last three were mostly corporate pop tunes, designed more to sell than to inspire: no different from those of the past line of highly produced stereotypic superstar female popstars.

I didn't want to be just the latest clone of Madonna. I wanted to be a true artist in the tradition of Carole King and Judy Collins. But I'd been corrupted, co-opted, and contracted.

I still owed the studio three more hit albums before my contract was up. Of course by then I'd be in my twenties, over-the-hill, with a new fresh teenaged wailer capturing the tender little hearts of the next generation.

Yes, it's sad to be so sage. I felt like an elderly woman on the edge of death, having already lived a long and full life, imparting wisdom to a horde of know-it-all young snotty kids. But I knew it was a futile effort. I was largely wasting my time. Driven by hormones and the natural stress of growing up, my screaming fans only knew what they wanted in the moment. They had no patience for what they really needed. They were too ignorant to stomach solid advice.

Still dancing and prancing, singing my heart out, I nevertheless felt cut-off from my performance, sad and introspective.

Even from a child I felt that way: as if I'd already lived several very eventful lifetimes, wise beyond my years. I'm sure that attitude and depth of insight was what made my early songs so powerful. Indeed, my over-active imagination had already dreamed up enough prior-life fantasies to fill several large science fiction books. Sometimes I even thought that those prior lifetimes were real: imagining myself traveling through time and space, chased by dinosaurs, or traveling to the moon and Mars in my very own spaceship.

Little did I know during that fateful, final concert: I wasn't so much seeing into the past but anticipating the future!

"It's great. You're doing fine. The filming's going swimmingly."

I was halfway through, at the one hour break. I had a full seven minutes until I was on again. The drummer of my band was out there doing a mind-bending solo. Without even being consciously aware of what was happening I'd breezed through six more numbers, four costume changes, and two scenery shifts.

Far from "bombing" in humiliation, collapsing in a trembling heap on the stage coughing up my guts—to that point it was the best performance I'd ever done! The audience was like putty in my hands as I molded their brains and emotions.

It was an awesome power.

For the first time in my life, the scary thought flickered through my fever-ridden skull that *maybe the super-conservative religious sects were correct:* popular music *was* a corrupting influence inspired by the Devil. Society had been a lot less chaotic and evil when music was mostly limited to Gregorian Monks stoically chanting their praise for God from within cloistered monasteries.

But things were wavering around me, going out of focus.

"Suzette, I've got a great idea and Maurice agrees. We can get him into the IMAX film if he appears instead of..."

I was gasping for breath, my head hanging down. I was weakly coughing, trying to clear my throat. Wiping at my mouth I saw blood smearing the back of my hand.

I shook my head slowly, trying to clear my vision. Who was talking? Oh, right. It was Darlene. She was blabbing at me as a flurry of activity surrounded me: someone handing me a bottle of water, Eun stripping off my wig and skull cap while fluffing out my natural hair and a team of wardrobe personnel dismantling my metallic robot costume while sliding me into "everyday person" clothes.

"—so what do you think?" Darlene concluded.

"I...sure, whatever you want...say, Darlene—do you happen to have another of those blue pills? I think the one you gave me before is wearing off and..."

"We can't have you slurring your words," she frowned. "The one I gave you should last through the concert. Just focus on the next number. You're doing fine. And ham it up with Maurice, ok?"

"Say what?"

But I was *not* doing fine! I felt myself steadily drifting down from the fluffy clouds. I could see the muddy ground rushing up at me. For Christ's sake, I was coughing up blood! Maybe one pill was fine for a healthy, relatively low-stressed "Darlene" but not for me. I was crashing to *start* with—and now after an hour of feverish exertions...

I was going to *crash*, hard!

"You're on in thirty seconds."

"Huh?" I gasped, grabbing the bottle and chugging it down in one long gulp.

But Sam wasn't paying me any attention. He was already out getting the rigging untangled for the next change of the giant props on-stage. A classical ensemble located in the orchestra pit was now ramping up a long violin sequence, ending in an ear-splitting *explosion* of cymbals, snares, and timpani all going off at once.

It was a glorious ending to the first hour and start of the last hour of the concert when both I and *Strinjet* would race back onto the stage.

But my legs were so weak I could barely stand, let alone run out to start another marathon session.

"Darlene, I really think..."

"Not now, Suzette!"

I suddenly realized that a *squad of police* was standing behind me, arguing vehemently with my manager.

"What's...?"

"Ten seconds!" Sam snapped at me, back at my side.

"No, we're *not!*" Darlene barked at the police, her hands on her hips, "No freaking way! It's not going to happen. We get these sorts of threats all the time!"

"Threats?" I gasped, perplexed.

"*Five... four... three... two...*"

My red electric guitar was slapped back into my trembling hands as I was pushed forward—and suddenly I was back on stage facing my 20,000 fans. They were thunderously clapping, all in unison, anticipating their favorite "classic" Suzette tune: "*Lost in Paradise.*"

At least I felt free. This was the one part of the concert where I briefly got to shed my silly costumes and dress like a real person. I now had on my iconic torn blue jeans, a white tank top, and a blue-brown plaid long-sleeved shirt with a brooch of fake amber jewels above its breast pocket. The brooch exactly set off my natural blond hair which now swirled freely around my head. Of course it was all still theater. The "persona" I portrayed was back to my early years: that of a teenage writer-singer strumming her guitar all by herself.

My song started just like that. A spotlight lit me as I waveringly stood in place before a fixed floor mike. Everything else, including my band, were in darkness, poised to start ramping up their accompanying rumbles at the end of the solo.

It was just me and the audience. I stood there silently—not playing, singing, or moving. The clapping slowed, softened, and then stopped.

It was another magical moment: no longer a big-prop theatrical production—just me, my guitar and my fans.

It was a carefully crafted intimate interlude.

I had a few moments for improvised "spontaneous" speech.

"Uh...you know...I almost didn't come out tonight. I've been feeling really puny lately."

I heard the thousands of fans all hush, listening intently. Each person was individually in tune with me.

"...but I knew I couldn't let you down..."

A rustle of appreciation swept through the giant concave bowl that was spread out before and above me.

"...and what kept me going," my voice grew stronger, "Was remembering the best time of my life."

A growing avalanche of applause swept through the audience.

In my best "little girl" voice I weakly began: "*We made love in the flowers of a lovely mountain meadow...*"

"WHERE THE STREAMS FLOWED PURE AND CLEAR..." the audience answered on the counterpoint...

"*—and Juaquin and I skinny-dipped in cold, pure water...*"

"ROMPING WITH THE BEARS AND THE DEER..."

"*It was Paradise...summer in the Catskills...a time that I will never forget...a time long ago...before I got old...*"

"*WHEN THE STREAMS FLOWED PURE AND CLEAR!*" both I and the fans belted out together.

"*But storm clouds were brewing...*"

And so it continued. It was a long ballad, ending in heartbreak and tears. I'd written it right after my family's disaster occurred, thinking back on our many happy "wilderness trips." Of course I'd never been out naked in a meadow having unprotected childhood sex with a kindly but incredibly handsome mountain-boy. That was a complete fantasy. But the feeling of being back in untainted nature, casting aside the pretenses of civilization, returning to my primal roots was compelling. Every time I sang it for an audience it surfaced that unforgettable pain, causing real tears to run down my cheeks. Its authenticity was undeniable, resonating with whatever terrible trage-dies large or small my fans had themselves endured. Many a face in the vast audience was wet with tears.

And then Strinjet cut in, softly at first and then more forcefully.

And the ballad smoothly changed from me and my guitar into a different sound: a *rock-and-roll* throwback I'd written that had the audience back to bouncing and cheering. I did my job. I didn't leave my people wallowing in their tears. I made a path for them to return to the joyful abandon of the *fantasy rock concert!*

As the full orchestra joined my band—the *magnificent noise* sweeping up everything in its path—I staggered off-stage for a sched-uled short break and next costume change.

I dropped to my knees, my head spinning.

Hands grabbed onto me, trying to get me back to my feet. I clung onto the skinny frame of the person nearest me, a wardrobe assistant we'd picked up in England. We'd gotten him off the street. He'd been hanging out in the West End outside the *Prince of Wales Theatre*, working for tips calling over cabs for the departing patrons. I took pity on him and offered him a job in our troupe. He was funny and peculiar, usually (obviously) "on" something, a real drug-head. But he was dependable and didn't mind traipsing all over the world. His name, I recalled, was George.

"Do you have anything?" I hoarsely whispered in his ear.

"Say whut, Miss Kingly?"

"Come on, George...I'm desperate. You've got to have something on you. I'm begging you."

"I don' won no trouble."

"You won't get into any trouble. I promise!"

"Well..."

"*Please!*"

He slipped me a greasy feeling tab.

I stuffed it into my mouth where it instantly dissolved.

"Thanks," I gasped, managing to get my arms out so they could be slid into priestly robes. Next I was due to become a *Goddess* ordering giant dragons around the stage in a mystical fog lit by sparkling golden laser beams. Yes, I know it was silly. But that was a critical part of the whole exercise: to let my young fans escape their problems and stresses for just a couple hours. Sure, I plucked on their heart strings. But I also tweaked their imaginations. I took them to *wondrous* places they'd never been before!

That was the essence of the best art. Even at that late date, as total disaster loomed before me, I still took pride in my work.

"PUFF THE MAGIC DRAGON, LIVED BY THE SEA..." the crowd roared out the first line to the Peter, Paul, and Mary 1963 famous song, prompted by the orchestra's melody and words scrolling across the giant Jumbotrons looming to the sides.

I danced out into the mists.

"*And he's my little, pretty, baby pet lizard!*" I sang back, inserting my own take on the number.

Out of the swirling mists a giant dragon head lurched upward, its toothy mouth opening, with fire erupting from its throat.

The crowd gasped but didn't stop singing.

"AND FROLICKED IN THE AUTUMN MIST..."

"*Who huffed and roared and barked and purred...*"

Still singing, I launched into an intricate dance number with my troupe. As I did so I had a strange sensation. Where before I was barely staggering along, I now felt light as a feather!

"*And turned into the Sparkling Four—my wonderful, wonderful band!*"

Strinjet's members, now highlighted beneath the raging beast, took brief solo turns as I introduced each.

"*Lift me up upon your back and take to the promised land!*" I bellowed out, racing over to the looming dragon and climbing up its waving tail.

This was totally unexpected. It wasn't anything we'd ever done before. My words were brand new. I was supposed to scamper around and through the band, kissing each of the members, not clamber up on the giant inflatable prop's unsteady tail! But the audience didn't know I was taking a dangerous detour.

"...IN A LAND CALLED HONAHLEE!" the crowd roared in delight.

"My baby dragon is my pet and he loves me like my very own Daddy!"

By then I'd reached the top of the neck. The rubbery figure wasn't meant to be climbed on. I was now fifty feet above the stage. My dancers milled about below, fearfully positioning themselves to try and break my fall if I slid off. Strinjet soldiered on, pounding out their rhythm and chords.

"Ain't that dandy?" I finished the silly song.

The crowd roared back its approval.

"This is new, folks!" I shouted. "This is just for you! You can ride a flying dragon too! Just imagine it and it can happen! Let your mind soar! Fly up away into the sky with me!"

Wow. That produced a sensation. Watching a wonderful production where every note is practiced, rehearsed, and set in stone is one thing—but witnessing "free form" spontaneous theater is something else again. The "act" becomes real!

I could see the IMAX cameras zooming in on me in my Goddess robe now holding onto the horns of the fire-breathing Dragon as I straddled its head. This was exciting!

...and it was totally out of character. I never did weird stuff like this. I always kept to the script. Any "improvising" was just a few words here or there in predetermined short pauses. But everything was so *dreamy!* Reality wasn't solid anymore. It was fluid. I felt that my very thoughts could change things.

Oh, right...ok. I realized what was happening. The tab I'd gotten from George had "energized" me, but not like the relatively tame amphetamines. Christ, I must have ingested some LSD or derivative thereof!

Ah well, might as well roll with it and enjoy the ride.

"*Look at me, world!*" I shouted as I *stood up* unsupported upon the flattened head of the green dragon.

The crowd collectively "gasped" as I slipped and fell, flopping down toward the hard stage, bouncing off a rubbery dragon-arm that broke my fall...

—from which my thankfully nimble dance troupe neatly caught me in mid-tumble and carefully lowered me back to the floor.

I saw some of them looking very scared.

"*Sing with me!*" I shouted happily, snatching up my red guitar to insert a whole new number into the production.

Damn the copyrights. I was going to sing with the audience the whole song from Peter, Paul, and Mary. Darlene could sort out the royalty payments afterward. And so we all together bellowed out...

"PUFF THE MAGIC DRAGON LIVED BY THE SEA...'

It was glorious.

It completely threw off the schedule, but my production manager cleverly substituted it for the tune we were supposed to be doing. Following the diversion we were right back on cue.

The lighting changed and the Dragon mutated from a cute, friendly giant into a glaring, roaring beast.

Its eyes flashed red laser beams and it swung down to bite me in half.

"*My Prince comes to save me from the bad Dragon!*" I shouted, turning to my dance troupe.

But where several scantily clad, well-muscled male dancers were supposed to rush forward, surround me, and carry me away—*one lone figure* emerged from the mists.

As the orchestra's soaring harmony captivated the entire arena, *Maurice* walked "heroically" toward me, arms held out, his head back and a big smile planted on puckered lips.

Yep, he wanted to kiss me.

I was stunned to see him there. He was totally out of place. But that must be what Darlene was trying to tell me earlier. I suppose if I could improvise for the IMAX audience, then so could he. I liked him, but had zero romantic interest in him. We'd picked him up in Paris along with his band. Darlene found them in the *Caveau de la Huchette*, a famous jazz/bar venue. They became our opening act when our original openers were fired due to excessive drinking. Darlene said he'd be a great "counter weight" to me, perhaps recording a joint album for our next outing.

He was only seventeen, a dreamy young Frenchman. He was lean, hairy, and perpetually horny. He played a mean acoustic guitar, wore a very short trimmed beard, sported solid gold dark glasses, and had golden-brown up-brushed short hair. Whereas I could tap into the experiences and dreams of every young girl, he could directly cream their pants. Darlene insisted we'd make the perfect pop team, coldly suggesting we should become an "item."

Well...a singing duo maybe. But a romantic interest, never. Yes, I admit I was initially attracted to him when Darlene brought him into the tour. But any serious romantic interest on my part was squashed by him immediately bedding whatever warm body (female or male) in the troupe that he could entice into a one-time "hook up." Though he tried to woo me I carefully stayed at a professional arm's length.

And here he was before 20,000 of my screaming fans arrogantly strolling out to "save me from the dragon" with a big, wet smooch.

Going "off script" were we?

With a big grin plastered across my face, fueled by reality-altering drugs loosing me from my normal constraints, I walked right up to him and *cold-cocked* him with a *knotted fist* straight to his chin!

He dropped like he'd been hit with a hammer.

I stood astride his twitching body, holding my red guitar above my head, and screamed out: *"Big girls can take care of themselves!"*

Jesus, it was beautiful.

The vast crowd around and above me was completely silent, stunned. And then they erupted into *thunderous cheering and clapping!* Hah! It was *glorious!*

As shocked roadies pulled the young Frenchman's slack body off-stage I resumed our normal routines.

In no time at all, we were at the final number. I'd already done two encores. This was the third and last encore, after which the production for that night would be finished.

It was a slow number. It was designed to leave my fans in a state of gentle euphoria. I'd returned to my "doo wop" theme from the beginning of the concert. This time, I did an adaptation of the 1954 classic from the Penguins: "Earth Angel."

My new lyrics were easy to remember and sing. Just to make sure the audience could join in fully, the words scrolled across the giant Jumbotron screens.

My outfit was now that of a beautiful, white-gowned, actual angel. As I strummed my red electric guitar, *magnificent feathered wings* slowly extended from my back.

"EARTH ANGEL, EARTH ANGEL, I'M YOUR EARTH ANGEL!" me, the backup singers, and my 20,000 fans sang in perfect unison.

Darlene, damn her manipulative soul, had somehow convince Maurice to come back onstage. Though his reddened jaw sagged a bit, he stood at a distance looking at me adoringly. An extra spotlight highlighted him. I admit it was a stroke of genius on Darlene's part. I'd turned the lyrics around such that the female was in control. And since he'd been roundly "put down" earlier by me his last-minute emergence to adore me fit in perfectly.

"MY DARLING DEAR, LOVE ME ALL THE TIME... EVEN IF I'M GONE... HOLD ON... HOLD ONTO YOUR LOVE FOR ME."

Nearly invisible wires that secured me to transparent cables above lifted me up into the air.

The audience "gasped" to see me floating upward, my beautiful angel-wings fully extended.

I continued singing with them: "LOVE ME FOREVER... FOREV-ER AND MORE... YOU'RE JUST A FOOL, A FOOL IN LOVE WITH ME."

Maurice, bless his horny little heart, played his improvised part perfectly. Centered in his spotlight down on the stage he cupped his hands and blew a kiss up to me.

"EARTH ANGEL, EARTH ANGEL, I'M YOUR EARTH ANGEL!" we started the chorus again.

"I'LL BE YOURS, MY DARLING DEAR, IF YOU LOVE ME ALL THE TIME..."

As I continued to sing I was now nearly *a hundred feet* up in the air, floating along seemingly unsupported out over the audience, my wings grandly flapping. A *rainbow of bursting fireworks* sprang up behind the Hollywood Bowl half-shell, lighting up the night sky.

Golden sparkles showered down on me, transforming me into an ethereal, magical apparition.

It was the perfect ending to a magnificent concert. It was a personal triumph since I'd nearly cancelled the entire thing. It required great sacrifice on my part, popping drugs I'd sworn never to touch, thus making the success all that sweeter. Yes, we'd done this final encore sequence in all our other venues across the world, but the Hollywood Bowl was perfect. I'd never been up this high before, nor so engulfed by sparkles. Still juiced by the fading amphetamines and still-potent LSD I truly felt like I was flying up into heaven, powered by the eternal energy of pure Love.

I had the smug thought that my lucky-charm marbles hidden in my inner pocket had carried me through. I was on top of the world!

And then the first *bomb* EXPLODED.

The audience clapped, thinking it was part of the act, but glancing behind me I saw that the massive half-shell covering the stage had crumpled in a blazing firestorm. Maurice was briefly highlighted on the extended runway as he tried to flee, only to be engulfed by the spreading inferno.

Then the next two *even more-powerful* bombs simultaneously DETONATED.

They'd been hidden inside the two giant Jumbotron screens furthest from the stage, instantly showering the thousands of fans with twin hailstorms of deadly shrapnel.

"No!" I gasped as I felt my side hit and the cables holding me loosen then sever...

Below me I heard a chorus of *agonized screams!*

—as I dropped unsupported into smoke, fire, and blood...

Fortunately I'd moved far enough into the amphitheater's ascending tiers such that I was then only about fifty feet above the bloody mess down below.

That's probably what saved my life.

The last thing I remember was plunging face-first downward with my smoking angelic wings trailing flames.

Chapter 3

THE LONG ROAD BACK

It's a long, long road
When you're dropped in the middle of nowhere
Thinking your family will always be there
They speed off and leave you all lost and alone
Out in the scary wilderness, shivering and cold...

Oh where, oh where, oh where did they go
And why did they have to depart?
When everything seemed to be perfectly fine
They casually rip out your heart.

Some day when the sun still hangs in the sky
And the moon shines bluely at night
When God is in heaven and everything's right
Perhaps I'll forgive their lies

But that's a bridge too far to go
A step too difficult now
I stand here sad, my eyes downcast
With no direction home...

The Suzette Anthology, Lyrics 3

I regained consciousness in utter agony.

It felt like I'd broken every bone in my body. I wanted to scream from the searing pain which throbbed in brutal waves through my arms, legs, chest, and pelvis. But I didn't have the strength to even

33

"peep." The drugs I'd taken earlier had worn off. I could barely breathe, my ribs fractured, my lungs congested.

Plus, I was severely burned. My head throbbed. Managing to inch some fingers up to my skull I found my wig and natural hair burnt off, leaving a big blistering sore in their place.

I knew I should be dead. I blearily realized the last two bombs had been placed such that the shrapnel blasts tilted downward, into the audience. Luckily I'd been high enough to avoid the main showers. But how had I survived the subsequence plunge? Had the mass of bodies below me cushioned my fall?

It seemed unlikely. A fall from that height should have killed me. But, regardless, I was still kicking, however weakly.

"...help...me..." I managed to whisper.

No one responded.

I feared I was dying. I was desperate to get help. My first task was to find out what was going on. Congealed blood covered most of my face, making it difficult to open my eyes. I grimaced and blinked until my surroundings came into view.

The first thing I saw was *my Dad and my brother Billy*. They were standing there beside me looking pitifully sad. Doubtless they'd come to usher me on to the other side.

"Not...just...yet," I grimaced, determined to hang on.

They vanished. I assumed their brief appearance was a lingering effect of the LSD I'd stupidly ingested earlier. They couldn't be at the concert. They were long dead.

What else could I see?

It was dark. How much time had passed with me unconscious I had no idea but it was still night. I was lying in and upon a heap of numerous bodies. The limbs that lay beneath or upon me were cold, motionless. Other similar heaps were all around me, piled over torn and shattered seats, descending down toward the still-smoldering orchestra pit. A faint glow in that direction marked where the giant half-shell stage had been. I could hear sirens in the distance, presumably fire trucks, police cars, and ambulances. Overhead I heard the steady "thwump, thwump, thwump" of a helicopter slowly circling the scene. A searchlight from above probed the darkness, briefly illuminating each heap of bodies before moving on.

In the distance I heard occasional screams and cries for help. It seems not many survived. I vaguely made out white uniforms of searchers moving through the night. Suddenly a bright light blasted down upon me.

I managed to jerk up one arm, weakly waving one hand in the air. *"There's someone alive here!"* an amplified voice blared down.

"...thank...God..." I whispered, exhausted by my effort.

As strong arms began untangling my mangled limbs from the bloody heap I gratefully slid back into unconsciousness.

I awoke in the I.C.U., "intensive care unit," of a hospital. Nurses and physicians hovered over me. They seemed surprised I was aware of their presence. I must have been doped up to my gills since I didn't feel any pain, though I glimpsed bandages, splints, and casts on my body. Tubes ran in and out through seemingly all my available orifices and blood vessels.

"Whuuuu....?" I moaned, trying to speak but failing.

"You're in the trauma center of the Cedars-Sinai Medical Center," a white-gowned physician sharply spoke at my side. That was nice of him. His overly enunciated voice penetrated the drug-laced haze in which I was lazily drifting. "It's been a week since the bombing at the Hollywood Bowl, located not far from here. We kept you in a medically induced coma until we were sure you were out of the woods. You have a lot of broken bones and damaged organs. But you're going to be ok. We've already done skin transplants to cover the main burned areas, mainly on your head, neck, and arms. There will be scarring, but no serious infections. It may take a few more operations and months of rehab, but barring unforeseen complications you should make a full recovery. *Do you understand me, Suzette?"*

I lifted my head, nodding. That was all the strength I had. I closed my eyes and slumped back down.

I saw the contents of my pockets in a clear plastic container on the small table beside my bed. In it I glimpsed my precious marbles. My "lucky charms" were still with me. I felt comforted. Though tragedy had fallen, I was somehow still alive. Though it was totally illogical, I was convinced my marbles had helped.

Even the "haze" felt nice. For the first time in years I had time to reflect upon my life without being crushed by the many urgent duties and responsibilities of being famous. The only thing I had to do now was lie on the bed, occasionally use a bedpan, and let my bones heal.

But I was not at peace.

How the hell did I end up here?—I grimaced.

Visions of the past swam around me. Was it when Darlene discovered me singing youthful-angst tunes in that seedy nightclub in Nashville? No, it was earlier. Was it when my Mom and Dad decided our family Gospel group was good enough to record a professional album? No, it was even earlier. Was it when Billy decided I was "hogging" all the limelight and quit singing with our family group, retreating into Dad's "research sheds"? Nope. Was it when I got my first guitar for Christmas? No, it was even further back. Ah, *now* I remembered...

The first time I became consciously aware I wanted to use my life to make music was in kindergarten. No, it wasn't because my class sang some cute kid song. No, it wasn't me blowing on the ubiquitous grammar school pan-pipe. Likewise, it wasn't me listening to some famous musician who came to visit our school. Rather, it was during recess out on the school playground.

They allowed us little kids out on the playground because it was very well chaperoned. Several teachers were always present making sure us kindergarteners were included in the various grade-schooler activities. But I was nervous. In fact, I now recalled that this was my very first day at school. I was wandering around, considering if I wanted to play dodgeball or hide-and-seek, maybe hopscotch or jump-rope?

"Come and play with us!"

I was a bit startled by an older teacher who was beckoning me. He was on his knees, hunched over a circle drawn in the dirt. He was looking up at me, with sly laughter in his eyes. He sort of reminded me of my Daddy, but a lot older. He had long white hair and a huge bushy white beard. I suppose I trusted him because he looked like every kindly wizard I'd ever seen in the movies. I know I should have been wary. I wasn't supposed to talk to creepy strangers. I didn't recognize this particular teacher. But we were on the playground with monitors standing around dutifully. How could there be any danger?

Around the circle were three other kids, one of whom I recognized from my class. She was Shaneeka, a shy but clever little girl with curly black hair and dark skin. There were also two older boys, both with slanted eyes, Chinese kids I think. They seemed to be brothers, if not twins.

"Why?" I boldly asked the old man.

"These guys need one more person and you'll enjoy the game."

"Uh, ok," I shrugged, delicately getting down beside him. I didn't want my brand new blue jeans to get dirty or grass-stained. "What do I do?"

"Take this."

He handed me a *pearly white, perfectly round rock*. It was very smooth and shiny. The sun glittered off its surface. It felt warm in my hand.

I was instantly intrigued. All the laughter and running kids and other teachers around me faded into the background. All I could see was that glistening, perfectly round rock.

"What is it?"

"It's your *Taw*."

"Hah...that's funny. What's a 'taw'?"

"Whatever you want it to be."

I frowned, looking up from the milky sphere in my hand at the old man. His eyes crinkled in their corners in a strange way. He looked like the manufactured "Wizard of Oz" simulacrum I'd seen in that old movie many times.

"Be serious," I sternly admonished him in my fully dignified five-year-old voice.

He laughed.

"It's your very own, best, shooting marble. I'm giving it to you to keep with you for always. Never lose it. Never bet with it. Always keep it on you."

That was strange. Why should I always keep a dumb marble with me? But it *did* feel very comfortable in my hand, very *soothing*.

"Ok, thanks. So what do I do with it?"

"Here, let me show you."

And right then and there he taught me and the others how to play marbles: the ring containing the target marbles, the parallel lines outside, the "lagging" to get nearest one of the lines to see who'd shoot first, "knuckling down" to shoot, whether we'd be playing "keepsies" or not, and all the various rules of the game.

And so we played, all of us—including the old teacher—laughing and joking. It *was* fun.

But what fascinated me most was the *incredibly beautiful marbles:* all different sizes, materials, and colors. So in grade school I became a marbles champion, even entering various competitions. I won and lost many marbles. But I never gave up my Taw, always carrying it in my pocket with a couple other favorite rollers.

They were my "lucky charms." But most of all, they became my very first personal *music.* When I shot straight and hard the "*CLINK*" of the colliding spheres was clear, sharp, and pure.

That became my personal mantra and goal: whether strumming a new song isolated in my bedroom or singing in an isolation booth at a recording studio or performing in front of ten thousand fans: to be CLEAR, SHARP, AND PURE.

And even though an incredible tragedy had struck me down, my goal remained the same as before.

With that thought in my mind I was comforted and focused: fighting there in the Intensive Care Unit to *clear* my agonized mind, *sharpen* my blurred abilities, and *deliver again* an *uncontaminated reality* that would pierce to the center of my audience's heart.

I was determined to yet again bask in their righteous applause.

I was in the hospital for a full six months, recovering. It took emergency surgery to repair my internal injuries, four more operations to get my bones back into alignment, and several minor procedures to do cosmetic enhancements on my savaged face. I nearly died several times, but clever surgeons and attending physicians managed to bring me back. I almost wished they hadn't.

The pain was unendurable. Though my organs and bones had been knitted back together it would take a long time for them to heal. I was on a constant cocktail of pain-meds, barely conscious most of the time.

I expected to see my greedy mother at any moment, come to demand yet another million bucks from me. I figured she'd appear in person since I was out of e-mail communication with her. Sure, I'd paid her off to stay away, acknowledging her partial claim on my career. She insisted I was still under the "family contract" from my Gospel singing days. I didn't fight the claim, but not because I thought it was valid. Periodically paying her off meant I didn't have to deal with her, especially not having to face her in court. But that was before the bombing. I'd almost welcome her face now, giving her whatever money I had left just to feel her supportive touch.

But that was me being weak and emotional. I didn't want anything from her.

Gradually I got better on my own. At long last I was strong enough to be moved out of ICU. That was blessing. I was no longer in a fishbowl surrounded by hovering medical professionals. I was given my own, private room. But being there also opened me up to receiving unwanted visitors.

I steeled myself by holding my "lucky charms" in my one good working hand, slowly rolling the marbles around against each other. The rhythm of their continual hidden dance and "clinking" soothed me.

But it was still tough.

The first to grill me were the police. Though they were polite, their questions were pointed: *What was your role in continuing the concert even though credible bomb threats had been received* (None); *Why were drugs found in your blood during the initial battery of hospital tests* (I thought they were prescriptions or over-the-counter legal stimulants); and *Were you aware that financially the Tour was in danger of closing, driving my company into bankruptcy* (No); or that *A huge insurance payoff was in the works if a catastrophic event occurred during your Tour* (What the hell?)

"We'll probably have more questions for you later," the Detective assured me as the battery of officials departed. "Don't go anywhere without informing us."

"I'm sure I'm not going far," I gasped, still bundled up in a half-body cast plus stinted right leg and right arm hanging from supports.

Next to arrive were the insurance adjusters and big-wig studio executives.

Darlene was dead, burned up in the inferno, so I heaped the blame as much as possible onto her cooked corpse. Yes, that was cold-blooded, but necessary. The survivors plus relatives of dead fans had filed a gigantic class-action suit. If successful, it would definitely bankrupt my contracted studio, the corporate underwriters of *Tour Six*, and my own personal production company "Suzette Records." Plus it would take whatever personal assets I had. The payout would be not in the millions but billions. And that wasn't excessive. After all, roughly 5,000 fans died in the overlapping, twin hailstorms of lethal shrapnel. And, of course, there was an equal number wounded. It was the largest mass casualty event at a public entertainment event in modern history. A number of financially intertwined institutions would be brought down settling the massive damages.

So by lying through my teeth and blaming Darlene for everything, I just managed to avoid going to prison.

There was no proof I was complicit in the chain of events leading up to the terrible attack. As far as the courts and public knew, I was just an "innocent performer" duped by a conniving manager, a greedy corporate entity, shady book-keepers, and criminal financiers. How the hell was I supposed to know that my "rocket to Stardom" had been fueled by *drug cartels* looking to use my musical career to launder their ill-gotten gains?

Hah! The irony of it all...*sigh*.

There I was the "pure" entertainer who never took drugs and my whole rise to fame was built on the illegal drug trade!

The working theory was that the drug cartels had mined the venue, perversely looking to get a giant insurance settlement while covering up their involvement. And then their scheme went too far. Bombs that should have only caused minor damage instead resulted in horrific destruction and death. Still, though, it didn't make sense. At first, no one could believe the outrageous claim. It was so much easier to believe that religious fundamentalist terrorists had staged the attack upon the "sinful" musical performance (after all, my opening scene was dozens of giant erect penises disguised as mushrooms!)

But more and more, the drug cartel explanation seemed the most logical answer.

I was especially incredulous—then shocked—when the investigators actually discovered supportive evidence for their working theory. Previously I had no doubt that my success was built upon pure talent, not criminals looking for a compliant "kid-act" to launder their ill-gotten goods! But it seems that Darlene had a long illicit track-record of dealing with the underworld to fund her cute little starlets.

Then there were the reporters requesting interviews. I did as many as I could, trying to get the story out that I was just an innocent musician caught up in a web of big-money, intrigue, and deadly criminal networks. I could tell that none of the reporters believed me. I couldn't be that dumb. But, yes, I *could* be! So I stuck to my story even as my public image took a gigantic nosedive.

Finally with the "official" matters taken care of, my "friends" could now come to comfort and encourage me. At least I thought they were about to arrive. But there were none...

—which was actually a relief.

I was still in terrible pain, an agony held-off only by the strong meds still prescribed to me.

And, gradually, the news story, investigations, and criminal prosecutions moved from the *Hollywood Bowl Tragedy* to other more-current world horrors.

So I became just one of a long line of sham successes, humiliated and disgraced. Even the mass-media scandal-feeds finally conceded that I was only a stupid pawn. But I didn't get off scot free.

Everything I'd earned during my three-year meteoric career was toast. My millions, my mansion, my private jet, my yacht—were all confiscated or sold-off helping to settle the class-action suits. I guess I should have felt lucky that at least my incredibly expensive medical procedures were all paid in full. But even that came to an end. It seems that the special insurance taken out by my recording company for the World Tour had (inserted in fine print I never read) a "lifetime cap." Since the policy was based in Geneva and not in the U.S.A., it wasn't bound by U.S. laws which prevented such caps. So after six months the hospital kicked me out, even though I wasn't yet fully healed or able to move without experiencing crippling pain.

With just a bottle of pain-meds and a wooden cane, I limped out of the hospital owning only the clothes on my back. They wanted to discharge me in my own wheelchair. But I could no longer afford the luxury of purchasing such. Instead, I just shuffled along carefully, with barely enough money in my pocket to hire a cab to take me to a homeless shelter.

I wore the same clothes I'd been brought in with six months prior. Though they'd been washed free of blood, they were torn and ripped.

I looked like a scrawny, bald-headed, burnt-up bum.

"Hey, honey," my Mom greeted me.

Ah, I should have expected her. She hadn't been paid my "charity donations" all the while I was in medical, legal, and financial limbo. So here she was, personally coming to get her "cut".

Regardless, I was stunned to see her. She looked good! Yes, her dyed red-brown hair was graying at the roots, but she was as spry and fit as I remembered. She was dressed in a matching all-black, long-sleeved outfit. Her piercing green eyes cut through me.

I hadn't seen or talked to her since I was sixteen. That was three-and-a-half years previously.

"Need a ride?"

She stood beside an ancient, classic, two-seater, red Pontiac Fiero. It was my old car from before I became famous. Though the paint was faded and peeling, the interior held together with duct-tape, with smoke occasionally belching from its tailpipe...it warmed my heart to see it.

—but not so seeing my Mother, *Sally King*.

"I was wondering when you'd show up. Sorry, Mom, I'm broke. I've got no more handouts for you."

"So I've read in the news-blurbs."

"Then what the hell do you want?" I snapped at her, levering myself over to a park bench at the cab-stand and sitting down heavily. Just shuffling the twenty feet from the hospital entrance had exhausted me.

"When I heard what happened I caught the first plane and rushed to your side, sweetie. I was there when you first came out of surgery."

I frowned, not wanting to continue this conversation. Unfortunately, no cabs were immediately available. I'd have to wait for one to pull in.

"*Sure* you did...I didn't see you."

"I knew you wouldn't want me there. So when you were out of danger, before you woke up from your surgery, I left. But I didn't abandon you. I made sure that your lucky-charm marbles were there beside you when you woke up. I know how much you love those things, how superstitious you are. And I've been in daily communication with your doctors. I briefly went back to Oklahoma to get your Fiero. I drove it here and I've been living in a nearby motel, monitoring your recovery."

Huh. If that was true...well, I'd be surprised. Did she really care about me? But, no, it was just another ruse. She was waiting for me to die so that she, as my closest living relative, could scoop up any of my remaining assets.

But it *had* been nice to see my lucky-charms when I first regained consciousness.

No, she was just a damn money-grubber!

"Well I'm ok now. You can go back to Oklahoma."

"Are you sure? From what I hear you're back to square zero. I could help you to..."

"Like you helped *Dad and Billy?*" I angrily barked at her, outraged.

She hung her head and bit her lip.

"Look, Suzy..."

"That's *Suzette!*"

She sighed deeply. "You didn't have to legally change your name, you know. You could still have a stage name and keep your real..."

"That *is* my real name now! I'm *Suzette Kingly*, the top pop female Superstar in the whole wide world and..."

"Whatever you say," she shrugged, cutting me off. She held out a keyring to me. "It's your car, sweetie. We got it for you when you got your license when you turned sixteen. I can easily get a rental. The gas tank's full. At least you can use it to get around on your own, look for a new job, whatever. Please take it. I've got the family van back in Oklahoma."

It *was* tempting. It *was* my car. But I didn't want to take any-thing from her—to be indebted to her in any way.

"Go away," I growled, staring down at the cane that I held in a death-grip in my trembling fists, refusing to meet her gaze. "You can have the car. Sell it to some junkyard. Mark that down as my last payment to you."

She took a couple steps over to the bench and put a card next to me. "That's the motel I'm staying at. If you change your mind, give me a call."

Without another word, Sally King got into my old car and drove off.

All I had left was the clothes on my back, my wallet with a few dollars that were inside when the bombs hit, and my lucky marbles.

I tossed her card into a nearby trash bin. Then I popped a hand-ful of pain pills and waited in a daze for the next cab.

Chapter 4

<u>REPERCUSSIONS</u>

What really matters, *when all is done*
Is it your victories, your great triumphs?
Or is it family and lazy days
Lost in a haze that does not fade?

It's more, it's more, it's more
A thing I can't define
Twisting, winding, in and out
Making channels in my mind!

Can you explain what drives you forward
When all you love just turns to mush
Is it compulsion that keeps you marching
Or just the shadows from the sun?

It's more, it's more, it's more
A thing I can't define
Twisting, winding, in and out
Making channels in my mind!

I wondered where the stars had gone
Entering the blackness of outer space
Or was it heaven or lurking hell
Sent there by a cruel fate?
The Suzette Anthology, Lyrics 4

"But I've got several new songs. They're really *hot* and..."

"Sorry, Suzette. I wish we could record them, *but*..."

The seemingly sympathetic executive shrugged apologetically. He was the head of one of the Imprints that had collectively held my various contracts. I knew he was a cold hearted bastard only concerned about the bottom line, but he was also my ticket to reinstatement in the small world of commercially viable pop music. He was *Mr. Louis K. Dimille*, the CEO of U.W.M., *Universal World Music*. Like Darlene he was of African-American racial background, having made his first fortune in the Hip-Hop revival two decades earlier. For the music industry he was old, in his mid-forties. But he wore his hair straight, dyed deep black, and slicked down along the sides of his head. He kept fit, wearing only the latest, trendiest clothes. At the moment he had on a translucent-red, plastic-looking outfit. He was the picture of youth and vibrant energy. But that wasn't the only reason he stayed at the top. The real reason he'd survived so long in a young-people dominated industry was by being *ruthless*.

As soon as the Bowl disaster hit the newscasts he'd cancelled his part of my contracts. He knew what way the wind was blowing: gigantic suits and company-busting settlements. Using carefully concealed "fine print" in my agreements (more stuff I'd never read and Darlene had never told me about) he was able to slither out from under the financial obligations that bankrupted every other organization associated with me or the Tour.

But I still hoped he'd see potential profit in me.

"A come-back album would be *huge*," I pleaded with him. "It's what you want, isn't it? You'd make a fortune!"

He just slowly shook his head in sad denial, a seemingly regretful smile on his face. But I knew his gentle smile was just a way to get rid of me without causing a fuss. I'd breezed past security and several layers of personal assistants to march myself unannounced into his executive suite office. I expected an enthusiastic welcome, being "back from the dead" as I was—and instead got the brush-off.

"It could...be dedicated to the survivors...and a big hunk of the profits going to an education fund for the kids of the deceased..." I concluded feebly, my voice trailing off.

He sighed deeply, leaning back in his ornate office chair, looking up at the high, polished wood ceiling.

"Well, right after the Event that might have worked. But things have changed a lot during your recovery over the last six months, Suzette. There's a new style of music that's the latest rage, *Jungler*. It goes back to primal rhythms. Your retro vibe mixed with classic orchestration just doesn't resonate anymore, Suzette. I don't mean to be blunt, but as happy as the public is that you survived—your music is old. It was already on the way out during your Album Six tour. Plus, people *don't* want to be reminded about the Bowl tragedy. The kids today want *diversion*, fresh faces...*not* old retreads. And, Suzette, let me be frank—you're looking bad, girl."

That cut me deeply, in too many ways.

"I'm getting better," I feebly objected.

He pointedly looked at my sunken eyes, sallow cheeks, and trembling lips.

"You're on drugs."

Jesus, how dare he accuse me of that! I was wracked by shrapnel and broken into pieces by a fifty-foot fall. I found out that the only thing that saved me was a suspension line that didn't quite snap and a pile of human bodies that cushioned my fall. It had taken six months in a hospital for me to get me into barely walking shape. I had plates, screws, and wires all throughout my body. It was still agony to try and climb a short ladder just to get into my top bunk at the shelter.

How *dare* he accuse me of looking bad!

And I *wasn't* taking drugs. I was taking *prescriptions!*

But I had to admit he'd hit a chord.

Besides being yesterday's news I, likewise, was shocked by what I saw in the cracked mirror at the Mission. I was no longer the sexy, powerful teen Diva I remembered. Instead, what I saw staring back at me was a bloated, scarred face, listless sunken eyes, uneven teeth, and random patches of dry hair sprouting here and there on a splotched head. I was *hideous!* But I wasn't deterred. I'd put in enough "make-up" chair time to know that even a hag can be transformed into a Princess with enough pancake, rouge, face paint, and a good wig.

Hell, after a few weeks rehabbing on the ancient universal gym at the Mission I knew my creaky, broken body would be back to its old vibrant form. Of course that assumed they'd let me stay there that long...but if not, I'd just find my own apartment. Sure, I'd probably never be rid of my limp. There'd be no more intricate dance numbers for me. But I was determined to put the Bowl disaster behind me and make a new start.

And I *was* weaning myself off the pain meds. Why, that very day I'd only taken...what, a dozen?

But, regardless, I could still sing and play my guitar better than most.

"But surely some spec work would...?"

"I'm so sorry, Suzette. We all miss Darlene, by the way. If you had her with you she'd likely find a way to get you back into the scene, however minor your 'comeback' might be. But, sadly, she's dead. And at the moment you're toxic. Maybe in a year or two—when you're cleaned up and back in form—well, who knows? You understand," he concluded, standing up from his chair as if to usher me out.

I knew that security guards already angry at me for having zoomed past were poised at the door. In a few moments I'd be kicked out on my sorry ass. This was my last chance to make my case.

But instead of a compelling "pitch" I *burst into tears!*

I'd never done that "pre-Bowl"—but now I felt frazzled, skittish, and incredibly fragile.

"For God's sake, I need some work, Lou!" I blurted, loudly snuffling and sobbing, "The medical costs and the settlements took everything. The only thing I've got left is pharmacy benefits. And they're just keeping me barely hanging on as it is. You've got to give me something—*please!*"

It was humiliating. I was literally begging the man.

"Well...maybe I *can* help you out."

At that moment I felt like throwing my arms around his tall, plastic-wrapped body and hugging him. Yes! Just let my creaking voice and bumbling fingers back into a recording studio and I knew that I could...

But he was pulling out his wallet and handing me a *twenty*.

Yep, that was barely enough to pay for a cab to take me back to the Mission.

I got my sobbing under control, wiping my tear-stained face with the back of the sleeve of the old shirt I'd been given at the Mission. I pushed myself to my feet. Staggering with my cane I turned toward the door.

"I don't need your charity," I managed to indignantly reply. "I'll be back on top shortly. Then you'll beg *me* to get my contract reinstated!"

"Hey, I hope so, kid...I really do."

I was thoroughly humiliated, but capable of one more act of principled defiance. I poised myself to turn and *slap* him right across his smug face! Well, maybe not...

I spun back at him, grabbed the twenty out of his hand, and fled.

The *L.A. Reformed Mission* was Jesus-based, a comfortable fit to my Gospel-singing days. They had a small auditorium for worship services. I sat in a rickety chair on the stage, strumming an old guitar I'd found in a corner. I was playing to an empty room.

"Jesus loves me, this I know," I feebly croaked, then stopped.

Appropriately "in tune" with my scarred face, my singing was likewise hideous. My voice box had also been badly damaged in the hail of shrapnel and subsequence plunge onto the stadium seats. Lucky for me the darkened auditorium was deserted. I wouldn't want anyone to hear me in this state. True, extended rehab by expensive medical and vocal experts might still restore my voice to something close to the powerful instrument it'd been a mere half-year before. But who was I kidding? Even if I had the money to pay for the specialized care, which I didn't, I knew my sound would never be the same. Just as Lou had brutally noted, I was a vocally handicapped has-been.

I wearily pulled out my bottle of pain pills and chugged down a couple, absently noting there weren't many left. I'd have to get a new prescription soon.

"FOR THE BIBLE TELLS ME SO!" a powerful, alto voice shouted from the shadows, startling me.

"Who's that?" I barked, dropping the guitar with a "clunk" as I jerked to my feet.

"I'm one of your backup singers. Don't you remember me?"

Since there was only a feeble, yellow stage-light illuminating me, I couldn't see anything out in the dark audience area. Squinting, all I could make out was a dusky figure standing at the back of the chamber.

"What...are you Florence, Jaseque, or Chandra? I thought you were all killed in the explosion!"

"No, no...I'm from much before them, Suzy."

Oh no, "Suzy" was it? I suddenly knew who this mysterious "back-up singer" was: my pesky, persistent *Mother!*

"What are you doing here, Mom? What more do you want from me?" I replied feebly.

I dropped the old guitar onto the stage where it made a hollow "clunk" sound. My head hung down as well.

She slowly walked down the central aisle toward me. Coming into the light she spryly hopped up onto the stage.

"I want you to come home."

I laughed bitterly.

"I like it here."

"No, you don't."

"Do so..." I protested weakly.

No, she was correct. It was awful. I was used to living in a mansion with servants taking care of my every need. Here, the management had reluctantly granted the "fallen world-famous superstar" a week to "get your act together." I was assigned the upper of a three-decker bunkbed. Just climbing up the ladder was torture. Plus the several nights I'd already spent there were disgusting: punctuated by screams and chants, knife fights, and occasional gunfire out on the street.

The Mission was in the worst part of town. Drunks, mentally ill, and deadbeats grabbed for me on the street outside. They recognized me and either pitied or despised me. To them I was either a busted has-been or somehow complicit in mass murder. Kids jeered at me, thinking I was one of those celebrity impersonators. Sure, there were a few nice folks who were civil, in the Mission because they were temporarily down-on-their-luck, but they were in the minority. Most of the rest of the "guests" were the refuse, rejects, and losers of society: kindly cared for and nurtured by the good religious folks running the Mission.

But space was scarce. Prior "world superstars" were assumed to have the means to move on quickly.

"Your room is just as you left it," Sally King calmly informed me. "I haven't touched anything. You can stay as long as wish, leave whenever you want. It's surely a better temporary solution for you than being here. I'll even call you 'Suzette' if that's what you want. What do you say?"

Going back to the little, peaceful town of Sulphur, Oklahoma no longer seemed so intolerable. Maybe I needed a short rest, away from the big city.

"I...still hate you," I gulped, pressing my lips tightly together to keep from sobbing.

"That's ok," she comforted me as she stepped closer, then hugged me tightly, "I understand."

Did she?

There's nothing worse than the conviction that if you'd just acted differently your Dad and little brother might have lived. Now to augment that personal guilt I could add 5,000 more. My mother would never really love me. My surviving previous adoring fans had all turned to other shinier, younger superstars.

Suzette was finished.

I was slinking back in disgrace to my "little girl" room in my parents' house.

It was so pure and yet perverse I didn't know whether to cheer or cry. Unable to decide, I did both.

"*Noooooooooo!*" I screamed at the sky, falling down on my knees, my arms stretched upward, my cane brandished at the offending effigy, "Those bastards! They did it! They actually did it!"

It was my best imitation of Charlton Heston at the end of the first *Planet of the Apes* movie, falling down in disbelief at seeing the half-buried Statue of Liberty thrusting up from the apocalyptic seashore.

Though it hurt my healing bones to grovel in front of the looming structure, it soothed my aggrieved sense of drama.

"Are you ok, lady?" a little kid asked me, wobbling up into my sight. His mother quickly grabbed him and hustled him away.

"Don't talk to strange street people," she admonished him as she bundled him and a couple other kids into a car and hastily departed.

I was at the little city-park next to the main drag that went through the small town of Sulphur, Oklahoma. An iconic artesian spring sprouted a white fountain up into the air. Right beside it— which I'd not seen until then—was a raised-up bronze statue of *me!*

I'd heard that the town had commissioned it to honor their newly famous "favorite daughter." The statue had become a great tourist attraction there alongside the fountain.

Now I saw it in all its glory: *me* frozen in a moment of passionate singing, riffing on my electric guitar, flannel shirt flopping, blue jeans ragged and tight on my pert ass, hair flying around my head, eyes closed and mouth open, standing on one leg with the other kicking out into the air.

God, it was beautiful.

And I'd never be it again.

The next thing I remembered in my shuffling excursion out of my lonely room in my Mom's house, I was on the edge of the Park sitting on a boulder beside Travertine Creek. It was a peaceful, isolated section of the *Chickasaw National Recreation Area*, known by locals as The Park. I was mere blocks away from my statue beside the main street, which was itself mere blocks away from my Mom's house.

"I've missed this," I sighed, finally feeling the stress and heavy responsibilities I'd carried the last few years slipping away. "Suzette lost too much when she turned her back on this place."

It was early springtime. New, green leaves covered tree branches arching over the peaceful glade. The greenery was lit by the setting sun. The water in the stream spread out into a wide pond. Cattails swayed in clumps, frogs splashing between them.

My right leg and side hurt terribly from the shuffling walk I'd done from my Mom's house. I was now several streets away, on the town side of the large Park, having had to limp under a bridge to get to this secluded spot. The pain pill I'd taken the night before was wearing off. I would need another "hit" to help me make it back home.

I pulled out my vial of meds and was shocked to see that it was empty. Wait. What? *Empty???* Oh, sweet Jesus, what would I do? I'd soon be crippled by excruciating pain!

"You come here often?" I heard a friendly voice from behind me.

Twisting to the side (almost toppling over) I saw a young man walking up. He had long brown hair that fell loosely to each side of his head. He had bronzed skin, high cheekbones, and wide expressive eyes. He wore a buckskin shirt over faded blue jeans. On his bare feet were leather sandals.

He looked to be a high school kid. He reminded me a lot of Billy: not this guy's "Indian" appearance but the jaunty walk. His cheerful greeting displayed a joyful acceptance of anything novel or interesting. I'd really loved my little brother's similar joyful attitude until he had that stupid falling-out with me. I wasn't "hogging" the limelight! Was it my fault that the audiences liked cute little me rather than dorky him? But back to this kid, clearly he was of local Chickasaw ancestry, perhaps even being a full-blood Native-American.

"Oh, hi there...I live nearby. I've been coming here all my life," I replied.

"That's funny—I don't remember seeing you around. I do a lot of jogging in the evenings out here in the Park."

"I left Sulphur nearly four years ago."

He grinned in a disarmingly boyish way.

"Yep, I would have been only around twelve years old then. My folks didn't let me go running in the Park by myself when I was younger. They were pretty protective."

"So you're fifteen now?"

"Sixteen in September...I'm getting old," he laughed.

From his appearance and ease at conversing with a stranger I would have guessed he was older. He was tall for his age. He'd probably top-out at over six feet when he was full grown.

"Well then, I guess that makes me a certified old woman. I'm nineteen, going on twenty. Say, you're just the age of a friend I had here, if he'd lived that is."

"Your friend was my age?"

"Maybe you knew him: Billy King?"

He looked like I'd hit him in his face, the jaunty grin immediately replaced by deep sorrow.

"Sure, I knew him. It was really tough when he died. We were in the same class at school. We even went to church together. He was my best friend. My name's Scotty Yanash, by the way."

I was shocked. I guess I should have known Billy's grade school friends. And, regardless, I should have kept up with the young people at church. But by that time I was completely immersed in my own budding musical career. I realized I'd been totally selfish, thinking only of myself. Maybe Billy was right to be pissed at me.

And perhaps this was a chance to partially correct my prior mistakes.

"Well, I'm glad to meet you, Scotty. I'm Suzette...uhm, I mean Suzy King."

"Hey, you're Billy's sister. You're famous!" he laughed, the easy grin back on his deeply tanned face. "I didn't recognize you...uhm...."

He caught the look on my face and rushed to apologize: "Oh, but of course you're just out of the hospital. I'm so sorry about..."

"No, no," I waved off his awkward apology. "I'm ok now. Give me a few months and I'll be as dazzling as always. And as to the bombing at my concert...well, bad stuff happens. Plus I'm not all made-up and in costume, like I am on my album covers, and..."

Christ, I was babbling. But even beat up and burnt to a crisp I was still *Suzette*. I wasn't some little girl getting all tongue-tied meeting a charmingly handsome new boy.

"I didn't mean...well, you look..."

"I'm ugly!" I snorted, owning it. "I'm still fat and bloated from lying on a hospital bed the past six months. Plus I've been on all sorts of medication that's shrunk my face and shredded my hair. It's just going to take a while for me to get healthy again. So I'm not shocked you didn't recognize *sexy Suzette* in my present beat-up body. And I'm not technically famous anymore, well maybe *in*famous. But all that is in the past. I came back here to Sulphur to get my head on straight. I don't want to make any trouble for anyone."

"Why would you be any trouble?" Scotty innocently asked, sitting down on a nearby boulder.

Well, that was welcome. I'd have expected him to stammer excuses as he tried to get away from the hideous has-been. Instead he looked genuinely interested in my sad situation.

"People associate me with disaster. They think if they get too close then they'll also get caught-up in terrible tragedies."

"That's not fair. I don't mind being close to you. It's an honor, really."

I liked this kid. He reminded me of my little brother, but from a more mature perspective. I never got to know Billy other than as a snotty little kid. He was only twelve when he died. This "Scotty" friend of his was clearly a smart fellow, starting to mature into an adult. I guessed he was a freshman or sophomore in High School. It brought a tear to my eye to think I'd missed all that with Billy. Though we had our problems, he was still my one and only little brother. Simultaneously, though, remembering what happened to Billy hardened my hatred of my mother, steeling me to move out of her house the second I got my feet back under me.

"Life's not fair." I gave the stock response, sighing deeply. "And I guess you've just got to take the bad with the good."

Christ, I was full of trite sayings, wasn't I? Couldn't I say anything original?

"I really like your songs," Scotty stated firmly.

That was affirming. It knocked me out of my sad ruminations.

"Oh? Which one do you like best?" I cheerfully responded, gently testing him as to whether he was being sincere or just polite.

"*Wind-song!*"

That caught me by surprise. "Wind-song" was one of my earlier, obscure songs. It didn't even make it onto any of my six albums.

"Where'd you hear it?"

"Billy would hum it all the time. He liked it a lot. He taught me the words. We sang them together from time to time."

"You sing?"

"Just the traditional tribal songs or church songs, is all. I'm not good enough to be a professional like you. But singing inspires everyone, whether they're good at it or not, right? It's like the Bible says, we make the best music in our *hearts*. I mean, when I sing I feel like I'm merged with Nature—like God is smiling down on me. When I'm depressed, singing picks me up. Your albums do that for me. I've all your songs as MP3's on my smart phone. But they're best when I don't just listen to them but sing along with them. I do that a lot."

Wow. The kid was a real fan. But that was probably to be expected. When I was a part of my family's Gospel group, we were locally acclaimed. Then when I went off on my own—immediately after the tragedy occurred—I heard I still remained a home-town heroine.

Well, my statue by the fountain certainly made the case. I wondered if they'd tear it down now. After all, I was now in the same category as civil war Confederate leaders: once revered but now denounced, once hailed for their victories but now reviled for their mistakes and defeats.

Ah, well...maybe I had one single fan left.

"Well, that's one of my favorites also—back when I was transitioning from pure Gospel to a wider perspective. You want to give it a try?"

"Could we? I'd *love* to sing it with you."

"Do you take the lead or sing harmony or both?"

"Me? Well, I usually cover tenor to base at church. But I can sing alto using falsetto and the soprano an octave lower, so..."

"I thought you weren't a professional singer? It takes real talent to chime in with whatever harmony or lead is needed."

"At church I'm a youth song leader."

"That's impressive, Scotty. Have you ever wanted to perform in a group of your own?"

He shyly ducked his head. "Sometimes I imagine I'm *you* with my own band."

Wow. This kid sure was encouraging.

"Ah, that's great, Scotty. But believe me it's not all it's cracked up to be. Sometimes it's magical, that's true. But then you get stuck in a rut, singing the same few hit songs over and over and over, night after night. It can get really boring at times."

"Oh, I didn't mean to bore you. We don't have to..."

"No, no! I'd like to sing some of 'Wind-song.' Out here in real nature without a recording studio obsessing over every note or an audience to please, it feels...right! Let's give it a try and see what happens."

Scotty grinned widely. He had a great smile. His teeth were perfect, pearly white, contrasting starkly with his bronzed skin. If he were a few years older I'd have been smitten. He was going to make a really handsome boyfriend someday for a lucky girl. But for the moment he was an unexpected friend when I needed one most, maybe my only true friend in the whole wide world.

"Sure," he enthusiastically replied.

"Ok, I'll start and you chime in whenever you want. Ready?"

"Ready."

"*There's an Eagle on the wind...*" I began.

"EAGLE ON THE WIND..." he echoed in deep base.

"*Looking for his love...*"

"LOOKING FOR HIS LOVE..."

"*As high as the sky and as deep as the sea...*"

"DEEP AS THE SEA..."

"*Could he find...me?*"

"Me...me...me...me," his voice trailed off, moving at each word up higher from deep base into tenor.

"Sing me a wind-song, calling to me," I sang.

He was silent. Then he joined on the repeat, harmonizing in falsetto at alto: "*Sing me a Wind-song, calling to me.*"

"Up into the blue, always being true, never departing, always together, flying in formation, wingtip-to-wingtip we sing...'

"—dream a Wind-song!" I belted out the concluding words of the first verse.

"—dream a Wind-song!" he echoed in tenor.

"—*dream a Wind-song!*" we finished together, he an octave lower and me at soprano.

We were silent for a minute, enjoying the harmony we'd created. I was pleased. This was the first time I'd really sung after the Bowl. I expected a few croaks but was pleasantly surprised my voice box produced a strong soprano. Maybe my throat wasn't as damaged as I thought. That hopeful revelation, the bubbling creek, isolation, and beautiful scenery made for a magical moment.

"Wow, that was great," he grinned.

"It probably would have been better if I'd had an acoustical guitar with me," I mused. "I usually hammer out a riff between the verses. Plus the chords are really striking on 'wind-song,' helping the words to soar. But, yes, that was very nice harmony. It works a-capella, that's for sure. I've actually never tried it that way before."

"I know all the verses. I even made up some new ones myself."

"*Nice* job, Scotty," I congratulated him. "You sang marvelously. Do you write original songs? If I ever get another group I'll hire you as one of my back-up singers."

He snickered shyly at the notion. "I'm not that good, but thanks for the compliment. I'd like to try writing my own tunes, but I'm too busy taking extra college-level business classes and working after school for my Dad. He's got big plans for me in running the family business."

"Well, that's as important as writing more silly teenage love songs. God knows there are plenty of those in the world."

I was tempted to start singing the second verse of *Wind-song*, but the magic was broken.

I suddenly realized that the beautiful glade was no longer a sunny paradise. Abruptly it was dark and gloomy. Looking upward I saw black storm clouds blocking the sinking sun. A few "thudding" raindrops were starting to fall.

It was the unpredictable Oklahoma weather throwing a damper on my parade: gently rolling plains allowing lightning storms to un-expectedly creep up on you.

"It looks like our concert is finished. It was really nice to meet you, Scotty," I said as I painfully levered myself to my feet with my cane.

"You too! See you at church this Sunday?"

I paused...the thought hadn't even occurred to me.

"Do you...think they'd want me back?"

"Why not?"

"Well...I've been away a long time...never came back after I got famous...moved from Gospel to singing the 'devil's music'...and my last official concert killed and mutilated thousands of people?"

"Oh, right," he frowned, brushing a hand at the now more-rapidly falling raindrops. I heard *deep rumbles* of thunder heralding fast-approaching lightning strikes. It'd be dangerous to stay out in the open much longer. "But isn't *Jesus* all about understanding people in trouble?" the young man continued, undeterred, as he also stood up. "...like loving our neighbor and even our enemies, offering them forgiveness?"

"Uhm...sure, Scotty," I answered, not wishing to douse his optimism with the truth: people are very unforgiving and rigid particularly supposedly religious people! "I'll think about it."

"Super!" he waved as he dashed off.

And maybe I'd just as quickly *forget* all about the possibility. What people claimed that they theoretically believed and how they actually conducted their day-to-day lives could be radically different. Yes, sometimes the worst hypocrites were self-proclaimed "righteous" people. It was true I had abandoned my roots. I wasn't proud of that. And my musical "heresies" had been uniformly condemned by most of the traditional churches—including my very own mother. Did I really want to return to face such narrow-minded bigotry, especially as I tried to regain my personal equilibrium?

A *cold wind* blasted into me, making me shudder. It was like a razor pulled slowly across my brow. All the suppressed agony in my body was emerging and multiplying! I'd better find a local Doctor fast. I *needed* a prescription renewal!

I painfully gripped my cane, beginning to slowly totter back home. There was no time for regressing to stuck-in-the-past fame. I'd done enough "rehabilitation" work staggering around for the day.

My peaceful interlude was over. A *bad storm* was about to hit.

Chapter 5

WITHDRAWAL TERROR

*It's **dark in the woods** at night*
Especially in the concrete jungle
Predators waiting to snap you up
Or mug you in a wicked rumble
But if you really hold me tight
I might not stray too far tonight
Staying where it's warm and safe
Far from the savage fight

So tell me the story of Jesus
Write on my heart every word
Tell how He loved those on fire
Healing every aching burn

But pain is a mighty motivator
Forcing me to seek soothing help
Or just to take the easy way out
Thinking only of myself

So please tell me the story of Jesus
Write on my heart every word
Tell how he survived his torture
Finding heaven even in the absurd...
The Suzette Anthology, Lyrics 5

61

"I don't need to go to the emergency room," I moaned, shoving my Mom's hands away. "I just...need to get my prescription renewed and..."

"You look terrible, Suzy. We're going to the hospital," she stated, bodily lifting me up in her strong arms and physically hauling me out to her black van.

I had just barely made it back to the house. As I stumbled along through the steadily increasing storm I progressively got weaker. My vision blurred such that I could hardly make out the street signs. Nearby lightning flashes were all that kept me on the right course. And it wasn't just the generalized pain of a healing body. I felt miserable, like a terrible bout of flu was ravaging me.

"Go...faster," I groaned to my mother.

"We'll be there in less than five minutes, Suzy. Hang in there," Sally King replied as we whipped up 12th Street to the light at Broadway.

"Good...I feel like I'm falling to pieces," I mumbled.

"Of course sometimes there's a wait at the emergency room before we can see a doctor and..."

"A wait?"

I'd never been sick-to-death before, except for right before my last concert. And even then a private physician (highly paid) came to see me in my trailer. There was no "waiting" involved.

"Depending on the other emergencies their dealing with, it could be hours before..."

"*No! No!*" I yelled in protest. "Can't we just stop by a pharmacy and get them to call up a doctor somewhere? The doctors back at the L.A. hospital would do it, I'm sure. I just need some more of my pain pills!"

"You don't know that, honey," my Mom stated. "Besides, the local pharmacies won't do that for you. A local doctor they know, maybe— but not out-of-state. You'll just have to see a doctor in person to get your prescription refilled and..."

I'd stopped listening to her. I was sweating profusely, trembling. Plus I was experiencing gut-wrenching stomach cramps. I could feel my heart missing beats. I couldn't get enough air into my lungs even though I was sucking air rapidly. I couldn't concentrate. The pain was so bad I literally felt like opening the door and jumping out into the road, letting myself get run over and killed!

"Please...hurry," I groaned, doubling over with pain.

"Suzy!" I heard her cry-out as we sped along Broadway.

I felt my eyes rolling back in my head as I passed out.

And that's all I remember until I woke up on a gurney inside a hospital. I was delirious, running a high temperature and feeling my muscles spontaneously knotting-up.

The muscle cramps were excruciating.

"It's ok, Susan," I heard a nurse telling me. "We're admitting you to the hospital. You're going to be ok."

Vaguely I saw quick FLASHES of light around me. Damn it! I knew what those were—the snapshots of "paparazzi." I thought the damn gossip sheets were done with me. I guess you can never really vanish from the sights of those scum-bags. Someone must have got a cool payoff phoning in I'd been brought into the emergency room.

"Whu...what's w-wrong with m-me?" I stammered. "Where's my Mom?"

"Get those reporters out of here!" I heard a sharp command.

I saw hospital security rushing past me, blocking off the corridor along which I was being wheeled.

"She's filling out your paperwork," the nurse kindly replied. "She'll be back with you shortly. Everything's going to be ok," she repeated.

"No, it isn't! I'm *dying!*"

As I tried to jerk away from the nurse I felt straps holding me onto the gurney. I couldn't get away. That was probably a good idea as otherwise I'd just have toppled over onto the floor from continuing convulsions.

"You're experiencing withdrawal symptoms," a deep voice spoke from the other side of my gurney. Twisting my face over, I blurrily saw a heavy-set older man leaning down into my line of vision. He had white stubble on his chin. He had on a pair of large black glasses. "I'm your family's local physician, Dr. Spencer. You may remember me from checkups when you were a kid. I wasn't as fat then, hah! It seems that the L.A. hospital had you on a fairly hefty dose of oxyco-done and..."

"Well then give me some more!" I barked at him.

"You don't need them," he tried to soothe me. "From the latest x-rays I distally accessed in your California file, your broken bones have all healed. Sure, you'll have discomfort now and then. But a postsur-gical requirement for severe pain relief is long gone. Don't worry, though. We'll get you on some other drugs that will help you 'detox' comfortably and..."

"No!" I argued, managing to grab his pudgy arm with a claw-like grip of my extended hand. "Just give me some more of what I've been taking!"

His other hand gently pushed back on my shoulder, keeping me from straining against my straps. He loosened the death-grip I had on his arm, finger by clawed finger.

"I can't ethically or legally extend your present prescription," he informed me. "But once you're through the main withdrawal symp-toms you'll find you won't need those pills anymore because..."

"I'm *sick!* I'm *dying!*" I screamed. "*Help* me!"

"It's not an illness!" he snapped at me, apparently trying to cut-through the panicked haze that enveloped me. "You are *addicted* to opioids. What you are experiencing are *withdrawal* symptoms. It'll be rough for about a week. But then you'll start feeling better and..."

"Me...a drug addict? No! I don't take drugs! Well, maybe a cou-ple just one time, but I'm not..."

"How has your IBS been doing?"

"What?"

"Have you had any bloating or diarrhea?"

"What the hell are you talking about?"

"Just tell me," he ordered me gently.

"I...it hasn't bothered me much...I dunno...I only have a few bowel movements a week but..."

"Solid?"

"I guess...examining my turds has been a low priority!"

Christ, what was he doing? I needed my pain medicine and he was babbling on about my guts?

"I'm just helping you be aware of your body and what you've been doing to it, Suzy. Oxycodone and similar drugs lock down your bowels. In your case, since you're naturally very loose, it's tamped down the IBS you've dealt with your entire life, almost bringing you back to normal function. Do you see this?"

"Ok, it's helping my IBS," I admitted, straining against the straps. "So give me some more!"

I was vaguely aware of them wheeling me into a room, orderlies unstrapping me and transferring my writhing body to a bed.

"The drug you've been prescribed is very similar to *heroin*, Susan. They both activate what are called 'opioid receptors' that release pleasure-inducing dopamine in your brain. They're both highly addictive. The pain of being cut off from them quickly eclipses the original bodily pain, creating their own need: i.e. 'addiction.' Now, I don't know why they kept you on oxycodone so long in L.A., but..."

"I had *every damn bone* in my body broken!" I now yelled, struggling against the orderlies who were strapping me down on the bed. "I had *multiple surgeries* over months. God damn it—give me some more of those freaking pills!"

Shockingly he just gently laughed, clinically observing me from the foot of the bed.

"This is an all-too-common situation, Susan," he informed me matter-of-factly. "People go in for bad injuries or illnesses and get prescribed opioids. Then either the physicians or the patients don't tail-off the dosage properly or promptly enough. The patients end up addicted despite everyone's best intentions. It just happens. They, like you, may not even be aware they've become a drug addict. In fact, we have a local epidemic of people in your similar situation. But..."

"I'll *kill* all of you!" I screamed, struggling like a maniac against my straps as I was firmly cinched down upon the firm surface. "I'm Suzette Kingly! I'm a *superstar*! You can't do this to me! You can't tie me down like an animal! Let me loose right now! And give me my pain-meds!"

But apparently they *could* tie me down like an animal.

I'm ashamed to say I was literally foaming at the mouth in my rage to get free and get more of my "fix." I was still struggling to surge upward and break free of my straps like a transformed green she-Hulk.

"You had severe injuries, that's true," Dr. Spencer calmly stated, "but you should not have been on oxycodone for six months. That might have been due to the Hollywood medical environment, often rather unethical, catering to the needs of—yes—the so-called 'superstars.' I take it that when you initially entered the L.A. hospital you were fairly wealthy?"

Unexpectedly that sobered me. Though I felt like I was about to vomit up all the meals I'd eaten over the last week, I was suddenly subdued. He was right. Despite the paparazzi's getting in a few "low blows" in my hour of misery, I was no longer a superstar or even a millionaire. I was just a little girl again, who'd behaved badly.

"I'm sorry," I whispered as I felt a needle roughly jab into my arm.

Thankfully it was some type of sedative. My eyes fluttered shut as I fell backward into an internal, burning, seething *hell*.

I was in the hospital detoxing for a full two weeks. For much of that time I was incoherent, alternating between sobbing uncontrollably and raging like a maniac. They gave me other drugs supposedly for easing the withdrawal, but they didn't do much. Apparently I was particularly sensitive to opioids like oxycodone. Methadone, buprenorphine, and naltrexone just put a lid on my suffering rather than easing it.

And, yes, my IBS returned with a vengeance. Every time I woke or twitched it seemed I needed to use a bedpan or lurch my way to the bathroom.

Auuugggggghhhhh!

But, after what seemed an eternity, I was ready to be released from the hospital...yet again.

I half expected a phalanx of reporters and paparazzi to meet me at the exit, but there was nobody. My brief flare-up of fame was snuffed out. A raging addict "has-been" was news, but a recovering Diva was not.

"—and take these whenever you feel any additional pain," Dr. Spencer was instructing me, handing me a vial. "And of course if you feel you're relapsing then contact me immediately. Your mother has my home number. As soon as you're able, you'll need to be in a long-term support group. There are several locally, many more online. Good luck to you, Susan."

I was hunched over in the wheelchair, half-buried under a thick blanket my Mom had brought for me. I'd barely eaten anything in the nearly two weeks I'd been in the local hospital detoxing. I'd torn out the i.v.'s they tried to give me. I was a shell of my former self. If I'd before looked like a hideous middle-aged rehab, I was now the picture of a shrunken up old hag in her eighties.

My, how far the Mighty have fallen.

"Thank...you," I managed to whisper. "And...thanks to the whole hospital staff."

"We'll send them a card," my Mom encouraged me. "Again, thanks for taking such good care of Suzy, Dr. Spencer."

"That's my job."

"Well, I so appreciate you coming so quickly to the emergency room and then monitoring Suzy's recovery."

"Well, I get to claim I detoxed a 'superstar,'" he laughed good-naturedly. "It'll look good on my resume."

I shuddered at what I took as his mocking tone, though I'm sure he was just trying to insert some much-needed humor in the situation. I grit my teeth together to keep from snapping-back at him.

As Mom helped me from the wheelchair into the passenger seat of the van I looked down at my fist tightly gripping the new vial of pills. My scrawny fingers were visibly trembling. It'd be a long climb back to the heights from which I'd fallen, if ever.

"You ready?" Mom asked me as she spryly slipped into the driver's seat.

I was bundled up in my blanket, my head just poking out, holding up the vial to my eyes.

"I guess," I gulped, trying to focus on the label of the pills.

It said: *Take 1 to 2 tablets every 4 hours while symptoms last. Do not take more than 12 tablets in 24 hours unless directed by a doctor. 235 mg NSAID per tablet for pain relief, aspirin...*

Aspirin? That damn quack of a doctor was prescribing me *aspirin?*

I could already feel the NEED building up in my body. The terrible PAIN I'd temporarily quelled over the last two weeks was *returning*, even more powerful than before.

"How are you doing, honey?"

I grit my teeth together, trying not to let her see how awful I was feeling. She just might turn the car around and get me readmitted to the hospital. Nope. I wasn't having any more of that torture.

"Not too good...but I guess it'll take a while to fully recover."

"Be patient, dear. You've been through a lot. You can't expect to be back in top form overnight."

As the van crept slowly along—apparently not to rattle its delicate cargo, me—I was ashamed to be dependent. It hurt me to be indebted to her. Sure she was my mother, but she was a *traitor* to the family. I *hated* her more than ever.

"I...don't think...my insurance will cover my stay in the..."

"Don't even bother your head about the bills," she stopped me. "You generously supported my work while you were on top. I saved enough of that support to take care of you now. You just concentrate on recovering, dear."

Outwardly, I nodded gratefully. Inwardly I knew that my "payoffs" to her were just to keep the press off my back in regards to familial obligations. If I'd been free to do what I wanted, not just to maintain my official "nice-girl" image, I'd have cut her off entirely.

Sure, she had her retirement income from her years teaching at the local high school, but that didn't amount to much. I'd been the real bread-winner for years now.

"Can I...have the window...down?" I hesitantly asked.

"Of course, honey," she said as she activated the control on the arm of her seat.

A cool breeze rushed over my fevered brow as the window fully opened beside me. Ah, it felt great. It was early evening and the air was dry. It sucked the sweat off me. According to Mom there'd been no rain over the last two weeks I was in my hospital room. That was fitting. I came in during a thunderstorm and I was going back out in a drought.

I was going from bad to worse.

Disdainfully I inched my hand up to the bottom of the opened window. Making sure my Mom wasn't looking I dropped the vial of aspirin out the window into the street.

I wouldn't need that weak crap.

If they wouldn't prescribe me the medication I really needed, then I'd just have to get it on my own.

The day before I escaped from Sulphur was a Sunday. I decided to go to church. It would lull my Mom into thinking I was recovering. Then, when she least expected it, I'd make my move.

"How are you doing, sweetie?" she asked. "Are you sure you want to go to Church today? You don't have to, you know. You can take all the time you need to fully recover. After all, it's only been three days since you got out of detox at the hospital."

I was sitting in the living room in a big rocking chair, bundled up in a thick blanket. Just my raggedly bald head poked up. I was trying to look "healthy." But beneath the robe I was sweating and trembling.

"I'm...doing better," I tried to grin at her. I'm sure my effort didn't convince her as she looked alarmed. She recognized my attempt to get my mouth into a stage-smile. "Going to...church services...singing with the congregation...will help me."

"Well, it's only two hours until services. I assume you're not interested in attending the adult Bible class?"

"Uhm...when I'm fully recovered, maybe...but for now...the Worship Service will be enough—if that's ok with you? I don't know how the congregation...will react to me. So maybe just one hour's exposure will...be best. I don't want...to upset them."

I could see she was touched that I asked how she felt about it. Up until then I just did stuff. If she liked it, fine. If she didn't like it, then that was too bad. I guess I wasn't much of a house guest. But she wasn't much of a mother.

But for now I had to keep up the pretense.

"Of course that's fine," she smiled gently at me, coming over to lay a hand on my exposed shoulder. I fought the urge to pull away. She put her other hand on my forehead. "But you're still feverish and...?"

"It's just this warm blanket. I'm sweating. I'll take a shower—but, say...?"

"Yes?"

"Do you still have our stage wigs?"

Even during our Gospel-group singing days we'd all had spiffy wigs we could slap on to give a bit extra "voom" to our numbers. Combined with outfits appropriate to the performance, that's what made us stand out from our competitors: professionalism.

"I do. They're in a box up in the antic that..."

"Maybe...I'll look less scary if I put on the short blond one. Do you think it'll still fit my head?"

"I'm sure it will..."

"Super!" I ended the conversation, wobbly getting up and slumping toward the bathroom. "I'll be out shortly."

"I'll have breakfast ready."

"Ok...great...*thanks*, Mom."

I could see I'd touched her with my pretend-gratitude. I saw she had tears in her green eyes as I shut the bathroom door behind me. I turned on the shower to full-blast, dropped the blanket, stepped out of my loose underwear, and looked at myself in the full-length mirror. I was a scrawny, hunched-over caricature of my previous Superstar self. I'd been sleek, sexy, and powerful. Now I was mottled, disgusting, scrawny, and weak. At least that's what my eyes saw staring back to me from the mirror.

I dropped to my knees, put my head in the toilet, and vomited.

"No...breakfast...for me," I muttered as I got the heaving under control.

Sure, I knew I should go back to the hospital or at least make an appointment with Dr. Spencer. But they wouldn't give me what I knew I needed. To get what I *really* needed, I'd have to go to Oklahoma City. I just had to make it through the day. After my Mom was asleep, I'd escape.

At least, that was my plan. Yes, it was crazy. But when your mind is contorted by an all-consuming addiction, your priorities get likewise twisted-up.

"Suzette! It's so nice to see you again. You're looking good."

It was Scotty in a suit. He looked cute with his fashionably wide tie. His long, wavy black hair was tied in a neat pigtail at the back of his head. His young-guy bright smile was dazzling, infectious.

I stoically shook his hand as we moved through the crowd into the auditorium proper. I nodded to others that greeted me. I didn't say anything in response to their seemingly kindhearted statements. I knew they didn't mean any of it. They were all out to get me. They wanted to change me back into what I'd been when I'd gone to their little church as a child: a carbon-copy of them—proper, obedient, and controlled...just like pretty-boy Scotty.

But I wasn't any of that. I was *Suzette Kingly*, their "bad girl" of Pop-Rock. Hah! But for the moment, I had to be contrite, polite, and quiet.

At least I didn't look hideous. I'd always taken pride in my appearance. The wig covered up my horribly scarred head. I had on a long-sleeved blue shirt and blue pants that concealed my scrawny limbs. And I'd used makeup to hide much of the splotches on my face, conceal the bags under my eyes, and fill out my shrunken eyebrows. Any close examination would see I was just a failed "detoxed" addict about to explode. But from a distance I looked presentable.

As we slid into a pew my Mom asked me: "I wasn't aware that you knew Scotty. He's such a nice boy. His dad, Losa Yanash, is one of the elders here now, you know. He was appointed a couple years back by the governing Board."

"Uh huh," I nodded politely, just trying to keep down the big breakfast she'd forced me to eat. It wouldn't do to vomit all over the people in the pew in front of me. That might be a "clue" to everyone that I wasn't doing as well as I was pretending.

"Scotty's going to lead the first song today," Mom observed, reading the order-of-service pamphlet. "He's a real nice kid. Everyone's very proud of him."

Yes, that was definitely a dig at me. Little Scotty's the darling and I'm yesterday's news. Well, I'd make them all pay! But for the moment I had to relentlessly execute my plan.

"I...saw him out in the Park when I first got back,' I explained. "He recognized me so I briefly talked with him. It turns out he was...Billy's best friend."

My voice trailed off in exhaustion.

She didn't reply. Good. I'd shut her up by bringing in Billy's name. Hah! She deserved it. Maybe I could shove the knife in just a bit deeper.

"I'll bet Billy would have been a good song leader here too."

She briefly nodded, stoically staring forward.

Yep, I saw the dig had cut her deep. Good!

It all went downhill from there. The service was awful. It was old, stale Gospel songs from centuries in the past. The audience's singing was flat. The band hurt my ears. The preacher droned on and on for what seemed forever. The "altar call" was prolonged, seemingly to give the "prodigal Suzette" plenty of time to go forward and "confess her sins." Well, I wasn't going to give them the satisfaction of seeing me grovel for their "forgiveness." To hell with them all! I needed neither their sympathy nor "healing."

My insides were turning to jelly and they were prattling on about the sweet love of Jesus! I needed honey and they were feeding me crap.

Agggghhhhhh! I felt like jumping up and screaming: *you people are all pitiful hypocrites with an unprofessional, boring show!*

But I managed to clamp my trembling jaw shut and sit quietly, waiting them out.

Finally it was over and we could head back home.

"So...how did you like the service?" Mom asked me as we drove the few blocks in our van back home.

"Nice," I lied.

"Well, that's good," she nodded. "You're looking a bit tired, Suzy. Would you like to eat lunch or just take a nap and get your strength back?'

"Yes...that..."

"Take a nap?"

"Right...thanks...I *am* tired. The preaching and singing took more out of me...than I'd thought it would...didn't sleep too good last night...don't wake me up if I crash, ok?"

"You sleep just as long as you want. You sure you don't want me to make you a sandwich first?"

I almost vomited all over the car seat at the thought.

I gave my Mom a wan smile, trying to reassure her.

"Not hungry..."

"Alright then, Suzy. You know where the 'frig is. Whenever you get up, take whatever you want."

I nodded. Yep, I'd do that alright. I'd take whatever I wanted. Once I got my strength back from my morning religious "torture" I'd take *whatever* I Goddamned wanted!—I mentally shouted to myself.

I was sick and getting sicker, sinking down into a bottomless black pit. And I didn't care what my mother or anyone else thought about me. They were irrelevant.

Chapter 6

<u>OKLAHOMA CITY</u>

For a brief taste of heaven *she lived life in hell*
That's what the prostitute claimed
When I saw her on TV being interviewed
Showing reality's perverted fame

Down in the hollers and the peaceful valleys
The cowboys and horses tend to their ranch
It's a hard-working vision of iconic dreams
Where life taunts the haunted damned

We'll eat it or drink it or breath it right in
Or stick it straight into a vein
It doesn't much matter however it comes
If it only takes away the pain

Well they say that I'm weak; they say that I'm stupid
They say that they're glad they're not me
But walk in my footsteps and you'd be even worse
Doing anything to get your next fix

I'd really like to give you a redeeming verse
Where the sad song becomes affirming
But all I can say to those in my shoes
Is: "Don't go to O.K.C.!"
The Suzette Anthology, Lyrics 6

I stayed in my room through the entire afternoon, evening, and into the early night. I heard Mom come and peek in my room several times. But I stayed huddled under my blankets in my bed, moving just enough that show her I was still alive. I didn't want to talk to her or even see her. I didn't even get up to go to the bathroom, holding in my pee until the pressure became unbearable.

Finally, hearing nothing else stirring in the house, I got up and dashed to the bathroom. I didn't flush the toilet, lest I awaken my Mom. I was mildly concerned to see blood in my urine, but didn't worry about it. I was going to fix everything soon enough. I quickly dressed. I put on my church clothes and wig so I looked presentable.

I made sure I had my wallet with all its i.d. cards, plus my lucky marbles to nervously fumble with in my pocket. The wallet didn't contain any money. As a last resort I could pawn my Taw for a few cents...but there was a better option.

It was pitch black outside. Only a few nightlights faintly illuminated the bathroom, living room, and kitchen. My Mom's bedroom door was shut. I could hear some sporadic sputtering. I didn't know she snored. Maybe I'd never noticed when I was a kid. Maybe it was just because she was getting older.

Back sitting on the toilet I again happily emptied my bladder. Shortly thereafter my bowels succumbed to explosive diarrhea. Strangely it wasn't disgusting but liberating. Afterward I felt lighter than air, relieved of a heavy burden. My stomach was growling. I was starving. But I didn't want to reclog my body with ordinary food. I needed something far more energizing.

"Where is it? Where is it?" I whispered, fumbling at the drawers in the kitchen.

And then I found it. There beneath the sliding wheels of the lowest drawer was a fat envelope. It was Mom's "emergency cash" that she'd kept there for years, just in case whatever terrible disaster she'd imagined actually happened.

With trembling fingers I opened it and felt crinkly, old twenties stacked up inside. There was at least a thousand dollars. That should be plenty to get me to where I needed to go.

"Good...and now for the keys," I shakily whispered.

I slowly edged open the key drawer, being careful not to make any more noise than necessary. I saw my keyring which had house keys plus my car keys. Yep, lots of keys. I snatched the keyring into my trembling fist.

"I'm not stealing anything," I whispered to myself. "I'm just taking back...a little part of what Mom extorted from me. And the car...well, it's mine anyway."

Creeping out of the house, I opened and slid into the raggedly driver's set in my parked-under-a-carport, beat-up old Fiero. It was spooky outside, quiet. Normally the residential area was full of honking cars, twittering birds, and barking dogs. Now it was past midnight. Everyone, even the damn dogs, was asleep. The gate to the yard was open. Starting the car without turning on the headlights I backed up and turned out of the gate. It'd been a long while since I'd driven on my own. During my Superstar years I'd always had chauffeurs. Now I had to remember which foot went where. But I quickly fell back into old habits.

In a few minutes I was gliding down the road out of town, headed west toward I-35. I was glad to see the gas tank was full. It'd take me to where I wanted to go without having to stop to fill up. I didn't want to chance someone recognizing me, getting suspicious, and calling up the police or my Mom. Hopefully before the night was over I'd be back in the arms of my sweet, soothing *Lover*.

And just like in an old-time, 1940's musical, I'd then magically "live happily ever after."

Hurray!

As I zipped up I-35 approaching Oklahoma City I was dazed and weak. But after the nearly two hour trip on the freeway I was also excited. I knew exactly where I was going.

After sleeping all day long and finally approaching my destination I was on an incredible natural high. But my body was fast deteriorating. My guts were knotted up with convulsions. I was fast filling the cab with putrid farts. I rolled down the driver's side window to let the cold night air blast into the car and flush out my stink. The frigid air also kept me alert.

"Ok...now I'm onto I-235...I'm almost there...gotta turn quick on-to East Sheridan Ave."

I swung out on the circle going off the highway leading onto the city streets. In my early career (three-and-a-half years ago) I'd done a tour of nightclubs across America. That was when most of the fundamentalist Christian churches formally condemned me, their former Gospel good-girl singer. One of the most vibrant clubs I appeared at was the "Chocolate Factory" in the Bricktown region of Oklahoma City. The club was in a renovated warehouse district where in the 19th and early 20th centuries four railroads had extensive freight operations. The area was decimated by the great depression. By the late 20th century it was mostly just abandoned, large buildings. But when Oklahoma City granted generous tax incentives for renovations the place became a tourist Mecca: including a ball park, waterway, monuments, restaurants, and nightclubs.

The most famous (or infamous) of the nightclubs was indeed the *Chocolate Factory*. Superficially it was a dance club that brought in some of the world's most upcoming bands and singers. But as I discovered when I played there, it had its seedier side. It provided ready access to gambling, prostitution, and drugs. The pimps and dealers blended into the crowds and approached any obvious marks. Since I was clinging to my "nice girl" image (for everyone other than uptight religious fundamentalists), plus was underage, I was carefully protected by my managers from the illegal activities. But I knew anything was readily available, right below the respectable surface, for everyone with the desire and the money to find it. And unlike many of the more reputable establishments, this nightclub was open 24 hours a day, 7 days a week.

I now had both the desire and the money. And I sure wasn't a "nice little girl" anymore.

"Chocolate...chocolate...chocolate *cake!* Hey, hey, hey, hey, and *hey!*" I sang wildly to myself as I turned off E. Sheridan into a parking structure.

The gate was open. You paid on the way out. I didn't even take one of the automatic tickets. I had no thought of leaving. I was going to stay there forever—or for as long as my $1,000-plus cash lasted me. And after that...who knew what depravities I might sink down into? But that wasn't what drove me relentlessly forward.

I had to have a fix.

Everything around me was a blur. Parking, following the signs, coming out to the ornate plaza, looking around at the stone columns, finding the entrance to the Chocolate Factory...it was all hard. Sticking a stage-grin on my face and smiling my way past the bouncers at the entrance was easy. I had on my blond wig and the nice looking blue outfit I'd worn to church. Glaring laser lights of every color flashed through swirling white fog inside. It made everyone garishly cartoonish, hiding any personal flaws. No one would take a second look at me. I was totally anonymous.

Though it was almost 4:00 AM in the morning, the place was packed with a gyrating, swirling mass of dancing and prancing humans. There wasn't a live band at that early hour, but the DJ was cranking it up high. The beat was wild and eardrum-shattering.

"Looking for some fun?"

In the crushing mass of hyper-humanity it was hard to make out who was speaking. But then I saw a lean Hispanic fellow with greased-down black hair leering at me. He had on a diamond-sparkling vest over an aqua-colored silk shirt. Several gold chains dangled from his wiry neck. He looked every bit the part of a pimp.

But I wasn't looking for sex. I needed drugs.

"I need some smack. Got some?"

"You want 'smack'? Hah! That's kinda nonspecific, old lingo, babe. I got you smokin' *h-bomb*, *squashers*, *cheese fries*, *chocachips*, *dirtballs*, *zippers*, *flick*, *jolly-rogers*, *swimmers*, and *cream*. What's yur pleasure, darlin'?"

"Straight injectable."

I wasn't playing around. I wasn't experimenting. I was all in. The LUST pounding at my body and brain was overpowering. And in this environment my body knew it was just minutes away from *satisfaction*. I was literally *drooling* with anticipation.

Sure if I'd had plenty of time I knew I could have found it in Sulphur. Everything's available anywhere if you know where to look, know the right people, and have enough money. But I didn't have time to screw around. I needed it *now!* And this was the fastest route to getting my agony and lust simultaneous soothed and satiated in one monstrous high.

"Oh yep, straight blast, huh? Got some real fine *brown sugar*, very pure. It'll cost you, though."

"How much?"

"Two."

I wasn't a total novice. Dealing with world-trotting musicians for years I knew the going rates. You didn't live on the road for months with hanger-ons, "peeps," entertainers and roadies surrounding you without knowing the basics.

"You're funny," I grinned at him, forcing myself to dance off to the side away from him.

I knew if I didn't at least make a pretense of playing the game he'd drag me off, kill me, and take everything.

But he was back at my side, doing a strange imitation of a mutated penguin walk in response to the blaring BEAT.

Oh yes, he blended into this raving, maniacal crowd just fine.

"*One*, then—for safe passage to the nest, clean needle, good security, medical monitoring, and deliverance back here after you're stable. Professional nurse administers the dose. Very safe, discrete—it's perfect for a sophisticated lady like you."

"Hah. And just who is it you think I am?"

He leered at me again, revealing gold-capped teeth.

"You be, with no doubt, a Superstar," he grinned widely, his head bobbing up and down like an insane duck.

"Damn straight!" I laughed, twirling around in a tight circle.

"Ready?"

"Let's do it!"

"Cash up front."

"You take me for a fool? That's insulting."

"Hah! Just testing you, foxy lady...ok, then...forty will do. The other sixty when I bring you back safe, sound, and higher than a kite. Deal?"

"Deal," I said as I reaching into my cash-packed pocket and drew out a couple twenties.

I followed him through the crush of humanity, past the marble-topped bars, and through a side door. Down a corridor and through a guarded entrance I found myself in what looked like an opium den. Though mostly shrouded in deep shadows, I saw under scattered dim lights many bodies strewn about sitting or lying on mattresses and pillows. Some were smoking. Most of the rest were just slowly twitching, lost in their own personal ecstasies.

"Here we be, girl. I leave you in good hands."

"Thanks. What's your name, so I know who to blame if this juice doesn't live up its billing?"

"Freddy. Jist say you want Freddy and I'll come running, Superstar. And don't worry. It's gonna be great. Would I lie to you?"

That should have scared me straight. But I was beyond caring about the dangers.

I waved as he vanished away. Hah. "Superstar." If he only knew I was "Suzette," a *real* Superstar. But it was best no one recognize me. If I ever had a hope for a comeback I sure couldn't do it as a user. That was the kiss of death in the teen pop market. And, like it or not, for a few months I was still a teen.

"You ready?"

"More than ready."

It all happened fast. One moment I was wobbling along toward an empty, clean-looking, silk-sheeted mattress. The next I was lying upright against some soft pillows, a white clad nurse-looking lady thumping at a vein in my arm. A rubber band was constricting my upper arm, making the blood back-up in my arm, expanding my vein. I approvingly noted that she was using a fresh 1-ml syringe/needle combo snapped directly out of its sterile plastic wrapping. She swiftly sucked up a brown fluid, swabbed my vein with alcohol, and then slipped the needle in. She expertly depressed the plunger.

"*Ouch...I...*"

She withdrew the needle, flicked off the rubber band from my arm, and placed a blob of white cotton over the puncture.

Then she cinched the blob down with a Band-Aid.

She moved my thumb to press down on the Band-Aid.

"Hold down firmly for five minutes so you won't get any hematoma," she kindly informed me. "I'll be back to check on you periodically. This is a high quality product. You should peak in two hours, be up for four, with a gradual fall after that. Freddy will take you back to the official rave whenever you wish. Enjoy!"

She moved on as I pressed down on my cotton blob. There was no pain from the jab on my arm. I was already feeling the effects of the injection. A wave of *pure bliss* swept over me. The nausea, all the crippling hurt, the fear, the intense cravings all faded away. My body felt like it was transmuting from a steaming cesspool into *wine:* an intoxicating, marvelous, bubbling fluid that could take any form. My skin felt electric, burning-hot in a marvelously erotic fashion. Pounding pulsations of *supernova energy* swept through me.

"Oh...yes..." I sighed, closing my eyes. It satisfied all the cravings of my missing oxycontin pills. But it was ten times better. This didn't just push off the pain but *erased* it. All the lingering aches of my abused organs and bones vanished. I was drifting on white clouds of pure pleasure. I never wanted to leave this heavenly place. I closed my eyes and gave myself over to the beautiful ecstasy.

Was this what I wanted? Was this what I'd been missing all my life? Was this the "end-all" and "be-all" of human existence? Was this what I *really* wanted?

Seemingly so...

But my blissful reverie was broken by *bright flashes!*

"What...?"

The next white flash almost blinded me.

"You! Get out of..."

There was a scurry around me. Guards were running after a person clutching a professional-looking camera.

But then the brief turmoil was past.

I didn't care. Whatever... That was likely just a fellow patron that recognized me. Even if it was a paparazzi, so what? Who cared about "Suzette" anymore, anyway? That photo would just go on some blog somewhere that no one would give a crap about...

"Time to go, Ms. Kingly."

Eh?

Was the nurse back? Was it Freddy? But how did they know my real name?

Then I heard the *screaming* and *gunshots*...

I opened my eyes to see black-clad, bullet-proof-vested Police rounding up the patrons, putting in-house guards up against a wall with their hands up. Oh, hell...it was the fuzz! It was a bust! Wow, I was rhyming—should I write a song? But wait...was plain old harmless heroin *illegal?* Rats! I vaguely realized I was going to wind up in jail, at least until I could make bail. But once again...so what? It didn't matter. Nothing mattered now that I'd finally embraced my *one true forever-lover...*

—who had bit me so sweetly on my arm, darling Vampire!

Hah. That was funny...

"Sorry, girl, Superstars don' come in every day."

I blearily saw Freddy standing off to the side, unmolested by the Police. I smiled at him and he smiled back. I liked the way the glaring lights from the Police flashlights shone off his gold teeth, making him look like a cartoon shark.

"You...recognized me?" I whispered.

He came over and knelt down next to me, gently taking my hand in his own.

"I got a lot more than 'one' out of this. The rags still pay for full tell-alls. You should consider it, girl. I was goin' out with a big payday even before you came, workin' with the cops and reporters. But seeing you moved up my timetable. I'm getting' six figures out of this bust."

"But...your business...?"

"—very dangerous for jist chump-change, taking bills off tourists. I'm getting' too old for it, don't 'cha know. I'm retirin' to the Bermuda's. Fun in the sun on the beach with the bitches. Settin' myself up with a new crew in Pembroke. I'm goin' 'legit' with my own 'modeling' agency, if you know what I mean. I was always more pimp than pusher."

"Sounds nice... I'm happy for you."

"I could always use young used-up famous bitches like you. Maybe you look me up after you get outta the slammer?"

"Maybe...who knows?" I smiled vaguely in his direction.

"Ok, then. Stay safe!"

"You too, Freddie."

I closed my eyes and let the Police bodily carry me out of the opium den. I was still too high to care.

"*What* were you thinking?"

I sat shivering on a hard bench, waiting to retrieve my personal possessions. I just hoped they'd not lost my lucky marbles. Without them to grasp and roll in my hand I felt unmoored, adrift on a burning sea of pain. I'd just spent two days in the Oklahoma County Jail. The heroin I'd shot-up had long since worn off. I was cold, mentally depleted, and deathly ill. I'd never been this low before.

"I...wasn't...thinking," I whispered back to my Mom. She stood there with a stern-faced officer who was taking out a set of keys to unlock my handcuffs.

"Then what were you doing?"

"...just trying...to get what I needed," I whined, my voice trailing off.

"Well, the judge let you off with most of the other 'customers.' Your sworn statements were enough to help convict the dealers at the establishment. But if you ever appear back in the drug court they say they'll throw the book at you. Suzy, you're lucky to be alive. People can *die* from injecting heroin the first time!"

"At least they die happy," I mumbled, rubbing at my aching forehead.

I had a huge, throbbing headache.

"*What?*"

"You heard me."

She locked her green eyes with mine. I was the first to break off the visual confrontation. It just took too much energy to maintain a fighting attitude. I was too tired. I just wanted to go home.

"What's really behind this?" she demanded.

I shrugged, wiping snot from my nose with the now-filthy edge of my shirtsleeve. I was still wearing the same clothes. They hadn't even given me a jail uniform. I itched terribly and stank. My wig was tattered and stringy. I'd have to wash it and give it a perm.

"What do you mean?" I sullenly replied.

"This isn't like you, Suzy. This isn't even like Suzette. She never would have allowed herself to sink this low. She hated drugs!"

"Live and learn, bitch..."

She slapped me hard on my cheek, glaring at me!

"You *don't* talk to your mother like that! Apologize, now!"

Around us were in-coming and out-going prostitutes, pimps, other drug users, various criminals, drunks, swanky high level corporate lawyers, overworked-looking public defenders, bailsmen, and many police. It was a strange place to have a confrontation with my mother. It felt like when I unwittingly took that tab of LSD: unreal. The processing-out area was a cavernous space filled with sad souls where sounds echoed and clattered and clashed: a "cacophony" of ugly noise. I could just pretend I didn't hear her.

But I was ready to have it out.

"It was *you* that killed Dad and Billy!" I blurted out, tears coming to my eyes.

The handcuffs slid off as I rose to my feet, freeing my aching wrists. I planted my fists defiantly on my hips.

"I thought that was behind us," Sally King replied softly.

Good. I'd set her back on her self-righteous haunches.

"It's never going to be behind us! I've had it with you. I never want to talk to you or see you ever again. I'm *not* going home! I still have some cash and I'm..."

"—that you *stole* from me! I should press charges and..."

"I gave you millions over the last few years, Mom. *Millions!* And that was all for what—'rescuing' some measly, useless, discarded cats and dogs? Instead of humanely euthanizing the excess beasts you pamper them until they die of old age? Where's the logic to that? Well, as long I was making a hundred million a year it didn't matter, 'good publicity' my manager Darlene told me. But I'm *not* making millions anymore since my whole career turned out to be just a criminal *scam* that ended up killing thousands of people! So what are a few hundred bucks back to me for the millions I gave to you and your stupid animal shelter? How dare you get mad at me and slap me! It should be me stomping *your* face into the dirt!"

Her eyes narrowed and she stepped back a couple feet.

"Well, come on then."

"What?"

"If you're really so tough, then take a swing."

I glanced around uncertainly. Everyone else was ignoring us, going about their various frantic businesses. The officer that had released me was walking away, his back to us.

"I can't hit my own mother. That'd be..."

And yet a second time she *slapped* me hard across my cheek.

Stunned, I put a shaking hand to my twice-smarting face. It hurt! The people around us paused in the rush and tumble of their own personal tragedies to watch. I saw flashes of cellphone cameras going off. Yep, a few videos and I'd be right back in the pity-news cycle, yet again.

This was a real screw-up loop!

I was about to launch myself at my Mom to pound her face to pieces when I felt my balled-up fists loosen and drop to my sides.

"Mommy..." I sobbed, falling into a heap on the floor.

I felt her strong arms around my shoulders, comforting me.

"We're going home. And then we're finally going to have a long talk. Ok?"

"Ok..."

Chapter 7

THE ANIMAL SHELTER

*Well they call it **puppy love***
When you're falling on your face
Drooling at his or her feet
Wanting nothing but their touch
Wagging your tail at lightning speed
At a smile, a caress, a brief hug
Willing to do anything at all
To know that they are pleased
Glad that you're around...

Could it be a better dream
Barking and yapping happily
Spinning, hopping, and prancing
Bopping paws and sniffing butts
Getting our glorious, sick fun
Behaving like raving lunatics
Finding our forever home
Never again to be alone!

The Suzette Anthology, Lyrics 7

"I remember it like it was yesterday," I whispered, my lower lip trembling.

I was incredibly weak, shaking. I should have put a jacket on since it was cool outside. But I didn't want it weighing down my flannel shirt. As it was, my skin felt dry and itchy. I was hyper-sensitive to anything touching me. Even my soft old jeans felt itchy and scratchy. I didn't even have my wig on, letting my nearly bald, burnt head stand out like a big sore.

My mother was there beside me, hovering protectively.

We were standing to the side of the crater in the empty lot behind our house. It looked like a small meteor had hit, excavating down twenty feet, throwing up a crater wall of fractured and pulverized rock. I was standing on the lip of the crater's wall. If I went forward a foot I'd fall down the steep slope. It was too deep to fill in. So we'd just let it go to nature. Already small bushes were growing around the edge. During the winter and spring it filled up halfway with water. Give it a few more years and we'd probably have a nice fishing pond.

"I know, honey, me too," she replied quietly.

My guts rumbled and twisted. I held in the gas. I didn't want to mar this moment of intense confrontation with my disgusting, IBS-generated farts.

"I could have saved them."

"There wasn't time. You'd have died also."

"You don't know that."

"Yes...I do."

I turned to look at my Mom standing behind me. I was surprised to see she had tears streaming down her cheeks. I thought she was cold-blooded, having long since put it all behind her. Though her speech was rock-steady, clearly she'd also not gotten over the tragedy.

"How can you know that?"

"I was told to let it happen—and to keep you away."

"What—by whom?"

She sighed, swiping at her eyes with the backs of her hands.

"Let's go back into the house. I'll tell you all about it."

"Whatever it is, why didn't you tell me before?"

"You wouldn't have believed me."

"And I'm going to believe you now?"

"I think you will," she sighed.

She turned away from the ragged crater that once was the center of the detached garage where Dad and Billy did their "inventing." It had been a place of delightful scientific adventure. Billy and I pretended we were assistants to a great scientist cracking the hardest secrets of Nature. We were merrily and naively pursuing *cold fusion* for unlimited safe power generation, *room temperature supercon-ductivity* for ready storage of all that massive energy, *artificial self-aware intelligence* for controlling *quantum-level teleportation* for traveling to the stars, *time travel* for mastering past and future history, and *medical miracles* to let us all live forever—solving any of which (pick your poison) was only one experiment away.

Magnificent scientific childish fantasies...*sigh*.

Was this what I really wanted? If so, I sure sidetracked myself pursuing Music. But little did I realize then that my radically different performing career would lead me right back to those seemingly impossible dreams!

But I should add that my Dad, Dr. David King, was realistic. He *wasn't* just a starry-eyed dreamer. He was a pragmatist, ever reassessing his radical theories in light of the latest data from his jury-rigged experiments. He used his packed garage and adjoined sheds filled with surplus scientific equipment wisely, chipping away at mysteries which reputable scientists in big, well-funded labs had long since dismissed as impossible or unsolvable. Though he'd relegated his active research career to just a fun night-time hobby as he taught physics at the local high school, he had unbounded enthusiasm. He didn't shrink from attacking any and all big challenges. But unlike established scientists, he jumped wildly from one idea to the other. He eagerly awaited new data while refusing to be discouraged by the inevitable negative results.

"Next time we'll get it!" I heard him laughing exuberantly in my mind, reading dismal printouts from the latest failed experiment.

Right... "Next time" he and Billy *died* while his supposedly faithful wife Sally King looked on and did nothing.

And I'd never forgiven her.

She brought me a mug of hot tea, putting it on the coffee table beside my rocking chair. I picked it up, cupping it in my hands. I now had a warm robe on over my long-sleeved plaid shirt and blue jeans.

I deliberately did not thank her. My momentary lapse when I was discharged from the County Jail was over. I wasn't "Mommy's little baby" crying on her shoulder. I still insisted in my mind that I was

Suzette Kingly, an independent grown woman—who *despised* my mother!

But the mug of steaming tea was welcome.

Ever since getting back from Oklahoma City I'd been cold. Even though the days were warm, I couldn't shake the chill that had settled deep in my bones. Dr. Spencer said it was one of the lingering effects of my prolonged addiction to Oxycodone. My internal thermostat was screwed up. He assured me it would gradually readjust to a normal setting. But I was prepared to be cold forever. I still didn't know if I'd be able to kick the addiction. But I was trying to recover—though reliving the brutal past wasn't helping.

I'd avoided the subject of my Dad and Billy's tragic death the last couple days, claiming I needed time to get my thoughts back in order. My Mom patiently bided her time, kindly affording me the space I needed, until now.

Thinking back to that awful tragedy, though, tempted me to run back into that glorious needle-induced euphoria.

Maybe I would. But maybe I wouldn't—though it'd be incredibly hard to keep on going cold-turkey "un-medicated." Dr. Spencer assured me this would be preferable to "cutting back." But *he* didn't have to endure the hell I was experiencing.

"So what's your story?" I bluntly cut-to-the-point, "Did 'God' tell you to let Billy and Dad die?"

Truth-to-tell, I'd lost my faith. It died the day that the cold, uncaring Universe squashed my Dad and brother. Except for the previous Sunday, I'd never gone back to church again.

But my mother, inexplicably, had the opposite reaction.

At least that was all I could figure out. Ever since we'd gotten back from OKC I'd puzzled over my Mom's cryptic behavior. And it wasn't just her nonchalance at my accusing her of murder. Even after the tragedy happened, she'd been strangely detached. I'd attributed it to the same awful shock that I myself felt at the time. But it was more. Even at the memorial service at church she'd seemed impatient, bored. It was like she was pretending to care, even when we placed roses on the empty caskets at the graveside service. Since Dad had left a generous insurance policy we did a full funeral. It seemed to mute the official inquiries that came after the event. Even the press seemed to back off, respectful of our elaborate grief. But she seemed preoccupied, more and more dedicated to a new project completely at odds with her previous interests: funding and building a sprawling state-of-the-art "no kill" shelter for Montgomery County's wayward, stray animals.

She'd never shown an interest before in the animal welfare movement. But now she became an official in the local Humane Society. She forged strong links to ASPCA and even to the more radical PETA and affiliates. As a certified, Ph.D. scientist she was embraced by those groups, one of whose main objectives was to put the brakes on the use of animals in scientific and medical research. True, her academic degrees were in theoretical mathematics, hardly an area that needed to test procedures and medications on animals. But her Ph.D. gave her a lot of credibility in advocating terminating animal experimentation.

And she remained fervently though quietly religious. She was active in the local congregation of our church, still singing occasionally with the house band. It seemed to me that she'd long since embraced the doctrines and traditions of fundamentalist Christianity. But, curiously, she wasn't evangelistic. She had firm beliefs but didn't try to force them on others. She held an expansionist view of "God": as the sum-total of the Laws of Nature, the breadth of known and unknown "reality," and the inner spark that drove both her and Dad to putter at their "impossible" quests.

I was convinced her Faith explained her awful prior actions.

She must have had some sort of "vision" that the "all-knowing" God in his "infinite Plan" needed my Dad and brother to get blown up in a failed scientific experiment to "test her faith" and that of the local community.

Hah! To me that was total bull-crap.

"No, it wasn't God," Sally King calmly informed me, leaning back and closing her eyes.

"Oh? If it wasn't the Lord then who was it?"

She paused, pursing her lips, as if considering what to reveal to me...

"Do you remember what happened?"

"Are you kidding me?" I snapped back at her.

"Humor me, Suzy. Tell me exactly what you remember."

I started to get up, go to my room and slam the door behind me...

"Please!" she begged me. "Let's get everything out in the open. I promise after this I'll never bring it up again—if that's what you want after hearing me out."

I groaned, settling back into the rocking chair and setting it in motion. I swung forward...back. Forward...back. Forward...back—a very soothing rhythm that caused a *massive flash-back* in my head.

"We were at the talent show in Nashville..." she prodded me.

It was actually the event that launched my subsequent career. I was only sixteen...*sweet* sixteen! Due to my submission video showing me recording with my family our first Gospel album, I'd been invited to participate in the opening episode of the newly revived series: *Nashville Teen Star*.

It's "catch" was featuring only youthful artists/musicians who would write in-house all the songs they'd personally perform on that season's show.

It was a "house entry" round, featuring twenty-four young hopefuls. Votes cast by the audience and judges would eliminate all but a dozen, who would then live together in a chaperoned "reality"-style house-situation for the entire run of the show. Each week the lowest vote-getter would be eliminated, until the increasingly elaborate productions resulted in only three remaining. Those last three then squared off for the title "Nashville Teen Country Star," winning a big recording contract.

I was determined to get into the show and become that season's Star!

"I thought you were ready for it, but your Dad didn't," Mom nudged my memory.

What did this have to do with the lab accident?

"Was that why he and Billy stayed behind?" I frowned. "I thought Dad couldn't get out of his teaching duties at the high school and..."

"Yes, that's partially true. He had a full teaching load, committee duties, and wrestling team coaching duties for that entire three days we were down in Nashville. Plus Billy had a whole raft of critical midterm exams at school. But the main reason was that we couldn't afford to send the whole family."

"But I thought that the show paid for everything?"

"Just you and one parent or guardian—anything extra had to be paid for by the individuals."

"I thought you and Dad were rich. You and he had all those patents on things you'd invented plus we had our two Gospel albums out that..."

She laughed. Despite my anger and suspicion it warmed my heart to see her green eyes twinkling. It'd been a long time since I'd seen her truly amused.

"Dear, we were just two high school teachers in Oklahoma. It's a low-tax but consequently *low service* state. By any standard, public school teachers are poorly paid. And raising two thriving kids plus all the weird science we were trying to do without any regular funding kept us barely getting-by, check-to-monthly-check. And the modest sales of our two albums didn't even pay the recording and advertising fees. We did well to lose money only modestly on our Gospel band career."

I nodded, sadly acknowledging the truth of her statement.

"Huh...I guess I got spoiled as a world-famous celebrity. My fans were knocking down the walls of the souvenir shop on my World Tours to get my pictures and do-dads," I shrugged. "I forgot all about my earlier career as a starving artist happy to get free singing time at the clubs."

Sally nodded, back to being sober. I could see she didn't think much of my nightclub performances. Certainly my last nightclub "appearance" in OKC had been traumatic enough.

"Anyway," she continued, "it was just you and me sharing a room at the local motel. Do you recall what happened the night of your dress rehearsal at the studio?"

"Sure. The limo came to pick us up at the motel. I was ready to go, dressed in my 'cow-girl' outfit, my guitar case in-hand, my demo song in my mind—but you weren't ready."

"No, dear. I was ready but something else happened. Remember?"

"I...oh, right. The limo was already crammed with kids. To take my guitar with me you had to stay behind. You said you'd take a cab. But then you never showed up at the practice session. When I got back you said you couldn't get a cab, they were all booked. But it turned out ok. The practice went fine. And then you were with me the next day at the actual taping session and..."

"How did I seem to you when you returned from the rehearsal?"

"Huh? Well, I was really excited about the set they had and the competition that..."

"Of course you were, honey. But what about me?"

"Oh...I was so excited I hardly noticed. But now that you mention it..."

"Yes?"

"You looked—shocked, unresponsive. I babbled on about all the details but you didn't say a thing. I'd thought I'd done well at my recording, but we wouldn't get to the actual judging until the next day. I thought you were just embarrassed at missing the session and wanted to let me describe everything. But, now that you mention it, you hardly said a word. And when we went to sleep in our separate beds in our motel room—oh, now I remember you making some noise. It was muffled, like you were crying into your pillow. But I heard you. I was so tired, though, I went to sleep quickly after that and forgot about it. The next day you looked normal so..."

"Something happened that evening, Suzy, beyond not catching a cab to the rehearsal. In fact, I lied about that. When I went back to our room to call one of the show-approved cabs so that I didn't have to pay for it, I had two visitors."

She stopped speaking, as if she were trying to control her voice, stay calm.

"Ok. You had a couple of visitors. So who were they? What did they say that upset you so much?"

She took a deep breath before continuing.

"They told me that something terrible was going to happen to your Dad and Billy. They told me I couldn't intervene. They said it was critically important that I keep *you* from intervening or you'd be caught up in it as well. They said I had to allow it to happen."

"What? They threatened our family? Did you call up the police?"

"I couldn't call the police. They wouldn't believe me. Even if I told you about it, you'd think I'd gone crazy. *You'd* call the police to get an ambulance to take *me* away!"

I was getting a bad feeling about this story. Did the death of Dad and Billy in the accidental explosion drive her over the edge? Despite her outward calm, did she go crazy? Did she make up some bizarre fantasy to justify her subsequent actions?

"Well...I'm listening to you now, Mom. Did you think that God or maybe Jesus came to 'warn' you about the impending disaster?"

"Hardly—do you think they'd tell me to let it happen if I had the chance to stop it?"

"Well..." I puzzled. That certainly didn't jive with my understanding of God and Jesus in the Bible. I could maybe believe that a heavenly vision warned her so she could *stop* what was going to happen. But why would they want her to not interfere?

"Alright, you've got me, Mom. Who was it that visited you?"

"It was Dave and Billy."

I almost burst out laughing. Surely she was kidding. My Dad and little brother came in person to warn her not to interfere with them getting blown into atoms out in the science shacks? They were 700 miles away in Sulphur! It would have taken them all day to drive to Nashville, as we'd done in the van. And even if they'd ditched all their responsibilities and classes to drive down to Nashville how could they possibly know the future?

"Did you think—you were under so much stress maybe seeing me have a chance at the big-time—you just imagined that..."

"I did *not* imagine it!" she yelled at me.

Wow. That set me back in my rocker, shocked at her intensity.

"Alright...alright...but surely you questioned their unexpected appearance at the motel door when..."

"Of course I did! But it wasn't your Dad and Billy that you or I knew. In fact, it took me a moment to even recognize them."

I shook my head, trying to get my thoughts unjumbled. She wasn't making any sense. Was she psychotic? If so, she was in worse shape than me.

"But then...?"

"It was *older* versions of your Father and Billy. Your Dad was frail and elderly. Billy was grown up. They both looked to be *fifty years* older than they should! They said time was short, gave me their warning, and then just disappeared."

"Uhm...disappeared?"

"They vanished. One moment they were there as solid and real as you are sitting there in that rocker—and the next moment they were gone."

I frowned, suddenly really scared to be there with her. Clearly she was demented with grief.

"You see? You don't believe me even now. There was no evidence they'd actually been there. I checked and there were no motel security cameras covering our room's door at that time. Without any hard evidence, if I'd told you what happened when you were sixteen coming off the audition of your life, would you have believed me?"

"Well..."

"I didn't do much talking on the way home, did I? I didn't even critique your audition performance, even though it was radically different from the judges' guidelines."

"They just wanted a variation on the currently popular Country Western stuff. I showed them real genius, blending in Jazz!"

"I agree it was genius, honey. But it startled them. They weren't ready for you to flout their rules and..."

"I couldn't just do insipid crap for them!"

"Sometimes it's best not to rock the boat. You've always been headstrong and..."

"That's not true! I'm very cooperative!"

"Sure, honey...but we're getting off the subject. Instead of focusing on you, try to remember *me*."

I frowned, trying to remember that ride. It was all a blur. I hadn't gotten into the show's house. But they said they'd send the videos of all of us losers to agents, just in case we could advance by that route. That was nice of them. Indeed, my future agent, Darlene, saw me and my off-beat music resonated with her later, causing her to come see one of my nightclub shows. The rest was history. But that was an unknown benefit. At the time I was just one of the dozen of applicants that got cut. It was incredibly depressing. I didn't want to chatter, just sat in the passenger seat staring out the side window. I felt like giving up. But then I got mad, determined to show those stupid judges they should have accepted me and let me win the contest. My righteous anger energized my subsequent escape to Nashville and meteoric rise through the nightclub circuit.

"I didn't do much talking either," I shrugged.

"I'm not asking you believe me!" she snapped at me, abruptly getting up. She grabbed my mug and carried it with her to the kitchen, dumping the now-cool contents into the sink. "But I now have *solid evidence* to show you. I couldn't show it to you earlier because I only got it this last week. I had to confirm it was true. But I'm certain of its validity. So get your coat on, Suzy. We're going for a ride!"

"Uh...ok...but where are we...?"

"We're going to the *Suzette Kingly Animal Shelter*. Grab your wig. We don't want to startle the workers or animals with your bizarre appearance."

By now I was thoroughly confused, even fearful. My Mom had clearly lost her mind. I might accept she just panicked when we returned from Nashville late at night to find the science sheds and garage lit up with a strange *electric glow*. I might have accepted that she feared for my safety as *explosions* began going off, *physically holding me back* from rushing out of the car to try to somehow save Dad and Billy! I might have accepted that she was already lost in grief keeping me in the car as the entire backyard erupted in a gigantic "boom" that left only a smoldering, deep crater. But I could *not* accept that she'd been visited by the *future ghosts* of my Dad and brother warning her *not* to interfere in their upcoming deaths!

It was ridiculous!

What I needed to do was call up Dr. Spencer and get him to treat my clearly insane mother.

But I didn't have that opportunity. I was weak and she was strong. As I snatched up my wig hanging on a hat rack by the door she grabbed me by the arm and practically dragged me to my beat-up old Fiero.

At least I still had my lucky marbles in my jean pocket. They reassured me as I took them out and juggled them in a trembling, closed fist.

Yes, she'd gotten my car back from Oklahoma City. It seems she was paying for its registration and insurance. She was the actual present owner of record, not me. So when it was discovered lurking in that parking garage they contacted her, charged her the fees and penalties, and released it to her.

For a crazy lady she was very clever, even devious.

I'd never visited the Animal Shelter I'd so generously funded. I had no idea it was named after me. I didn't even like the fuzzy little pests, let alone wanted to spend millions constructing them a lavish "retirement estate." But that was exactly what it turned out to be.

We drove down 14th Street leading north out of town in silence. I vaguely remembered this was the way to the Oaklawn Cemetery. The empty caskets of Dad and Billy were buried there. At least their scattered atoms could claim gravestones acknowledging they'd once existed as living, breathing, human beings. Now, though, I wondered if perhaps my mother were on her way to joining them there, dying from a hysteria-induced stroke!

The worst thing of all was that I'd never had a chance to reconcile with my little brother. For all I knew he died still resenting my success. The cemetery sure brought back some bad memories...

Likely my Mom was thinking the same. She was muttering and spitting, as if she were debating with herself. Plus she was zooming along far past the speed limit. She must have been doing seventy! I guess that's why she took the old Fiero instead of the van. I was learning a lot of new things I didn't know about my Mom that day. I held onto the side grip for dear life, slung about as she swerved erratically back and forth.

And then I saw the cemetery zip past on the right as we headed into open farming land.

She jerked the wheel to the left and we skidded onto a plain dirt road leading into the fields. Topping a rise I saw what looked like a big farm ringed by a cyclone fence with razor wire on the top. She slammed on the brakes and we slid up to a security gate. Beyond it I saw a big parking lot. Though it was late afternoon, the place was packed. There must have been a hundred cars already there!

What the hell was going on? For an animal shelter stuck in the wilds outside a sleepy little town this was an incredible amount of people.

"Ma'am..." a guard greeted her through her rolled-down window. "You'll have to—oh, Dr. King."

"This is my daughter. She's cleared for access."

"Of course—I'll open the gate."

We zipped on through into the big parking lot as she gunned the motor. I saw signs which directed visitors where to go with their animals, or for tours, or for information.

And most of all I was surprised to see patrolling military personnel, carrying rifles! They wore army uniforms.

And was that a *tank* parked beside the main entrance to the central building?

Wow, that was an awful lot of security to protect a few measly stray animals...?

"Get out!" she yelled at me as she skidded to a stop, barely avoiding crashing into a couple of already parked cars.

Running around to my side she jerked the door open and hauled me to my feet.

"What's the big rush?" I complained. "I'm coming! Let me keep up!"

I was hobbling along, leaning heavily on my cane, panting.

Jesus Christ, I was just a few days out of the hospital!

Looking around I just had time to study the large, dome-shaped building in front of me. To my right I saw what looked like a modern zoo, with big natural-appearing enclosures. Maybe that was why there were so many cars. Perhaps they were visitors coming to see the various sad, cast-off critters?

Behind the main building was what looked like extensive fields with high electric fences closing off different sections: some with trees, shrubs, or flowing creeks.

And off to my left was a big rectangular, power plant-looking building. Wow. If that was a true power plant it looked big enough to run an entire city!

And then we were marching into the curved glass-lined domed building.

A security station faced us, a magnetic-arch scanner complete with stern looking armed guards. What? Well, I suppose that made sense for a place doing animal research...uh. But then again...they *weren't* doing animal research, right? Didn't Mom support legislation to *restrict* animal research? This looked like administration, but also halls were marked out, exhibits?

"What's...?"

"This is check-in, medical quarantine and isolation wards, veterinarian offices, surgical suites, visitor greeting, administration and the like. Animals don't stay here long. They're moved out into natural or minimally managed habitats as soon as possible. A few have to stay in isolation in smaller exhibits due to psychosis or medical conditions or compatibility issues, but most are returned to environments very close to pure Nature."

"But what's this got to do with...?"

Startled, I heard all the *alarms* going off, all at once!

"You'll have to be wanded, Miss," a bald headed, beefy guard informed me as I froze in the middle of the magnetic scanner.

"Huh? Don't you recognize me? I'm Suzette..."

"Just cooperate with them, Suzy."

"It's stupid, Mom. I'm not a terrorist!" I sputtered as I was led off to the side. "The whole united states government and even FBI testified on my behalf at the official investigation."

"It's standard protocol. Everyone gets patted down or wanded if the alarms go off, which are very sensitive. Some of your implants contain metal, after all. We use diffuse x-rays plus infrared plus..."

"Isn't this a bit excessive for an animal shelter?" I complained, groaning as I extended my aching arms upward.

"You'll have to strip down, Miss," the guard ordered me as a couple female guards moved up to join him.

"Say what?" I gasped, shocked.

"There's no need for cavity probes, Frank," Mom laughed, bringing up some charts on a nearby screen. "Here are her medical records. You can correlate your micro-scans with the various pins, plates, and wires in her body to prove nothing extra's been placed inside her. She's undergone extensive surgery recently."

"Ah, ok...we'll do that, then."

He sounded disappointed. Either he was a pervert or very diligent at his security job!

It took a full ten minutes carefully correlating my medical records to their scans, but finally they were satisfied I wasn't sneaking a bomb into the facility inside any of my various body cavities.

"Christ, Mom, that's way too much!"

"Our visitors appreciate the security. It's the same at all the other buildings. *You* certainly know all about terrorists and bombs, correct? It's much easier to prevent tragedies than to clean up afterwards."

I shut my mouth, hobbling after her deeper into the large building. Somehow I got the idea that she wasn't just talking about the Hollywood Bowl bombing...

"We're going through continual facial recognition scanning. We'll have to do iris scans to get into the elevator. Then to exit we'll have to do thumbprints at a detection pad. We've got great security here."

"Elevator?"

"We're going down to the 'basement'."

"What's the big rush?"

"I was informed before we left that a critical procedure was happening. I need to be there for..."

"So what's in the basement?" I interrupted her, now getting annoyed by all this "cloak-and-dagger" stuff.

"It's our AERF—or as our workers like to call it the 'arf-arf'...a little dog joke."

"Oh...so you *do* conduct animal research? That's what all the heavy security is for? But I thought you didn't..."

"It's called the 'Animal Ethical Research Facility.' As a scientist, I sponsor programs where we enlist animals into 'humane' research. We don't just do research, though, we develop the programs and protocols that other scientists at established research facilities can use for their own objectives to which even strict groups like PETA can give their stamp of approval."

"I...didn't think that was possible. I thought PETA was against all animal research and...?"

"Ah, here we are. Step inside, Suzy."

The elevator opened smoothly, green lights blinking above.

"But it didn't...?"

"You were scanned extensively. I have all your parameters already loaded into our database. The central A.I. knows who you are."

"GOOD AFTERNOON DOCTOR KING, MISS KINGLY. WHERE ARE YOU GOING TODAY?" a vibrant, disembodied voice hurt my eardrums.

"Take us to the sub-basement, please."

"TRANSIT TIME WILL BE TEN MINUTES."

"I thought you said we're going to the basement?" I asked, startled by the computer voice. It sounded friendly and competent, even intelligent. "Either your basement is really deep or this is the slowest elevator I've ever heard about."

"We're going *through* the basement to the deepest levels. All of that AERF stuff is actually just a cover."

"Say what? A cover? You mean it's not real?"

"Oh, it's very real—and acclaimed. We've not been in operation for long, of course. But we're starting to publish papers in respected journals. It justifies our power usage, money expenditures, and scientific personnel. Our true work is hidden, down in the 'sub-basement,' which only a select few know of or have access to."

"Does the Humane Society and other groups know about the 'other' work?"

"Of course not. But our ethical protocol development is genuine and strongly supported by the Animal Welfare Movement. You see, we don't use animals—even lowly critters like mice or rats—in mass trials in tiny cages. Our trials are similar to clinical trials used on humans. For instance, we enlist older dogs in cancer research dealing with treatments of their actual disease. Their owners substitute for informed consent. We draw on veterinarian input from all over the world. That's just one example. We've pioneered free-range clinical trials of rodents and..."

"But you're still imposing your needs upon them," I stopped her, spitefully arguing with something that actually sounded really impressive.

The elevator kept moving downward. It seemed slow. But then again, I didn't know how deep this "sub-basement" was actually situated.

"Wherever possible, we get the animal's direct cooperation."

"Say what? You talk to the animals?"

"Oh, things like enjoyable psychiatric research: puzzles and problems with excellent rewards. If the animals enjoy it they indicate they want more. If they don't like it then they can withdraw from that particular trial. And the animals get to go home to their owners, back to their natural habitats here, or to loving caregivers in our wards. In other words, they're not treated as living test-tubes but feeling, thinking fellow beings."

"But you're still deriving benefit from tricking lower forms of life into doing what they can never truly understand. How is that 'ethical'?"

"They benefit from it. Most of the time, they even enjoy what they're doing. It's *not* unethical," she frowned at me.

"So *you* say," I argued, happy to irritate my mother. "If they were somehow brought up to our level of intelligence, would they agree?"

"That's impossible."

"But it's the basis of our 'ethics', isn't it—to treat them 'humanely', as we'd like to treat ourselves?"

"Suzy, I didn't bring you here to argue about..."

"What the hell? This is *my* facility, isn't it? My name's on the sign outside, right? I paid for this place! Don't I get a say on the 'ethics' of what you're doing?"

She sighed deeply, clearly trying to control her anger at my pigheaded stubbornness.

"We're the wiser, more evolved species. As long as we're not causing undo pain or suffering, we have the right to use lower species however we wish."

Well, that was rather blunt.

"So you ascribe to the fundamentalist belief that 'Adam and Eve' were given the 'Garden of Eden', Nature, to use for their enjoyment rather than to be responsible caretakers?"

"Oh, get real, Suzy," Sally King sighed again. "We can do both."

"So 'might makes right'?"

"In a sense, yes, I guess it does. We need medical research and rather than do initial tests on us humans we do it on animals."

"That's not the view of PETA, is it? Don't they take the 'high ground' fighting against *all* animal research?"

"They're also humans. The whole point of their agreeing to my 'cover activity' is to find ethical loopholes that allow us to do what's needed."

"So it's ok for superior, higher-evolved *aliens from outer space* to come and use *us* however they wish, as long as they don't cause overt pain or suffering?"

She looked at me curiously.

"Where did that thought come from?"

"Nowhere!" I snapped. Then, more thoughtfully, I explained: "I remember you telling me once that testing an equation often involves driving it to the extremes. They you can see if it breaks down or holds up."

She nodded slowly.

"Yes...good point...but we have to deal with the present reality: creating a complex enough 'cover story' to hide our true activities. I leave higher speculation to philosophers."

"But still...doesn't your approach give skewed results?" I now asked seriously. "I thought the idea of inbred animals in tightly de-fined living conditions was to have consistent test subjects to more easily find mechanisms, eliminate potential harmful conditions for humans, and point to subgroups that would benefit from some treat-ment."

"I thought you were totally consumed in being a world-famous musician, Suzy. How do you know details of clinical trial design?"

"I read, Mom!" I huffed at her. "Every week I go through the latest Science issue. Its first half is always articles for us knowledgeable laymen. I find all kinds of science fascinating. I try to keep up with what's going in medicine, chemistry, physics, astronomy, and..."

"Mathematics?"

"Uhm...sure, Mom, somewhat...but that's not really a separate discipline, is it? I mean, it's used throughout all of science, of course, but..."

She poked a finger into my chest, shoving me flat back against the wall of the elevator.

"Are you forgetting that I hold a Ph.D. in Theoretical Mathematics from the University of Oklahoma's Department of Mathematics—the very University that you cavalierly skipped past in your headlong rush to fame?"

"Uh...no, Mom," I sheepishly answered. "But you were just using your degree to teach Algebra, Trig, and Calculus at the high school, right?"

She just shook her head at me, briefly shutting her eyes.

"Sometimes I'm not even sure you're my daughter," she sighed deeply.

The elevator stopped. Wow, that ride seemed to take forever. We must be really deep beneath the surface. The door awaited our thumbprints on the yellow-flashing exit pad. As Mom put her thumb on it I followed.

The door opened and we stepped out. Another guard station awaited us. And beyond that was...

"*Jesus H. Christ!*" I somewhat disrespectfully gasped

I saw a large chamber filled with many personnel in white smocks working at elaborate computer consoles attached to massive equipment. I recognize strangely wound huge magnetic coils, superconducting collider conduits, and a *perfect white sphere* in the center *levitating* above a black platform.

This was my Dad's "science sheds" on steroids!

A low "hum" filled the air.

"What...the hell...is *that?*" I pointed, my finger trembling. It sure wasn't one of my favorite marbles, though it looked amazingly like the Taw in my pocket. It had a piercing glow, a faint haze close to its surface, and was the size of a small car: glistening and shining, twirling and spinning!

"It's a time machine," she curtly replied. "And we're going to use it to save your Dad and brother."

I wobbled over to a lab bench and sat down heavily on an empty stool. I put my arms on its cool surface and lay my head down.

She wasn't sure I was her daughter? I *damn well* wasn't sure she was my mother! How had I missed all this? Was I so self-centered in my musical career I couldn't see what was right in front of my face?

She sat down next to me, putting a warm arm around me.

"Would you like some tea before we get started?"

That sounded wonderful.

Chapter 8

SAD RABBITS

Hoppity, hoppity, hoppity, BOP
*Do the **happy rabbit hop***
Bippity, boppity, hippity, stomp
Jump in the air then do a flop!

You're a fluffy, bouncy, animal doll
Big long ears and twitching nose
Giant legs that make you jump!
Wish I had a pair of those...

Making babies lickety-split
Little bunnies cute as ticks
Wish I knew where they had gone
I'd join them in a goodbye song!
The Suzette Anthology, Lyrics 8

"So they're not really dead?" I gasped in disbelief and relief.

"I don't think so."

"Then what happened, Mom?"

We were in a small canteen, sitting at a table in a corner. There were several other people getting hot meals out of dispensers, sipping at mugs of coffee, or talking to each other. This was an amazing facility, buried deep beneath the ground. It looked to be a thriving, "big science" research operation.

Oh, Dad and Billy would have really loved this!

For a moment she looked down at her mug of hot tea, pursing her lips.

I was totally blown away by it all. I'd expected her to show me some blurry long-distance photos from security cameras of nearby buildings to the motel we stayed at in Nashville as her "evidence," not this!

"They were testing excitation parameters of our latest exotic-energy generator."

"Say what?"

"Your Dad was fixated on getting his cold fusion matrix to work. He'd been tinkering with it ever since he graduated from Harvard. He developed its initial, unique palladium-based structure for his Ph.D. in physics."

"He spent most evenings puttering around in his 'science-garage', but I never knew the details of what he and Billy worked on. I thought all that stuff failed, that he was just having fun doing weird experiments that would never come to anything. That wasn't right?"

"They wouldn't succeed—without my help, that is."

"But you're a mathematician, right? That's not *physics* that...?"

She glared at me like she was going to say something harsh. Then she sighed, smiling at me.

"Suzy, *mathematics* is the most fundamental science of all. It underpins everything. It's the foundation upon which the Universe is built. It describes the Laws of Nature. If you know the math, then you not only understand a situation, you know where to intervene to *control* it."

"So you were helping Dad?"

A couple of uniformed military people came into the canteen, a man and a woman. The woman had three stars on her shoulder, the man two. I didn't know much about the military, but they had to be generals. What branch of the service they were, I wasn't sure—but what were *generals* doing here?

I noticed that the two of them didn't get any food or drink, but just sat at a table on the other side of the room from us. Mom glanced at them and they nodded back to her. Clearly they wanted to talk to her but were respecting her time with me.

I was doubly impressed with my Mom—that Generals would hold her in such high regard and deference.

"He was great experimenter but not the greatest theorizer. I added to his experiments updates on the theory governing the interaction of the atoms within his matrix's unique chemical structure."

"Wow..."

"Yes, it was a fun hobby. We never expected it to produce anything significant. We were both just exercising our creativity beyond teaching our introductory high school classes."

"So you taught high school to have a job—to pay the bills—to take care of Billy and me. Otherwise, you'd have been at some big University with your own real laboratories?"

She reached out and took my left hand in both of hers.

I noticed that the Turtle Tattoo on her left wrist plus the identical one on my own left wrist seemed to briefly glow as we touched.

But maybe it was just my imagination.

When I was just a kid I'd gotten the tattoo from one of the elderly patients at the nursing home beside the Park, a few blocks away from us. I did it on a dare, the other kids at school knowing my Mom had tattoos on her arm. I wanted to be like my Mom, especially in regards to the most-visible one, the cute little Turtle on the inside of her left wrist.

My parents were angry with me for doing it without their permission. They even went to the nursing home to complain, but the skinny old goateed man that'd done it had moved out the previous day. My tattoo was permanent. So they seemed to forget about it. I liked it. It "branded" me as "the daughter of the Lady teacher with the Turtle Tattoo: *the Girl with the Turtle Tattoo*"...hah! Those were the days, before my Mom betrayed our family and I hated her, ran away, and became a world-wide singing sensation.

Similar stuff happens to all kids, right? Well, maybe not...

"We never thought of it like that," she quietly but firmly reprimanded me. "You and Billy were always our pride and joy, worth more than any scientific achievement, prize, or job. In fact, we'd both been part of the rat-race of scientific laboratory life for years and were sick of it. Settling down to a low-paced, relatively easy teaching job in a small town where we both had relatives was what we wanted. Puttering with our surplus lab equipment out in the science-sheds wasn't an obsession, just a fun hobby."

"But why were you working on something as dangerous...as *this?*"

I vaguely waved in the direction of the spinning, humming, levitated, giant Sphere!

She shook her head in denial, her red-brown hair flopping around with the force of her emotion.

"At first our experiments weren't in the least bit dangerous. At most what we were attempting, if successful, might warm up this cup of tea I hold in my hands. Under normal environmental conditions it was impossible to produce an explosion or any other dangerous products."

"But things weren't 'normal' that night we returned from Nashville?" I prodded her.

She gulped, looking down at her hands gripping mine. It was getting painful. Realizing she was squeezing too tight she let loose, sitting back.

"I'd given Dave a new set of equations to program into the equipment generating his oscillating electrical fields. It had to do with distorting the subatomic vibrations of the interacting atoms."

"Atoms make vibrations?"

"If you get right down to it, Suzy, everything is just vibrations of energy fields. So-called 'solid' matter is mostly just empty space punctuated by coherently vibrating nodes or 'strings' of energy. Of course that's not apparent on the level we exist. But for theoretical physicists it's all too real—dealing with subjects like 'quantum entanglement' for one, by which objects can interact instantly across vast distances."

"But I thought that the speed of light was inviolable. Didn't Einstein prove that?"

"Yes, that's right. And subsequent cosmic observations and on-earth experiments backed it up. Nothing can move faster than the speed of light. That is, at our level of existence..."

"You keep saying that."

She nodded, glancing again at the two generals who seemed to be getting antsy at their table, as if something important was happening they needed to talk to her about.

"Should you...?" I began, looking over at the generals.

"They can wait. You're far more important than them."

"Ok...so...?"

"What I realized was that for your Dad's cold fusion experiment to produce a sustained exothermic reaction I must *change the level of reality* within which it existed."

I nodded as if I had the foggiest idea of what she was saying, encouraging her to continue.

"You see, Suzy, it had to do with the nature of Time."

"Uh huh..."

"It's rather complex."

"I guess so."

"We all think we understand Time because we live in it every second of our lives."

"Right."

"It goes forward at a set rate and doesn't go backward."

"Sure..."

"But in true reality at both the cosmic and subatomic levels, Time is chaotic. It can speed up or even stop. Plus there are possibilities for subverting the flow and turning it backward."

"Ok..."

"Are you following what I'm saying?"

"Nope—not a bit."

She laughed, fondly patting my hand.

"Well, you said you remember Einstein, right?"

"Sure, his 'Theory of Relativity', $E=mc^2$?"

"That's exactly right, Suzy. He showed how time and space aren't separated. They are two aspects of the same thing, space-time. And depending upon the present properties of space, Time can be altered."

"Uh...but in that formula there isn't any 'time' value, is there?"

"The speed of light can be solved in terms of the different characteristics of Time."

"And that means...?"

"Time can be 'diluted'—flowing at different rates for people moving at different speeds."

"So for me Time might be the same as always but for you it speeds up or slows down?"

"Yes."

"So you figured out a way to apply this to Dad's experiment?"

"Actually, time dilation was already well understood. What I did was find a way to quantify and specify the different time-states in the 'm' or Mass variable of the equation."

"But how did that...?"

"It opened a simple window on the subatomic level that we could exploit to speed up the fusion rate of deuterium atoms in Dad's unique matrix. All he had to do was alter certain 'catalytic' atoms while tweaking precisely the electromagnetic field that contained them."

"Super..."

"You're still not following this, are you?"

"I'm getting the 'take-home' message, Mom. That's all that really matters at this moment, right?"

She sighed. "I'd hoped you'd acquired more of my genetics and would find this fascinating."

"I did! I am!" I hastened to assure her. "But it's really tough to concentrate on it, particularly when that...*thing*...is out there!"

She laughed, visibly relaxing.

"Yes, that 'thing' is rather daunting, isn't it?"

"What is it really? You said it's a time machine. But it isn't like any 'H.G. Wells' time-machine I ever saw in any movie."

"What does it look like to you?"

I gulped, hesitant to reply.

"Go ahead, Suzy—this isn't a class at school. You're not going to get marked down on a test for a wrong answer. Say what you think."

I knew it was crazy but with her encouragement I went ahead and said it: "It looks like animated representations I've seen in space doc-umentaries of a *neutron star*...perfectly circular, hanging in space, bright white."

"That's not far off, Suzy, because..."

"Dr. King, we need you. We're about to begin the latest test runs. The scientists tell me that they are worried about unexpected fluctua-tions in the zeta-field and..."

The two Generals were standing beside the table I was sitting at with my Mom, looming impatiently over us.

"*Tell* them I'll be there *shortly*," she snapped at them. Then more controlled, she added: "Thank you for informing me. I won't be long."

"But...?"

She glared at them. They backed off, leaving us alone.

"Wow...you order Generals around?"

"It's a long story."

"Tell me!"

"I will, when we have time. But right now..."

"Ok, then," I sighed, intrigued and now not wanting her to stop. But I realized my 'retired' Mom had heavy duties. "Those generals sounded really worried. You probably better go and see what's wrong. But first tell me what that white Sphere is. It's sure not a machine—at least not like anything I've ever seen."

"We think it's the stabilized end of a *wormhole*."

"Oh...*Jesus*...really?"

"No, I'm lying to you," she grinned, starting to get up.

I snorted, glad to relieve the tension.

"But...how could you contain something like that? That validates my prior conclusion. It's incredibly dangerous! And how can something as *stupendous* as an active wormhole be here, hiding away underneath an animal shelter outside of Sulphur, Oklahoma?"

She just shrugged apologetically.

"I'll tell you all the details later, at least as much as you'd like me to go into. For the moment, the answer is 'yes'—it's incredibly dangerous. In essence I helped your Dad's experiment stabilize and extend a few naturally occurring *microscopic* wormholes in the matrix of his experiment, altering the flow of time enough to increase the deuterium fusion reaction rate. You saw what happened that terrible evening at our house. What you now see in the cavern here is far larger and proportionately even more powerful."

"So...if something went wrong?"

"Let's just say we wouldn't be around to know what happened."

"We'd...be evaporated?"

"—us and the entire North American continent."

I was stunned.

"I guess that explains the heavy military presence outside...this is very, very *scary!*"

"Suzy, I can get an aid to take you up to the basement level to tour our official AERF experiments. Or perhaps you'd like to visit the surface facility. There are some mighty cute animals up there. Or I can call a limo to take you back home since you're in no shape to drive yourself. I'm afraid I have to be here for a while to..."

"I want to stay with you."

She smiled, holding my elbow to help me stand. I was still very wobbly, not-to-mention *totally discombobulated* by the incredible story she was telling me!

"The Generals and other officials won't like it, though," she sighed.

"Why not?"

"This is all highly classified. You normally need the highest top-secret clearance to even see any of this."

"Aren't you the boss? Just tell them I'm authorized!"

"It's not that simple, dear. There's a process. I've started it for you, but..."

"There's always a way to do something if you want it bad enough," I petulantly frowned.

"Well, maybe if you don't mind having guards following you around all the time and..."

"Nope. Back when I was famous—a few months ago—I had body-guards around me all the time. What's the difference?"

"Not much."

"Ok, then, it's settled. The guards will stop me from being a bad girl and touching anything I shouldn't."

"It's not just seeing everything—it's *understanding* what's really going on and..."

"I've already seen it. You've already told me the main 'take-home' messages."

"True enough, dear. I'm sorry to burden you with all of this but..."

"I need to know *everything!*"

Technicians around us were startled by my loud shout, looking at us worriedly. More concerning, security guards looked menacingly at me.

But Mom waved them off.

"And I absolutely will tell you everything. You can't imagine how much I've wanted to share this with you, both the frustrations and the triumphs. Alright, then, we'll find a way. But right now we've got to go and deal with this emergency and..."

"—just one more thing!"

"Yes?" she said, again waving off concerned guards.

"Where does that 'wormhole' lead to?"

She smiled broadly, keeping a firm, steadying hold on my elbow as we walked out of the canteen back to the giant chamber holding the captured wormhole.

"Potentially, anywhere we want."

Flanked by two burly armed guards, my new "bodyguards," I followed my Mom to a *giant electrical coil* situated close to the hovering, so-called "time machine."

I was still in shock, trying to sort out what was happening. This was all impossible! It wasn't just the claim of time-travel, but this huge research facility situated beneath a freshly constructed animal shelter—all built in the space of three years? Ridiculous!

But the "wormhole" Sphere was undeniable: hovering silently only a hundred feet away from us. It looked like a perfectly round, giant white pearl ten feet in diameter. It seemed to be spinning. Squinting at its smooth surface I could vaguely make out the outline of shapes zipping past. Perhaps it was some sort of projection device? But if so, it was light-years ahead of any special effects or props I'd used on-stage in my World Tours.

It was simultaneously awesome and ominous.

"...vector resolution, shifting the galactic coordinates? If so, then we don't have control of the right ascension. The declination appears to be stable, but..."

I was vaguely keeping track of what some scientists in white lab smocks were telling my Mom. They were arguing about some complex multi-colored graphs on a computer screen that kept shifting. The only thing I understood was that they were trying to track some-thing within the "galactic plane" then alter its position with various fields they were generating: electrical, x-ray, and something else I'd never heard of before.

Christ, were they talking about the other end of the wormhole?

Apparently satisfied, my Mom walked back to me.

"We're ok," she assured me. "We'll wait over here for them to arrive."

"What? Dad and Billy?" I excitedly asked her.

"No, dear...if that ever happens it's still a long way off. We're first doing some tentative exploratory experiments."

"Experiments?"

"Last week we sent two apples three days into the future. It was our first transportation experiment. It worked. Now we're waiting for our *second* experiment to arrive. It's a crucial step."

I was momentarily dumb-struck.

"Mom, if that's one end of a wormhole how can it be here? I thought from I've read in Science that they only occur on a subatomic level. Anything big enough to manifest into our level would be so dense it would warp the space around it and...oh!"

"You're fast, Suzy. What do you think's happening here?"

"It really *is* warping space! And that causes it to have its own envelope where space-time is different, wrapped around it like a skin. So since gravity isn't affecting it like normal objects, then...?"

"Correct, Suzy. It seems to 'float' in the air, levitating."

"But you can't actually send things through it like they do in science fiction movies, right?"

"Yet again you're correct, Suzy. It's super-dense, reaching beyond our local space-time coordinates. Nothing can pass through it without getting squashed into subatomic particles. But along its 'skin' where time-space is folded around it..."

"Ah, I see!" I excitedly interrupted her. "You can send signals along its surface to interrogate its full-length orientation in space-time. And...is that how you 'transport' things, using it like a cable you walk on instead of trying to magically pass through? And what about the resonant frequencies, like the metal strings on my electric guitar? Can you induce vibrations that bias it toward...?"

"The government bureaucrats aren't going to like it, Suzy," she interrupted my enthused babbling, "but I'm hiring you right now as a consultant. You'll deal with the 'music of the spheres,' as a verse in the Bible puts it. A fresh introspection of what we're doing, taken from a knowledgeable layman's perspective, can be very valuable. I and the other scientists here can easily get what's called 'tunnel vision' where we focus too much on the details while losing sight of the larger issues."

"I've got a job?" I grinned, elated.

"Yes, dear."

"And you mean like 'not seeing the forest for the trees'?"

"Exactly."

"Wow, that's great, Mom," I smiled. Here I thought I was a useless failure—and now I was a science consultant on a big-research physics problem! "So did you say you successfully transported *apples?*"

"Yes. Would you like to see them?"

"That'd be awesome."

She walked over to a totally glass-enclosed area, speaking through a microphone to "space-suited" technicians working inside.

They walked over to a refrigerator and keyed in a security code. One of the techs opened it pulled out an ordinary Tupperware container. Inside were two red apples. Through the glass and plastic they looked fine, crisp and ready to eat.

"See?"

I nodded: "Two apples."

"They're composed of organic molecules, similar to what's inside you and me. We tested biopsies. See the holes? It's like tiny worms were chewing on them."

I again nodded.

"Are they...edible?"

"There's no change as far as we can see. So the next step was to send something alive and see what happened."

"Alive—you mean, like, animals?"

"Yes, two grown rabbits."

"I thought you were against forced animal experiments. Did you get their informed consent?"

She shrugged, "I won't tell if you won't."

"Ok."

She laughed, signaling for the space-suited technicians to put the apples back into the locked refrigerator.

"That was a joke. Seriously, though, those two particular animals love doing travel experiments. When they get out of a centrifuge, maze, or new jet being tested they hop over to their reward tray. When we put out the container for the test they actually got into it on their own. They *wanted* to go."

"You're kidding me again, right?"

"Not at all."

"I thought animals just wanted to be warm, feel safe, eat well, and occasionally breed, you know—satisfy their internal instincts."

"You mean like us?"

"Uhhh....you're not saying they wanted to be *time travelers,* though—the first rabbits to take 'a great hop forward'?"

"Well, to get a reward for doing fun stuff, certainly. In a sense, they did volunteer for the experiment."

"I'm not so sure that PETA would agree."

"Nor would any of the PETA members be willing to take their place," she replied glibly.

Yep, that was true. Most people still figured a human life was worth more than that of a mouse or a rat, or even a rabbit. "Ethics" clearly depends upon one's evolutionary status.

"So what happened to the bunnies? Did they get what they wanted?"

"We're going to find out in five minutes. That's when they're due back. Their transport container should materialize right beneath the wormhole. Only seconds will have passed for them, though for us it's been three days. That is, if everything went as hoped."

"So that floating pearly round manifestation is functioning as both the beginning and the end of a wormhole tunnel? It began in the past when it was the 'present' there and is ending now in the future which is now again the present?"

"Yes. That's quite astute of you to realize, Suzy. We determined that this would be the simplest function we could test. But we have the ability—we think—to adjust the coordinates to send something to any place or time within the known Universe. It goes back to my new *Theory of Time* which has several interlocking formulae describing the temporal, physical, and subspace fields in play. We influence the wormhole with ordinary electromagnetic fields that then affect its new emergence point within the Universal matrix. That's what we were just now adjusting. We were trying to zero-out other possible exits, such that the emergence point for the rabbits is right here, not inside a black hole on the other side of the Universe, or inside if you or me."

"Uh huh...but didn't you set it to emerge here to begin with?"

"Unknown fluctuations are randomly occurring along the wormhole length," she worriedly informed me. "We're continuously readjusting, but it's almost like something else is trying to take control."

"That is rather...unsettling—both the randomness and the possible interference," I gulped.

"Yes," she agreed. "Our Sphere has the potential to wreak havoc on Earth if it's erratically functioning. If we can't control the wormhole then we'll have to turn it off. But that wouldn't be a disaster. I'm sure I can create another, if needed. But the 'interference' may be just coherent resonances we've yet to fully understand, the 'music of the spheres' that you're being hired to investigate, remember?"

"Ok...but..."

"But?"

I was beyond impressed. I had no idea my mother was a mathematical and physics genius. This was mind-boggling. This was Nobel Prize-winning type work!

"Why do I have the feeling you're holding something important back?"

"That's because I am," she frowned. "We haven't had time yet for the full 'back story' that..."

"Dr. King, sixty seconds," a gray-bearded man nervously nudged her, pointing to the floating white Sphere.

Indeed, something was happening. A *blue fog* formed beneath the pearly globe. Flashes of *green lightning* interweaved within the fog.

A loud "pop" startled everyone.

I felt my wig almost ripped from my scarred head by a blast of air.

Then the fog cleared beneath the Sphere and there stood a closed, sealed container.

Smoke was rising from its top.

"Space-suited" technicians gingerly approached it. They grabbed it from a dozen feet away with a long mechanical arm then gingerly carried it back toward us.

"Now the veterinarians will examine the animals," Mom informed me.

The technicians entered the glass-sealed decontamination chamber and opened the container.

Outside, the scientists and officials crowded against the glass barrier collectively "gasped."

Inside, the two rabbits looked perfectly fine, sitting side-by-side.

But they weren't moving.

"They're dead," a flat voice sounded over the speaker. "We'll have to do an autopsy before we can give you the cause. But they don't appear to have panicked. And the clock in the cage reads just a minute since we put the container into the distortion field three days ago."

"Is...that what happened...to Dad and Billy?" I whispered to my Mom.

"I don't think so," she glumly replied, turning away. "I told you I saw them, alive and well, looking fifty years older than we remembered."

"But that was before their lab exploded," I relentlessly pressed her.

"True...I suppose it could have been just a stress-induced hallucination...and the rest was only a bizarre coincidence."

She looked deflated, overcome with doubts and disappointment.

Maybe I could finally be of real help to *her*.

"But I saw them too."

"What?" she gasped, grabbing me by my shoulders and peering intensely into my eyes. "Why didn't you tell me this before?"

"I thought the same thing," I slowly admitted. "It was after the bombs at the Hollywood Bowl went off, when I just recovered consciousness. At first I thought they were ghosts coming to escort me to the other side. But they only appeared for a second or two, so I figured it was just—like you said—a trick of my mind."

"What did they look like?"

"Uhm...they certainly weren't old.   Billy was a bit taller.   Dad looked the same also—maybe a little grayer is all.   But like I said, it happened so fast I didn't think they could be real.   But now..."

"We can't draw conclusions from just two data points, Suzy.   But we have to consider that somehow they're still alive and...aging backward."

"That's...crazy."

"Yes," she whispered, hugging me close so the others couldn't hear us. "In my new equations, Time can have many strange attributes—including flowing backward, sideways, and even stopping dead in its tracks: real 'quantum-foam' type stuff."

"That's...spooky."

She seemed to slump downward, such that suddenly I was holding her up instead of her supporting me.

I heard a muffled "sob."

Then she straightened up, a steely look in her eyes.

"It'll take a while for the vets to do the full gross and molecular autopsies of the rabbits," she stated. "What do you say we go and take a grand tour of your Shelter?   I can tell you more of the events that led me here, with your crucial initial funding.   What do you say?   We can even get some ice cream at the concession stand."

"I have to be very strict on desserts," I mock-seriously squinted. "Us 'superstars' gotta watch our figures."

She grinned at me saying "us."

"Chocolate?"

"Oh, that'd be great!"

Chapter 9

HEAVENLY MARBLES

Rocking and rolling, spinning about
Flashing and sparkling, turning around
All the world's there for taking today
If you're just in the game to stay

You win some and lose some
But that's not the goal
It's all about having some fun
You're not in a fight
It's just harmless play
As you're trying to find your way

Helping each other, doing what's right
That's not a wicked, fierce pain
Shooting straight while finding your aim
Gives you the greatest gain

Winning or losing, it's all the same
When you're on that incredible high
Don't be afraid of trying too hard
When you're placing the bets of life!
The Suzette Anthology, Lyrics 9

We were on a kid-sized train, slowly "chugging" along a track that wound through the extensive aboveground compound. It was built with a miniature locomotive in front and ten two-person sitting carts trailing along behind. I was sitting in the front cart while my Mom sat right behind me in the second.

I was absently juggling my lucky marbles in my front jeans pocket.

Their faint "clicking" sounds soothed me.

We'd gotten a nice lunch at the Visitor Center and were now taking the Tour.

"This is just like the first Jurassic Park movie," I laughed as I licked at my chocolate ice cream cone "dessert." Normally I didn't indulge myself in high cholesterol, high fat, high saturated-fat confections—but they soothed my IBS-ridden guts. Here I was finally reconciling and working with my mother. We were actually together having fun! I didn't want to stink up the place with smelly blasts of intestinal gas.

I was still giddy from the incredible experience of seeing actual time travel happen in the sub-basement cavern. Yes, it wasn't working optimally. If a person tried to do it he or she would probably end up the same as those two unlucky rabbits, stone-cold dead. But the very fact that the mysterious floating orb could throw objects ahead in time was amazing. Now if they could only reach backward to when Dad and Billy were in the burning shacks and pull them forward.

Wait, what if that was what actually happened?

"I'm afraid not, Suzy..." Sally said from behind, sighing.

What, was she reading my mind?

"—no giant T-rex is going to come charging at us," she finished.

Oh, right. She was replying to my "Jurassic Park" comment.

"I was just amused by this track that goes around the enclosures and..."

"Yes, I put in all the 'bells and whistles' to make this facility a real tribute to your marvelous career. It's a family-friendly place where even kids can have a blast. I envisioned it as most zoos should really be, on a large farm with fenced natural sections—and, yes, similar to the Jurassic Park movies for resurrected dinosaurs. But here we're limited to existing species."

No one else was there with us on the train. It was automatic, running on an electric motor. A robotic "conductor" sat in front of us, turned toward us to give us a running update on whatever we were viewing. Mom had turned him off so only his mouth moved without making sounds, such that we could talk without his interruptions. He looked like the stereotypic robot guide, all silvery and metallic. I was reminded of my garish stage show. Clearly I'd inherited my flare from my like-minded Mom.

I was beginning to appreciate her more and more.

But the incredible "highs" of this outing were taking a terrible toll on me.

I was now too weak to walk, even with the help of my cane. My whole body ached. My guts felt like they were twisted into knots, despite the soothing ice cream trickling down my throat. Dr. Spencer told me I'd be in pain for months fighting to get my amped-up addiction neurochemistry back to normal.

I just had to keep myself diverted from the beckoning, blissful siren song of the seductive *needle*.

"So Mom, how did all this happen? I can't believe you put all this together in just three years on the seven million dollars I sent you. I mean that's a good amount of money for a small animal shelter, but it'd only be a drop in the bucket to fund what I saw beneath us."

We were chugging along through a meadow. Short trees around us provided welcome shade. A creek gurgled along over black rocks. All around us dogs and cats of every size and shape ambled along or peacefully basked in the sun. Boulder-shaped large enclosures plus food bowls were never far. This was a true pet retirement home, a cast-off-pet paradise.

I should come and join them, toss off my clothes and go back to nature.

But I never liked the hairy critters that much. Sleeping in a big pile of them would be too itchy.

"It was my Turtle Tattoo."

I wasn't sure I'd heard her correctly. The locomotive had just given out a large "*toot, toot!*" Apparently that was so if any person or golf cart vehicle were crossing in the upcoming gated area of the low cyclone fencing tunnel through which the railroad ran they could get out of the way.

"Your Tattoo made all this happen?"

"Yes, Suzy. You see, soon after the explosion at our house it led me here."

I heard several dogs barking in response to the Toots. But they quickly put their heads down and went back to sunning themselves.

"How?"

"It flared up on my wrist, burning me—except when I pointed it in this direction and moved this way. It led me to this very plot of ground. At that time, three years ago, it was empty grazing land. The ranch it was part of was up for sale. That's when I pressured your agent for some donation money. Your first million allowed me to buy the entire ranch. It's 300 acres. It was large enough to contain both the free-range shelter and my covert activities."

The two-person cart I was sitting in bumped and rumbled beneath me.

"How did your Tattoo get smart enough to lead you here?"

"I don't know," she sincerely answered back. "But ever since I got it as a young teenager I've felt I had a destiny in which it played an important role. I've always had strange dreams at night: going to other dimensions, space travel, even time-traveling...but thought they were just the product of an over-active imagination. However, I think they were somehow caused by the Tattoo."

"Just like mine...all these strange visions in my head?"

"No, dear—your singing and writing talents are genetic. You can't blame the same Tattoo as mine, which you got without my permission as a little kid. It's the same creative drive that fueled your Dad's extremes: his brilliance and obsessions."

"Maybe...but did you feel anything before Dad's research was destroyed?"

"Nothing overt, just the dreams I mentioned. But I knew what to do at this site: I had to *dig deep!* My Tattoo pointed my arm *down* into the earth. So since Murray County lacks a really excellent 'no-kill' animal shelter, I used that as my cover story. My increasingly successful brilliant daughter was funding an animal rescue effort, validated by strong humane society approval. And since you kept giving me money I was able to quickly design the facility, get local contractors lined up, and dig deep."

"And?"

A flock of bright red and yellow parrots flapped close over the cyclone fence tunnel. Apparently dogs and cats weren't the only type of animal rescued here. I was glad to see some exotics.

"As a certified scientist I quickly brought in the various societies to support the idea of alternative, 'ethical' research in which the animals are happily involved as willing participants. Most of the medical and scientific world thought I was nuts. But the animal societies were intrigued. With matching seed money from the Chickasaw Nation I lined up a number of other donors, particularly from the animal rights societies. Whether or not it made much sense, it allowed me the excuse to dig deep and wide, building a well-protected subterranean facility. So I had a lot more money than just your millions, honey."

"I still don't see how you accomplished all this in such a short period. Even if you had decades, it'd take *hundreds* of millions, maybe *billions* to..."

"Let me finish, Suzy. While excavating a deep pit I discovered the cavern that..."

"Cavern? There was a natural cave down below? I don't recall there being caves around Sulphur."

"There are some, yes—such as 'Torture cave' near Turner Falls in the Arbuckle Mountains not far from here. So I wasn't that surprised. But it turned out to *not* be natural."

"Say what?"

"The excavators found an opening about a hundred feet down. It was a crack that led to a yet-deeper chamber. I crawled into it and found myself looking over the edge into a huge, perfectly spherical cavern. The rock was still warm from being melted. It was recently formed."

"But there's no volcanic activity around here that could..."

"It wasn't volcanic. The thousand-foot high chamber was brightly lit from within."

I looked up at several cats sitting atop the cyclone tunnel, staring down at me with slanted-pupiled eyes. Their eyes were lit from within. Miracles could happen.

"You're not making sense, Mom."

"There was a *white, glowing sphere* levitating at its center. By the radioactive ion decay rate, we later determined it formed the crater by its explosive appearance. Molten rock drained down onto the bottom of the vaporized chamber, hardening into a flat floor. It was perfect for housing a hidden research facility."

"It was—the *time machine?*"

"Yes...and it formed right when your Dad's experiments detonated."

Oh, Christ...that thing was directly linked to my Dad and Billy's research!

"And then...?"

"Well, I had no choice. I had to bring in the military and the government. Like you said, we were no longer talking millions to keep your Dad's work going. To pursue this mind-boggling result might take billions! And that's when everything became 'super-top-secret.' I revealed most of my new mathematics on time travel, covertly holding back enough so they'd have to keep me in charge of the research."

"That's amazing, Mom. I had no idea you could manage such a giant project, achieving so much in such a little time."

"Thanks, Suzy," she smiled at me. "I take that as a compliment. I was happy for your Dad to take the lead before, freeing me to do what I enjoyed most—working on the theoretical underpinnings of the physics. But I always had the feeling I could handle administrative duties if I had to do so."

"You could be the President!"

She snorted. "That's not a job I'd want."

"But I bet you could do it!"

"Maybe—but not because I'd want the headaches. I'd have to be forced into taking on those heavy responsibilities."

"Yes, it's tough to be the Boss," I sighed, remembering the huge operation I myself ran before the Bowl Bombing. It wasn't a lot of fun. It drained the joy from my creative efforts. I doubly respected my Mom for my having endured all the headaches of managing this present giant project.

"And because of its theoretical implications plus the obvious manifestation," Sally King continued behind me, "a flood of necessary large research components came streaming in. There's been no limit placed on my budget for either equipment or personnel. Since I'm still the only person who understands the underlying mathematical principles, I'm the boss. The military, of course, calls the shots for security and such. Balancing all the various factions and their needs takes a lot of diplomacy. So I guess I do have a talent for political maneuvering and governing."

"Wow."

"Yes, indeed—'wow'...and we've made tremendous progress in a very short period of a couple years, as you saw. We still don't understand exactly what we're dealing with or how to control it, but the implications are staggering."

"I'll say."

We were into another compound of the large ranch which I now saw contained a small lake. This section was meant for large animals. There were scattered groves of high trees where big animals could safely hide. The silently jabbering robot probably had a lot of fun facts to tell us, but I saw with my own eyes what was most important. We were inside a large-animal free-roam compound complete with small herds of older horses, some ostriches, a few exotic antelopes, a couple camels, and even some big cats.

Lurking ominously in the high grass I saw three *lions* and two *leopards*—even a *tiger* prowling amongst the cattails of the shallow lake.

I was glad the train was now chugging through another cyclone wire, enclosed tunnel.

"You let predators roam with their prey?"

We were moving into some woods, where I glimpsed monkeys swinging high up in the branches.

"Most of the big cats are grown-too-big pets, who are house-trained to eat dead meat. The keepers feed them with supplied carcasses. It's rare that they bring down one of the other occupants."

"Still..."

We were back in the sunshine, emerging from the woods.

"Animals killing animals is considered a 'natural' part of ecology, Suzy. It's only when humans start slaughtering them for food, hides, entertainment, or forced research that some of us 'higher-minded' humans get concerned."

I laughed. It seemed the fitting response, though I saw Mom frowning.

"But we're animals too," I mused.

"True enough," she now laughed with me. "But..."

A very loud "pop" sounded in the woods behind us. I felt a blast of displaced air. It felt very familiar, the same as what happened in the research sub-basement when the dead rabbits reappeared. This blast, though, was much *larger* than what had happened with the transported test cage. The sudden gust actually *ripped* my wig off my head!

"What was that?" I gasped. My hands were grabbing at my scarred, bald head as I twisted around in my seat to see what had happened...

—and a *Tyrannosaurus rex* came lurching at us. I didn't have time to even shout. I had the momentarily thought that my Mom had been holding out on me. I thought I was the Queen of "big stage effects" and here she had a mechanical dinosaur ready to jump out of the big trees and scare the piss out of the kids and parents riding the "choo-choo" train! Hah! Great effect...

—except it wasn't an effect! Slashing *dagger-like teeth* made short work of the cyclone wiring protecting the train track, *massive legs* kicking at us! It was trying to get us! Our entire train was smashed to the side, throwing me and Mom into the bushes.

That's probably what saved us.

The giant "thunder lizard" went stomping past. It was on a rampage, apparently not seeing us tangled up beneath some shrubbery. The big cats ran in terror, squealing. The large herd animals nearest to us stared in bewilderment as they were torn to pieces. The T-rex greedily ripped hunks of bloody flesh from the carcasses.

"Compound Four...on the s-south side of the l-lake," Sally King stammered into her cellphone as she lay beside me. "Probably two h-helicopters with snipers, b-big game caliber and..."

"You're going to *kill* it?" I gasped in disbelief, trying to stand up.

"Stay down!" she barked at me, grabbing my arm and pulling me back beneath the shrubs.

She stopped speaking into her cellphone as we untangled ourselves and hesitantly sat up. In the distance I heard several helicopters "thwumping" closer. I had fresh aches and pains, maybe some ligaments stretched too far, but no broken bones as far as I could tell.

I peered wide-eyed from our concealment behind some bushes.

"Is that what I think it is?" I gasped.

"We c-can't let it get l-loose...our f-fences couldn't hold it in. It's too massive to try to c-contain."

"But Mom, it's a real *dinosaur!* It's got to have something to do with the time-sphere down below."

"Yes, o-obviously...but what we do h-here is top secret. We can't let that be compromised, even by a relic of the p-past."

I heard deep *'rat-a-tats'* of assault rifles as the helicopters swooped down, followed by several *'booms'* of grenades going off.

The roaring giant dinosaur tried to escape, bounding away on its two powerful legs. But it was quickly brought down, tumbling into the dirt. It tried to get up...then collapsed.

As the military helicopters circled watchfully above, I pushed my Mom's restraining hands away, shakily stood up, limped painfully across the meadow, and then staggered up to the huge beast. It had several bloody holes blown into its towering side. Apparently it's not that hard to kill a T-rex with modern weapons.

I put a hand on its green, scaly side.

The flesh was warm, trembling beneath my hand.

Flat on its side, its piano-sized head wobbled feebly. It glared at me with one exposed reddish-brown eye. Hot breath "snorted" across its extruded, limp tongue. Its teeth were covered with blood from the prey it'd just devoured.

I lay a hand on its muzzle as its one visible eye clouded over. With a last violent shudder, the animal died.

I contemplated the amazing width and breadth of Nature.

"That was a shame," my mother's voice sounded behind me as she walked up. Her voice was back under its usual tight control, no more stammering. "We'll take tissue samples and do a full study of the carcass. It'll be a paleontological scientific breakthrough. But no one outside of a small circle of government scientists will ever know it existed. Lucky we were by ourselves on the tour train when it materialized."

"Did you try to get the Sphere to snatch something from the past?" I gasped, moving back a couple steps. "Can you try this on Dad and Billy?"

She tentatively stroked the giant scales of the monster, marveling. The entire animal stretched out there in front of us was a full forty feet from the tip of its tail to its nose. I guessed it weighed around ten tons.

"This was totally unforeseen. But, yes, it gives me hope that we might eventually do what we've seen happen here. How we'd deliberately accomplish it, though, I have no idea...at the moment. We'll have to study the event. This is very disconcerting. The Sphere is more dangerous than we ever thought, lurching about through the past millennia!"

"This can't be random."

"What do you mean?"

I grabbed her arm, more to steady myself than get her full attention. My cane was off in the bushes somewhere, ripped away from me when the dinosaur smashed into the train.

"Think of the probabilities, Mom. If the Sphere is randomly scrambling time, what are the odds it would grab a T-rex and place it here exactly as we're passing through on a tour train? This had to be deliberate. That dinosaur was meant to kill us!"

"We don't know that for sure, dear. You're speculating."

"That's what you 'hired' me to do, right? Or was that just a lie to get me to accept your charity?"

"Not at all Suzy, but..."

"But there's something even worse than an assassination attempt implied here!" I finished her sentence.

"Oh?"

I reached forward and touched the dead animal's huge head, making sure it was real and not an impressive holographic illusion.

"It's just like you said. If the Sphere is going to randomly scramble Time, should you let it continue to exist? Isn't it a terrible danger to our present timeline? What if one of these extinct critters plops down into a schoolyard? The *kids* would be just tasty appetizers."

"It's too late for that kind of consideration, Suzy. The government is involved. Mastering time travel will give our nation unparalleled power to change the present and dictate the future. We just have to accept and learn to manage the risks. It's the same for any new technology that..."

"I'm scared."

Though it was warm in the sunshine, I was shivering. Plus I felt like I was going to throw up. The dinosaur's opened jaws stank terribly. It seemed that T-rexes didn't brush their teeth near often enough. Its pointed six-inch long daggers were visibly rotted at their roots. I guessed there weren't that many dinosaur dentists *seventy million years* ago!

Christ, that time-machine Sphere was powerful.

"I'm sure it's just an unanticipated reaction to our recent two stabs at perturbing the timeline, Suzy. Maybe the Sphere somehow keyed into the presence of our two Turtle Tattoos."

"So you think my Tattoo isn't just a harmless copy?"

She frowned, as if debating whether to answer me or not.

"I never did, Suzy," she grimaced. "I've always felt there were unseen forces manipulating our family."

"And now they want to kill us?"

"I don't know. But my Tattoo is what led me here in the first place, remember? Maybe being together doubly focused the 'discharge' upon us, by a physical mechanism rather than some conspiracy?"

I saw she was grasping at straws. She obviously didn't want to believe that we were in the grip of unseen forces.

"Once we understand what happened, we'll be able to compensate or better control for unintended consequences," she continued.

"Really?" I replied skeptically.

"It's all a matter of immutable Laws of Nature, Suzy. I'm sure I can expand my time-theorem and latest derivative formulae to cover this contingency. I'm continually updating, refining, and tightening our control over the Sphere. We've already discovered a lot about its control functions."

I turned away from the dead dinosaur and violently *up-chucked* my ice cream cone and lunch all over the grass.

I wasn't so confident.

I should have gone looking for my wig, but I was overcome with trembling. I fell to my knees, my vision blurring.

"Suzy!" I heard my Mom cry out.

"I'm...ok. I just want...to go home."

Mom called for a government van to drive me home. I was much too weak and woozy to try to drive myself in my Fiero. A black-suited Federal Agent met us at the parking lot. I didn't ask his name. I was too sick and bone-weary to care one way or the other.

Mom told me she'd let me know the results of the rabbit autopsy when she returned home. She kissed me on my forehead, and handed me over to the Agent.

I hoped he'd just drive me home without any conversation.

But he was too polite to keep quiet.

"I'm F.B.I. Agent *Arthur Anderson*," he introduced himself in a deep, rumbling voice. He handed me a plain white card with his contact info on it. "I'm to be your personal assistant. Just give me a call, Miss Kingly, if you need anything. I usually operate behind the scenes, but I'm happy to be of service to such a talented person as you. We're all very happy you've joined the Project. I'm a big fan, by the way. I have all your albums."

Wow. He was really friendly. And I had an odd feeling I'd met him previously. But if I had, I'd surely remember it. He was a big, hulking, intimidating presence. Nope, didn't recognize him.

"Ok," I grimaced, my head spinning. I slipped the business card into my pocket. By habit I grabbed my marbles and began slipping them around in my fist as I waited to get into the van. Their faint "clinking" calmed me.

"You play marbles?"

"What?"

"Sorry, I heard them in your hand."

That was nice of him, to be interested in my particular hobbies. Somehow, though he was a stranger, I felt an urge to open up to him—to tell him things I'd never told anyone else.

"Oh...right," I shrugged. "It's just my 'Taw' and its faithful companions. Working them around in my hand helps when I get nervous, like just before a performance. When I was a kid I was pretty good in competitions. I won a lot of stones when we played 'keepsies', but only kept a few of the best and..."

My throat closed up and I momentarily couldn't speak. I was too tired, even for talking about my childhood passion.

Truth-to-tell, I was sick of fans pestering me. My forced "retirement" had been something of a relief. Before the Hollywood Bowl disaster I'd even stopped carrying a cellphone. The most valuable thing to me then was the profound relief of just being by myself. Now I had that "pleasure" all the time...

—except for a few diehard fans like this middle-aged guy.

"Me too," he grinned widely. "We should play sometime."

He seemed really nice, however—not the typical overeager fan starving for attention. He didn't even mention my grass-stained, disheveled, and wigless condition. I must have looked hideous, not at all like the young, pretty Diva on my album covers. He acted as if I were still "Suzette Kingly", soothing my ruptured ego.

"I...don't play anymore, not even the guitar...my fingers are kinda burned and broken..."

He soberly nodded.

"I'll get you back home in a jiffy," he rumbled at me. "And don't you worry. I'll protect you."

That was so nice to hear.

"Please go slow," I managed to groan. "I'm sick—my Mom drove me out here much too fast."

"No problem, Miss Kingly. But still please put on and buckle your seatbelt when you get in. Safety first!"

I focused in on the middle-aged gentleman. He had a short haircut and big dark eyeglasses that wrapped around his head. Did he say he was F.B.I.? What was the F.B.I. doing at this research facility? But, whatever, he politely held the back passenger door open for me. That was kind of him. I almost felt like I was back to being a world-famous Pop Superstar being chauffeured around. But I knew I was in reality a shriveled, cane-wielding, scared, vomit-smeared recovering addict.

And my guts were bothering me again. I felt that pesky gas building up in my intestines. Not letting loose nasty blasts was a chore. But I'd be home soon enough. I could "go potty" and let my irritable guts calm down. But for the moment I was in pain, fighting to contain my lethal farts.

"You mind if I turn on the radio?" he asked from the front seat. "Even though I get privileged updates over my ear buds, I like to keep up with the public newscasts. It keeps me grounded in the present reality."

That was an odd thing to say.

"Please don't," I sighed, closing my eyes and slumping down. "I have a terrible headache," I muttered.

He ignored my request. Either he didn't hear me or he wasn't as nice as I'd thought. I heard the radio start up, a bland N.P.R. reporter listing all the current world conflicts, pandemics, and crises: the "normal" world news summary.

The car started up and we pulled out of the parking lot through the opening guard gate.

I tried to tune it all out. I didn't want to hear the news, but he had it turned up too loud. Terrible things were happening all across the globe. The world was screwed up and getting more dangerous by the minute. But the world had *always* been screwed up. The world would always *continue* to be screwed up. What's "new" about that?

I was in an abysmal mood, getting more and more depressed by the moment. Little did I imagine that things were going to get a lot worse a lot faster than I'd like.

"I think Dr. King will benefit greatly from your presence back here in Sulphur," Agent Anderson volunteered from the front seat as he leisurely steered us at a moderate pace down the road toward the Cemetery. "She's a genius, you know. But even geniuses need to have solid moorings or they can drift off into 'coo-coo' land. She's missed you during your touring years. You can be an important anchor for her now that we've entered the active stage of the Project."

I didn't need to hear this. He seemed awfully intrusive for a "behind the scenes" government agent. His deep voice jarred on my brain. I just wanted to get back home, climb into my bed, and sleep for twelve hours straight. The trip to the "Animal Shelter" had exhausted me.

"*...breaking news—there's been another concert bombing, very similar to the Hollywood Bowl incidence at...*"

"What the hell?" I gasped, sitting up straight to listen closely. "Is this fake-News? I thought they caught the drug money launderers who were behind my disaster?"

"I'm getting secure reports over my earbud," he added. "It's real, happening as we speak."

"*...tens of thousands feared dead. London is in turmoil, the streets tied up with first responders rushing to the Wembley Stadium. Survivors say the stage blew up first, followed by denotations of the central hanging screens. Similar to the Hollywood Bowl bombing, a hailstorm of lethal shrapnel rained down on the audience that numbered over 90,000. They were there for the joyful memorial tour of 'Concert for Diana,' an event meant to celebrate lost youthful beauty and energy. Instead, mass carnage erupted that...*"

"I think to be prudent we'll turn back to the secure base where..." Arthur began as I felt the van slow...

THWAPPP!

I cringed down in my seat, the loud sound reverberating in the interior of the van.

Peering back over my shoulder I saw that the glass of the rear window behind me was now fractured into a spider-web pattern.

What—had a passing car kicked up a rock? Glancing behind us I saw two side-by-side cars fast approaching, blocking both lanes. Looking forward through the front window I saw the same: two more cars coming straight at us, one in each lane.

Was that a man with an *assault rifle* leaning out of a window to fire at us from behind? Even more worrying, emerging from the rolled back top panel of one of the cars zooming toward us was a black-clad person hoisting what looked like a *bazooka!*

We were lethally pinned in!

"*Hold on!*" Agent Anderson shouted as he suddenly spun the vehicle to the side...

Another "thwackkkk" made me duck down as the rear window *shattered* into a thousand pieces, spraying me with sharp glass fragments.

"What's...?"

"*...the Luzhniki Stadium in Moscow, Russia has also been hit. Fire bombs blended into the grand finale fireworks, engulfing the audience of 80,000 souls in a raging inferno. They were enjoying The Argo-Spacers, Eastern Europe's hottest ziffler band when...*"

I was stunned to hear the radio announcer announcing the death of one of my favorite zifflers. I'd caught one of their concerts in Munich. We'd just arrived there to start setting up our own show, just as The Spacers were finishing their last performance in the Olympic Stadium. It was awesome. They had state-of-the-art sonic-vibratons that augmented their traditional instruments, inducing trance-like visions in enraptured fans. I was close friends with their female lead singer, Shanna Katina. She was jarringly bitchy, but sweet when she wasn't on drugs. They were the latest rage in music, now *incinerated* along with their fans.

"Hey!" I yelled. "What are you...?"

"Help is on the way!" Anderson yelled back at me. "I'm cutting through the Cemetery to..."

I felt the jarring thud of a huge EXPOSION that tossed the entire van up into the air. I seemed to float for an eternity in "zero-g" before *SLAMMING* down hard into the ground.

The world spun around as we rolled several times before coming to a shuddering stop.

Stunned, I undid my seatbelt and crawled from the ripped-open side of the van. My seatbelt and the padding on the back and front seats had saved me. I saw that Anderson was embedded in an inflated airbag, trying to cut himself free with a knife. The radio was still on in the crumpled vehicle. I heard the N.P.R. reporter getting uncharacteristically agitated, shakily announcing that there were *four more* near-simultaneous bombings being reported. The latest concert bombings were scattered around the world at giant venues: in *South Africa* at the Cape Town Stadium, in the Beijing Concert Hall in *China*, at the University of San Marcos Stadium in Lima *Peru*, and at the Tokyo Dome in *Japan*.

"*...seems to be maximizing casualties for world impact, timed to when the largest number of people were entering, attending, or leaving the simultaneously overlapping events. Officials say it's too* *early yet to assign blame or assess how such powerful explosives were placed in the most secure mass-gathering sites ever where..."*

I momentarily blacked out.

"Are you still alive?" a gruff voice roused me, a firm hand shaking my shoulder.

I looked up into the dark eyeglasses of Agent Anderson. He was the one who should be dead. He had a deep cut across his cheek, spurting red blood. One of his arms hung limp at his side, clearly broken. But the other hand released my arm to grab up a heavy black gun. I was lying against a large marble tombstone.

To the side was the crumpled van, which was wrapped around a tree.

"Just barely," I managed to reply. "This is turning out to be a very eventful day," I coughed, trying to clear my lungs.

"They'll be on us in moments. Clearly they don't mean to take any prisoners. They're likely part of this world-wide terrorist event aimed at inflicting mass casualties. I imagine they're trying to finish the job they failed to accomplish at your Hollywood Bowl concert."

"So it really *was* terrorists behind the bombing?" I gasped, stunned. "Are they...going to kill me?"

"Not if I can help it. We've just got to hang on a few more minutes for our troops to arrive. Do exactly what I tell you. Agreed?"

I nodded.

"As I draw their fire, get behind this stone and head *directly* back from it to the next monument. Use it for shelter, assess the situation, and keep moving further back. Stay under cover of the upright grave stones and monuments, heading for those woods behind us. Got it?"

"Yes, but...?"

"They're almost to the van. When I say 'go'—get your skinny little butt out of here."

Hah...he thought I was skinny. What a nice guy.

He suddenly grabbed my left arm and gently *kissed* the back of my hand. I was shocked, not knowing how to respond. My Turtle Tattoo felt warm. It was visibly glowing!

"Whatever happens, I want you to know I'm *sorry*—for everything."

"Say what?"

"*Go!*"

I took a deep breath, scrambled behind the gravestone, and then scuttled away, headed for the next one further out.

I ignored the pain of my bruised, battered body. I moved as fast as I possibly could, crouched down low.

I heard a raft of *gunshots* behind me. Several bullets whizzed by my head. The assassins were hot on my tail.

"Oh, Christ!" I gasped as I glanced back from behind my last gravestone. I was panting, out of breath. I was barely able to move. I couldn't go on. They were going to catch and kill me!

Indeed, at least five masked gunmen were approaching from the rear. Agent Anderson was nowhere to be seen. I feared he was dead.

"There!" I ordered myself, trying to summon up the last of my strength for one more furtive dash.

At the outer edge of the graveyard sat a *casket* lit by the warm, yellow light of the sinking sun. It was made of brilliantly polished wood, maybe Mahogany. Beside it I saw a pile of dug-out dirt, signaling the presence of a fresh, open grave. Beside the grave lay a human body, unmoving. I saw red blood covering his face. He must have been there doing final burial preparations when one of the bullets cut him down.

I ran for it.

"*There* she is!" a shout came from behind me as I ducked lower, adrenalin powering my desperate sprint.

I "zigged" and "zagged" to try and obscure my path.

"Where'd she go?"

I heard thumping boots as the gunmen ran up to where I was hiding. I was struggling to be absolutely silent though I was sucking in air by the bucketful. I just managed to get a hand in my jeans pocket and pull out my lucky marbles. If I ever needed luck it was now.

"It's locked from inside."

I heard gun butts smashing into the side of the coffin.

"It's too thick to break open!"

"Then get the damn lid up."

"We can just riddle it..."

"We've got to make sure she's in it. We can't botch the job again. The Commissioner would have our heads!"

"Stand back, I'll shoot off the lock."

I cringed as several blasts hit the side of the box.

Then the top of the coffin was ripped to the side.

"Where is she? There's just some old corpse."

At that moment, my mistreated guts decided they'd had enough.

Brrrrraaaaaaappppppp!

Oh, God. It was a massive one... The evil smell caused me to gag.

"She's in that fresh grave! Take off the cover."

Yes, I was cowering down inside the deep hole. After pushing up the lid slightly to the coffin I triggered the inside lock and let it close forever. Well, that was what was supposed to happen. Fortunately I'd used a similar model in one of my stage bits and knew how it was configured. I figured it might buy me a few seconds. Then I pushed up a corner of the covering tarp of the grave, squirmed beneath it, and dropped to the fresh-dug dirt at the bottom. I sprained my ankle falling the ten feet to the bottom. But I hardly noticed. A terror unlike anything I'd ever experienced gripped me. Sitting there in *my own freshly dug grave*, I knew without a doubt I was about to die.

Simultaneously as the cover above me was ripped away a "chittering" helicopter swooped low overhead letting loose a lethal *machine-gun blast!* The gunmen above me snapped their attention to the sky, firing back.

Momentarily all was quiet. I breathed in a shuddering sigh of relief until I saw a *slack hand* appear above me at the edge of the top of the pit. Loosely held in the hand was a *grenade*.

"Oh, hell," I moaned, futilely thrusting up *my lucky marbles* as my one and only defense.

I absently noticed the pin was gone as the hand-grenade slipped from bloody fingers and dropped seemingly in slow motion down toward me.

I closed my eyes tightly as it *exploded*.

Chapter 10

PRIMITIVE BEATS

*Tapping out the **rhythm of the road***
Trains, trucks, cars, or motorcycles
That "thrum," "thrum," "thrum" of the motor
Evoking the pulse of the heart and the soul

Or ten thousand stomping feet
Rocking the stadium at countless concerts
A mass herd roaring, elevating the individual
Into a mindless, stampeding beast

Or a mighty armada's rolling thunder
Tanks, soldiers, battleships, or airplanes
Crushing and smashing all their enemies
In a raging orgy of conquest and blood

Hence that sad refrain of "the drums of war"
Satisfying a deep primeval urge
Smashing, breaking, and brutally hard
Permitting our worst instincts to surge

Or mimicking the penetrating thrusts of sex
The male performing its biological duty
Transmitting the sperm of varied life
Earning a period of blissful rest...
The Suzette Anthology, Lyrics 10

I lowered my shaking hand, surprised I was still alive. Wow. Those marbles must really be lucky!

Absently, I slipped them back in my jeans pocket, trying to figure out what had happened to me.

I'd never been in a gunfight before, let alone a military-style assault facing anti-tank rockets and hand grenades. From all the war movies I'd ever seen when a live grenade drops into a foxhole and explodes—the soldiers in the pit get blown to pieces!

Instead, I was stunned at what I saw...

"What the hell?"

Stretched out before me to the horizon was a *green-blue tropical ocean*. I could see *several small islands* close to the wide shore upon which I sat. Under my butt was *warm, soft sand*. Surrounding me were *towering palm trees*, their green fronds waving gently in a steady breeze. I saw *brown coconut clusters* above me. Behind me, inland, I could see *black lava mountains* rising up through swirling mists.

Holy crap! I sure wasn't in Oklahoma anymore!

"*O cei o iko?*"

I jerked to my feet, whirling around. I saw a young boy looking at me, holding a flopping fish in one hand and a small spear in the other. He looked as startled as I felt. His eyes were wide in his brown-black face, his teeth gleaming white in the sun. He wore a dried grass "skirt." I later learned that his words were quite straight-forward: "Who are you?"

"Uh...hi there...I'm so glad to see you. I'm Suzy. I'm kinda lost. But could you maybe help me to find...?"

Screaming repeatedly "*E dua na marama vulavula!*" he dropped his fish and ran away into the surrounding jungle.

If I'd known he was shouting "A white lady! A white lady!" I would have been more concerned. Instead, I found it kind of amusing. One moment I was about to be blown to pieces and the next I was scaring some little kid who was obviously just out fishing on his beautiful tropical island.

"Should I run? Should I hide?" I muttered, looking around, feeling the warm sun on my skin.

Jesus, this place looked like a paradise! I expected to glimpse secluded villas of a 5-star luxury resort set off from the dazzlingly white sandy beach. But there was just the wall of towering palm trees, waving in the breeze.

How did I get here?—I desperately thought to myself.

It had to be the Sphere. Somehow I was connected to it. That T-rex appeared right next to me. Then it attacked my "choo, choo" train. Could it be my mysterious Turtle Tattoo telling the Sphere what to do? I looked down at it, expecting it to be glowing. But it wasn't. Now it just sat there on my wrist, smiling shyly up at me.

"Come on, you damn thing!" I ordered it, shaking my wrist. "If you made the Sphere throw me here then make it yank me back. I appreciate not having gotten blow up by that grenade, but now I want to return!"

I shook my whole arm, trying to get the Tattoo to do its thing.

But nothing happened.

All I knew was that I'd been thrown somewhere quite different from land-locked Sulphur, Oklahoma. Where was I? But another, even scarier, question popped into my mind: "*When* was I?"

For all I knew I was thousands of years in the past or the future.

"*Kakua ni yavala, vulavula na tevoro, se o sa mate!*" (Don't move, white Devil, or you are dead!)

A *band of natives* burst from the bushes, wildly brandishing spears and clubs. They looked like a passing band of hunters or warriors startled by my sudden appearance. They were burly black-skinned males, naked except for grass skirts or loin cloths. They all sported bushy "afros." Some had on what seemed like war paint or tattoos: blue etchings on their face and torsos.

"Oh, Jesus!" I laughed, suddenly grinning at them. "I know what you guys are. You're native re-enactors, right? Nice job—you're very authentic looking. Hey, I'm...from the resort. That's right. I'm just a tourist. I was out surfing, lost my board, and washed up on your beach. If you could just help me get back to my resort I'd really appreciate your..."

They snatched me up, tightly bound my hands and feet with vines, slid a pole through, hoisted me up on their shoulders, and triumphantly marched away into the surrounding jungle with me dangling in the middle.

"...or not," I sighed, swaying back and forth beneath the pole. The unexpected pressure on my limbs and hands was very painful. Clearly they weren't native re-enactors from a local luxury-resort.

They lustily chanted as they marched along through the thick brush, as if they'd captured a valuable prize. Well, I certainly felt I was precious enough for them to take me to their Chief. I was good at negotiating contracts in foreign lands on my World Tours. This was just some misunderstanding. We'd get it straightened out. Whatever, at least things couldn't get much worse.

—or so I thought.

"Uh, guys? Where are we going?" I tried to get someone's attention, pulling myself up on the pole.

My head rang from a club unceremoniously "bopped" onto my noggin. Clearly they wanted me alive. But they didn't want me making any trouble.

"*O na cakava e dua na kakana talei me baleta na levu!*"

"Uh, ok," I groaned, hanging limply, trying to wriggle my extremities to keep some blood flowing to my hands and feet.

I'd have been more worried if I'd known then what the words meant: "You will make a fine meal for the Chief!"

I tried to track our movement through the jungle. If I need to escape from my captors I'd have to find my way back to the shore. The sun was setting to my right, so that must be to the West. And we were going steadily uphill. I noticed they were taking a defined path through the jungle. Also, they were avoiding certain grassy areas. I thought that was curious until I saw a snorting hog suddenly dart across our path. It ran into one of the clear areas, fell through a covering of branches and leaves, and was impaled on sharp spikes.

Its dying squeals were terrifying. A few of the warriors broke off to harvest its meat.

As we continued on up the mountain slope I saw more warriors hiding behind boulders and up on the slopes. Clearly we were approaching a well-defended village.

"Wow," I gulped as I hung upside down, impressed.

We were there. The jungle opened up to reveal thatch huts and larger structures. Hordes of women, their breasts naked and flopping down, were working at open pits busily roasting meat. It smelled good. I suddenly realized I hadn't eaten for a while and what I'd consumed last I'd vomited up. My mouth watered at the barbeque smoke drifting at me. Lucky for me they didn't offer to feed me. My psyche would have been scarred for the rest of my life. The "meat" wasn't from hogs, birds, or fish...

But then again, I guess protein is protein.

Ceremoniously garbed men were entering and exiting a central, large structure. It was raised up on a partial pyramid of stacked stone slabs. It was a square building with a very high thatched roof. The men there had elaborate necklaces, arm circlets, and red sashes across their chests.

It looked like I'd arrived at a particularly eventful gathering: maybe of local chiefs and priests.

Whatever, when they saw me dangling from the carried pole a great shout went up!

"*Me vakacaucautaka na Kalou! Me vakacaucautaka na Kalou! Eda sa rawata na qaqa!*" (Gods be praised! Gods be praised! We've won the victory!")

By now I was barely conscious, the blood drained from my limbs and pooling in my poor, swollen head.

I couldn't even protest as the band of warriors hoisted me up steps and into what I later learned was called a *Bure Kalou* or temple. Inside I was surrounded by dark walls. Hanging on the walls I recognized many weapons, all stained black by smoke from the central pit. There were battleaxes, spears, and clubs. Ominously, a platform sat against the further wall, stained red with dried blood.

I was dumped on the floor, the pole pulled away from my bound hands and feet, and roughly tossed up on the platform. Then the room was filled with chanting and dancing as the warriors presumably celebrated their great "victory." I *moaned* from the platform.

And as I lost consciousness I remember hearing outside, beating louder and louder...*drums!*

"Please...Miss...wake up!"

It was a gentle, soft voice in my ear, rousing me from my nightmare. Was it Mom? I'd just had a terrible dream where I'd been captured by savages, tied up like a hog, and tossed up on a ceremonial platform. My feet and legs hurt something terrible.

"Uhnnggg..." I groaned, trying to open my eyes.

By the light of the central fire-pit I saw *big brown eyes* inches from my face, set into a round, soft-skinned, black face. They belonged to what looked like a young girl. All she had on by way of clothes was a grass skirt strung from a waistband. Her breasts weren't yet fully developed. She must have been about twelve years old, just going through puberty. Her black, curly hair was cut short. She had a beaded necklace around her throat.

"Here...drink this...it is good."

I got my head up and sipped at a half-shell coconut filled with what I thought was coconut milk. But it wasn't a watery-sweet, cool fluid. Instead it was a greenish, thick, hot fluid that initially made me gag. But realizing I was parched and needed fluids, I managed to choke it down.

It was hot and soothing, warming my body and mind.

"What...is this?" I asked after draining the container.

"It is...Kava," she whispered as she set it to the side. "It will make the pain less."

"Thank you," I grimaced, trying to sit up. But my hands and feet were still bound. "Can you untie me?"

"Yes...but be very quiet...they do not know I am here."

"Thank you."

Outside I could hear the monotonous but frightening beat of the drums. Plus there was a lot of chanting and shouting. Strange things were happening outside.

And then I heard the *screams*...

A chill went through my spine as I recognized them: the sounds of my mutilated fans at the Hollywood Bowl being shredded by flying shrapnel, moments from death.

"What is that?" I asked as she undid my feet and hands. I wobbly sat up on the edge of the platform, rubbing at my wrists.

The feeling was starting to come back in my hands and feet. It wasn't as painful as I figured it should be. True to what the young girl told me, the drink she gave me was deadening the pain. I decided right then and there I could trust her.

"It is prisoners. They are being..." she seemed to struggle for a word.

Then she made like she was holding a knife and slashed up-and-down at her arms and legs.

I gasped. "Their limbs are being sawed off?"

She nodded.

"But why?"

"Fresh meat."

Oh...Christ. They were *cannibals!*

"Is this...the Fiji islands?"

She nodded again.

"And what year is this?"

"Year?"

"Yes! Time! The Christian date!"

"You mean, English time?"

"Yes!"

"Ah...it is, how do you say, eighteen hundred...and sixty plus seven..."

"It's 1867?"

"Yes."

Oh, hell. I'd been thrown back in time to the 19th century! If I remembered my homeschooled world history high school classes correctly, this was a time when the "cannibal isles" were being converted by Christian missionaries. But the Fijians had an existing strict religion that recognized many gods and condoned eating the flesh of one's enemies. Cannibalism wasn't just a means of finding extra protein, but part of a long and cherished religious tradition.

Naturally enough, many of the tribes on the Fijian islands hated the white people with their new religion that sought to up-end their native societies.

And I was right in the middle of it.

But why the hell was I here? I couldn't believe this was by chance. There was some *purpose* to me being put here. There *must* be! Either that or Lady Luck was a sadistic bitch.

"How is it you speak English?"

She smiled at me as she helped me down off the platform and wobbly stand.

"I was taught...by Missionaries."

"Are they here?"

"Not here...I was captured by this tribe...will help you escape...you help me return...they be glad to see you...no think me spy."

"Thank you. Or course I'll help you get back in the good graces of your Missionaries. What is your name?"

"I am Lelea."

"That's a very pretty name, Lelea. My name is Suzy."

"Sooz-eee?"

"Close enough."

I stumbled and almost fell. My feet were still numb, unresponsive to my brain.

"We must hurry...it is almost time for *Wate*. The men already do the *Cibi*."

I groaned, my limp legs giving way beneath me. I could barely move. My feet needed time to get blood back into them.

"We must leave now!" she insisted. "The Chiefs come back soon for you."

"Me?"

"They kill you last. You are the best Victory—over the white people who take our land."

"Ok...I get it," I gasped. The pain in my legs was crippling. I was sitting on the hard floor by the glowing embers of the central fire-pit. Being inside the Temple was really creepy. The soot-covered weapons—likely used to smash, pierce, and dismember many hapless victims—dangled all around me. Every fiber of my being wanted to slink out into the surrounding jungle and run like the wind. But my body just wouldn't cooperate.

"Yes, we rest, for a minute," she nodded, sitting down stoically beside me.

"What's the Cibi?"

"Oh...it is *Death Dance*. The warriors celebrate...a great victory over other tribes...feast on their flesh."

"Alright. And what's a Wati?"

She ducked her head down, visibly shivering.

"Lelea? What's going to happen?"

In a small voice she said: "The women take off everything...dance for men, naked...then men take us."

"They take you?"

"Just after big victories...other times not. It is...reward for the warriors."

"They're going to take *you?* But you're too young for .."

"Yes, me, tonight, first time! Not marriage. Not one man—*many!* They drink Kava now, *much* Kava."

Jesus Christ! She was talking about being gang-raped by a drunken, victorious army!

"Oh, good God, Lelea. That's terrible! You're right We have to get out of here, whether my legs work or not. Can I maybe lean on you and...?"

"*Na cava e yaco tiko eke? Kauti ira! Kauti ira ruarua!*" (What is happening here? Take them! Take them both!)

Warriors rushed into the temple, snatching away Lelea and pinning my arms to my sides. They carried me bodily out into the village's central compound. I saw with relief that Lelea managed to slip out of the grasping arms and scamper off into the darkness.

It was night now. Hopefully that would help her escape these savages.

"Thanks for trying to help me, Lelea! Run away! Save yourself!" I shouted after her.

The Kava was starting to wear off. I discovered I had a pounding headache that the monotonously beating "war drums" didn't help. Behind the many glaring torches and drunkenly dancing warriors I noticed a line of six-foot-long Lali along one edge of the compound. I knew of the Lali from my *South Pacific Tour* of Album Two. It was a large or small hollowed out log, open at the top. Beating on it with thick sticks created the deep, booming sounds I was hearing. The large ones were for war and signaling. Smaller ones produced a higher tone for dancing and chanting. I saw a lot of those scattered around, adding to the same steady beat.

"Ah hah!" I muttered knowingly to myself, "This is nothing more than a drugged-out *grunge* rock concert!"

I'd always strived to have my giant concerts as "family" Pop events that even little kids could enjoy (yes, sometimes giant mushrooms are just mushrooms). But I enjoyed attending fellow artists producing the hardcore, "triple X" versions. I didn't participate in the drugs or casual "hook-ups" but enjoyed the raw, sexual thrust of the musicians. The contemporary grunge-revival had contributed to my being denied a "come-back" album, but I wasn't bitter. Grunge was a fusion of the viciously relentless beat of *punk* combined with the exquisitely variable electric guitar riffs of *metal rock*. What I saw in front of me based in primitive drum instrumentals, was grunge without the fine-tuning of metal: a formalized version of punk. I saw older men with their red sashes carefully monitoring the "concert," doubtless to make sure their tribal and religious traditions, rituals, and norms were followed.

"I've *got* you bitches," I grinned as I dangled from the strong arms of the guards.

I knew just how to take control of the situation.

Maybe priest-ordained formalized punk rock music was possible at the start of this ceremony, but the guards were hauling me out at the peak moment: when all the young people (there weren't many middle aged or older people, likely due to constant war and untreatable diseases) were thoroughly liquored up. Their Kava wasn't alcohol, but whatever plant they brewed it from was definitely euphoric. The kids were in control!

"*Look!* It's *Elvis!*" I shouted, twisting my head to the side and forcing my eyeballs wide.

Startled, my guards relaxed their grips just enough for me to squirm free.

I dropped to the ground and scampered on all fours like a spider, away from my captors and through the chanting mob of leaping feet.

"*Tarova na tevoro vulavula! E sa na rawa ni!*" (Stop the white devil! She's getting away!)

But I wasn't running for the jungle. I knew that with this horde of juiced-up warriors I'd be cut down by spears or captured within a dozen paces. If I somehow eluded a whole village full of its occupants plus victorious hosted armies I'd either get hopelessly lost or fall into one of those spike-pits. No, escaping through the jungle was impossible. Instead, I was headed straight for the line of large Lali.

"Hey, buddy—can I take a turn?"

Startled, the afro-headed drummer dropped his sticks as I snatched them up and took his place at the central Lali.

Transfixed by this unexpected drama, the entire dancing throng came to an abrupt stop. The drums large and small ceased. Everyone was looking at me.

For that split instant I had them in the palm of my hand. And I meant to keep them there.

"*Let's get this party started!*" I shouted as loud as I possibly could.

To hell with their "war drum" monotonous beat! These were young people. They were the same as any other hormone-dripping, drugged-up, authority-rebelling kids of any other time or place. Though they were on the verge of a drunken orgy, I could give them something even better: *Suzette Kingly* unleashed!

I began beating on the Lali with a wild and varied beat, using the different parts of the hollowed out log to produce a stunningly exotic rhythm. But I kept the basic "*1-2-3-4*" cadence, motioning for the other war drums to join back in. With a bemused nod from the head Chieftain they did so.

Fortunately I'd often taken a turn on the drums in the middle of my concerts, to the delight of my audiences. I wasn't as good as the expert drummers, of course, but I certainly knew my way around the sticks and this was no different.

Ignoring the pain and numbness in my hands I set about laying down a dizzying, mind-bending, blazing pattern.

"*E dodonu me da kukuva koya ka vakamatei koya?*" (Should we grab her and kill her?) I heard one of the guards loudly ask the Chief, confused by what was happening.

"*Eda na kania vua e muri,*" the Chief imperiously ordered, sweeping an arm through the air. "*Meda raica na cava e rawa ni cakava na tevoro vulavula e na caka.*" (We will eat her later. Let us see what the white devil can do on the drums.)

"Come on! Let's get some *clapping* in here!" I shouted, setting aside my sticks and leaping up on top of my Lali.

I almost toppled off because of the blazing pain in my sprained ankle and still-recovering legs. But I managed to stand upright, again commanding their attention.

I pointed to the approaching crowd of naked ladies as my fellow war-drummers kept up the new, faster beat. Likely also juiced up on Kava, the horde of females put their hands up in the air and began loudly clapping. I was amused at their beat-synchronized bouncing breasts. You didn't see that in actual rock concerts...well, not to that extent anyway.

"Hey—and when I say, let's do *clicking!*" I laughed, spotting kids with stones in their hands. I made the motion of slapping rocks together. They happily chimed in.

Now the war drums were punctuated by thunderous clapping and ear-slitting clicking.

"And you *rappers* get ready!" I yelled, pointing to those holding sticks in both hands, making rapping-together motions.

Their stick-slammers joined in like a cloud of angry, buzzing insects.

"And you *stampers*, let's do it too!"

I'd spotted a number of Derua in the crowd. They were hollowed-out bamboo tubes of various lengths closed at one end. When stamped hard down onto the ground they produced various tones different from the Lali and other instruments.

"Yes! Yes! Yes!" I enthusiastically cheered them on.

They now added to the beat, making a *magnificent noise* that rocked the entire village and surrounding jungle!

And like a Tarzan orchestra conductor I stood upon the Lali and directed them all in turn, dropping to take up my wild beats on the giant hollowed out tree trunk as needed to keep the variety roaring along.

I worked them up from a starting *frenzy* into a mindless *ecstasy* of excitement. By the light of the glaring torches I saw the thatch huts and houses visibly *vibrating* from the incredible synchronized noise. It was just like one of my best rock concerts!

God, if I'd had a few less scruples I could have embraced the new retro-grunge diversion, making millions more greenbacks continuing my career. But I guess, like poor doomed Elvis, my folk and Gospel roots were just too deep.

Having seen enough, the Chief stepped into the middle of the compound to try and restore order.

But a swirling mass of now enthusiastically writhing young people swept him aside.

And that's when things turned ugly.

A *shower of arrows* suddenly plummeted down from the sky, skewering fornicating couples, guards, and chieftains alike. Torches toppled as warriors tried to recover their wits and grab up their weapons. A vicious mob of different, still-sober warriors erupted out of the surrounding jungle, shouting and chanting as they surged into the compound.

Other lit arrows arched eerily down, lodging into the thatch roofs, setting the structures on fire.

I guessed that their "defeated" enemies hadn't been as vanquished as this coalition of villages had thought. A counterattack was mounted when their enemy was at its most distracted point: right at the moment of mutually enthralled mob-rape. Yes, Lady Luck is a bitch. When my captors were about to have a victorious orgy they were royally screwed from behind. Served them right!

I dropped my sticks and fell back, exhausted, cowering behind my Lali as war-whooping enemy natives leaped over me into the bloody melee of the besieged compound.

"Soozee," I heard an urgent, soft voice from right behind me.

"Ah, Lelea—I thought you escaped?"

"Come with me. Come fast!"

Without a moment's hesitation I limped after her into the night.

Chapter 11

<u>CIVILIZED LAGOON</u>

Warm sunshine on a cool beach: SHIMMERING
Bathers in briefs and bikinis: SPLASHING
Crystal clear wavy ocean water: CURLING
Little kids making wet sand castles: PLAYING

Surely a period of blissful vacationing: RELAXING
Sipping margaritas to soothing music: LISTENING
Sleeping, eating, and dancing: LAUGHING
Swinging in a soft hammock: SNORING

Knowing beneath the waves are sharks: LURKING
Tidal waves poised to sweep away the shore: HOVERING
Conniving thieves at the gambling casinos: STEALING
Tons of money needed to pay the bill: DRAINING

But for the moment laughter and smiles: DISARMING
Leaving behind the turmoil and stress: RELIEVING
Riding surfboards, canoes, and rafts: PADDLING
Never wanting to go back but resigned: DREAMING...
The Suzette Anthology, Lyrics 11

Lelea led me unerringly through the dark, spooky jungle. The going wasn't as difficult as I'd feared. Most of the time, we were headed downhill. Gravity can be a great assist to abused bodies. The screams and shouts of the slaughter in the village behind me faded, though the raging fires from the burning huts lit the upper nighttime horizon.

"Where are we going?" I asked as she led me by the hand

I was sure there were many snakes, spiders, anthills, jagged boulders, and booby traps all around me. But Lelea seemed to know exactly where she was going, leading me step-by-step. She paused and hid us on occasions, letting marauding bands of whooping warriors pass by without seeing us cowering there in the gloom.

"We...almost to shore," she whispered back, leading me more slowly forward.

I tripped and fell on my face in the moist undergrowth.

Tangled up in my feet I felt something moving...

"Soozee? Oh no!"

I looked at my feet in the dim moonlight and saw a thick-bodied, six foot long *snake*.

Lucky my eyes were adjusted to the gloom. I saw it had a reticulated, brown-red and orange pattern, flattened pointed head, and wasn't trying to strike at me, just crawl away.

I almost laughed as I got up to my knees, reached down and lifted its thick body, placing a couple coils over my shoulders.

Wide-eyed, Lelea looked like she was about to attack the critter or run screaming away!

"No problem," I whispered, letting the now-calming snake's head hang over my arm as I gently supported its neck. It flicked its tongue out onto my skin, tickling me. "This guy's not dangerous, Lelea. It's a Pacific Boa. They're not poisonous. I know about them because my Dad was an amateur herpetologist. Snakes aren't my favorite pet, but I learned enough from him to know how to handle them."

"You...play with snakes?"

"You're afraid of them?"

"Yes! My Tribe's God—*Degei!*"

"You had a snake-god?"

"We had...deep hole...many snakes..."

"A pit with snakes?"

"Yes! Those who were bad...thrown in pit...die screaming!"

"Wow...rough tribe to be from," I shrugged as I gently directed the boa to crawl off me back into the surrounding jungle-growth.

"We go!" she urgently ordered me once the snake was off me, pulling me onward.

Well, that was fun. Back to work.

Yes, I saw we were almost out of the jungle, back to the seashore. In front of me I caught a glimpse of the vast ocean. Under the silvery light of the just-risen moon it looked like molten glass. I smelled fresh salty wind coming off the warm water. It smelled like freedom. But I also heard the laughing chatter of warriors. I peeked around a bush and saw *a fleet of boats* pulled up on the sand. That must have been how the army presently invading the mountain village arrived undetected. The dozens of crafts were guarded by a small band of Fijian warriors.

"One of those?" I whispered to Lelea. "Is that how we're going to get away, take one of the ships?"

"Yes."

Well, they weren't really boats or ships. They were in actuality, glorified outrigger canoes. But they looked sturdy, sea worthy, and some capable of carrying dozens or hundreds of passengers. The largest ones were giant double canoes held together with a central wooden platform holding up a cabin. And they weren't dugout logs, but plank-built hulls, quite sophisticated. Each ship had a furled sail. A few of the sails were still deployed, probably late arrivals whose passengers hurried to the battle. I saw the typical triangular shape of a Fijian ocean vessel's sail.

"We can't handle the big ones," I whispered as I crouched beside Lelea.

"No...*Drua* too big," she agreed. "We take small one—*Camakau*."

I saw a few small craft amongst the armada which were only large enough to hold one or two people. That looked ideal. They were single canoes with rudder, two tent poles, and a furled sail.

"How far are we going?" I asked.

"Across water...to next island. We can do it, Soozee."

"You've done this before?"

"Yes...with my brothers...we fished in the ocean."

I was very encouraged. The ocean out there looked flat and serene. But I knew that it could be very dangerous getting away from the shoreline. What might look like a little jaunt to a nearby island could wind up being a death trap in raging seas. I'd never been out on the water before except at the small "Veterans Lake" close to my house. And even then we'd been on a row boat fitted with a gasoline engine. Floating in the ocean at the whims of the wind wasn't my idea of fun.

But remaining on that island wasn't an option. As if to emphasize the matter, a *giant green spider* walked across a broad leaf right in front of my nose.

Plus *mosquitoes* were biting into the flesh of my face and arms.

"How do we get it?"

"I get guards away. You push into ocean, paddle out far as you can. I swim after you."

"What, but...?"

And then she was gone, racing barefoot down the sand, screaming at the guards: "*A lako I vale duka na vuaka! Se au na vakamatei kemuni kece ka kania na matamuni!*" (Dirty pigs go home! Or I will kill all of you and eat your eyes!)

Startled, the guards grabbed their weapons. Then they relaxed, seeing it was but one lone girl. They laughed at her: "*Lako mai sivia tale! Eda na qito vinaka vata kei iko!*" (Come on over! We will play nice with you!)

She skidded to a stop, just yards from them, throwing up a cloud of sand. Then, as if suddenly realizing the futility of her charge, she turned and ran into the jungle.

"*Yalovinaka kakua ni mosi vei au!*" she called back. (Please don't hurt me!)

Grinning at each other lustily, the young warriors dashed after her.

I ran for the nearest small outrigger. It bobbed on the waves, right between two giant double-riggers. That was great because it was somewhat hidden between the two towering structures. I hastily untied a mooring rope that held it to one of the big ships, threw the rope onboard, then pushed as hard as I could to get its one end off the sand and into the water.

Behind me I heard shouting and laughing. I desperately hoped they'd not caught Lelea to have their way with her. But there wasn't anything I could do but carry on with the jury-rigged plan. What could I do against a whole band of burly, well-trained warriors? Suddenly I heard *screaming*. My heart dropped. Poor Lelea! I wanted to turn back and help her. But I was too afraid.

I kept pushing until I was up to my neck in the warm saltwater, pulled myself onboard, found an oar, and started paddling as hard as I could out to sea.

I wasn't making much progress. Any of the warriors could easily catch up to me in any of the other small Camakau. On the smooth sea I stuck out like a sore thumb.

"Soozee," a black head popped out of the water to the side of the boat, water streaming off curly hair.

"Lelea, thank God! I heard screaming..."

"Wasn't me," she grinned as she pulled herself aboard. She showed me a thin, blood-stained steel blade. "This came from my missionary friends. It is best for cooking. Good also for slicing throats. I only killed one. The others look still for me, but not for long. Soon they will see us."

"Ah..." I nodded, not knowing what to say. My pretty little friend was a cold-blood killer. "I'm sorry you had to do that for me."

"Is not a problem," she matter-of-factly replied. "We taught as children how to kill enemy. Many times my tribe brought enemies to practice on. That was before I was taught by Missionaries. Love of Jesus is much better."

"As children you were taught how to kill people, even the young girls?"

"Not as fighters...we help...kill wounded."

Wow. They were taught as children to be murderers, even the girls. Lelea must have had a brutal upbringing.

"Uh...I'm not going very fast," I said, still paddling hard while changing the subject to the most urgent priority. "How can we go faster?"

"The sail..." she curtly replied, already loosing knots and pulling on ropes. In a jiffy our triangular sail popped up, was secured in place, and we were zipping along on the breeze. With the moon now over our heads we slipped away from the island into the surrounding ocean.

"If it's ok...I need to rest just a bit," I wheezed, giving the rudder over to Lelea.

Every muscle in my body felt like it was torn loose, my bones cracked, and my guts roiling.

Plus I was as weak as a kitten. Other than the Kava I'd had nothing to eat or drink for much too long for a civilized gal.

"You sleep, Soozee," she smiled gently at me, "We safe now."

I teared up as I snuggled down in the rocking center of the canoe. Coming off the most intense "concert" of my life, it was good to know I had murdering friends like Lelea.

The sun was high in the sky, blazing relentlessly down upon us.

We were still in our lonely canoe, bobbing up and down on a windless vast ocean. We were long out of sight of the island we'd left, not yet in sight of our destination. Lelea said we were on track. She'd guided us by the stars as I slept through the night. But sailboats aren't very useful when the wind goes away. How long it'd be this way she had no idea. All we could do was pray for wind and wait.

My lips were cracked and dry. My tongue was swollen. There wasn't any water or food in the small canoe. We were huddled next to each other in the shadow of our limp sail, trying to stay out of the direct sunlight. But the blistering light was reflected by the smooth waters all around us. I knew I was badly sunburnt, my skin red and blistered.

Lelea wasn't in as bad shape as me, due to her sun-resistant dark skin. But she was also suffering.

"Maybe it will rain?" I wanly grinned at her.

There wasn't a cloud in the sky. All I saw up in the brilliant blue expanse was a few high-circling birds. Hopefully they were seagulls and not vultures.

"Maybe...but then big wind comes."

"Oh, right...but won't it blow us to the missionary island?"

"Big boat, maybe. But this one very small—mostly for fishing close to island, not going between."

"So we'll...?"

"Sink. To bottom of ocean. Fish will eat us."

"Right..."

It was quiet out there on the ocean. All I heard was the sound of small waves lapping up against the sides of the canoe. Once in a while a fish jumped out of the water off at a distance. Other than that, it was very peaceful.

Lelea smiled back to me. She seemed irrationally peaceful. I suppose she was happy to not have been gang raped by the drunken tribe's warriors or killed by the attackers.

"I like your hair," I stated feebly. I was trying to take my mind off the mental image of our sun-desiccated skeletons drifting for years on the ocean.

"Hair?" she said, putting a black hand up to her naturally curly Afro. "Why like?"

"Well...it's so healthy looking and springy. It fits your head very well. It matches your nice skin. You look very pretty with it."

"Thank you, Soozee," she answered politely. Then she stared at my head. "Why you no hair?"

"Well...it's a long story."

"I have time."

"Ok, then..." I shrugged. Well, why not. We were probably going to die on the ocean, anyway. A person can live for up to a month without food, but only a few days without water—especially while being baked in a hot sun. We might as well be in the middle of a dry desert. Trying to drink the salt water around us would kill us superfast instead of just fast. "It all began when I discovered how to play marbles..."

"Marbles?"

I fumbled into my jeans pocket and pulled out my lucky-charms.

I held up my Taw, admiring its pearly round gleam in the brilliant sunshine (a *china*). I rolled it around with my four other favorites: one blue-white with a red-yellow band in the center (a *catseye*), one clear blue (a *clearie*), one with a swirling rainbow of colors (an *onion skin*), and another with a mixture of gold and yellow (a *Lutz*).

"What...do with these?"

"It's a game. Kids play it. You make a circle, put some of these inside, and then see if you can knock them out with your shooter."

"I like that one."

"Which?"

"The sun marble."

"Ah, yes, that's very beautiful. It's called an 'Onionskin Lutz.' It's made of glass in which is embedded Lutz copper or goldstone."

"I...don't know those words. But I like the colors."

Even then I was reluctant to do what I did. I prized those lucky charms almost as much as my life. Almost, but not all the way—and Lelea had, indeed, saved my life...twice!

"Here. I want you to have it."

I handed it to her.

"Really?"

"Yes, please keep it with you forever. If I should die or vanish, you can remember me by it."

"Vanish? What is vanish?"

As I put away my precious remaining marbles in my jeans pocket with my left hand, I opened my closed right hand with fingers suddenly extended.

"Poof! Gone! Disappeared! *Vanished!*"

"Why...vanish?"

"Oh—like what happened to my hair. It was there then it was gone. Nothing left. Just gone."

"Oh, like with marble?"

"What?"

"No hair on marble."

"Ah..." I nodded in the affirmative. "Yes, bald like my marbles."

I winked at her.

"What did you do?"

I snorted. "It's called a 'wink', silly!"

"What does it mean?" she asked seriously.

Ah, she was a smart one.

"It means we share an unspoken connection, one that others around us may not understand or see. It communicates this without us having to speak. I just said: 'I'm beautiful like a Lutz even if I'm ugly like a smooth-headed fish.'"

"Hah," she laughed politely, obviously not fully understanding my words.

"It's a joke—between the two of us."

"Ah...a 'wink'..." she nodded, slowly closing one of her eyes at me.

"What does that mean?" I kidded her.

"It says...we both sisters under the skin...both of us golden."

"I like it!"

"Yes, it is most beautiful," she grinned, holding it up to the glaring light. The gold and yellow elements glittered within the clear glass.

"Onionskin Lutz Marble," I pronounced.

"Lutz..." she grinned brightly as she slipped it into a pouch attached to the waistband of her grass skirt.

So that was where she carried that small knife.

"Good enough," I grinned, relieved not to have to explain my whole life story to Lelea with her limited command of English. My life to-date had been much too complicated. And I was very tired. I just wanted to close my eyes and slip away, gently rocked by the endless waves.

Thank God for ocean currents. We were stuck in the "doldrums" for three whole days. Doldrums is a maritime expression for a calm period at sea where the winds disappear completely, trapping sail-driven ships. We almost died.

But on the third day I realized our canoe wasn't rocking anymore. Managing to open my crusted-together eyelids I saw we'd drifted up onto a sandbar. Not far away was the seashore of a tropical island. I hoped it wasn't the very same island we'd left four days before. That would be sad irony, to almost die at sea just to return to be eaten by the cannibals we'd thought we'd escaped.

But, no, the group of people gathering on the shore was dressed in western garb, a mixture of black skinned and white skinned people. And one of them was wading out to the sandbar.

Through my blurry eyesight I saw a pale-skinned, black haired man reach into the boat and gently lift out my unconscious companion.

"My dear God!" he exclaimed. "It's a miracle! It's Lelea!"

She opened her eyes and smiled.

"Reverend Baker," she whispered. "I'm so sorry I..."

"—nothing to be sorry about! The raiders were to blame for the abduction, not you. We are so glad you found your way back to us. Thank the Lord!"

"I...can...come home?" she whispered.

"Or course! We were so worried about you and the other children who were captured. We searched as best we could but..."

"Soozee...she helped me escape."

"Ah, rest, my dear child. We'll get you back to the settlement and get you healthy. 'Soozee' you say? A white girl? How amazing!"

"I'm...from a shipwreck," I croaked, lying. I didn't know how they'd react to me claiming to be a time-traveler from almost two hundred years in the future. "I almost got eaten by cannibals on a nearby island...then Lelea saved *me* and..."

He handed off Lelea to another person. Then he hoisted me out with his strong arms. I couldn't even move I was so weak from hunger and thirst. But by his words and demeanor I knew I was now in safe hands. I was with Christian missionaries. Sure they'd done terrible things across history, forcing whole societies to abandon their traditions and beliefs in order to "get saved," putting a high-minded gloss over cultural enslavement. But at least they weren't going to eat me.

I drew the line at people eating me.

Long story short, I was there with the missionaries for six months.

They readily accepted my story of having been on a trading ship from the United States of America. I told them I'd hit my head during the shipwreck on the coral reefs and had amnesia. That accounted for my not being able to tell them much of my past life. The main thing that clinched my story was, well, my being there in the South Pacific—plus my white skin, command of English, and American accent. Everything else was just unnecessary details. They promised to get me on a ship back to America whenever one came around, which unfortunately was rare.

That was ok with me. I was content to stay in their island paradise until I could find a way to travel closer home. They'd already converted to their form of Christianity most of the costal tribes located there on the largest Fiji island, *Viti Levu*. The missionaries were headquartered at a small English settlement. So there were plenty of tasks I could help with to earn my keep. I tried various things and settled on being a cook's assistant. It was an easy, pleasant job cooking for the English settlers. The island abounded with different kinds of tubers, fruits, wild pigs, and seafood. Though, I must admit, I had nightmares of cooking detached human legs and arms. But those faded quickly as I became used to my new routine.

Also, I happily attended Reverend Baker's local church where they had regular worship services, singing with incredible passion and intensity. The music was wonderful. I joined in happily. It reminded me of my fundamentalist Christian upbringing, but with the fervor of true converts. Reverend Baker didn't have to force the native tribespeople to convert since they did so enthusiastically. After all, they'd been raised from birth in a strict regime of extreme fear. Fighting with their neighbors to the death was a solemn religious duty. Few lived to old age. And here came this Englishman who was kind, generous, and preached a loving God that just wanted you to have a great, long life.

They particularly identified with Jesus, both his loving teachings and his extreme sacrifice. It was so different from their traditional many gods that had little regard for humans except to cause the people misery then laugh at their suffering. Jesus was tortured to death *for* them instead of causing *them* to be tortured to death! So they readily converted and heartily embraced the Christian doctrines, tossing aside their centuries-old gods and rituals.

Also, I was relieved that they'd accepted English clothes. Though the hot, humid climate justified going around half naked, it soothed my sensibilities not to have to see everyone's flopping dingdongs and nipples.

In other words, I found it pleasant to get back to my engrained norms of civilization.

But the natives were not just recipients. They had great talents and achievements to trade for their new-found serenity. One of those was an ancient mix of healing herbs that Lelea applied to the burns on my body, particularly my hideously scorched, bald head. She insisted on doing it herself, twice a day. I also had to eat a batch of it once a day—yuck! It tasted awful!

I told her she wasn't my servant and I could do it myself, whenever I wanted, trying to get out of doing it. She said she wanted to make sure I had the treatment twice a day. So I humored her, not expecting much from it. But after a month I was astounded to find *fresh new hairs* sprouting out all over my scalp! Also, new skin was marching across my scars. When I asked her what was in the nasty goop, she was apologetic. The elders of her tribe wouldn't reveal the exact mix of herbs, except to admit to the presence of Kava. Ah! That awful tasting, euphoric "tea," which the tribe still used during their native ceremonies, could grow hair! Who knew? And, strangely, the continuing pain from the brutal damages I'd suffered inside my body were easing as well. Was it due to her herbal goop or living in a peaceful, beautiful paradise?

Or perhaps I was just finally getting rid of the remnants of my drug addictions.

Who knew? I certainly couldn't conduct a controlled, double-blinded clinical trial on the Fiji islands in 1867. So my miraculous improvements had to remain anecdotal.

Regardless, I was delighted that after two months I was back to my healthy old, pre-Hollywood Bowl health. It was an incredible gift from Lelea and her tribe for which I was very thankful. And supplying "magic" treatments wasn't all that the coastal tribes freely gave the Missionaries. They also brought their energetic singing and powerful instruments to the worship services. Incorporated into the regular church routine were their Lali war drums, smaller chanting drums, Derua stamping bamboo tubes, clicking oval hand stones, striking sticks and hand clapping. This transformed the staid Christian ceremonies into powerful celebrations. It was a joy to attend the church services. Tribal members came from miles around to be part of the weekly gatherings.

So things were going great! A ship from America was expected in a month. Reverend Baker said he knew the captain and would vouch for me. I'd be able to earn my passage as a cook's helper. By now, having spent nearly six months with the missionaries, I was part of their extended family. The prospect of leaving them, Lelea, and her friendly tribe made both them and me sad. But they understood my desire to return home—even though my true family was almost two hundred years in the future. But I had a feeling that my path home led through America. I couldn't just give-in to the allures of the Fijian paradise.

But then the Reverend announced he was going into the mountains to convert the hill tribes.

I had a very bad feeling about it.

I vaguely remembered his name from the world history classes I'd home-studied for my high school G.R.D. But I couldn't remember the details... Damn it! I didn't know if I should be discouraging him or cheering him on. What was the good of being from the future if I didn't remember how history turned out?

So for once in my life I chose to be conservative, banking on my personal experience: "Thomas, you shouldn't go," I insisted, by then on a first name basis with him. I was addressing him during an official meeting of the missionary steering committee. Several of his assistants plus natives were present, both males and females.

"But I must, Susan. It is my holy job. It is why I came to this place. It's what I do!" he smiled triumphantly. "I've spent eight years insuring that the costal tribes are inside the embrace of our dear Lord and Savior. Now I must push further, evangelizing the inland heathens."

"But is this what you *want?*" I asked.

He tilted his head, a puzzled look on his face: "I want to serve God."

"Really? Is that what you want the *most?*"

His expression turned hard, patriarchal. Guest though I was, I was also a mere woman questioning the male leader of the local Church.

Also, he wasn't used to anyone probing his deepest motivations...

"Of course that's what I want," he snorted indignantly.

A gentle, warm breeze was blowing through the opened windows of the house. I could hear children playing down on the beach. Women were singing a Gospel hymn as they prepared the evening meal. But I knew it could all be *snatched away* in a moment's notice: a sudden raid by savages from the inland or the sea, carving us all up into a cannibal tribe's next bloody meal.

"I know it's your job," I continued to press my argument, now less confrontationally: "but as you know I was captured and taken to a mountain village when I was first shipwrecked in these islands. I directly experienced the intolerance of outsiders and rigid adherence to tradition of mountain tribes. I was lucky to escape with my life. Their leaders fiercely protect their heathen beliefs and so-called gods. And

I hear from my native friends that the closest mountain tribe to here is particularly fierce, ruled by a savage Chief. He is renowned for the number of enemies he's eaten. For God's sake, he's said to be addicted to human flesh! You must tread carefully if you wish to challenge his authority. The mountain tribes are definitely not as easy-going or open-minded as the costal tribes who are used to dealing with seafaring strangers. I would respectfully advise you to wait until the coastal confederation, with the aid of your guns, outright defeats them before..."

"All good points," he interrupted me, "but..."

Lelea spoke up, uncharacteristically interrupting the Reverend. "I agree with Soozee. We fear the inland tribes, for good reason. They, in turn, hate us. If you approach them at this time they will identify your small party with us. You will not be welcomed, indeed quite the opposite."

I was amazed at how much her English had improved in the last six months. She seemed a different person than the half-naked savage who rescued me on the other island. She wore a demure, cotton dress with long sleeves. Except for her round, black face she could be a young English girl. I'd "rubbed off" on her. Part of her remarkable transformation was doubtless because she'd spent most of the last six months with me. Though she identified with the local tribe she wasn't actually a coastal native. She herself had escaped from one of the inland tribes. She apparently felt more comfortable with me than even her adopted tribe. Either she was helping me learn to cook the local dishes or she was facilitating my interactions with the local natives, as I simultaneously learned more about them. She was highly intelligent, continually learning better English from me as I was learning native Fijian from her. Although I wasn't yet fluent, I could now communicate on simple terms with most of the natives, understanding most of what they told me.

"I'm sorry, ladies, but God has called me to this ministry."

"You *can't* help them find God if you're *dead* and *eaten!*" Lelea snapped at him. "Please do not go, Reverend! I'm begging you! I escaped from them. I was about to be killed and eaten myself—when all I did was fail some of the tests put to all the children."

Everyone at the wooden table was taken-aback by her fierce tone, including me. I agreed with what she said, but knew her angry tone was exactly the wrong one to take. Once Thomas Baker felt he was on the defensive he became stubborn as a mule. It was his one weakness: the very *inalterable determination* that had driven him to become a minister volunteering to preach the Gospel to the most dangerous heathens on the planet might well be his undoing.

"Lelea, I appreciate your concern," he said. His long white face was set in a stern expression, his high forehead wrinkled as his normally soulful eyes narrowed. "But the matter is settled. My expedition into the interior will begin one week from today. All the rest of you, please make the arrangements. I will not risk any other white people on this initial trip. But I ask for eight volunteers among our Fijian followers to accompany me. In that way, the hill tribes will see familiar faces vouching for me."

"You must take a larger party," one of the Englishmen at the table insisted. "We can supply a sufficiently armed expedition to..."

"That's out of the question!" Baker snapped at him. "They must see friendly visitors, not a war party. We do not bring Jesus at the point of a gun, as do the Spanish. We are different. We offer the love of God on its own merits."

"I still think it's a bad mistake to..." the other European continued.

"Then I volunteer to be one of the Fijian believers," Lelea insisted. Take me with you. I was raised among them. They will listen to me!"

"I will not risk your life, dear Lelea," Baker dismissed her offer. "God has saved you twice already. We should not tempt the Lord a third time. They would likely want to punish you for your escape, or think we participated in stealing you from them. You must remain here where you are safe."

Another of the Fijian females tentatively chimed in...

"The Reverend is correct, Lelea. You must listen to him," she spoke authoritatively. She was one of the few older natives, with gray showing in her dark Afro. "Also, taking any of us women would be seen as a sign of weakness. Here, females such as you, Lelea, and our guest Soozee, are honored as equal members of the Christian family. But, as you yourself said, the hill tribes are very traditional. The

Christian belief of spiritual equality between men and women is foreign, even repulsive to them. Perhaps in subsequent journeys as they
warm up to us we might join other expeditions to..."

Lelea slammed her small black fist down on the tabletop, startling
everyone.

"Then I will not see you again," she sobbed, abruptly standing up,
tears running down her cheeks. She ignored the others while staring
Baker in his eyes. "I love you, my Reverend leader—and I cannot bear
to see you go to your death. Thank you for all you've done for me.
Goodbye."

She stalked out of the room, weeping as she departed.

Right then and there I determined to accompany the expedition,
whether they wanted us women along or not. They would need
armed backup. I'd been practicing with some of their primitive rifles
over the months, growing better and better at target practice. I could
tag along behind them, an unseen sniper, ready to intervene if they
got into trouble.

So I didn't protest further. When the meeting broke up I just
went off and made my own preparations. The English settlement
kept an armory. One of their latest acquisitions was a Snider-Enfield
rifle. It was just starting to replace the Enfield muzzle-loaded rifles in
the British army. It was more efficient because it loaded at the
breech. So it was much faster to fire. A trained soldier could shoot
ten rounds per minute versus only three with the muzzle-loading pre-
decessor. I'd not shot it myself, but carefully observed its operation.
Also, it was more accurate. Doubtless the custodians of the armory
wouldn't allow their jewel to be taken away. So I determined to break
into the armory the night before the expedition departed and "bor-
row" it for the duration.

Reverend Thomas Baker was a genuinely nice person who
thought the best of people, including heathen cannibals. But I'd personally heard the screams and smelled the roasting flesh carved from
limbs severed from still-living victims. If I had anything to say about
it, he'd not face the mountain tribes with just the Gospel and his
bright smile.

If necessary, I was ready to blow some heads off. If Lelea could
kill to protect me, I could do no less to protect my English benefactor.

Perhaps that's why I was there in the 19th century—to ensure his survival. Helping spread *The Love of Jesus* wasn't a bad purpose.

I'd caught the missionary "bug."

Chapter 12

SNAKE IN THE GRASS

He and me, **linked** ***in a dream***
Floating on fluffy clouds in the sky
From all our problems we're finally freed
Knowing we'll never more suffer or die

Our own little log cabin out in the woods
You, I, and wee baby make family three
Gonna live happily singing our tunes
Old-time guitar-strums and simple drumbeats

In our own peaceful "Garden of Eden"
Our vegies grown in our own little garden
Hunting and slaughtering critters no need
Malice or evil not even a hint

Except in the lush meadow's greenery
Lurking to bite a misplaced foot
The fangs of a poisonous, hidden fiend
Sinking through futile and useless boots

But the lethal strike is an affirmation
Of Nature just doing its normal thing
Where everything eats everything else
Seeking dynamic equilibrium...
The Suzette Anthology, Lyrics 12

The morning that the expeditionary party was due to depart for the mountains was ill-omened. The sky was dark with storm clouds. At the island, tropical squalls routinely poured down buckets of rain then vanished as quickly as they'd appeared. But this was different. It looked like a typhoon might be upon us.

The leaders of the settlement begged Baker to postpone his trip into the mountains. But he was resolute. He said God had ordered him to depart that very morning. The bad weather was just Satan trying to slow him down, confirming the importance of his venture.

He and his eight Fijian converts, loaded down with heavy packs, set out on the jungle path leading upward toward the distant, looming mountains in the island's brooding interior.

Lelea, true to her word, was nowhere to be seen in the waving crowd of well-wishers seeing the missionaries off. But I was waiting out in the bush, carefully concealed. I hadn't abandoned my mule-headed Christian friend. Sitting beside me was my own heavy pack, plus sheathed rifle. I had enough bullets with me to put down a whole war-party of heathens.

Giving them fifteen minutes head start, I crept out of the bush and followed them up the narrow jungle path.

In the distance, I heard the deep "booming" of thunder. I saw sizzling flashes of lightning illuminating the roiling clouds. I knew what I was doing was stupid. Despite my frequent "adventure" trips with my parents as a child I knew next to nothing about surviving all by myself in a real jungle. Plus even though I was now healed up and healthy, I was still only one slight female. I was unable to carry much more than a jug of water, some hardtack to nibble on, and ammunition. If the expedition lasted more than a few days I'd be in real trouble.

"You thought you could go without me?"

Startled, I looked behind and saw Lelea trudging determinedly along, her own heavy pack strapped onto her back.

She was out of her English clothes, back to wearing only a short grass skirt, half-naked.

Her boobs looked larger. She was quickly maturing.

"You!"

"I will guide us, Soozee," she flatly stated. "I saw you steal the rifle. I will help you get in position to help our friends. Without me you'd be lost, captured, or killed by my former tribe's fierce warriors. They always have many lookouts to stop approaching enemies."

I smiled at her, incredibly relieved she was there with me.

"Thank you."

I noted she still had her pouch at her waistband. Doubtless she still carried her prized Lutz. If I fell into a snake pit and died from their venom she'd at least have that to remember me by.

And so we marched on together. It was a lot more difficult climbing upward than going down. Six months ago, with just the clothes on my back, it was like I was floating in air escaping the savage mountain tribe, running down the mountainside. Now it felt like we were climbing a sheer cliff, the heavy packs pushing down like boulders on my back as each step led us higher.

"It'd be nice to have a parka."

"What is a parka?"

"It's a hooded garment to keep the rain off."

"Why?" she shrugged as a torrent of rain pounded into us.

I hoped the ammo was waterproof.

Even though Lelea seemed to think that this storm nothing to worry about, I was fearful. This wasn't regular warm tropical rain. It was chilling. And the lightning was now flashing all around us. We might be electrocuted!

Wow. "God" sure didn't seem to be blessing this venture...

It was the morning of July 20, 1867.

We'd hiked through the day and spent the night in the jungle, off the beaten trail. Interpreting drums heard in the distance, Lelea told me the mountain tribes knew the expeditionary party was coming. The drums were calling together local chieftains. Either Baker would have a great audience for his fervent Godly appeal or provide a high-status dinner crowd a hearty feast.

We'd fallen far behind. Traveling through the thick jungle was much more difficult than following a well-beaten trail. But I wasn't worried. For some reason I didn't expect any trouble on July 20. Something was nagging at the back of my mind.

Lelea and I were huddled together in a hollow protected by huge, centuries-old trees. Jungle vines covered everything, hiding us from the view of even nearby passing warriors.

The sun had just risen. We were preparing to depart. It was early in the morning, July 21, 1867.

Somehow, that rang a bell in my mind...?

I was getting very uneasy, though I couldn't yet identify the cause.

"Hungry?" I asked, passing her some hardtack.

She grimaced but took some, delicately nibbling at the tough biscuit. It was unappetizing but nourishing, a staple of maritime expeditions.

She, in turn, passed me some fresh fruit. Truthfully, her provisions were much tastier.

"They should have reached the nearest mountain village yesterday," I said, musing. "Something about...something about..."

"What?"

Then it struck me. I *wasn't* trying to recall my world history class. My subconscious mind was struggling to bring up a *news report video* I'd seen on youtube. In 2003 a whole village in Fiji had hosted the descendants of a missionary, begging for forgiveness. It seems that when departing their village on the 21st of July, 1867, their ancestors, two accompanying Chiefs, had suddenly turned on Baker and his party, killing him with a battle axe! In moments, the rest of the village made short work of Baker's Fijian accomplices, except for one that'd fortuitously escaped to carry the tale. In the coming months the coastal tribes banded together to conquer the mountain tribes, forcibly putting an end to the cannibalistic religion and imposing Christianity throughout the Fijian islands.

But Baker and his party was long dead.

Why didn't I remember this before?—I groaned to myself.

Ah, it was just one of those seemingly trivial things jumbled amongst a million other memories—until the events of this morning and the date jerked them to prominence in my mind.

"I know where we have to be!" I exclaimed, jumping up.

"Where?"

"We need to be poised within shooting distance of the road leading out of the first village up ahead toward the next mountain village."

"Why?"

"It's there that the Reverend and his men will be murdered!"

"How do you know this?"

"I...*God* told me! Please believe me, Lelea. How soon can we get there?"

"We will have to leave behind everything except your rifle and ammunition. We can be there in thirty minutes."

"Let's go!" I said. I dropped my backpack, extracting my ammo pouch.

And so we set out, Lelea in the lead. We still avoided the path while scampering across boulders, roots, and thickets. I wouldn't do for posted guards to spot us on the beaten trail and stop us. All around me loomed jungle-shrouded ridges and black volcanic out-croppings. It was a surreal place. By myself I'd be totally lost, floun-dering. But Lelea seemed to know the rocky slopes like the back of her hand, knowing just where to step and jump to continue at a breakneck pace.

At times I lost track of where she was, following her only by the sound of her steps. But then she'd reappear, urging me to hurry. Once I was lost her for ten minutes, afraid I'd fallen hopelessly be-hind. But then she was back, holding my arm to steady me.

So in less than thirty minutes, heaving and gasping for breath, we were poised on top of a leafy outcropping. We had an unobstructed view of the beaten path leading out of a fortified village.

And right there in front of us, walking single-file was the Rever-end with his men. They appeared unharmed. Two Chiefs, identifia-ble by their red sashes, accompanied them, one walking in the front with Baker and one bringing up the rear.

It seemed that the Chiefs were providing an "honor guard" to the Missionaries. But I knew better.

The battle ax held by the front Chief was not for decoration. In mere moments he would almost decapitate Baker. And the club of the trailing Chief would smash into the head of the last in the line of Baker's men. But he would escape because a box of supplies he was carrying blunted the blow. Villagers would rush out and murder all the rest of the men.

And I could *stop* the massacre.

I flopped down, positioning the rifle's barrel on a flat stone, carefully aiming. A round was already in the chamber. I could pick off the front Chief. Then I could reload, get the other Chief, and as the villagers ran out, drive them back as well.

I'm going to change history!

"Lelea, get ready to hand me…"

A lot happened in the space of a few seconds. The rifle was snatched out of my hands by suddenly appeared stocky warriors. I was hit on the side of the head by a war club, causing a huge ringing in my ears. It seemed I was watching a silent movie around me: now helpless to change anything.

Down below I saw the following Chief at the end of the line *slam* his war club into the back of the man in front of him. Hearing the blow, Baker spun around only to be near-decapitated by the leading Chief's war ax.

I didn't see what happened next as I was pulled away by the band of warriors, but I assumed it was just as I'd remembered on the video…just as history had recorded.

I'd failed.

I was dragged in front of the tribal council. They were arrayed in a circle around the central fire pit inside their village's Temple. It was "*déjà vu all over again.*" I couldn't believe it was happening. I was back in a mountain village's Temple captured by cannibals!

I couldn't see clearly. Blood from the wound on my head kept running into my eyes. Strong warriors to each side of me kept my arms locked in brutal grips. The war drums were beating outside. I doubted I'd be able to pull my "concert appropriating" trick a second time.

But I had to try! I kept squirming back and forth, trying to slip free.

"You are wasting what little time you have left."

I blinked rapidly, clearing my vision. I saw *Lelea* standing beside the leading Chief, not as a captive but as an honored member of the group!

I was dumbfounded and helpless. I was surrounded by savages, the dangling soot-covered war-weapons of the temple, and officials. I recognized the "holy" Priests by *snakeskins* wrapped around their upper arms.

Right—Lelea had told me they worshiped a Snake-god. Lovely...

"Lelea," I rasped, unable to believe what I was seeing. "Did you *betray* the Reverend?"

The Chiefs present nodded to her, allowing her to speak to me.

"I respected him. He believed in what he was doing. He had courage. I did not want it to come to this. You saw I did my best to convince him not to come here, to not confront us."

"Yes, that's true...but you also betrayed *me!*"

"I am sorry," she answered dispassionately. "I like you. But my assignment was not to be your servant, Soozee, but a scout. As we ran here I slipped off and told my people where we were headed. They met us at the outcropping, preventing your interference with what had to occur."

"So...you didn't really 'escape' from...?"

"I was sent by my tribe to spy on the English, to learn their tongue and ways. A raiding coalition from another Island unfortunately captured and carried me away. You helped me escape and return to my original assignment. I am grateful. But I saw with my own eyes what happens to Fijians that accept the sweet seduction of the Missionaries. That must be stopped, even if it means white devils die—including you!"

"And...just what is it you saw with the coastal tribes that was so terrible?"

She snorted, turning up her nose as if something stank.

"They are neutered. They lose their drive, their energy. They become meek slaves and servants, *cooks* like you and me! Their land is leveled and turned into cotton plantations. Their music is watered down into 'gospel' accompaniments. As your Bible and Jesus say so well, they become sheep, not wolves. What good is it to live as a sheep if your heritage, your very identity, your *pride* is destroyed?"

"You...speak...excellent English...far better than you pretended."

"I learn fast."

She held her head high. It was obvious she believed every word she uttered. There was, indeed, a *hard glint* in her brown eyes that

I'd not seen before. Well, maybe when she sliced open the throat of that guard as we escaped the seashore.

I sighed deeply, ceasing my struggling. She'd conned me, pretending to be the little innocent escapee. She'd won!

"Will you remember me?"

For a moment her stern expression softened as she fingered the pouch at her waist.

"You are not sheep. You are a true warrior, Soozee. I will be honored to eat your flesh. All of the mountain tribes will remember you as a worthy opponent."

"Oh...that's just dandy...I'll make a tasty snack."

"*Vinaka! Sa tomana nan a vakayacori!*" The Chief beside Lelea pronounced. (Enough! Proceed with the execution!)

"*Sa levu sara na lewe ni manumanu taudaku oti. E rairai ed me wawa kina?*" a priest replied (We have much meat already outside. Perhaps we should wait?")

"*E rui rerevaki me taura tu na kena oqo. E kaya o Lelea e dua na liganiwau qaqa. Vakamatei koya oqo!*" he replied regally, sweeping a muscled arm at me (This one is too dangerous to hold. Lelea says she is a mighty warrior. Kill her now!)

"*Tamaqu, me 'u sa na dokai?*" Lelea interjected, half-bowing to the Chief (Father, may I have the honor?)

He paused, as if considering. Turning, he picked up the new rifle I'd brought, fingering the ammo that now lay loose in a big bowl at his side.

"*O sa cakava vakavinaka, na luvena yalewa. O kauta mai vei keda na nodra iliuliu me ra vakamatei. O kauta mai vei keda na iyaragi talei oqo. Lo, o me vakamatea na marama,*" he nodded, folding his muscled arms together (You have done well, daughter. You brought us their Chief to be slaughtered. You brought us this fine weapon. Yes, you may have the honor of killing the woman.)

"*Qai au cabora noda meca dokai na digidigi ni na e kena ibalebale ni nona mate,*" she pointed at me (Then I offer our honorable enemy the choice of the means of her death.)

Looking me straight in the eye...she *winked*.

I licked my lips, thinking. I'd followed enough of what they'd said. The powerful warriors to each side of me had me trapped. The

Chief was expecting a meal. And the Priests were expecting a sacrifice, yet uncertain how they'd handle this unexpected embarrassment of riches. And even though the Chief granted his daughter authority in this matter, he didn't seem happy about it. Clearly, this was a patriarchal society where women did not give orders but rather did as directed.

"*E dua na ka! E dua na ka! Au sega ni via! Ni o vakayagataka e dua na kalavo se na icoga! E sega ni dua na ka vei au! Me kakua ni yalovinaka...*" I sobbed, seeming to break down (Anything! Anything! I don't care! Use a club or arrow! It doesn't matter to me! Just please don't...)

"*Kakua ni cakava na cava?*" the Chief asked, frowning thoughtfully, apparently impressed by my unexpected command of their language (Don't do what?)

"Don't throw me into the pit of snakes!" I yelled in English. "Lelea told me what you do to your worst enemies. They fall into a writhing mass of poisonous snakes to get bit over and over then die in agony— over hours or days before their meat is finally harvested. Just give me a quick death. Don't make me suffer like that! Please, I beg you— *don't* throw me into the *snake pit!*"

I broke down in sobs, wailing pitifully. Out of the corner of my squinted eyes I saw that the entire council was greatly impressed with my performance, looking at each other in surprise and curiosity.

"*Na cava a kaya na vulavula ni tevoro?*" the Chief asked Lelea (What did the white devil say?)

"*A vakatakekere vua me kakua ni ra viritaki ki na qara ni gata,*" Lelea shrugged (She begs not to be thrown into the snake pit.)

The priests looked at each other knowingly. It would be the greatest vindication of their religion, tossing the "great warrior" to their Snake-god. Also, it would likely keep my body alive for a while so they wouldn't get indigestion eating too many human bodies at once. Likewise, the warriors and gathered Chiefs seemed to like the idea. Instead of a quick death I'd suffer prolonged agony. Plus it would defy the wishes of their enemy, dealing me the ultimate insult.

"*Viritaka koya ena loma ni qara na gata!*" the Chief imperiously ordered, waving a hand at my captors (Throw her in the snake pit!)

"*La, na Tamada! O tukuna au rawa...?*" Lelea tried to protest (But, Father! You said I could...?)

"*Luvei keirau yalewa, o rawa ni o ni na dua mo na biliga koya,*" he barked at her as he turned away and my captors dragged me out of the Temple (Daughter, you can be the one to push her into the pit.)

I let out a blood-curdling *wail*... "Oh, dear God! No! No! Please don't do this! Hit me with a battle axe! Stick knives in me! But don't throw me in a pit with hundreds of *snakes!* Jesus Christ! You can't do this! Have pity! For the love of God, *have pity!*"

They all grinned at each other as they dragged me from the Temple.

I broke down in tears, *screaming* in apparent terror.

Hee, hee—I was really turning the screws. This was one of my best performances, ever...

—until my giddy self-congratulation was instantly chilled as I saw the heap of *dead, mutilated, naked bodies* in the village's central plaza. I now sobbed in real grief. Their genitals were cut off, hanging on a nearby post as trophies. Women nearby were sharpening knives for the butchering, while laying out leaves to wrap the meat within. Ovens were being stoked to their highest temperatures, smoke bellowing up into the sky. And on top of the pile lay the body of Reverend Baker, his sightless eyes staring at me accusingly.

I could have saved them, if only I'd not trusted Lelea so blindly.

Truly, a clash of civilizations could be disastrous—to both sides. Before a new equilibrium can result it seemed there had to be horrendous pain, suffering, and death.

Why were people so evil?

Was this characteristic limited to humans, or did all living creatures share this defect? Even the supposedly benign, loving Missionaries fell prey to their own "hubris"...thinking they knew best for others.

Still musing on the stupidity of us humans, I found myself outside the village proper, marching down a well-beaten trail in the jungle. My hands were tied tightly behind my back. At my side, steering me along with a hand on my arm was Lelea.

Behind us came several of the gathered Chiefs, the main Priest, and a troupe of warriors. The Fijians were happily belting out a war chant as other villagers, following along further behind us, beat on their small portable Lali.

"So how did you *really* know what would happen to Baker and his men?" Lelea demanded as I stumbled along, jerking painfully on my arm.

"I *told* you, *God* revealed it to..."

"Do you think I am stupid?" she snorted. "Your God never did anything in the English settlement except send more Missionaries to enslave my people."

"Well...you wouldn't believe me if I told you."

She pushed aside giant green fronds growing down over the path so we could continue forward.

"Before you sleep with the Snakes, I need to know!"

"Why?"

"My Father is old. When he dies, I plan to replace him. I want to know if this is a wise move. You saw what would happen to Baker. Now I want to know what will happen to me."

I stumbled on forward, every muscle aching.

"From what I've seen, your plan is impossible. In your patriarchal society, women can't be Fijian Chiefs."

"I have learned much from the English and their Bible," she snapped back. "I like seeing women with power. I have many young friends here who will support me. In a few years I *will* take my rightful place as Chief, bringing all the mountain tribes under my rule!"

"*This* is what you want?" I asked, genuinely curious.

"Did I not just say it?"

I hadn't slept much the night before in the jungle. Climbing up the mountains had been a chore. Then racing to try and save Baker had drained me of what little energy I had left. Being clubbed on the head, with blood matting down my newly outgrown hair didn't help my mood. I had no desire to encourage my previous "friend" who'd so brutally betrayed me for her own people.

"Well, you won't have to worry about it," I growled at her.

"What do you mean?"

"*Screw* you and the horse you rode in on," I muttered angrily.

Behind me the chanting and drums were increasing both in pace and volume, reaching a crescendo. The *snake pit* must not be far away. My head throbbed. I just wanted it all to be over.

Lelea grabbed me by my throat, choking me as she *slammed* me against a moss-covered tree trunk.

"Tell me!"

Her dark eyes drilled into my own. She was one fierce young lady. I glared back at her, but then relented, looking to the side—if only to get her to loosen her grip so I could breathe freely again.

"Within...(cough)...six years from now your mountain villages will all be burned to the ground, most of your people killed in battle or hung by the English authorities. The few that survive will be sold as slaves."

She backed off a half-step.

Behind us, the accompanying warriors paused, seemingly impressed by her ferocity toward me. They didn't understand our English words but they certainly recognized and applauded her slapping me around.

"How do you know this? And do not try to tell me again that your 'god' told you. I am right here. I know that no god is speaking!"

She wanted the truth? Ok, then—I'd give her the truth!

"I am not of this time," I spat back at her. "I came here from almost *two hundred years* in the future. In my schoolings I studied the history of the world, including the Fijian islands. The last hold-outs to colonization here were the mountain tribes. You fought well in many battles, against both your own Christian converts, the Europeans, and the Americans. But in the end you lost."

"Lost?"

"Yes...everything! You were all forcibly converted to foreign religions. Your battle axes and clubs were retired to dusty museums. Your land was taken, made into cotton plantations. You adopted European clothes and mannerisms. In the year 2003 your few descendants left at this very place apologized for the murder of Baker and his men, *begging* Baker's descendants for forgiveness. In my time your dances, drums, and chants only serve to amuse drunken tourists at fancy resorts where your people are *still* the servants."

Their future wasn't actually that bad. Eventually Fiji obtained independence and self-rule. But I wasn't going to tell her that.

"It doesn't matter," she growled as she jerked me back on the path, shoving me forward. "I know the foreigners are too numerous and mighty. But we will *still* fight to the end, dying with honor."

"So that's what you *really* want, 'honor'?"

"What else is there?"

It was hardly a time for a philosophical discussion. I was about to be executed. And I still hadn't answered the question myself.

"Well, don't say I didn't warn you," I concluded lamely.

And then we were there. In a cleared glade in front of us I saw a deep hole in the ground. It was at least a dozen feet wide, from lip to lip. Looming trees surrounded it, making it seem we were cut off from the rest of the world. Of all the Fijian "holy places" I'd experienced, this was the most awe-inspiring. And twenty feet down, obscured by shadows, I glimpsed a *squirming mass* of captured snakes.

We paused at the lip, her hand on my back poised to push me in.

The followers behind us all fell silent, expectantly holding their breaths.

"So...why did you allow me to trick them into permitting this?" I asked.

"You know why."

I sighed deeply, frantically scanning below for a fairly clear spot to land.

"You *love* me, you *know* you do!" I taunted her.

The hard hand on my spine seemed to soften, rising to settle warmly on the back of my neck.

"You are...the nicest foreign devil I've met," she reluctantly admitted. "If your God does exist, then perhaps He will intervene with *Degei* to save you. Otherwise, I hope to see you in the next life, Soozee. Goodbye!"

With that she shoved me over the lip.

I seemed to fall for an eternity, though it was probably only a second. Lelea hadn't tossed me in, just gently pushed. So I still had my legs under me rather than tumbling uncontrollably. I instinctively leaned back, bowing my legs to absorb the shock...

—still *slamming* down hard on the packed dirt at the bottom of the twenty foot fall, my already hurting head bouncing off the dirt wall behind me!

My legs felt all bruised up and aching. But I didn't feel any broken bones.

I was stunned but still with enough wits about me to begin instantly *screaming* as loud as I could: "Oh my God! They're *biting* me! Oh, God! It hurts, it hurts—it *hurts!* They're killing me! Oh, God! It hurts so *bad!*"

They were doing nothing of the sort. Down that deep into the ground, the temperature was cool, making the exothermic critters stuck at the bottom of the pit sluggish. Plus, as soon as my eyes began adjusting to the gloom, I saw there were only three types of snakes present: many captured white-and-black banded *sea snakes*, a few small black *bolo snakes*, and a couple large *pacific boas*. Though highly venomous, I knew the sea snakes had such small mouths it was unlikely they could even break my skin if they wanted to bite me, which they didn't. The bolo snakes might be poisonous but their main food was insects and earthworms. They didn't see me as prey. The boas weren't poisonous or large enough to constrict me dangerously. Regardless, all the poor snakes trapped down in that pit were so malnourished and sick I knew they'd only strike at me if I grossly threatened them.

The previous "victims" of the snake-god tossed into the pit probably died of fear-induced heart attacks or from landing on the snakes, causing them to strike in self-defense.

Instead of scaring them, I had managed to steer my path to land in a clear area next to the wall. But—as I continued yelling like I was being eaten alive—I dragged over with my feet a big boa and squirmed underneath its cold coils.

Yes, enemy though she'd proven to be, Lelea had saved me from being immediately executed—knowing I was adept at handling snakes.

Maybe she actually did "love" me.

Above, I could see a few of the Fijians peeking over the lip of the hole, looking down in fascination.

"*Oi, o koya e se bula,*" a deep voice spoke happily (Ah, she is still alive.)

I let out a few additional howls of despair, flopping back and forth but not enough to alarm my sluggish new boa friend who was seemingly constricting me.

"*A sa rarawa sara vakalevu!*" another voice answered excitedly (She is suffering greatly!)

"*Eda na lesu mai ki na moto ni veivakararawataki, ka na laveta cake kina na yagona ena mataka,*" I recognized the Priest's surly voice (We will return to spear and lift out her body in the morning.)

As I heard them stomping away I let loose a few more blood-curdling screams for good measure, then slumped back down in the cool, muddy ground, totally exhausted.

Jesus Christ, this had been a rough couple of days! But I felt relieved I hadn't had to kill anyone. Though I was resolved to defend Baker and his party with that sniper rifle, I didn't relish the thought of blowing the heads off a number of the natives.

After all, they were only doing what they thought best to defend their ancient traditions and territory.

Still, my successful rescue of the missionaries would have been better than my being trapped at the bottom of a pit with hundreds of snakes. A glance upward told me the steep walls of the pit would be difficult to climb. They were slick with rain, sporting few if any handholds or protruding roots. I'd have to carefully plan my assent.

But I had until the next morning before the Fijians returned for my body. Since the sun was just getting to its zenith, that meant I had the rest of the day and most of the night to plan and execute my escape.

At least I had a respite from my brutal exertions. I was exhausted. My tied hands were trembling. I squirmed out of the mud-slicked woven vines. Then I dug in my pocket, pulling out my Taw and its companion marbles. To calm myself I rolled them in one hand.

Then I got a great idea.

"I know," I muttered to myself, as my heavy eyelids began fluttering closed, "I'll carefully pick up and toss out most of these snakes first. Then when those savages come back for me they'll be in for the scare of their life. In the thick grass above me they'll walk right into their own critters, now warmed up and ready to strike. And I'll save the longer boas for living ropes, if needed, tossing their heads up to grab onto something, using their strong bodies to pull me up. And when the natives finally get to the pit and see me gone, they'll think that I supernaturally overcame their trap and not pursue me. Ah— what a great plan!"

It might have even worked. Unfortunately, the next thing I knew voices were arguing above me.

What the hell?

Oh, Christ—I was so exhausted I'd fallen unconscious and slept away the entire previous day and night! It was now early morning and the Priest plus some helpers had already returned to harvest my tortured, dead body.

"*Na dali sa semati ena vakacobari vakavinaka?*" the surly voiced Priest irritably asked up above (The ropes are tied on securely?)

"*Eda sa vakarau tu!*" several voices answered in unison (We are ready!)

Totally helpless I lay prone looking upward as *several heavy spears* came plummeting down straight at me...

—as I instinctively shoved up my hand, still holding my marbles, in futile defense!

Chapter 13

FUGITIVE

Why do they hate me so?
I'm really not that different from them
Taken a few wrong turns, gone a bad way
They'd do the same if they got broke
Smashed up on the shores of fate's blind whims
Driven out to sea on sucking riptides
Wanting more than anything else to remain
But long ago having given up on that hope
I beg them to give me another chance
But that ship has long ago sailed
And all they see are my many sins
Real or imagined, they signal "thumbs-down"
The universal sign for the condemned
Placing upon me their own collective guilt
Yep, I'm their "scapegoat"
Blind, selfish, bastards!
Why do they hate me so?
The Suzette Anthology, Lyrics 13

A *glaring light* blinded me.

"Suzy!" I heard a cry of delight and amazement.

I was hauled out from beneath a burning "sun," hustled away over to the side, and wrapped up in a pair of tightly hugging arms.

My vision was starting to clear.

It was my mother, Sally King, wearing a wrinkled white lab coat. All around me were instruments, giant towering machines, and computer consoles.

"Where did you come from? We thought you were dead! Oh, my God—we've got to hide you."

"Hide...me?" I gasped, pushing smeared mud away from my eyes.

"If they find you here they'll either lynch you or put you in prison. During the experiment they've retreated to the safety of our in-house bunker. I do all the fine tuning out here, exposed. But they'll emerge any second."

"What's...going on?" I hiccupped, disoriented.

"We'll talk later. Here, put on this containment suit. Hurry!"

I managed to slip my muddy jean legs into the freshly unfurled, pristine-white, disposable plastic suit. Then I got my trembling arms into the sleeves, donning the hood with its darkened faceplate.

She zipped me up in the back and sealed my head covering. And then several military types came around the corner of a huge super-conducting conduit.

My guts were bloated from the stress of the last couple days, gas building up in my intestines.

No, no! Not now! I can't fart now! The noise will draw all their attention to me!—I ordered myself to resist.

I struggled to hold the wicked gas inside my lower guts.

"Did it work?" a General sporting two stars curtly demanded.

Sally helped me stand up.

"What happened to you?" a lady-Colonel at his side asked suspiciously. She was frowning at my Mom's now mud-smeared white gown.

"It was some sort of blow-back. There must be something wrong with the flux capacitors, squirting out lubricant. It knocked down my assistant here. I'll figure it out and fix it before..."

"You'd better!" the General barked at her. "You know full well that the Pentagon is demanding results. The President is getting impatient. And the general public is rioting outside the grounds. We've got to have tangible deliverables!"

Boy, he sure knows his business talk—I giddily observed, still disoriented.

"Yes, I know all that," Sally King snapped back at him. "We're working as fast as we can. But trying to go backward in Time is much more difficult than tossing things forward. Do you want us to blow this entire place up, including you?" she pointedly concluded.

Oh, God! I'm going to blow it all out my ass!—I groaned, clutching down tight on my sphincter.

My Mom's words apparently sobered the gray-haired General.

Me, I was just trying to come to grips with not being in a snake-pit about to be skewered by plummeting spears. Instead, I had apparently returned back inside the secret research facility located deep beneath "my" animal rescue shelter. And, yes, there in the middle of the big chamber was the same hovering Sphere...glowing, pulsating, with flares of red fire drifting off its gleaming white surface.

It was *so* impressive!

It actually soothed my cramping guts, seeing again the mysterious remnant of my Dad and Billy's failed research project.

"Alright, but the launch was successful?"

"I think so. At least the rabbit box vanished. The beacon is still sending bursts along the wormhole network. So it's intact, wherever it's now located."

"And that is?"

"For God's sake, General, give me a minute to figure it out. We just launched the test subjects. Plus, we had this unexpected blowback. But at least the box didn't *disintegrate* like it did the three previous attempts at sending subjects into the past. We're making progress!"

His already hard expression became even fiercer.

"Must I remind you it's your own daughter behind this national emergency?" he growled. "If you don't help solve this you'll suffer her fate as well: vilified and labelled as *public enemy number one!* If you want to remain head of this Project you damn well better give us something better than just 'making progress.'"

"That's how science works!"

"You're not the only scientist available," he sneered at my Mom. "You're a dime-a-dozen, Doctor. Don't forget that!"

"I'm the *only* one who understands the fundamentals of what's happening here! Are *you* forgetting it was *me* that derived the formulas allowing us to control the wormhole? Try and replace me and you'll put yourself a year behind the present schedule."

"I'm not convinced that's true, Doctor. Perhaps we should 'test' your theory?"

The lady Colonel stepped between the two of them. "Please, let's concentrate on the present test. If we can't defeat *Phoenix* in the present then we must cut them off in the past before they ever gain traction. If the rabbits made it into the past then we've made a giant leap toward that objective. If we can find out where they landed, our troops can search for their present corpses, bones, or whatever remains of them. Let Doctor King proceed with her work, General. And you, Ma'am, we need your report within the hour."

Wow. She sure had a lot of authority to be giving orders far above her rank. But then I saw a "U.N." insignia and realized she was representing the world community, not just the United States. What had happened in my absence?

They abruptly turned away, my Mom breathing out a sigh of relief.

And I finally allowed the gas to dribble out my rear end and *fill up* my suit...oh God, it was disgusting!

I could see my Mom was shaking with barely repressed fury. I was impressed. She seemed ready to rip those soldiers to pieces.

"Let's get you into the examination room," she grated through clenched teeth, supporting my arm as I tried to shuffle a few steps but almost fell down.

She bodily carried me away.

And then we were hidden away within the sealed containment chamber.

"Where have you been?" Sally gushed, hugging me again. "We're not going to have a lot of time before they discover you've returned. We've got to come up with a plan."

Hah...that was funny, a "plan." Whatever it was, I hoped it would work better than my previous plan I'd failed to even start some two hundred years in the past a few seconds ago...

Wow—that thought was *so* confusing.

I fumbled at the self-sealing tape holding my hood on, finally getting the two layers to fall apart.

I yanked the hood off and let it fall to the floor. I was sitting in a chair beside an examination table. I noticed that the transparent wall had gone opaque. My Mom was trying to conceal me for as long as possible.

But...why? What had I done so terrible I'd apparently been labelled as "public enemy #1"?

"Oh, dear—you stink, Suzy! Is your IBS acting up again?"

I gave her a withering stare: "No!" I lied. "I've been out running in a jungle for a couple of days."

"What?"

I took a deep breath and in a gush gave her the "take-home" message: "I was somehow transported from that grave in the Cemetery to the Fijian islands in 1867. A couple of times I almost got eaten by cannibals. I was in a snake pit about to be hit by spears when I found myself back here," I succinctly summarized. "Do you think this...has something to do with...the *T-rex* that materialized beside us on your kiddy ride?"

She peered intently into my face, studying me. In turn, I studied her.

To me, she seemed markedly older. Yes, her hair was still dyed reddish brown but the roots that had been gray were now white. Her normally twinkling green eyes were subtly clouded, almost like she was getting cataracts. And she looked very, very tired—as if she'd been working nonstop for months.

"Suzy, your hair—it's regrown! And your burn scars, they've healed!" she marveled. "And yes, the dinosaur was caught up in what I call a random 'loop' from the Sphere. Somehow it 'imprinted' on us, you more than me. Just how long were you gone?"

"A loop?"

"Here, a year has passed since you disappeared, Suzy," she rushed on. "I've learned a lot during that time. Your Dad cracked open subspace, which allowed the Sphere to emerge. I believe it's a node of subspace that reaches not just to one wormhole exit as I originally thought, but into a *network* that has many possible exits. With the proper electromagnetic stimulation the Sphere can be induced to carry a passenger to almost any place or time. I'm just now beginning to understand where and how, though it's still very uncertain as to..."

"Ok, I get it, Mom. It likes me—maybe because of my Turtle Tattoo. It makes sense that it's somehow *imprinted* on me. It can toss me through time. I'm duly impressed."

"And you need a good bath."

"Do you think? You've got a mother's probing eyes, and nose..." I grinned at her, pausing in appreciation, "—to see under all this mud. I *desperately* need a shower and a meal, fast! Then you'll see that I'm actually back to full health. I don't even need a cane anymore. And to answer your question, I was there for over six months. During that time a 'friend' gave me a secret, native herbal treatment. It had a dramatic, rejuvenating effect."

I started to unzip myself from the containment suit to show off my new muscular body.

"We'll get you cleaned up as soon as possible, sweetie. For now we've just got to figure a way to get you out of here undetected. Maybe you should stay inside that suit for the moment."

"Ok," I sighed, feeling incredibly sticky and filthy locked inside the clinging plastic garment. "I—you say it's been a *whole year* since I got thrown back to the Fijian islands?" I gasped in unbelief. "What about Agent Anderson, did he survive the attack? He was nice to me and did his best to defend me but..."

"Yes, he's alive and well," she said, grabbing some bottled water and handing it to me from a small in-containment frig. I guzzled it greedily as she continued: "He was severely wounded and in the hospital for several months in a coma. But he's back to work. In fact, he's outside right now. He's in charge of security."

"I need to see him," I stated, setting the emptied plastic bottle to the side.

"If we can," she agreed. "But he's got his hands full trying to hold off the demonstrators and activists. It's getting to be a war zone around here. I haven't dared travel to our house for two months. I'd be lynched if I tried to leave the compound. So far the general public doesn't think I conspired with you, but being your mother is damning enough to them."

I closed my eyes tightly, trying to calm down, to figure out what was going on before totally freaking out.

"Please...start at the first, Mom. Tell me *what the hell* happened in my absence."

"It's actually a long, complicated story that..."

"Give me the 'cliff-note' version!" I snapped at her. "I could tell you a *lot* more about what happened to me in Fiji. But I summarized that all up in one crisp paragraph."

"Yes...yes...you're right," she nodded, now pacing back and forth in front of me. In the distance I heard muffled "booms" going off. What was so powerful up on the surface that I could still hear it buried deep down underground?

"Please start with that attack on the road that drove us into the Cemetery," I requested.

"Right...that was the first direct attack from *Phoenix*. It was timed to complement their world-wide simultaneous Concert bombings."

"I heard that on the car radio as it happened," I nodded. "But the commentators didn't know who was behind the attacks."

"Phoenix immediately claimed credit for the attacks," she explained. "They're a loose association of the worst 'fundamentalist' groups across the world, attracting extreme members from all religions and ideologies. They claim that *music* is the prime corrupting influence of all societies throughout history. They say they're shutting down music, for everyone, everywhere."

I was stunned.

"A world without music...is that even possible? But where do I fit in? And if what you say is correct, then *I* was their first victim at the Hollywood Bowl."

"They claim you were secretly working with them and set the bombs off yourself."

"What? That's ridiculous!"

"Of course it is, Suzy, but they claim since you were intimately familiar with your own tour mechanisms you could easily place very potent plastic explosives and small detonation devices—then set them off while you were in the relatively 'safe' location of flying above the crowd outside the main blast radius."

"I blew myself up?"

"I know, I know. It's ridiculous. But they say you observed firsthand the 'terrible corrupting influence' of your and others' music on society and—deriving from your own 'fundamentalist' religious background—you were convinced that nothing less than a violent revolt would purge the so-called awful effects of music from the world."

"But then I was seemingly killed in the Cemetery attack...?"

"Your body wasn't found. Phoenix claimed that their armed forces managed to 'rescue' you from the clutches of the American F.B.I. agents. You supposedly then you went on to head up the continued attacks."

"*Continued* attacks?"

"All music-sharing online sites have been devastated by extremely sophisticated self-evolving viruses and other means," she explained. "Churches where music is a central part of their worship have been bombed, both by real explosives and cyberattack. In the last year, many organizations have learned that if they go about their business without using any form of music they're left alone. Stores no longer play mood music. Elevator music is a thing of the past. Recording companies have shut down. The only music you hear now is inside private homes. And even that's become 'iffy.' When word gets out of music-'orgies' in particular homes, the adults find their bank accounts emptied out, the kids no longer enrolled at their schools, and their credit cards declined."

"That's all impossible, Mom. The malware and anti-viral companies would..."

"They're stymied," she shrugged. "The attacks by Phoenix are bafflingly complex. There's no defense—except to comply."

"So...just don't play music and everything is fine?"

"You'd think so, Suzy, but their plan is deeper and more insidious."

"Like what?"

"One by one they're taking over the governments of the world, using their incredibly powerful cyber-war techniques. They can hold the entire electrical grids, transportation systems, and militaries hostage: hijacking all their critical computer systems. Apparently they mean to establish a world-wide theocracy, imposing strict ethical and behavioral standards upon everyone. Their genius is in not insisting on one single 'God-given' set of rules, but letting the rules vary from region to region according to whatever faction is in control. The more technologically advanced secular governments are fighting tooth-and-nail, doing everything they can to resist the attacks, but smaller and less sophisticated nations are falling to Phoenix, one-by-one."

"Jesus Christ! That's beyond awful. But how could anyone believe *I'm* behind it? All this time I've been back in 1867 on an island being chased by cannibals."

"Look..." she said, switching on a monitor.

There *I* was on the computer screen, calming explaining the demands of Phoenix. *Shut down all forms of music and things will be fine. There will be no further attacks. Life can go on as usual. People can get back to their normal lives. Resist...and your life will be destroyed. Even ignoring the use of music by others will implicate you. So turn in your neighbor if you hear them playing a musical recording late at night.*

"That's monstrous!"

"Yes, I knew it wasn't you. The continuing videos of you supposedly on their Central Council helping direct Phoenix are total fakes. But for people without a Mother's knowledge of you, it makes sense. Since most people like their music and not being told what to do, you've become the most hated person on the planet."

"So that's why you can't leave the compound."

She nodded. "I'm guilty by association. But so far I'm not directly implicated. There are a lot of people who pity me, agreeing that the 'sins of the children aren't caused by the parents.' But just about everyone has accepted the supposed 'fact' that *you're* the cause of all their misery. For the remaining intact secular governments, you're public enemy #1."

It was beyond incredible. I was stunned.

"Oh, Jesus...but why are people attacking the animal shelter? Wouldn't even biased, ignorant conspiracy buffs realize that innocent animals shouldn't be blamed for the person who bankrolled their care?"

"That's not who is besieging us. Animal lovers had no thought of attacking the shelter just because your name was on it."

"Huh? Then who...?"

"It's Phoenix. They leaked the information that our hidden research facility exists. They've roiled up the crowds against us. It seems they somehow found out we're experimenting with the means to go back in Time and stop them before they started. Since they've proven their invulnerability to our best intelligence and offensive institutions, they've arrogantly bragged of their initial founding and formation. According to them it all began at *Woodstock*."

"Woodstock? Do you mean the folk-rock festival at the end of the 1960's?"

"Yes, exactly," she said, bringing up news accounts of that event. I saw huge crowds sitting in front of a roughly constructed stage, upon which rock groups were performing. "It was a time of epic unrest. The young people of the U.S.A. were being sent off to a mindless, violent war in Vietnam. The world was rocked by social unrest: feminism, civil rights, the sexual revolution, and rapid technological changes. Nuclear annihilation loomed above everyone's head, part of the cold war between communism and capitalism. Society was ripe for subversion. It's there that the seeds for the present radical extremist religious revolution began."

"I still can't believe it, Mom. That was the 'hippy' generation who was 100% opposed to controlling other people or dictating how others should behave! If I remember my music history—which I've studied in depth—their theme was *freedom* in love, sex, and drug usage...not more rules and regulations!"

"True, but somehow Phoenix originated there."

"Even so...how could we change Time? Isn't history fixed? Have you even succeeded in sending living animals back in time? What about those first two rabbits that died when you just tried to send them *forward* in time?"

She nodded, settling wearily into a chair in front of mine.

"We discovered the cause, Suzy. The Sphere was disturbing the quantum resonance of the subatomic particles in the animals' molecules. Once I adjusted for that, transmittals into the future worked fine."

"And into the past?"

"Like you heard, tonight was our first successful launch. Going back in Time is going against the natural flow. I had to build into the 'cocoon' a protective counter-ripple that..."

"Too much detail, Mom. So you think that you can deliberately send live animals into the distant past? What about humans?"

"We don't know yet. It's much too early to consider such. I first have to check out and perfect a number of..."

"Wait, *I* did it! I made it to the past and back again to the present. I'm proof it can be done!"

"Yes...that's true. But we don't know *how* it worked with you. If I attempt to force the Sphere to do such, it could be a disaster. And if we reveal that you succeeded, you'd at best be imprisoned, at worst torn apart by the angry mobs."

"Then send me back, now!"

"What?"

"Send me back to Woodstock! I'll find the conspiracy and root it out, preventing any of this from happening."

Sure, it was a great idea. But I conveniently didn't find time to tell her that I'd failed to stop the murder of Baker and his party. I'd already tried to change the future and failed. I hoped that wasn't a set rule of time travel.

"I have an idea how to fine-tune an exit point in the past, Suzy, but only the outlines of a potential procedure. I wouldn't trust myself to make such a precise insertion or..."

"I'm willing to take the risk, Mom."

"But as you yourself said, we've no proof that History can even be changed, Suzy. It's much too risky. We just have to..."

A huge "boom" rocked the room around us.

"What was that?" I gasped, falling from my chair as *large rocky hunks* fell from the high ceiling of the cavern, crashing down around us!

A burly, short gray-haired man burst through the isolation door, panting heavily. I recognized his dark eyeglasses and suit. It was Agent Anderson.

"Doctor King, Phoenix is bombing us! They've taken over a U.S. Air Force base, capturing bunker-buster bombs. I've got to get you away from...*Suzy?*"

I waved at him: "Hi Agent Anderson. Thanks for saving me at the Cemetery. The Sphere rescued me, snatching me away and..."

"No time! I've got to get both of you out of here. The entire facility is about to be reduced to rubble!"

Another huge BLAST sounded above us, rocking the flooring beneath us.

Outside of the now ripped-open containment room I could see violent *arching electrical discharges* as coils were damaged.

"No! You've got to send me back in time to Woodstock, Mom. I'll change history! I'll somehow stop Phoenix from being birthed. You've got to send me back to 1969, right now!"

"That's impossible. We can't risk..."

"I've already proven that I can survive the trip. Before we lose power down here, you've *got* to do it! Look, if we can't stop Phoenix then what's the point of trying to rescue Billy and Dad? If the Sphere is destroyed by the bombing runs then we've got *no* chance of reaching backward in Time to grab them!"

Anderson nodded: "Doctor King, the girl makes sense. It may be a desperate toss of the dice, but it's our only play. I've got faith in both her and you. She *will* make it back to Woodstock. But you've got to do it quickly. Can you get the Sphere to cooperate before we're buried down here forever? I for one don't want to live in a world where our lives are dictated by narrow-minded fools, a world without music. Suzy *has* to go back to Woodstock!"

"Then it's settled," I said, puzzled about Anderson's unexpected strong support of the idea but not having the time to question him further. I peeled off the constricting plastic suit from my filth-encrusted body. "Mom, set the Sphere to send me back."

Sally King nodded, tears in her eyes.

And minutes later, as a *roiling electrical charge* built up around the Sphere, I lay scrunched-up in a small container beneath it, praying...

"Dear Lord," I whispered, closing my eyes tightly. "Please help me see the Truth—whatever it is and wherever it may take me. And help me survive being stuffed into this damned-tight rabbit hutch!"

And as the ceiling of the cavern crumbled downward, I was yet again tossed back into Time.

Chapter 14

Woodstock

__Peace and Love__ not just for now but forever
Sounds like a beautiful world for us humans
Maybe it's not possible when we're hurting
But wouldn't erecting its framework be fun?

That old vision of the Garden of Eden
Where the lion lies down with the lamb
And all God's critters dance together
Joining paws and minds in innocent harmony

Renouncing war and crime and atrocities
Swearing off pain and suffering and dying
Embracing the most beautiful, fulfilling music
Carrying our spirits up high into the clean blue sky

Way up there above the mud, grime, and icy storms
No more sickness, sorrow, suffering, or pain
Effortlessly taking on whatever psychedelic form
This "heaven on earth" rejecting the legacy of hate

But then trapped again in the clinging webs
We say "goodbye" to our teenage fantasies
Clothed yet again in a fabric of constricting threads
Gray heads swamped with duties and responsibilities
We cherish the delicious taste of yesterday...

The Suzette Anthology, Lyrics 14

I jerked my body out of the tight container and knocked over an *acoustical guitar*.

"Hey, watch it!"

"Oh...I'm sorry...I didn't...?"

"Hey, no worries, little missy—it's a mess anyway you cut it, right? But you gonna take a nap, you should go to one of the tents, not crawl into an amp cover. It's too crowded out here."

"I...sure...right..."

I looked up to see giant rigs. It was nighttime but the platform I was on was well lit. I was off to one side, almost buried amongst stacked electronic components. I instantly recognized my amazing new situation. High metal-frame towers supporting giant speakers and lights loomed in the night. Directly above me dangled a couple giant tarps that protected the stage with its scattered collection of musical instruments. Glaring strobe lights shone down on me from above. This was a Concert Stage.

And out in the darkness I sensed a *huge crowd* beyond the edge of the Stage, stirring like a hungry beast eager for its next meal. I heard rain thudding down on the canvas above.

"Ravi's on next, girl," the man declared. "You best get off the set. What you been doin', wallowing around in the mud?" he grinned at me playfully.

I looked down at my mud-saturated jeans and shirt. After two days fighting my way through a jungle then sleeping in a deep pit I definitely didn't smell very good. I had to find a way to get a shower and a change of clothes to...

Then I stopped obsessing on my clothes and squinted at the man. He looked familiar.

"Do I know you?"

"I dunno...I'm Arlo!" he replied cheerfully.

He was a handsome young man with a full head of curly brown hair. He had a mildly cleft chin, turned up nose, and soulful eyes. In the fingers of one hand he held a half-smoked joint. I was breathing in second-hand sweet smoke.

"Arlo?"

"Arlo Guthrie," he happily stated, reaching out and shaking my hand. "I gotta go help out Joan. She's just setting up for later. The latest performance list for tonight is Ravi, then Melanie, then me, then Joan. The bosses keep changing the set order, but I think they've got it down now. Lots of the performers just can't get here by land. You were lucky to make it through. The rest are going to miss the festival or have to come in by helicopter. Man, this thing is out of control! There was supposed to only be 50,000, total. I hear it's already twice that number, with more arriving every hour."

"Joan?"

"Yep, she don't move around so well now that she's six months pregnant. Hey, I didn't do it!" he laughed as he turned away. "It was her husband David, not that I wouldn't have liked to knock her up myself. But please don't kick over my guitar again, eh? I've got backups, but it's my favorite."

Arlo Guthrie...Joan—*Baez?* Jesus Christ, did it work? Did I actually make it to *Woodstock?*

Arlo was the son of the famous folk singer Woody Guthrie. Arlo was a premier young folk singer in his own right in a mighty tradition. Joan Baez was his young female contemporary, beloved for her exquisite voice and lyrics.

Yes, the opening night of Woodstock had been devoted to the still-vibrant folk singing traditions of the 1960's hippy generation. My Mom had set me down smack-dab on the "X"!

And, yes, the festival was definitely already "out of control." I remembered that the audience ended up around 400,000 people. The largest crowd I'd ever performed for in one place was around 30,000. Woodstock was gigantic, the seminal event of the 1960's "hippy" generation.

But was this all really true or was it just a vivid hallucination while the research cavern collapsed down upon me? I had to confirm I'd actually made this incredible jump...

"Wait just a second!" I called after Arlo.

He paused, turning around.

"What's today's date?"

He laughed like I'd said something funny. "You been smokin' something a lot stronger than what I'm havin'? Anyway, girl, it's Friday night, August 15."

"The year?"

"Wow, you're really gone, baby. It's 1969. What other year should it be?"

So it was true. I was stunned to realize the Sphere had thrown me nearly a *hundred years* into the past.

"Ok then..." I gulped. "Thanks."

"No problem. You one of the backup singers?"

"Uhm....right, that's exactly right. I'm a backup singer."

"With whom?"

"Uhhh..." I paused, my mind racing to remember the lineup at Woodstock and where my claimed identity might fit in... "Jefferson Airplane!"

"Oh, cool—I totally see it."

"You do?"

"Sure! You're a spitting body-double for Grace Slick—the same height, similar face, and sexy figure. You sing as good as her?"

"Better," I glibly grinned at him through the mud still streaking my face. "I mean...when she's sick, that is. She's got a sore throat and might not be able to sing, so I'm here to..."

"Ok, then—see you around."

A great roar went up from the unseen audience as I saw *Ravi Shankar* and his group walk into the middle of the big stage.

A lot of people hustled around me onstage, moving in and out of the lighted areas. I was sitting cross legged on the bare floor next to one of the big stage speakers that began blaring out an ear-numbing drum sequence. Actually, it was from just two small drums played with naked palms. It hit me there the incredible importance of *electronic amplification*, which I'd taken for granted all my life.

The *beats* that once rocked only small villages could now rock entire cities.

So that which otherwise would have been a pleasingly soft small-venue performance was now being *blasted* out as *soul-stirring* vibration to over a hundred thousand people!

And then Ravi joined in with the distinctive, mind-altering complex rhythms, tones, and harmonies of the *Indian Sitar*: a hollow seven-string guitar-like instrument with sympathetic additional strings.

It was hauntingly mesmerizing...

I'd made it! I was without a doubt back in 1969 at the start of the Woodstock festival. Now I could try to find out where the Phoenix conspiracy began and foil it. But in this gigantic crowd, how would I even start to proceed? My task seemed all but impossible to...

PING!

I was abruptly snapped out of my reverie by the sound of something striking hard next to me. Jerking to the side I realized that Arlo's guitar was again off its stand and lying on the wood flooring beside me. It had a neat round hole through its front side. The back side, though, was almost completely blown out.

"Oh, wow," I gasped, startled, "Arlo's going to be really pissed..."

THWAPPP!

Wood splinters from the speaker beside me showered my face as I realized someone was *shooting* at me!

Oh hell...it appeared I didn't have to worry about finding the conspirators. They'd already found me!

I ducked behind the still-working speaker, peeking up into the glaring lights, shadows, and dark girders above and around me. Where was the sniper?

FWIP! FWIP! FWIP!

Three more bullets in quick succession burst through the back of the speaker right above my head, showering me with wood chips.

I dashed away from the stage lights and into the shadows at the back of the stage. There I saw a burly man in a yellow-orange jacket with "security" written in big red letters. He had a closed-over holster on his waist that might or might not have a gun in it.

"Someone's shooting at me!" I said, panting hard.

He looked at me suspiciously. Stinking and covered with mud I probably didn't inspire a lot of confidence. "You say you saw someone firing a weapon?"

"Yes! With a silencer or from a long distance! It hit Arlo Guthrie's guitar and a speaker right over there," I pointed...

But his guitar was gone. Had someone picked it up?

The speaker was still blaring out its rocking drums beats, apparently functionally undamaged.

And as far as I knew, there'd been no further shots.

He peered upward at the surrounding high towers. But there weren't any obvious rifle-pointing snipers lurking in the dimly seen steel frameworks.

"And just who are you, Miss? You don't have a Stage Badge. If you're an audience member, I'm afraid you can't be back here and..."

He thought I was a backstage-crasher, maybe even a hallucinating acid-head to boot.

"No! No!" I implored him, now afraid I'd be ejected from the stage area. I knew that I needed access to the performers. I'd just have to try the same story on him that worked with Arlo: "I'm a back-up singer for Jefferson Airplane. I just got here by road. It's way tough out there, dig me? Anyway, our bus broke down and we had to change a tire in the mud...man, what a bummer! But we just got in and..."

"Alright, alright," he cut me off. "Just let me see your Performer Pass. Then we'll get to this gunshot business."

"Well..."

He was a very big man, with the darkly tanned skin of a steel-worker. He was probably six-foot-five, weighing in at over 300 pounds, physically able to toss me over the front wood fence protecting the stage if he wished.

All around us the surreal alien music of Ravi made it seem I was in a bizarre musical, playing the part of a lost waif trying to get help from an uncaring policeman.

"Oh, right, 'Performer Pass'!" I grinned, hopefully disarmingly. "That! Well, we were in this big group and I just followed the others and things were confused and then they said I had to be on stage and..."

"So you never picked up your Performer Pass?" he skeptically asked.

"...uh, that's it! I thought someone put a Badge around my neck and we moved on and...but with all the mud...no time to clean up and get changed...so..."

"Ok, then let's go get it."

"Oh...sure," I hesitantly agreed. "That'd be great. If you could just point me where to go and..."

"I'll take you there," he politely but firmly informed me, grabbing me by my arm.

"Oh...that's not necessary."

"I insist."

"Uh, sure...thanks," I gulped.

Trapped, I walked beside him down a long wooden ramp to a crowded group of tents and trailers. Stopping at a busy tent, we went inside.

"She says she's a backup singer with Airplane," he informed a cheerfully smiling middle-aged lady sporting bright red framed plastic glasses. She wore the distinctive Woodstock T-shirt that had been issued to the stagehands and other crew members. I recognized the iconic white dove sitting on a guitar neck highlighted against a red background. "She needs her Pass."

"That's cool," the lady brightly responded, bringing out a long sheet of papers. "Could I have some identification, please?"

I gulped, starting to shake. The suspicious guard hadn't let loose of me. There was no way I could run away from him. I wondered if the nice lady would take a driver's license from nearly *a hundred years* in the future.

"Alright, then..." I sighed, fumbling into my back jeans pocket. I pulled out my slim pocket wallet. Fortunately it was one of those zippered, lady-friendly types. It'd already gotten drenched in the South Pacific, baked on a boat on the ocean, immersed in a mud pit, and blasted through a time tunnel. But, amazingly, my wallet was still there and sealed tight.

I unzipped it, opened it, and fiddled around with the cards...

"Here you go."

I handed her my *Oklahoma Driver's License* on which I'd "accidently" smeared some mud that covered up my birthday and expiration dates.

She glanced from it to me then back to the license.

"This is amazing. How do they get that watermark to look like it's three dimensional?"

"Ah...new technology...Oklahoma's on the cutting edge of everything digital and..."

"Digital?"

"Uh, I mean *driver's*...license...stuff," I concluded weakly.

"Ok, then," she said, handing it back to me. "Suzette King-ly...Suzette Kingly," she repeated, scanning her lists.

I prepared to try and jerk away from my captor and bolt for the exit.

"Ah, here you are. Yes, you're listed with the Jefferson Airplane party. Just fill in your name and group at the lines indicated on your Performer Pass. Here's a pen..."

Stunned, I silently accepted the pen and card. It was black-and-white, with the dove/guitar-neck silhouette in a corner plus big letters boldly stating: "An Aquarian Exposition, Performer Pass."

I wrote in my name (Suzy) and group (AIRPLANE).

"That's it," she cheerfully smiled. "Here's your badge holder if you want to put it around your neck. Be sure and not lose it if you go out into the audience. Without it you won't be able to reenter the stage area. Next?"

I moved to the side as a group jostled up behind me.

"Sorry about being rough," the burly Guard apologized, removing his big hand from my arm. "With this many people we can't be too careful and..."

"No problem, no problem," I muttered, clutching my prize and retreating in a daze.

How the hell is my name on the performer list with the group I just pulled out of the air only a few minutes before?

Whatever, someone was trying to kill me and simultaneously put me on stage at Woodstock! Ah, right—they were making sure I was an easy target.

"So about that supposed weapon's firing..." the guard began.

"You know, now that I think about it—maybe it was just the sharp drum sounds," I grinned at him. I needed to escape into the crowds. I couldn't afford to get caught up in some official inquiry. "Thanks for your help!"

I beat a hasty retreat as he frowned down at me, his arms folded suspiciously.

"Oh, please to be excusing me!" I heard a cheerful voice.

I'd bumped right into someone.

"No, no, it's my fault," I hastened to apologize, trying to not make a fuss, just move on past. "I wasn't looking where I was going and..."

I stopped, mesmerized. In front of me at arm's length was a dark-skinned Indian-looking gentleman in a pink robe. He had long gray-brown hair falling past his shoulders, a huge bushy gray-white full beard and mustache, a gleaming smile, and warm brown eyes.

If I didn't know better, I'd think he was an aged, Indian Jesus.

Wait, I remembered who this was...

"No, it is entirely my fault, child. I should have been looking through your eyes as well as mine. As I've often proclaimed: '*If we only look within, we will see the Light as if we were seeing our own image in a mirror.*' But then we bang into our innocent neighbors. I am so sorry."

"Uh...ok...very n-nice to meet you, S-Sir," I stammered, not having the foggiest idea what he was talking about.

I escaped into the crowd of frantically working stagehands.

Wandering out into a fenced-off green grass area beside the mammoth stage, I welcomed the rain splattering down from the night sky. If I remembered properly, this was the helicopter landing zone. It was the last area where the previously thick grass remained, now thoroughly trampled down and destroyed elsewhere. In the dark I doubted the shooter would see me amongst the many others milling about or running to do their various jobs. The first thing I had to do was find some food. I was starving! The last thing I'd eaten was some hardtack back on the Fijian island of *Viti Levu*.

I saw a carefully guarded gate that exited into the milling crowd outside.

Showing my badge with my Performer Pass to the guards I slunk through, immersing myself in a chaotic mass of cold, wet, and miserable humanity.

I now didn't want to stay with the Performers and stagehands any longer than necessary. Whoever had given me my secret identity likely didn't magically insert my memory into any of those people. It'd be too easy for me to slip up and be discovered as a fake.

Out in the audience I'd be just one more person amongst many thousands. In fact, I wouldn't even need a ticket to the concert. Since the preparation for the event had proved much more difficult than expected, flimsy fences went down quickly. Many thousands of people without tickets poured in and the organizers acknowledged the reality, declaring it a "free" concert.

It was a confused and miserable start to an iconic, magnificent gathering of "old" and "new" musical talent. Both performers and audience alike were bombarded by icy cold rain and wind. They huddled miserably beneath makeshift tents, tarps, and plastic bags.

As I wound my way up the hill of the natural bowl in which the concert was set, careful not to slip and fall, I marveled at the mix of humanity thrown together in the mud, trash, and rumbling thunder. The slowly transiting searchlights from the towers revealed *little babies snuggling* in mommy's arms feeding on hot tits of naked breasts; *joyfully jumping up-and-down* slender young men naked to their waists reveling in the combined blast of nature and amplified music; people of *all racial types* and skin colors; *little kids* darting in and out of the crowd, having the time of their lives; *kissing couples* writhing in passionate embrace beneath wet blankets; old white-haired men and similarly wrinkled women with *fists raised in the air*, swaying with the youngsters to the seductive timeless rhythms of Ravi's convoluted Sitar melodies; and *countless joints* lit and flaring in the night like psychedelic fireflies.

Now hallway up the long slope I paused and turned back.

I let the pounding rain pour down on me, standing straight, my elbows out with hands placed on my hips. My hair was plastered down on my head, my flannel shirt slicked down over my pert breasts, and my jeans hanging loose over my slender hips.

At least the mud in my hair, on my face and clothes, was being blasted away by the downpour.

I almost felt like cutting loose from all constraints, slipping out of my clothes, and running naked through the crowd. I could become one with nature, humanity, and the transcendental music!

Almost, but not quite...hah! My "civilized" constraints held me back from making a flaming fool of myself.

But I was amused to see it didn't stop others, who were doing just as I'd fantasized. The flitting naked bodies were uniformly young people—from little kids to people in their twenties—reveling in their newfound freedom to do whatever they wanted whenever they felt like it.

"It's both amazing and horrifying," I whispered to myself.

I widened my view and saw a huge mass of humanity huddled under plastic bags, blankets, small tarps, and an occasional umbrella.

"And it's so primitive," I mused, truly shocked. But I wasn't commenting on the crowd, but the venue.

The stage was just a raw wood platform. The "protection" for the performers was just a loosely tied giant tarp fluttering above. The speaker towers were jury-rigged steel frameworks hastily bolted together. How the people onstage weren't being all electrocuted during the lightning storm was unfathomable.

It certainly wasn't the type of concert I was used to hosting. Where were the Jumbotrons to each side showing close ups of the performers and details of the instrumentation? Where was the holographic projection onto artificial mists, surrounding people in drifting images? Where were all the giant special-effect builds? Where were the elaborately choreographed dance numbers? Nowhere! From this distance you could barely see the tiny performers down on the stage.

Yes, this whole event was back at the very start of huge, amplified rock festivals. But what it lacked in slick effects it gained in substance: *pure, unadulterated, POUDING music!*

My ears were bombarded with an incredible array of brilliant, intricately interwoven *noise*.

Woodstock would fly or fall upon the quality of the performers. And since the organizers had assembled some of the contemporary best in the world—though at the festival, at that moment, it all looked like an abysmal failure—it would still become the defining event of a whole generation.

I saw how this could inspire not only rabid participation by fans, but *shocked horror* from aggrieved conservatives.

"Groovy, huh?" a deep voice resonated richly behind me.

I turned and saw a tall man standing beside me. He was over six feet tall, forcing me to look up at him. In the shifting searchlights I couldn't make out his exact features, but I saw long brown hair held back with a white bandana across his forehead. Though it was nighttime, he had on prominent dark glasses. A handlebar mustache ran over and beside his full lips. Slung by a strap over his wide shoulders he carried a field bag. He had on an old military shirt, opened at the chest to reveal curly dark hair. A denim jacket was tied around his waist. The insignia on his arm was that of an army staff-sergeant. The name above his shirt pocket said: "Hartley."

"Well, Sergeant Hartley, I guess it depends on how you define 'groovy.'"

He laughed, holding out a big hand.

"I'm Cleve. My friends call me Cleve."

I laughed in return, accepting his firm handshake. He looked very familiar. I couldn't place it, but I had a feeling I'd seen him before. Of course that made little sense as I was a hundred-some years in the past...?

Ah well, I was here to blend in until I discovered Phoenix's roots. Best to try to look and act as normal as possible...

"I'm Suzy. My friends call me Suzy."

"Hi, Suzy."

"Hi, Cleve. Say, you've got a great base voice. Are you a fellow performer?"

"Sadly, no. I can't carry a tune in a bucket. But hey, I saw you come out of the stage entrance," he explained. "I hope you're not turned off by this, but I followed you here. Are you a performer? You certainly are photogenic."

Ah, maybe I'd spied him backstage, or knew him from videos I'd studied on the history of the Festival. Woodstock had always fascinated me. But there were so many people milling about and working here I couldn't remember exactly.

"Well, I'm a backup singer for..."

"Cool. Do you have a minute to talk?" he continued.

Wow. That was a lame "come-on" for sure. But, then again, maybe I was due for a bit of romance. After all, this was free-love-preaching *Woodstock*.

I grit my teeth, forcing my mind to focus. I could not afford to be distracted by a dreamy hunk. I was there on a mission: to *change History*, not get entangled in juvenile fantasies.

It was likely my Mother was killed in the collapse of the research cavern under that final bombardment from Phoenix. I had to save her by preventing that attack from happening, stopping that evil organization from ever starting! My short time at Woodstock was *deadly serious*.

"Maybe you should tell me who you are, before I answer."

"Ah, of course," he smiled, pressing closer to me. He undid the denim jacket wrapped around his waist and slung it over his and my head, gallantly protecting us from the still-pounding rain. "Better?"

Of necessity, I was pressed up against him. He was warm and solid. He must work out with weights. He had big muscles. Unlike the suspicious burly guard I'd encountered, he didn't look like he had an extra ounce of fat on his lean, muscled body. And it definitely felt nice huddled there against him, somewhat out of the icy wind and rain.

"Thank you," I primly answered, still waiting for his answer to my question.

"I'm a freelance reporter, on special assignment here from *The New York Times*," he explained. "Here's my Press Pass."

With his free arm he revealed a badge that'd been hidden inside his opened shirt. Yep, there it was: his name on the official, orange Press Pass: "Cleve Hartley."

Again, I was amused it was so primitive. It didn't even have a picture i.d. on it. That badge, granting him all sorts of entry throughout the festival, could belong to anyone. The security here was appalling—not-to-mention an *unseen killer* who was still out there stalking me!

"That could belong to anyone," I coyly articulated my misgivings while still enjoying his warmth and unexpected companionship.

He reached into his bag and briefly pulled out a bulky camera followed by a blocky cassette tape recorder, then a bound notebook. He stuck them back in as raindrops splattered on their surfaces.

"That's my gear," he explained. "I'm here for the news."

"Not for the music? You're not a fan of us sexy performers?" I replied, startling myself with my coy response. It wasn't like me to flirt with strangers. He was having a peculiar effect on me.

I felt more than saw him shrug.

"The music's ok," he diplomatically replied, ignoring my "sexy" comment. "But the underlying political currents are my main interest."

"Well, *I* sure do love this music—but I guess I'm also here for deeper aspects."

"Well then, I'd *love* for you to give me a few minutes of your time," his deep voice rumbled directly into my ear, apparently subtly turning my flirting back at me. "I'm trying to put together a series of 'off-views' concerning the concert. That is, if you're now convinced I'm legitimate and...?"

"I'm convinced," I sighed, grabbing onto his surprisingly slender waist. My own even slenderer waist was filled with churning guts *screaming* at me: "I'M HUNGRY! FEED ME!"

"Great! Then we can..."

"Look, Cleve," I interrupted him. "I'm exhausted and starving. If you happen to know somewhere that's out of the rain where we can sit down to eat a meal—then lead on."

He hugged my shoulders with his free arm, the other holding the coat above us both as we resumed walking up the slippery slope. We wound our way through the crush of cheering, jiving, dancing, snoring, prancing, singing, smoking massed humanity.

"I know a great place," he assured me. "It's not far."

"I'm afraid I don't have any money...any that's acceptable here, anyway."

"Naw, you celebrities never do. It's my treat."

"You're sure?"

"I've never been surer."

"Then I'm all yours."

Chapter 15

DECADENCE

__Sweet love__, the start of the hunt
Yes, you say you love me my dear
Until my needs conflict with your wants
And I crumple into a heap of tears

That beautiful, intricate mating dance
Which the male or female uses to attract
Garnering the favor of the opposite sex
Presumably to produce better, fitter babies

Then, having run its course, fleeting passion
Changed into pressing duties of fathers and mothers
Finding a new object of affection, the children
Raising them up to revitalize the herd

Ah, the dear sweet babies, kids, and offspring
Unbreakable familial bonds easily shattered
Fragile emotions fired as spurts from primeval genes
Until we sit back and wonder what happened

All that frantic coupling and cleaving
Whether in contracts, affairs, or outright sin
Naked bodies writhing and merging together
Making and raising little "mini-me's"
Who grow up to do it all over, yet again...
The Suzette Anthology, Lyrics 15

I was so weak I could barely make it the last few steps. It seemed to take forever, but we were finally past the huge press of the gigantic crowds in the viewing area, past the medical and commercial tents, past the jammed-together trailers and cars, and all the way to some small covered tables in front of a busy food truck.

Even though it was late, all the tables were filled. Other patrons were still standing up or lounging on fallen trees on the slope. The people in the truck were feverishly working to fill the orders.

"What's your pleasure, my lady?" Cleve asked as a small table briefly opened up and he blocked a surge of people toward it with his big body. He helped me to wearily collapse onto a seat.

"Food..." I moaned, barely conscious, "—and maybe a milkshake if they have one, *vanilla*...it's been five hundred years since I've had one."

He laughed, thinking I was wildly exaggerating. I wasn't. He moved away to a long line at the food truck. I think I fell asleep, my head lolling down onto my arms...

Next thing I knew there were incredible, luscious *smells* right in front of my nose.

I raised my head and saw a steaming sandwich piled high with lettuce, tomatoes, and pickles covering a greasy hamburger patty. A heap of hot French fries sat alluringly beside it. And an extra-large Vanilla Milkshake loomed above it all.

I *devoured* them.

As I've mentioned previously, normally I'm a low-fat, no saturated fat, no cholesterol, health nut: translation, a "low-fat vegetarian." The closest I usually come to "comfort food" is a no-fat yogurt and a plain bean burrito. Actually, that's a great diet for a performer to stay slender and fit on, or for an elite athlete, or—for that matter—any human being. But starvation has a habit of destroying careful consumption rules: if it's digestible it's edible.

And that *high* fat, *high* saturated fat, *high* cholesterol food was the most *delicious* meal I'd ever scarfed down!

"Woh, you *were* hungry," Cleve grinned at me, still thoughtfully chewing on his half-eaten burger.

"It's been hundreds of years since I ate last," I repeated, leaning back contentedly, my belly pleasantly filled. Off in the distance I distinctly heard deep beats booming from the viewing area. The audience was clapping along, a rhythmic "slapping" that seemed to jar the cold night air around us.

Then I heard the far off singing start. Actually it was ending. I had trudged or slept through all of Melanie and most of the next set. It was probably midnight now. I heard the closing number from *Arlo Guthrie*. I heard him there at the food truck at a comfortable volume, as if he were coming from a small radio sitting up on the serving counter. He was sweetly singing "Amazing Grace."

As Cleve leisurely popped fries into his mouth, I joined the far-off folk singer, spontaneously harmonizing with his lead alternating at low tenor, then middle alto, then high soprano, then super-high falsetto:

> *"Amazing Grace! How sweet the sound...*
> *That saved—a wretch like me!*
> *I once was lost, but now am found,*
> *Was blind but now I see..."*

A pixy-looking older woman at a nearby table tossed me an acoustical guitar. I snatched it in midair and continued without missing a beat, augmenting my singing with a staggered beat using the heel of my palm while riffing on an alternate, sweetly clashing melody.

> *"Through many dangers, toils and snares*
> *I have already come*
> *It's Grace that's brought me safe thus far*
> *And Grace will lead me home..."*

I motioned for all the people at the other tables to join me, giving them permission to enthusiastically join into the words of this well-known song. I raised my volume so the harmonies I was singing augmented the local folks and Arlo's far-off, raspy, boyish lead.

> *"When we've been there ten thousand years*
> *Bright, shining as the sun*
> *We've no less days to sing God's praise*
> *Than when we first begun..."*

"Everybody on the lead!" I yelled, stopping strumming as we all sang the chorus in full-throated unison with Arlo:

> *"Amazing Grace! How sweet the sound...*
> *That saved a wretch like me*
> *I once was lost, but now am found*
> *Was blind but now I see*
> *Was blind but now I see!"*

—and at the end of the words I launched into a wild remix and distortion of the lead with just the guitar, alternating between riffs and chords, going from low to higher, higher, *higher*...

Then plunging to the deep resonate strings and singing breathily and harshly: "Was *blind*...but now...I SEEEEEEEEEEEE!" sustaining the last note and rising up into falsetto.

BANG!—I hit the last chord and handed the guitar back to the nice older lady, who looked at me wide-eyed.

For a moment there was utter silence.

Then wild applause and cheering broke out from the tables and everyone else within earshout. And they weren't applauding Arlo's rather whiny, weak rendition. They were applauding *me!*

I grinned back at everyone, bowing my head mock-humbly as I held my hands up in the air triumphantly—turning back to Cleve.

"That was 'amazing,'" he wryly but sincerely stated, squinting at me as if he were seeing me for the first time.

"That was definitely fun," I laughed, feeling better than I'd felt in several hundred years... *I just performed at Woodstock!*

"It was...so different," he mused, frowning.

"Different?"

"Well...most of the rest to me is just noise: much-too-loud noise, in fact. But what you just did—it was mesmerizing, entrancing. How did you connect with everyone like that? When you all joined together I felt something I've never felt before, a pulsating power. And then you enhanced the meanings of the words with all those extra notes and harmonies within your one single instrument. I think I saw some new colors!"

I felt greatly honored by his strange analysis. It felt like he was revealing a carefully hidden part of his soul.

But I keyed-into something that might be critical to my Mission.

"You say you find *folk singing* to be just noise? I can understand people saying that about soul, jazz, or rock—where loud instrumentation often dominates, but folk singing?"

"To be truthful, yes, I do."

"But what about the messages, don't they move you?"

He shrugged apologetically, looking down at his half-eaten burger.

"What kind of music *do* you like?" I probed deeper.

"I...not any, I suppose."

"How is that possible?"

He thoughtfully fingered his handlebar mustache, looking from me up to the overhead tarp over the tables.

"Are you going to eat that?" I asked, looking hungrily at his half-finished meal.

"What? Oh, no I'm not. I'm full. You're welcome to it."

I grabbed the half-burger and jammed it into my mouth, luxuriating in its fat, salt, and meat.

He had a half-smile on his face watching me devour the remaining food.

"To answer your first question, I grew up in a family that didn't play much music, if at all."

"Ah—a strict fundamentalist family?"

He nodded.

"Yes...but even more than that: within a society that frowned on displays of emotion or related subversive activities."

"Music is subversive?" I frowned, speaking around a mouthful of greasy fries.

"Isn't it?"

"But it's uplifting, noble, beautiful, and..."

"Look around you, Suzy. There are people openly fornicating out there, running around naked with their sexual organs flopping in the breeze—in front of little kids! They're smoking tobacco, drinking, dulling their brains with marijuana, and then popping dangerous hallucinatory drugs. Did you hear the announcement about not taking the 'brown acid'?"

"No...?"

"It was from physicians here that were seeing 'bad trips' twisting people's brains."

"Well..."

"And the music here is directly fomenting *insurrection*."

Ah! Now I was onto something. The roots of Phoenix were definitely mired in insurrection!

"So? I thought you trying to do the same thing."

He frowned, pursing his lips before thoughtfully replying.

"Yes, I'm advocating change, but only through peaceful, intellectually persuasive means—not inciting people to mob violence! Sure, our leaders can make terrible mistakes, often for what they think are the best of reasons. The ongoing Vietnam War is the prime example. But that doesn't mean we burn down the world to try to rebuild on its ashes. We're not a magical Phoenix that rises full grown from its own funeral pyre! Societies must have viable institutions in order to exist. *That's* what's needed to construct a better world: good people working within their own enabling frameworks, with continual improvement. In the U.S.A. you *tweak* the Constitution, not rip it to shreds to start over from scratch."

Phoenix...he actually said the word! This was starting to make some sort of twisted, perverted sense. *How* did the future rabid anti-music religious radicals decide on that name?

Did Cleve inadvertently start Phoenix?

He said he was a freelance writer commissioned by the nation's most prominent 1969 newspaper: The New York Times.

How influential will be his series of articles?

If that was true—if *he* was the source from which Phoenix eventual sprang—then my Mission was simple: *stop* him by any means necessary!

The horrible prospect of *killing* Cleve came to mind. That would be terrible. But to save the future...?

For the first time I wished I had a smartphone connected to the Internet so I could research all his future newspaper articles. Unfortunately, the Internet and smartphones did not exist in 1969.

Best to slowly draw him out...

"Yep, you sound like a true conservative, Cleve—a smart, intellectually honest one, but still a 'be a good citizen' enthusiast," I cautiously observed.

"Well, maybe I am. But permissive 'music' like we're witnessing here endangers all our normal, healthy constraints. It 'frees' our very worst instincts!"

"Even what I just did with the people here at the food truck?"

He paused in his rant, clearly questioning his own argument.

Perhaps I didn't have to "eliminate" him: just persuade him of a deeper, more-meaningful viewpoint on the merits of Music.

But I didn't know if I could disagree with his argument either, at least in some cases. So I chose to change the subject.

"This 'restrictive society' you were raised within, was it here in the United States?"

"No...I was raised elsewhere."

"Ah, you mean like Saudi Arabia. They claim to adhere to strict religious fundamentalist standards—and yet have a long, rich history of Eastern music."

"Something like that..." he abruptly broke-off, standing up. He seemed to realize he'd gone too far with our enthusiastic discussion. "Say, I've got to use the port-a-potty...hold my place here?"

"Sure," I mumbled, turning my attention back to his unfinished meal. I filled my mouth with more of his incredibly delicious grease-soaked fries, "—and then I'll go when you return."

"So why *did* you go in?" I soberly asked Cleve.

We'd been discussing his background, how he came to be at Woodstock. He'd gone back at my grateful insistence and gotten us fresh milkshakes. We were nursing them sitting across from each other at one end of another, larger table. A loud group of youngsters occupied the rest of the table, giving us a sort of 'cocoon of noise' to speak within, leaning into each other. He had out his recorder, insisting he tape our discussion for his series of articles. He wanted to know my background, but I insisted he go first.

He sighed deeply, looking up at the close tarp before proceeding.

"Lots of reasons, I guess," he began, sounding pensive. "I was just out of high school, trying to figure out what I wanted to do with my life. Like I said, I was from a military family that moved around a lot, raised to be very patriotic. I sincerely believed my government when they claimed we were fighting communists overseas to keep the U.S.A. free. I thought I was doing something noble enlisting instead of just waiting to be drafted. And I guess it felt really macho, learning to be a 'warrior' and all. But, to tell the truth, I didn't have a real choice. If I'd waited I'd been drafted."

"So did you see any action?"

Now there was a long pause. "Too much... I wasn't a gung-ho killer, so I didn't want to be battling hand-to-hand. I managed to become a medic. But that turned out to be even more dangerous than being a regular soldier. When anyone got wounded I went out to try and retrieve them. Most of the time I found a way to haul them back to safety, when they were still alive that is...not blown to pieces or shredded with bullets."

"You said you didn't reenlist. What soured you on the War?"

He laughed bitterly, looking down at his big hands knotted together on the tabletop. His cassette recorder was rolling. I felt like I was interviewing him instead of the opposite.

"Well?" I prodded him.

"War's hell, right?" he answered quietly. "We weren't winning, still aren't. The 'democratic' government we fought and died to prop up over there was corrupt and brutal. 'Charlie' wasn't the devil we'd been led to believe he was, just regular guys fighting a civil war against us. The communists weren't marching through Asia, just co-opted by the Vietnamese people to help throw off their colonizers when we ignored their pleas for freedom after WWII. It took a while for me to realize all this, of course. In the meantime I got a lot of blood on my hands, saw my friends and comrades broken for life or hideously slaughtered. Does that answer your question?"

"You still wear the shirt."

He shrugged ruefully. "It's both an honor and a protest. When my 'Uncle Sam' told me I had to go to Vietnam, I did my duty. I respect those who went to prison for not obeying their draft notice—like Joan Baez's husband David—or those that left the U.S.A. to become Canadian citizens, but I answered the call. I discovered I was lied to by my own government. And now as a freelance reporter I'm doing what I feel is my duty to make that plain to everyone. Hopefully my principled opposition both in person and in my news reports will help to finally bring this pointless conflict to an end."

For me, the Vietnam War was ancient history—like World War I or II. It wasn't "my" war. To hear it from a person who was actually there in the middle of the quagmire was fascinating. Indeed, much of the violent turn of American music from gentler folk tunes as sung by Arlo to the psychedelic, transcendent guitar riffs of Jimi Hendrix featured at the "grand finale" of Woodstock was because of the seemingly endless, ruthless military draft.

As Cleve said, he had no real choice. He graduated from High School to risk getting his legs blown off in jungles half the world away for a purpose that he didn't understood or agree with. A whole generation of young people was traumatized and squeezed: expressing their fear and anger in brilliant new forms of music!

"I feel your pain," I whispered to him, putting both my small hands over his big ones.

He shrugged. "So, then, I've told you about me. Now it's your turn."

He was grinning, the tape was rolling, and I was feeling very warm and cozy even though the night was long and cold.

"What do you want to know?" I obfuscated, knowing I couldn't tell him the truth.

He smiled at me. I wished I could see his eyes. But he steadfastly refused to remove his dark eyeglasses, insisting they were part of his "image."

"Same questions as you asked me, Suzy. Where did you come from? What's your background? How'd you get here? What are you trying to achieve? What do you think about this whole Woodstock thing?"

"Right..."

I took a sip at my sweet, smooth, vanilla milkshake. It was so good! I could sit there and sip at it all night long. But I had an uneasy feeling that things were brewing right beneath the surface, waiting to explode upward. I had to figure out how and why someone was shooting at me, why I was apparently *expected* here—and most of all what I needed to do to stop the future Phoenix movement.

I considered giving Cleve the same story I'd told Arlo, the guard, and the pass-lady.

But then I realized that wouldn't be fair to him. He'd opened up to me. Maybe I should do the same for him...after all, what was the risk? There was no way he'd believe what I'd be telling him. And if I made out like I was joking, then perhaps I could safely unburden myself.

I desperately needed to tell my story to someone. And if he was truly the kernel from which Phoenix malignantly sprouted, then maybe I could use my tale to change his mind.

"You want the truth?"

"Of course!"

I grinned at him in what I hoped was a playful expression.

"Then I'm from the *future*, Cleve—almost a hundred years from now. This is all ancient history to me. In the future I was one of the performers you see up on the stage here: world-famous, rich, and arrogant. Then, somehow, everything went wrong. The world started to disintegrate around me, both personally and collectively. My Dad discovered a new scientific advance that had an unexpected side effect: throwing me back into the distant past. I spent six months in 1867, in the Fijian islands. I almost got eaten by cannibals, twice. But during that very horrible time I also learned a lot about *drums*. By *experiencing* the roots of my future world I'm learning the true meaning of *music*."

I paused, considering if I should tell him the whole truth, about my Mom and Phoenix.

"If you're a world-famous musician, don't you already know the meaning of Music?" he asked mildly. I saw that he was making an effort to not "diss" me, keeping his voice neutral. That was nice of him.

"I thought I did," I sighed. "But now that I've been transported here, back to another 'nexus' in musical history—all wrapped up in civil rights, governmental overreach, savage war, nuclear confrontation, civil unrest, and societal turmoil—I'm no longer so certain. And to make things even worse, someone or something here is trying to *kill* me!"

I'd gone shrill on that last sentence. I fought my emotions, trying to get my story back under control.

I shrugged, smiling wryly at him. I was glad that the loudly chattering crowd around me couldn't hear what I was saying. Over the distant giant speakers I heard *Joan Baez* sweetly warbling "*I Shall Be Released.*" She was the last singer of the day. It was now 1:30 in the morning. She was performing an incredible, iconic set which I knew would be replayed far into the future.

Yes, that was another of the musical revolutions stirring the Music "zeitgeist" of the 20th century: exquisitely reproducible *recorded* music. All throughout the prior history of mankind, Music had to be produced "live." You might only experience your favorite top performers a few times in your lifetime. Now you had instant access to any of your favorite Music. It was yet another piece to the puzzle of Phoenix beginning at this point in history.

But even though anyone could hear terrific music at home, seeing it performed live in front of you has its own magic. Still reprising the fading folk singing scene, Woodstock was striking deep into the souls of everyone in attendance, including me.

Woodstock represented far more than just sung words and played instruments. Would I be "released" as Joan was so beautifully singing? Or was I trapped in a maze beyond my understanding?

"Someone's trying to kill you?" Cleve responded, interrupting my wandering train of thought. I could have hugged him for not laughing at my ridiculous "time-travel" story. But we were both boxed-into our seats at the table. If I stood up we'd be swept away by others jumping for our chairs. It seems that the late attendees were surging out of the listening amphitheater in search of "munchies." Having used up their present stocks of "weed" they needed to feed their ramped-up metabolisms.

I told him about discovering myself cringing up on the stage, inventing a story to explain my presence, then almost immediately being fired upon from afar. I'd decided to omit my side trip from the Fijian islands back to the 21st Century.

"That's really serious," he grimaced angrily. "The organizers insisted that this event would be peaceful."

"I guess not," I shrugged again. "But I don't think I'm going to find the answers I need here at this food truck. I surely do appreciate the meal, Cleve, but I've got to get back to the stage. I need to search for evidence, once Joan is finished with her set and they shut down for the remainder of the night."

"Then I'm going with you," he insisted. "I've got a Press Pass. They'll let me in with you."

"That's...so nice," I smiled.

I didn't have to do this alone. I had a friend. But—how could he accept my bizarre claims without question? Surely he must think I was a looney-bin character straight out of an insane asylum.

"You...believe I'm from the future?" I pressed him.

He grinned. He had a great smile. It warmed my heart.

"I believe that *you* believe it, Suzy—and that's enough for me."

"You know, I really *am* from the future," I insisted.

"If you say so."

"I do...I say so!"

"Ok," he shrugged.

Now he was making me mad. I knew I shouldn't be short with him, especially when I expected him to not believe me. But I couldn't help myself.

"Look, I have proof."

"What?"

I reached in my back jeans pocket and pulled out my waterproof wallet. Zippering it open I grabbed a twenty dollar bill and "smacked" it down in front of him on the tabletop.

"Compare that to a contemporary twenty," I ordered him.

He extracted a twenty of his own and compared the two, side-by-side.

"Hmmm...there *are* differences...the '20' in the right lower corner is raised—and changes color with the angle of viewing!—and Jackson is large, out of the oval...and the 'series' is from *2013*."

"See? It's proof I'm from the future."

"Or that you've got ahold of a cleverly forged fake note."

"So don't believe me!" I snorted, snatching my twenty to put back in my wallet. I started to get up and leave...

"Don't go, Suzy," he grinned at me. "I told you I believed you. I'm just saying no one else would. That's all."

I settled back down, pulling out my remaining four marbles and placing them on the tabletop.

"What are these?"

"Since I can't pay you back for lunch with 'fake' money then these are the most precious things I have. They're also from the future. In fact, they're magic!"

He laughed, rolling them around on the tabletop.

"I do like the blue one," he mused. "It reminds me of what we're missing today: a beautiful blue sky."

I laughed, glancing outward at the still-thudding rain. "It's called a 'clearie' and it's yours."

"I can't..."

I closed his big fist around it. "Always keep it with you and it will bring you luck, just as it has for me."

He shrugged, slipping it into his pocket.

"Alright then," he gave me a broad smile. "You've proved it. You're a magic-marble toting time traveler from the future. I will cherish your sky-marble."

I was certain he didn't believe any such thing. But it was nice of him to go along with the running "gag."

"So do you have any 'reporter' questions for an actual time-traveler?" I asked him flippantly.

"Oh, sure—what's going to happen with the war?"

"It drags on and on and on for years."

"But doesn't Nixon stop it? His 'Vietnamization' policy seems hopeful."

"He gets reelected in a landslide and then gets impeached for stupid presidential overreach, resigning in disgrace. But before he's thrown out he eventually did extricate the U.S. from Vietnam—only to have the Northern communists move into the South and take the whole place over."

"So we lost?"

"Totally lost—but then we became friends with them. Vietnam became a popular tourist destination."

"So all the tens of thousands of our people who were mutilated or slaughtered...?"

"—all for nothing...more than a million people died in total. Well, maybe the war did prevent communism from surging across Asia, but that's an academic argument made only by a few diehard conservatives. Eventually the current political leaders in the U.S.A. admitted they were wrong about pursuing the war. Hah, fat lot of good that did all those like you who returned permanently scarred."

"That's...both amazing and horrifying. But then after suffering such a terrible defeat, I imagine the government avoided further no-end conflicts, ushering in an age of peace that..."

"Nope! Wrong again. After that it was just one stupid conflict after another. We didn't learn a thing."

"But this Music—the 'Age of Aquarius' peace and love, surely...?"

"The mellow pot and mind-expanding LSD 'heaven' turned into a cocaine and heroin *hell*. A number of the performers on stage here are dead in a few years from overdoses. Both Janis Joplin and Jimi Hendrix die from drugs a little over a year from now. 'Peace and love' became profit and pain. The 'music' became more and more hedonistic, simplistic, and wild. The 'hippy' generation became the 'hopeless' generation—turning inward to nationalism, fear, and rank selfishness."

He pursed his lips, considering my words as if he really believed I'd been to the future and knew what was going to happen.

"In your...vision...of the future, does religion have a comeback? The formal churches are all in decline. Does increased evil in the world at least bring people back to God?"

I saw that he wanted some sort of vindication, a rationale to make sense of the horrors of war, an ultimate justification to his strict religious upbringing.

But his feeble hope was futile.

I was ashamed. My own behavior as "Suzette" put the lie to his hope. I'd started out singing Gospel as a kid with high ideals, only to become selfish and shallow. I myself turned to hard drugs, rejecting formal religion. In a microcosm, I was my own worst example.

So I decided to continue with the truth.

"Nope, just the opposite happened, Cleve. As the formal traditional religions died out, newer modern-music rooted ones grew up. But even then the so-called 'praise' music became a watered-down, formalistic, self-serving, weak version of Gospel. Instead of conveying the 'real' Jesus it exalted the 'comfortable' Jesus. It avoided doctrinal controversy by focusing only on two things, repeating over and over '*God is great*' and '*Jesus is great.*' True, the Praise Music did draw in people, but it didn't have the deep audience-participation of Folk, the 'soul' of the Blues, the rampant experimentation of Jazz, the biting edge of classical Western, the mind-expanding qualities of the various hard-Rock offshoots, or the raw reality of Rap. And at the same time, young people flocked to ear-rupturing hardcore beats, fueling the AIDS epidemic and illegal drug usage."

"Uhm...'Rap'...AIDS?"

"Oh, don't get me started," I groaned. "If you don't like Folk you'd surely not like Rap. And just always use a condom whenever you casually hook-up with someone, ok?"

"Uh...sure."

"Look, I know this all sounds crazy," I said as I stood up and carried my trash to a nearby over-flowing waste barrel. Behind me a fight broke out as people vied for the empty seat. "I don't blame you a bit for cutting loose from this zonked-out, hallucinating gal."

He was right at my elbow, tamping-down the barrel with a big boot while inserting his waste there also.

"I'm intrigued. If you'll have me, I'd still like to tag along with you."

"Suit yourself."

"But before we leave, there's one more thing," he continued, leading me over to a log beneath a tree. The night skies were clearing, at least for the moment. The rain had stopped. "I'd like your recorded reaction to the benediction given last evening at the start of the concert by *Swami Satchidananda.*"

"Ah, you're referring to the Indian mystic who counseled the Beatles and gained an American following. I actually ran into him earlier and..."

"I recorded what he said. Just a minute," he said as he fumbled in his shoulder bag and found a labelled cassette tape. Popping it in place of the one that he'd been recording on, he punched the machine to "play."

"Listen, Suzy."

"*My Beloved Brothers and Sisters,*" the tape crackled through the small speaker. The voice spoke with a strong, "sing-song" India-derived accent. "*I am overwhelmed with joy to see the entire youth of America gathered here in the name of the fine art of music. In fact, through the music, we can work wonders. Music is a celestial sound and it is the sound that controls the whole universe, not atomic vibrations. Sound energy, sound power, is much, much greater than any other power in this world. And, one thing I would very much wish you all to remember is that with sound, we can make—and at the same time, break. Even in the war-field, to make the tender heart an animal sound is used. Without that war band, that terrific sound, man will not become animal to kill his own brethren. So, that proves that you can break with sound, and if we care, we can make also.*"

Cleve switched the tape off, pulled it out, and reinserted the one he'd been recording on, punching it back into the "record" mode.

"Well?" he asked me.

"Bull crap!" I snorted.

"What?"

"Music isn't what drives us, the Universe, or anything else. Music is a *symptom* of what we do. We can't blame music for our victories or defeats. Sure, it's a powerful means of communication—though 'speaking' *not* in its superficial lyrics but its transmittable, underlying *emotions*. Yes, it strikes to our hearts, but Music alone can neither save nor condemn us."

"Then...can we do without it?"

Uh...was that what I meant to say?

I seem to be going in circles!

I was shocked to realize that after all my experience on top of the music business I didn't know what I was talking about. How could I "convert" Cleve to a better way of thinking if I didn't even know what I myself believed?

"Who the hell knows?" I gulped, looking down in confusion.

"Would you live in a world without music?" he pressed me.

"That's impossible," I again snorted, cowardly retreating into absolutes. "Music is part of who we are. It goes back to birds tweeting love songs, wolves howling to mark their territory, or whales calling for mates across oceans. Music is in our genes."

"What if it were somehow taken away?"

"Then we wouldn't be human anymore," I firmly concluded, relieved to finally hit on a positive argument—no matter how tenuous—for not doing away with music. "And now I'm going back to the stage. Coming?"

"If that's what you want, then..."

"It's not a question of 'want', Cleve. It's a matter of *duty!*" I replied grandly.

"So who's the ex-military soldier now?"

"That's not fair," I replied peevishly, again looking down at my shoes. "Stop teasing me!"

"Hah. *I'm* teasing *you*, the sophisticated, world-spanning time-traveler?"

He got me there.

"You are one fascinating performer, Suzy," he nodded, putting the recorder carefully back in his shoulder bag. "Just try and get rid of me. Besides, I need to file my initial report to the Times."

"You've already got it written? I heard there's a bank of phones somewhere further out that..."

"Yep, your interview will figure into my later articles. Fascinating stuff, Suzy, I really appreciate your help. And yes, I could use the public phones in an emergency. But they'll be monopolized with teenagers telling their anxious parents they're still alive. There's a press tent located in back of the stage, just for us reporters."

"What's your headline for the first day of Woodstock?"

He laughed: "*Hippy Festival Mired in Mud and Filth.*"

I sighed. "I hope your headlines get better."

"So do I."

Chapter 16

<u>COSMIC RIPPLES</u>

Time keeps on flowing, keeps on flowing,
Keeps on flowing along, like a river
It goes downhill and it never turns back
Sweeps you up and spins you around
Sucking you in till you think you'll drown
Then spitting you out like a stinky wet cat.

You can fight, fight, fight, fight, fight...
Try to fight against it, but you'll lose
You start out young but you end up old
You're body's warm and then its icy cold
You're smooth as a baby then wrinkled and spotted
Giggling at first then coughing up phlegm.

Or you go with the flow on a magical boat
Surfing the waves and speeding along
Dashing and spinning and bouncing up high
You merge with the water and make it your own
Evaporating upward into the sky
You drop as rain and start all over again
Knowing that you'll never, ever have to die!
The Suzette Anthology, Lyrics 16

The moon peeked through a gap in the dark clouds above as we made our way through the sea of massed humanity back toward the stage. Clouds still drifted across its face, but at least we had some celestial light to illuminate the darkness.

235

"That's rather romantic, isn't it?" Cleve asked me. We were carefully winding our way through the mass of seated or sleeping people. A number were leaving, making their way back to tents or trailers. But many others apparently had no place to go or didn't want to lose their spots, choosing instead to huddle miserably on the muddy slope throughout the long, cold night.

He paused and looked upward in wonderment, as if he'd never seen a silvery moon before.

In the moonlight Cleve Hartley looked to me like a marble statue of some Greek God: pensive, long hair sprayed to each side of his thick neck, his white bandana a crown, his mustache a frowny slash, his dark eyeglasses alien goggles, his opened shirt flaunting chest hairs like coppery metal shards.

"Naw..." I lied, smitten. "A moon is a moon."

Joan Baez was still up on stage. She was just finishing *"Let me Wrap You In My Warm and Tender Love."*

We stepped over several couples buried beneath blankets who were obviously taking her advice.

"So what's your plan once we get back onto the performers' side?" Cleve asked, taking my arm as we neared the carefully guarded gate.

"Uh..." I gulped, feeling confused. He was having a definite effect on me. There was strange warmth in the pit of my stomach different from the digesting lump of fast-food. God, was I falling in love? "I think once Joan finishes we'll be free to inspect the gear still stored up on the stage. If we find the speaker that caught the four bullets, maybe I can gauge the direction the shots came from and..."

He stopped dead in his tracks, staring entranced up at the stage.

"What...?" I began, looking up as well. Then I stopped speaking, likewise mesmerized. Only one single blue spotlight was on, ethereally illuminating Joan Baez standing all by herself. Her youthful, soulful-eyed face was highlighted beneath her uncharacteristically short-cropped black hair. The applause to her last song was dying down. She unslung her guitar from her shoulder, set it to the side, and began singing a-capella, totally unaccompanied: *"Swing Low, Sweet Chariot."*

Her warbling, seductively vibrating voice transgressed the entire music scale with impunity. The giant speakers on the towers changed her already powerful voice into that of a celestial angel. Her transcendental tones soared up into the stratosphere, taking us with them. And the images evoked by the simple, timeless words of the song hung about us like living objects.

"Amen," she firmly concluded.

"That was...exceptional," Cleve gasped.

"I couldn't have done better myself," I ruefully admitted. "She's a tremendous singer. But just *why* do you find it so 'exceptional', Cleve?"

"It's...not noise...and not instruments?"

"Yes, Cleve, that's exactly right," I patiently explained to him, huddled against him as Joan launched into her final number. "The finest music needs no accompaniment—emanating from our very souls. The *best* musical instrument *is* the human voice."

Baez's last song was a powerful rendition of "We Shall Overcome"...in which she invited the whole huge audience to join her in "*we shall be alright*"... then "*we shall live in peace*"... then "*we are not afraid*"... and finally a powerful reprise of "*we shall overcome!*"

The incredible singing of Joan backed up by *100,000 people* rumbling all around us swept through our minds, causing even Cleve to sway to the beat.

I was getting to him. If he was somehow involved, directly or indirectly, in Phoenix's birth I was *touching* him.

But then, abruptly, he was back to being "all business."

"Your plan sounds dangerous," he stated, patting his shoulder bag.

"What?"

"Suppose your shooter is still up there, looking for you?"

"Uh..."

"I've got an '*m' nineteen eleven* in my bag. I'll protect you."

"What's an M1911?"

"It's the standard pistol issued by the US military. I kept mine when I was honorably discharged from the Army."

"You stole it? That doesn't sound very 'honorable', does it?"

"Let's just say it was part of my reward for surviving the Vietnam War."

"Oh...ok...you certainly deserved it...but just how will you get a *gun* through security?"

"I've got my Press Pass. They won't search my bag like they do for random, unknown people. I've also got a bowie knife from my service days in my bag. Once we're backstage you can take it if you want. It wouldn't be a bad idea for you to be armed as well."

"No thanks," I turned down his offer. I didn't want to be burdened with an unfamiliar weapon. I'd much rather just run fast away from danger.

"Suit yourself."

"But won't the magnetometer...?" I started to ask then stopped speaking. I remembered that metal screening didn't become a routine procedure for several years into the future, "—nothing! Your riding 'gunshot' for me sounds fine, Cleve. But I doubt whoever was after me is still lurking up there. I just want proof that I wasn't imagining the attack."

"Still, Suzy, I'm locked and loaded. I keep the safeties on while it's in the bag, but it's ready to fire within seconds. In a crowd this big there's bound to be a few crazies. Since I came here to confront people with my recorder and my pointed questions, challenging their viewpoints, I wanted to be ready for all contingencies. I'd only shoot someone as a last resort of course, but I'm prepared to do whatever's necessary."

"Good to know," I gulped, pulling my arm away from his. That was a buzz-kill for sure, effectively counteracting the "romantic" moon now shining unobscured down on us.

He smoothly untied his denim jacket from around his waist, whipped his arms into it, and flipped the attached hood up over his head.

"Are you cold?" I asked.

All the energy we'd been expending making our way through the crowd kept me warm, even though the night was chilly.

"I prefer to be 'incognito' with the organizers, workers, and performers," he stated. "They're less defensive if I they don't recognize me as a reporter."

"Uh...ok," I shrugged. I didn't know how putting a hood over his head would make other people more talkative, but he was the reporter here, not me.

And the moon did make a very bright light above.

But then the silvery heavenly body was again hidden by the still-roiling black clouds. The lights were going out on the towers. The stage was dark.

We walked together to the gate.

It was now past 2:00 AM in the morning of Saturday, August 16th, 1969. We were tracking a *potential assassin* at Woodstock!

And, yet again, it began to rain heavily.

"Are you ready to give up?"

I groaned, stretching. My back hurt from bending over examining the still-present loudspeakers on the crowded stage. I was getting very sleepy. The slow searching allowed my body to get cold. We'd been at it for over an hour.

The few remaining stagehands didn't question my looking for "a lost earring" amongst the piles and jumbles of musical equipment. The stage was originally meant to have a circular, rotating area in which the front half would hold the active performers while the back half was being broken down and set up for the next. But the mechanism failed after the first few attempts. Thus there was a mad scramble to disassemble and reassemble the next performers' instruments and equipment during each and every changeover instead of smoothly rotating in-and-out. So in the confusion, lots of things got lost or scrambled up. And the speaker I was looking for was nowhere to be seen.

Likely it had been already removed from the stage.

Or I'd just imagined the whole thing. In my eagerness to nail down and stop Phoenix I may have mistaken broken strings or thrown rocks for bullets. But I'd *heard* the loud hits and *felt* the flung wood chips!

Either way, there was no evidence remaining of an "assassin" trying to kill me. At least we hadn't attracted unwanted attention, what with the renewal of pounding rain driving most people undercover or off the stage.

"Thanks for humoring me, Cleve. I guess I'll just go and try to find some tent to crash in for the night."

"I'm happy to help you find a pad," he shrugged. "But first I've got to file my report to the Times for tomorrow's paper. It'll only take a few minutes once I get on a phone."

"With your help and contacts I'll have a lot better chance of getting someone to give up a few square feet of a nice, dry tent," I acknowledged. "You go do your thing, Cleve. I'll wait right here, on stage. For me this is an incredible, lifetime experience to be on stage at Woodstock. And this is the most peaceful time to be here, with most everyone else asleep."

"Ok, then, Suzy. I'll be back shortly."

"Thanks, Cleve," I smiled at him in the gloom. "It's funny, but I feel like I've known you all my life—you're a good friend."

"You too," he acknowledged, lithely slipping away.

I sat down on a big amplifier, moving its attached cables and electrical cords to the side.

Yes, it was insanely peaceful. The moon had just come out again. The clouds above were finally breaking up, showing patches of bright stars. The audience was mostly asleep. A fire burned here and there up the distant slopes, where huddled groups were trying to keep warm. Random bongo-drums were "popping" out scattered beats, as isolated groups tried to dance-away the chill of the night.

I could almost believe that everything was right with the world, people weren't still being slaughtered in Vietnam, and the future would take care of itself.

"Move and you die."

Startled, I jumped to the side...

—only to be *enveloped* in an excruciatingly painful *cocoon* of *crackling electricity!*

"Unnggg..." I moaned, convulsing face-down onto the wet wood planks. I was vaguely aware I'd peed myself.

"I warned you, 'Suzette'," a harsh female voice penetrated the red haze of pain blocking my sight. "I tried to scare you off when you first materialized, though I didn't expect you to appear right up on the stage. Rather, I'd anticipated you sneaking in and first getting the Performer Pass for which I'd snuck your name onto a pre-ordained list. I thought a few bullets might convince you to just enjoy the music. My gun can shoot this era's ammunition or revert to its primary mode. Rest assured I can 'taser' you as often as I wish until you're soaked in your own urine or dead, whichever."

"Who...are you?" I groaned, painfully rolling onto my back and looking up. My vision was clearing.

In the gloom I saw a *slender oriental lady* holding a big black gun. She had on one of the Woodstock T-shirts outside her regular clothes, with a stage badge dangling from a red cord around her neck. Otherwise she was clad in a black "ninja" outfit.

"Let's just say I'm a 'friend' telling you to enjoy the festival and 'cool out' over any supposed conspiracy theories."

"You're...one of them...the *Phoenix* terrorists."

She sighed deeply, slowly crouching down above me.

"That band of narrow-minded religious bigots won't exist for decades."

"Then...you helped to start the movement...you're from the future, just like me."

"Right! Right! And *right!*" she laughed. "But no, you're completely wrong."

"I don't...understand," I coughed, still randomly convulsing from the intense electrical charges I'd just suffered.

"They're just convenient patsies," she stated. "I'm with the organization that's really pulling the strings, looking to pacify the 21st Century's human society for our invasion."

"By banning Music?" I gasped.

"That's a big part of it, yes."

"Why?"

"The Commissioner is extending her territory."

"Who?"

"She's tired of the chaos in your Dimension, so nearby my own. We have a very orderly, peaceful, and productive world. One of the keys to achieving that gentle societal framework is a strict ban on Music, unlike your chaotic, violent, permissive world. And what with your very own mother discovering the *Principles of Time Travel* you've become an escalating threat to us. We tried to stop you earlier, but you were...are...resilient."

"The T-rex...?"

"Yes, that and other attempts to gently divert your pesky family across the Dimensional Divide that..."

"Wait...*my* 'Dimension'? There's another?"

"Yes! You really must listen more closely, Suzette. We've mastered Time Travel for a goodly while now. I'm actually an officer in the *Time Keeper* Corp. We exist 'out-of-time', protecting the most desirable Timelines—which *you* came here to *disrupt*, did you not?"

"If what you say is true, then you already know everything."

"No, not everything," she mused, standing upright while still aiming her gun directly at me. "Timelines are notoriously unpredictable and 'fuzzy'. It has to do with 'quantum uncertainty.' Your mother could explain it to you. Your tiny, little song-writing brain isn't advanced enough to understand what's happening. Regardless to say, though, you've already upset the balance sufficiently for me to have to make major corrections."

"Cleve..." I whispered.

"Yes, that 'reporter' was supposed to write the critical articles that would push fellow outraged radical religious conservatives over the edge, initiating the secret alliance that would eventually become Phoenix. But you've already modulated his thinking sufficiently that his further articles are more balanced. Even if I killed him right now, it wouldn't stop you having already toned down the negative articles. Terminating him would just affirm the absence of the desired inflammatory articles. Follow me?"

"I guess...but what happens now?"

I was beginning to regain control over my quivering muscles. My red-hazed vision was almost back to normal. I was starting to breathe normally.

"Well, my dear future pop-rock Superstar, I first need to know the exact means you used to time-travel here to Woodstock," she coolly informed me. "I have to be certain this disruption will not reoccur. Did you arrive here by accident or was it a deliberate transport?"

"And if I tell you—what then?"

"Then, sadly, I still must kill you," she shrugged. "We try to be delicate in altering Timelines, but your bumbling has to be stopped. But your reward for telling me what I need to know is a painless execution instead of extended, excruciating agony. I'll just set my gun to a lethal discharge. With all the water on the stage plus lightning storms tonight, your death will be deemed an accidental electrocution. You won't feel a thing. But your death probably won't even make the national news, sorry."

"And just how will my being 'electrocuted' correct the timeline?" I gasped, desperately trying to prolong my life.

"Oh, it won't. It'll just truncate your uncertainty factor. Dead, you won't induce further uncertainty, right? Your Mother was actually the main Time-Twister that we were proscribed from directly harming. She's a real 'pistol,' scrambling all our predictions and creating a time-fog around her actions that we can't easily penetrate. *You*, though, are just a pesky footnote on the Timescape who..."

I lashed out with my legs, catching her on her shins and knocking her down.

"Take *that!*" I sneered, trying to spring to my feet...

—which buckled, causing me to immediately collapse back to the floor. Too soon after being electrocuted...

"Well..." she growled at me, her slanted eyes nearly squinted shut as she painfully got back to her feet. "In 'that' case your death *will* be agonizing."

"Then I'll die happy, knowing I stopped Phoenix!"

"Not at all," she sneered at me. "Even if you'd somehow killed me with your feeble attempt at a karate kick, I've already started the countdown on a *bomb* that'll blow this entire heathen song-orgy to bloody chunks. It's equivalent to one of this era's small tactical nukes. Over *two hundred thousand* people will die!"

I was aghast at her claim. It was the Hollywood Bowl all over again, except much worse!

"What, your terrorist puppets didn't kill enough concert-goers in the future?"

"Yes! That's exactly right. You're catching on, Suzette. Doing the same thing to this seminal rock festival in 1969 will *advance* the future anti-music efforts by decades. Where the Commissioner would have required years to fully subvert the Phoenix religious control, in the new Timeline it'll only take months. The blast here will be attributed to governmental secret operatives looking to squash the anti-

war movement, fueling both societal distrust of government and fear
of musical concerts. The future will be ripe for my beloved Commissioner to *step across* the Dimensional Divide and *directly* take charge
of your pitiful world!"

"Bite me!" I spat back at her.

"With pleasure," she grinned, pointing the nozzle of the gun again
directly at me...

I closed my eyes.

BANG!

I grimaced. I was somewhat annoyed she'd lied to me. She said
she wouldn't shoot bullets at me again and...?

I was still alive!

I opened my eyes to see she was tottering above me, the gun
dropping from her slack hand, a red smear of blood spreading across
her chest, before she *collapsed* down on top of me.

"Suzy! Are you ok?" I heard a welcomed deep voice.

It was Cleve, shoving the still-twitching body of the woman to the
side and helping me to my feet.

"I...she..."

"I heard most of the incredible stuff she claimed. I got back right
after she blasted you with that electricity gun. I was angling for a
clear shot through all this piled up equipment. Sorry I didn't return
sooner."

I lurched forward and hugged him tightly. I was trembling uncontrollably.

"Thanks," I managed to whisper to him. "We've got to tell the organizers what happened, call the police, the F.B.I., and..."

"No!" he retorted. "They'd never believe us—just arrest us as
murder suspects."

"But...she said there's a *bomb!*"

"Then we've got to find it and defuse it."

"Just us? We need to shut down the festival, get all these people
out of here! And..."

"Their only hope is us finding it on our own."

I stopped trembling, pulling away from him. Fortunately no one
had yet responded to his gunshot. Presumably the "bongo" playing
out in the crowd had drowned it out or camouflaged the brief "bang."

We still had a few minutes until we were discovered by patrolling guards.

"What about her body?"

"I'll take care of it. You clean up the mess."

"Oh...right..."

I saw a thick pool of blood beneath her body staining the wooden stage. Who knew dead bodies could bleed that much? "I guess I can find a mop and some rags to..."

He'd already snatched up her body and dashed away into the darkness.

Just like a man—leaving a woman to do the housework!

I giggled hysterically, searching around for the "broom closet." At least *I* wasn't the body being carried off. I momentarily felt sorry for the poor, dead "Time Keeper," realizing I didn't even know her name.

"I'm *so* tired," I complained, barely able to keep my eyes open.

"Maybe that woman was just trying to get a last dig at you before she killed you," Cleve shrugged. He was sitting on a boulder looking out across Leon's Lake. "There may not be a bomb at all."

We were about a quarter mile from the Stage, at one of the main "skinny dipping" sites at Woodstock. Throngs of hippies were gleefully stripping off their clothes to get a welcomed swim. The sun was beating down mercilessly. Heat stroke victims were being helped out of the main throng at the stage. But clouds were still surging over the horizon, occasionally dumping more rain to make things even more miserably humid.

Woodstock was definitely not as romantic as it'd been remembered.

"We can't take that chance," I insisted. "We have to keep searching."

We'd been at it all through the night and into the morning. We trudged through all the obvious places you'd hide a bomb powerful enough to kill the claimed 200,000 victims. Cleve crawled beneath the stage throughout all the supporting timbers and concrete slabs. I went to the base of each of the sound and light towers, trying to see any "unnecessary" objects other than the giant speakers and lights.

After that fruitless search we joined up to peek into most of the nearest trailers and tents, and then back up the slope to the major covered structures around the natural bowl.

We found nothing suspicious. But the bomb could be hidden anywhere inside thousands of buses, trailers, and tents—not-to-mention buried under the soil beneath our feet. If that woman was truly from the future, the bomb might even be something we couldn't imagine: so small we'd never suspect it until it detonated.

"I'm open to suggestions," Cleve replied. He looked as exhausted as I felt. His handlebar mustache was drooping. His white bandana was askew across his forehead, his army shirt smeared with mud. Even his ubiquitous dark eyeglasses were askew.

"We've got to take a break," I flatly stated, looking at the alluring, blue water of the lake. "We can't accomplish anything if we're too frazzled to think straight."

"Sounds good to me," he sighed. "I could use a short nap and..."

"At *Woodstock?* Are you kidding me? Even if we get blown up, this is the thrill of a lifetime. It's no time to take naps!"

Off in the distance, Saturday's music was just starting to boom out across the audience. I remembered it was "Quill"—a regionally popular but nationally obscure rock band.

"Maybe for sex, drug, and rock-and-roll addicts—but not for me," he griped, slumping backward until he was flat on the ground.

I grabbed his arms and dragged him back to a sitting position.

"Come on, Cleve. Let's go skinny dipping."

"No way," he grunted, pulling away from me.

"It'll be fun."

"What—join those silly hippies displaying their sexual organs for all to inspect?"

I glanced at the splashing, laughing groups. Yep, they were doing exactly what he so aptly described: flopping their breasts, penises, testicles, and butts in their public nakedness.

But they were also washing off all the mud, plus getting cool.

"It won't be like that. Most of the time we'll be in the water, with our junk safely concealed," I insisted. "Come on, man—yank off those trousers and shirt. Drop your shorts and toss away those dark eyeglasses. Let's cut loose. We're at *Woodstock!*"

"Go if you want. Just leave me here. I'm past saving, Medic. Leave me behind," he joked, grinning wryly while clutching doggedly at his eyeglasses least I try to wrest them off.

It was endearing that after all the terrible things he'd endured in the War he still had a sense of humor.

"Alright, then," I laughed. "But you'll be sorry when you see me swimming like a nude porpoise."

"I'll guard your stuff," he sniffed primly.

I'd just been joking. I didn't want to detract from our desperate search to have frivolous fun. But I *did* achingly need to take a bath and get cooled down. So I stripped off my shirt, jeans, and shoes to make a mad dash for the shoreline.

No, I wasn't nude. I didn't need to invite any of the horny boys splashing naked in the water to gang-rape me, not that it was happening to anyone. Everyone seemed to be having fairly innocent fun running around sans-swimsuits. But I wasn't taking any chances.

Still, I glanced behind to confirm that Cleve was sneaking a peek at my t-shirted, panties-clad, semi-naked sleek body.

I was glad that back in Fiji I'd finally gotten rid of the flab accumulated during my future hospital and drugged-out months. I was back to being trim-and-fit, with a nice head of naturally blond hair flopping cutely in the breeze. I was sure Cleve was having a treat fantasizing me completely naked.

I splashed into the cool water and plunged beneath the surface.

It was the most refreshing "bath" I'd ever experienced.

"Wahoo!" I shouted as I surfaced and Cleve waved weakly at me. "It's great! Come on in!"

But he just slowly shook his big head in the negative, flopping backward onto the still-green untouched patch of grass we'd found.

"Is he your boyfriend?"

As I ran my fingers through my hair, washing out mud and grime, I saw a brightly smiling girl next to me. She was completely naked, her small breasts bobbing up and down in the water.

She had nice tits, firm and perky.

"Uh...not actually; well maybe," I admitted, simultaneously intrigued and embarrassed by the notion.

"What's it like to date a famous musician?"

"Say what?" I was taken aback as I ran my hands over the rest of my body, splashing away the coated grime. Was she referring to me? But no one knew who I was back in this time period. And though I resembled Grace Slick, my hair was blond. I'd have to have a dark wig on to be mistaken for...

"That's *Country Joe McDonald*, isn't he? What's he doing out here with us when he's onstage playing in less than thirty minutes? And why's he not out in the water with us? The three of us could get real friendly in the water."

Country Joe—Cleve *did* look a lot like him. In fact, he looked *exactly* like the young version of him that was next in the lineup onstage. No wonder he'd looked so familiar to me when I first met him! Country Joe, though not one of the most prominent performers at Woodstock, had struck an iconic profile in many of the historic videos and pictures I'd seen of the Festival over the years.

"Naw...he's just dressed up like him," I curtly dismissed the chatty teen. "Joe's a hero of his, is all," I made up an excuse for his appearance.

"Ah, too bad," she sighed prettily. "I'd sure love to screw him— that is, if it were ok with you? I mean, if he's not the real thing he's sure close! Wow, I could really dig feeling that big mustache on my..."

"Not available!" I curtly dismissed her unwanted advances, turning my back on her and marching primly out of the water.

I flopped down beside Cleve, luxuriating in the feel of the hot sun drying my freshly cleaned skin.

"I admit that was rather spectacular," Cleve laughed from beside me. "Your body puts all those other women to shame."

Wow. That girl in the water was totally correct. "Joe look-alike" would be a catch to screw! But what I was feeling for him was much deeper than a pseudo-celebrity thrill. I feared I was *falling in love* with the endearing hunk.

"What, next to all those big boobs bouncing in the water? I didn't even have all my clothes off."

"Well..." he pretended to carefully consider my objections, pursing his lips and furrowing his brow, "—it's true there are a lot of large breasts, thick nipples, bushy pubic hair, and big butts on display...but *you*, young lady, are trim, fit, and athletic. Next year after having their first kids—likely conceived here at Woodstock—those sexy young ladies in the water will weigh twice as much, loaded down with ugly fat."

"So you think I'm boyish?" I teased him.

"No, I think you are the ideal female."

"Really?" I asked, now definitely not believing his flattering words.

"On a scale of 1-to-10 you're a *one hundred*. Long after most of those splashing naked females turn into cellulite and wrinkles you'll still be beautiful."

Wow. This guy was either smitten with me or giving me the most outrageous "come-on" trying to get into my pants.

"Take off your shirt," I ordered him.

"Uhm—I didn't really mean to..."

That was nice to hear. He wasn't actually just then trying to make a move on me...

"I'll take it down to the water's edge along with my own shirt and pants," I explained primly. "They're all filthy. I'll wash them out. Also, give me your mud-caked boots. The water in the lake's still clean enough to use to rinse out clothes and such. I didn't see anyone peeing while they were swimming. And even if that did happen, there's sufficient volume to dilute out the excrement."

He grimaced but nodded in agreement.

"Good idea," he said. He undid his shirt completely, pulling out his arms and handing it to me. His broad shoulders, bulging pecks and biceps were impressive.

I paused as he untied the laces to his boots. I needed to ask him a serious question.

"You know, some girl commented that you're a spitting image for Country Joe McDonald. Is he perhaps a relative of yours?"

He gulped as if I'd caught him in some lie, looking away from me briefly.

Then he grinned and glibly replied: "Not as far as I know, but he's one of the few rockers I've followed, with his strong country bent. I wanted to blend into the festival, so I patterned my hairstyle and clothes after his hippy style. If I came here with my usual military buzz cut I'd be marginalized at best as an ex-Vietnam soldier. So I grew out my hair as I planned for this expedition. It's just lucky for me there's a general resemblance between the two of us."

"You say you've been preparing for this for a while, growing your hair out?"

That didn't seem plausible. He would have had to know about the festival before it was publically announced...?

"Indeed. I'm taking this Woodstock phenomenon very seriously."

"Even making yourself look like Country Joe?"

"That's correct."

"Huh. So then you must enjoy his famous 'FISH' chant."

"Oh, right—love it!"

"Well, he's on in a few minutes. You'll want to join the crowd in the chant, right?"

"Oh, absolutely. It'll be a thrill."

One of the highlights of Woodstock had been Country Joe's "F-I-S-H" audience chant: in which he unexpectedly and spontaneously changed the *give me a...*"I" to "U", the "S" to "C", and the "H" to "K"— then "*what does that spell...? What does that spell...? What does that spell...?*"

Yes, it was a more innocent time, when people could still be titillated or offended by crude public language.

I was sure his uptight, conservative butt would be shocked. I didn't believe he knew Country Joe as well as he pretended.

This "Cleve" was an odd cat, seemingly an open book but mysteriously evasive.

I hoped I'd be finished with my "house-keeping" chores down on the lakeshore in time to see his expression at Country Joe's chant. Hah! Cleve Hartley was a walking contradiction. He claimed to have participated in the most horrendous war battles imaginable, yet kept his language prim and proper. He said he was a pacifist but carried a gun, not hesitating to kill a threatening woman. He said he was a protestor yet balked at seeing hippies displaying their bodies. He denounced modern music yet adopted the clothes and hairstyle of the rocker Joe McDonald.

Who was he really?

I hoped I'd get to find out before we all got blown to Kingdom Come.

Chapter 17

DOWN THE RABBIT HOLE

*In the garden of life there's **a deep black pit***
A shaft below the flowers and the honey bees
Down where the worms and snakes all live
Where light is darkness and stones can bleed

Why would you duck down that spooky tunnel
Just to escape the pressures of gardening
Duties and responsibilities so terribly heavy
That you'd turn your green world an icy blue?

Gulp the one pill and shrink into an ant
Pop the other one and you grow into a giraffe
Do nothing at all and you're a jabbering monkey
Always too silly, thin, or fat

Alice don't dirty your pretty white skirt
Don't follow the tempting, prancing rabbit
If you do you're in for a world of hurt
Eating bad medicine just makes you sick

Your sweet, fine, excellent loving
So exquisite, warm, and divine
To blossom into roses needs lots of room
And soil to nourish deep roots
Down where the sun don't shine
Only the cunning can survive...

The Suzette Anthology, Lyrics 17

I let the strong arms of Cleve wrap me up. I only intended to join him in a quick nap huddled beneath a sheltering small tree. But nestled against his steadily beating heart I drifted off into an exhausted stupor. He was *such* a comforting, protecting *force*. I slept like a baby in his arms.

The next thing I knew I was jostled awake by a passing troupe of mantra-chanting *Hare Krishna*. They had on dirt-stained yellowish robes, sandals, gleaming bald heads, and were strumming guitars.

They were bizarrely lit by carried candles which jerked rhythmically as they pranced along. Jesus Christ, it was nighttime!

"Wait...how long have I been asleep?" I gasped, sitting up and stretching out my arms.

Cleve was tending a small fire beside us.

"Hey, Suzy," he smiled gently at me, offering me a stick upon which he'd been roasting a hunk of meat. "I bet you're hungry."

I snatched it and gulped it down, grateful.

"What is that?" I asked. "It's delicious!"

"I caught a chicken," he matter-of-factly replied. "It probably got lost from a nearby farm. The poor thing was terrified by all this upheaval going on around it. So I put it out of its misery with my Bowie knife and butchered it. I already had my fill. Not bad, considering."

I was violating my eating standards "big time," not only eating meat but wild-caught, not the way God intended: neatly packaged from a grocery store!

Ah well, protein was protein.

"Oh, Jesus Christ," I groaned. "Did I sleep through the whole day?"

"Yep," he acknowledged, "—all day long and half the night. It's past midnight now. *Creedence Clearwater Revival* is onstage. They just finished singing 'Proud Mary'...intriguing lyrics."

"But—the bomb! And didn't you say you needed to file your next report to your newspaper?"

"I wrote up my next article while you were sleeping," he nodded thoughtfully, holding up his thick notebook. "And, yes, we should work our way back to the Stage so I can get to the Press Tent. Though

I doubt the bomb even exists, we can still keep our eyes open for anything suspicious."

"Oh man," I groaned. "I missed all the concerts today."

"You needed the sleep. But I have to admit there's been some intriguing music today. I've also done some additional recorded interviews while you were sleeping. Did you know that the Hare Krishna folks' main message is 'Peace and Love,' just like for the Festival? I'm surprised there aren't more of them here. But the motorcycle gangs seem less than impressed by their simple chants, choosing to taunt or attack them."

"That doesn't surprise me," I nodded, "the Krishna seem trapped in the same type of thinking as Monks doing Gregorian chants a thousand years ago: repetitive, simple, few or no harmonies, and largely unaccompanied. In other words, for today's sophisticated musical audience it's massively boring."

"Regardless, I'm now giving equal time to the inspiring words and occasional amazing instrumentation of the performers. Objectively they should count for as much as the clear negatives of the Festival."

"Hey, that's real open-minded of you, big guy. I'm proud of you!"

He grinned in a boyish way I found charming.

"But back to the supposed bomb," he continued, "if it does exist I fear we're not going to find it. We looked in all the obvious places and nothing out-of-place jumped out at us. So we might as well just enjoy the positives of the remainder of the Festival and hope for the best."

He looked uncertain, like he had some other option in mind.

"What are you thinking?" I asked, still busily gnawing all the last morsels of meat off the chicken bones.

"Well...we *could* beat a hasty retreat and find a ride out of this hell-hole," he stated thoughtfully. "What do you think, Suzy? After I file my present article I'll have completed my minimal duty on this assignment. Anything more is just 'icing on the cake.' We could leave all this crap behind us, 'riding off into the sunset.' What do *you* think?"

Ah, he'd turned my own words back on myself! He was a tricky hunk for sure. In fact, he was playing right to my deepest emotions. If I were to "give in" to my genetic imperatives, he was offering what I most desired...perhaps. Here was a thoughtful, talented, handsome hunk of a man offering to sweep me off my feet.

Isn't that the fairytale ending all young girls yearn for?

"Well..." I paused, seriously considering his offer to join him in a strategic retreat. My immediate reaction was to argue against him wanting to prematurely leave the Festival. But I guess I'd also accomplished my Mission: moderating, through him, the radical reaction to Woodstock which according to the dead time-traveler began the Phoenix movement. Perhaps what I'd done was sufficient. And if, as he reasonably concluded, the "bomb" threat was likely an empty threat why obsess on it? The fact was I was stranded there in 1969, probably for the rest of my life. I was very tempted to take Cleve up on his offer to "leave all the crap behind" and "live happily-ever-after" wrapped up in his seductively strong arms.

After all, I had no way to get back to the future. My mission was likely complete. So why not just take up a new life in a "simpler" time making my own "peace and love"?

It was so *very* tempting...

"No!" I snapped at him. Then, less harshly, I continued... "I've seen firsthand what terrorist bombs can do at a concert, Cleve. I can't have this on my conscience as well. If *two hundred thousand* people die here then *that alone* will for sure trigger the formation of Phoenix. We've got to continue the search to the last possible moment. We've still got a full day left to find the bomb, assuming it is set to go off when the most people are present toward the end of the Festival."

"Just what is this 'Phoenix' thing?" he mildly replied, stirring the small fire. "That time-traveling lady seemed to think I helped initiate it. I take it that it's some sort of anti-music organization in the future?"

I nodded, moving closer to the small fire. I was getting chilled in the night air. I now missed the blazing heat of the sun.

"They're a collection of radically conservative religious groups that somehow acquires terrible software that can't be defended against. The whole Internet structure is in danger, paralyzing corporations, militaries, and nations alike."

"Uhm, setting aside I don't know what some of those words mean—what do those Phoenix people want?"

Ah...we were back to that key question yet again: *"What do you want?"* It seemed that if we could only probe our deepest motivations, understand our own minds, we'd have powerful insight into taking charge of our own destinies.

"Their first demand is to cease all forms of Music. I know, it sounds crazy. But when I got thrown into the past they were well on the way to taking over the governments of the world to impose *all* their restrictive religious rules upon society. Then that 'Time-Keeper' who tried to kill me said something about a 'Commissioner' who is pulling *their* strings and wants to advance her schedule for subverting Phoenix and..."

"I don't think we can believe much of what Sanako said."

I stopped speaking, puzzled.

How did Cleve know her name? *She never told me what her name was!* Did he somehow know her from before she attacked me that last time? Or, more likely, was she not quite dead and spoke to him after he hauled her body away?

But even that explanation didn't make any sense. She was clearly dead. His shot went right through the middle of her chest. She bled-out on the floor—a massive amount of blood that I had to clean up!

Or did she mutter her name and I just missed it?

"Oh? And why is that?" I responded, my suspicions again fully engaged. I could have just asked him, but that would have revealed my mistrust.

"I examined her 'gun' as I was burying her body in the soft soil underneath the main stage."

"What did you find?" I replied, careful not to confront him about knowing the Time-Keeper's name.

"It was just a fancied-up, military-issue 'Taser'. It wasn't some futuristic energy weapon at all."

I frowned, warming my hands at the fire. *Oh, Christ, why is he making it so hard for me to trust him?*—I groaned to myself. I *wanted* to trust his gorgeous ass! But what he said didn't sound right at all. I hadn't felt any barbs sticking into me or seen any electrical wires. And the *energy cloud* that enveloped me was far more than just an electrical shock jolting my eyeballs. It was almost a living entity unto itself.

And if I remembered correctly, the Taser wasn't completed until the early 1970's.

"It's a military weapon?" I cautiously replied.

"Well, some civilians are working on a version that police can use as a nonlethal alternative to guns," he answered me. "But the military research arm is far ahead of the civilians. I'm pretty sure her story of 'time-traveling' and a 'parallel dimension' are just obscuring lies from a *federal military agent* sent here to spy on or sabotage this Festival of anti-war hippies."

"What, she was 'lying'—like *me?*"

"Uhm, I didn't mean..."

"Sorry, I appreciate your humoring me," I hastened to add, pausing to think it through, "—but even if she *was* lying through her teeth, Cleve, her *threat* could still be true. Wouldn't the F.B.I., C.I.A., or military *want* to disrupt this 'subversive' event?"

"Suzy..." he said as he took me by my shoulders and looked me straight in my eyes, "—despite the common notion that us veterans who went to Vietnam are 'baby-killers', we're *not* murderers. The government would not under any circumstances sanction killing its own citizens, especially its children."

I choked back a response citing the Kent State massacre of college kids by armed National Guard troops. That awful event hadn't occurred yet, but would fatally smear the war effort in less than a year. Plus there were many other examples into the future of governmental officials condoning or participating in violent suppression. *Anyone* was capable of *anything* under permissive conditions, including governments.

"Can I see it?"

"What?"

"Her gun."

I half expected him to make some excuse, like he lost the gun or buried it with her body. Instead, he reached into his shoulder pack and drew out the heavy black weapon. He put it in my hands.

"It's warm," I noted, surprised. It wasn't the cold metal weapon I expected. And it was subtly *pulsing*, as if it were alive.

"It's still got a powerful charge," he replied, looking down at the ground. He now seemed to be deliberately not meeting my eyes. "Zapping you didn't drain its batteries."

It didn't look like any military gun I'd ever seen. Superficially it did resemble a handgun. But it didn't appear to have an exit hole for a bullet, just a small silvery metal plate. I supposed the plate might move aside to allow a bullet to emerge. I saw an obvious safety lock on its top, a transparent snap-over cover protecting a small switch that flicked from one to five stars. It was set on one star.

"Can I keep it on me? It sounds like a good defensive weapon for me to have if there are more of those agents and I should get separated from you and..."

He snatched it out of my hands, sticking it back into his bag.

"Sorry, Suzy," he firmly rejected my request. His voice was steely. His dark eyeglasses seemed alien, chilling. "It's too dangerous to be in untrained hands. If accidently set to a higher discharge it wouldn't just 'tase' people, it'd kill them stone dead."

"Oh..." I gulped, relenting. "Secret military stuff..." I verbally agreed, though I knew better.

"Should we get back to the Stage?" he asked. "If you need to relieve yourself, there are some good bushes here by the lakeshore. The rest of the ground in the Festival is rapidly turning into raw sewage. The port-a-potties are too few and too far away."

"Sure," I agreed, walking out into the darkness as he tamped out and buried the small fire pit.

That wasn't a secret 1969 military weapon. It was from the future. And "Cleve Hartley" was lying to me.

It was much more difficult returning to the stage then when we last left. The crowded natural bowl was now packed solid with humanity. Cleve told me he heard that the roads into the Festival were all shut down. Not only had the massive influx of cars caused huge backups, clogging and preventing forward movement, but the police were actually turning late arrivals around.

The viewing area of the natural bowl was a sea of people jammed in elbow-to-elbow—swaying, dancing, and singing like a giant living organism.

We had to fight our way forward inch by inch, alternatively apologizing and threatening people to get them to move aside.

As we finally approached the now doubly heavily guarded entrance gate, *Janis Joplin* was onstage, singing a fervent take of "*Try Just a Little Bit Harder.*"

I was in awe.

Janis was my childhood singing heroine even though she died long before I was born. She rose from nothing, wasn't particularly cute or pretty (taunted in high school as being a "boy"), had a harsh, rough voice, drank heavily and smoked like a chimney, took about every addicting drug known to man, and died young of a heroin overdose. And yet she turned her problems into assets, pouring her heart out through her song: becoming a distinctive and unique performing sensation.

Her iconic brand of wailing/screaming blues echoed down through Time to me.

And here she was, alive and at the peak of her career!

Up on the stage, Janis was lit by alternating blue and orange spotlights, belting out a tune backed up by a diverse band which included harmony singers and horns. It was inspired and soulful *thunder* as she writhed back and forth on the stage, laying out her bleeding heart for the audience to poke and ponder.

In turn, the hundreds of thousands in the audience sang along with her as she screeched "TRY! TRY JUST A LITTLE BIT HARDER!"...repeating that theme over and over, like a mantra.

Cleve squirmed into his denim jacket, flipping the removable hood up over his head. I now knew he did that because he didn't want stage personnel spotting his "Country Joe" disguise.

"*How is that awful noise even called music?*" Cleve yelled into my ear. He was holding me close against his side as we fought the last few remaining feet forward.

The music was so overwhelming I couldn't even hear the rapturous singing of those closest to me. Lucky Cleve's voice was so deep it easily penetrated the din.

"*It's a fusion of classical blues, rock, and pop!*" I shouted back to him over the roar of the massive crowd. "*It's brilliant!*"

"*All I hear is mind-numbing screeches!*" he shouted back.

"*Block out the instruments! Listen to her voice!*"

He hugged me close, putting his head flat against mine.

"I'm trying! But all I hear is a *scream*, like a wounded screech-owl!"

"Yes! Exactly! That's what it is! It's a *screech of agony* because she's losing the love of her life! And she knows that if only he/she were to try *just a little bit harder* they could succeed! But he or she is either unable or unwilling to go those extra inches! For the lack of just a *little* bit more effort they are losing something precious! And it's driving her insane!"

"Ah..." he grunted as the roiling crowd right up next to the fence slammed us one way then the other, "—I think I see it I still don't understand it completely. But, yes...it *is* brilliant!"

I grinned to myself, letting him pull my entire body even closer to him. Whoever he truly was, I was finally getting through to him.

Having made it back through security, yet again—as best we could—we thoroughly searched the stage and backstage areas. Cleve again crawled beneath the stage platform. We sneaked through the associated structures, continuing on through the night. Several times we had to make up quick stories to not get thrown out or arrested. But between my Performer Pass-fueled "lost earring" story and his valid on-the-spot recordings of "how's it going" interviews, validated by his Press Pass, we kept out of trouble.

But we found nothing suspicious. As far as we could tell there was no bomb. However, a nagging thought was knocking at my brain: *my own experience* in the far, distant future.

The main blasts that mutilated and mangled my audience at the Hollywood Bowl came not from the stage but from *within* the nearby, strategically placed Jumbotron screens.

"I think I know where the bomb is," I said to Cleve as we sat to the side of the main stage, exhausted.

"We've looked everywhere it could be," he shrugged, his big shoulders swaying to the hypnotic music.

The Who was just getting to the end of a giant set of twenty-three songs, a two-hour performance. It was almost 6:00 AM in the morning, Sunday August 17th, 1969. They were singing a rousing, frenetic take of "*See Me, Feel Me*" starting off slow and mellow, then progressively accelerating into booming "*In you...on you*" verses describing the glory of the interaction of the singer with his/her lover.

"Not quite everywhere," I began to explain.

"*Shhhhh...*" he silenced me, placing a finger on my lips.

Cleve's arm rested over my shoulders, drawing me closer. As the music crescendoed, he used his free hand to gently turn my face to his.

"I get it," he whispered.

He kissed me.

It wasn't a light, friendly kiss. It was a deep, passionate meeting of our lips and souls.

I closed my eyes, mentally seeing *brilliant fireworks* bursting across an alien horizon.

At that moment I would have done anything for him. If he wanted to "ride off into the sunset" I would have happily become his saddle or even his horse.

"Suzette! We've got to get you into costume!"

I jerked away from Cleve, momentarily bewildered.

"Huh?"

"You're Suzette Kingly, right?—sent here by the studio to be a stand-in, if necessary, for Grace Slick?"

A chubby woman was pointing to my badge where bold letters proclaimed my name—SUZY; and group—AIRPLANE.

Other stagehands were standing around observing. Several security guards lounged nearby.

"Uh, yes...that's me."

"Good! They're on next. We've got to get you ready to fill in for Grace in case she can't continue. She's got a bad case of the flu. She thinks she'll make it through the set. But the organizers can't have her out there on stage puking her guts out! Everything's being recorded on film for a documentary. You've got to be ready to take over for her at a moment's notice. The studio assured us you know all the songs they're doing this morning. That's right, isn't it?"

I smiled at the nice lady. *Of course* I knew all of Grace Slick's iconic numbers. I could do them in my sleep. From childhood, along with Janis Joplin, she'd been one of my top female rock heroines. But

I never dreamed I might have the chance to do those numbers at Woodstock.

"I'm *ready!*" I proclaimed, jumping to my feet doing my best impression of SpongeBob SquarePants.

Lucky for me SpongeBob wouldn't appear on TV until thirty years in the future. My pose wasn't that good of an impression.

"Great!" she answered equally enthusiastic, as she dragged me away.

I gave Cleve a rueful smile.

In reply, he gave me two "thumbs up."

Wow. At that moment I really loved that conniving lying man—whoever he was.

"That's just amazing, Ms. Kingly," the chubby make-up woman, Meg, complimented me.

We were looking into a full-length mirror in the cramped trailer. Peering back at me from the other side of the mirror I saw a slim woman with long dark brown fluffy hair (an excellent wig over a bald cap), wearing a low-slung white sleeveless shirt with long tassels at the arms and waist, plus matching white pants. My eyes were made up with natural-looking dark highlights. I was the spitting image of one of the reigning rock female superstars in the world. If you didn't look too close or know Grace personally you'd never guess it was me and not her.

"Nice work," I complimented Meg back.

"Let's get out there. They're about to go onstage!"

A number of stagehands and fellow performers waved at me as we made our way, apparently convinced I was Grace. I waved back, not wanting to disappoint them. I was enjoying my "star-turn" whether or not I was actually needed onstage.

"Better put on this raincoat," Meg said, holding out a black slicker.

"Right," I nodded, slipping it on and pulling the hood over my head. I wasn't really a 1960's rock star, just a backup in case I was needed. Only if I actually went onto the stage would I need to pretend to be Grace. There couldn't be two of us there!

And then we were standing in the wings as *Jefferson Airplane* launched into their iconic set, which would last for better than an hour and a half. I looked around for Cleve but didn't spot his also-hooded hunky body. Likely he was down in the Press Tent, filing his latest article with the New York Times.

It was 8:00 in the morning, Sunday August 17th, 1969. The huge crowd was exhausted from lasting through the prior night's incredible concerts. But they were still responsive and appreciative.

Everything went fine until Airplane left the stage after their tenth song. It was the encore break, after which they'd be "forced" back onstage by the thunderous applause, finishing with three more songs.

"You're on!" Meg breathless informed me.

"What?"

"Grace says she can't return for the next song, too sick! She's throwing up. Maybe if she gets better she can return in a few minutes. You've got to sub for her until then!"

Oh, Christ! This was real! I wished Grace all the best, but I felt a burst of adrenalin at the idea of actually going onstage at Woodstock. Lucky for me the next song didn't feature me. All I had to do was wiggle around prettily beating on a tambourine.

I joined the band as they broke out in a powerful rendition of *"Come back Baby."* They were so deep into their playing and singing I don't think they even noticed a slightly different version of Grace onstage with them. It was exhilarating! I'd seen it and the next two songs many times in historic videos. I knew every move and word that Grace performed in the songs. All I had to do was replicate her words and motions...

And then "Come Back Baby" was finished and we started the famous *"White Rabbit"* song. It was one of my all-time favorite songs, ever! The psychedelic, hypnotic chords and words were the inspiration of my future "Down the Rabbit Hole" montage for my Album Six World Tour.

Suddenly in a panic I looked over at Meg, hoping Grace had recovered. She slowly shook her head in the negative.

I'm on for real!

In the warm morning sunlight I took the microphone off the stand and launched into Grace's famous solo number: *"One pill makes you larger...and one makes you small...and the ones that your mom gives you don't do anything at all...go ask Alice...when she's ten feet tall..."*

My voice blasted out through giant speakers to a half a million fans. The words came without conscious thought since I knew the song so well. I belted it out in an exact duplicate of Grace's powerful unique voice.

"...*feed your head! Feed your head!"* I concluded as the gigantic crowd of pot and acid-heads erupted in approval.

"Thank you! *Whooo!"* I smiled back at them.

The band then broke into the final, military-banging tones of "The House at Pooneil Corners," their last song. I saw Meg beckoning at me from offstage so I slipped into the crowd as the real Grace Slick emerged, giving me a brief "thumbs-up" before seamlessly taking over.

I ducked into my black raincoat hood, saw the handsome head of Cleve over to the side, and ran over to him. He was grinning from ear to ear, his big mustache flared out. And for once his dark eyeglasses were off, letting me see his eyes!

I caught him up in a huge hug, practically lifting his muscular body off the wooden deck.

"Did you see me? Did you see me?" I laughed. "I performed on-stage at Woodstock!"

But he didn't hug me back. Instead, he seemed confused by my exuberant embrace. I looked into his frowning blue eyes. Something was *different*...? For one thing, his bandana wasn't white, but pink.

We both simultaneously blurted out: "You're not Cleve!" and "You're not Grace!"

Oh, boy. I'd really goofed up. In my enthusiasm I'd hugged the *real* Country Joe who happened to be standing there.

"Oh, sorry," I apologized. "I thought you were someone else."

"Hey, no problem, baby," he grinned at me. It was a sexy grin, to be sure, but not the thoughtful, penetrating scrutiny of Cleve Hartley. "Yep, I heard Grace brought a backup," he continued. "I'm glad she's able to finish her set. Saw you out there. You did a bang-up job on White Rabbit, super good singing!"

"Thanks!"

"You look parched. Here, have some juice."

He handed me a glass jar filled with what looked like orange juice. I hadn't thought I'd exerted that much energy, but apparently the morning sun plus the adrenalin had really drained me. I was completely dehydrated.

"Oh, that's great," I thanked him, upending and draining down the whole contents.

"Hey, take it easy, baby. That's potent stuff!"

"It hit the spot."

"Maybe we can..."

"Gotta go!" I brightly answered, running offstage back to the trailer where I'd left my regular clothes. I quickly changed, shook out my natural hair, and went out in search for Cleve. I was sure I'd find him in the press tent.

But I was wrong.

"Cleve! Cleve Hartley! He sort of looks like Country Joe McDonald. He's a big guy with long dark hair, a handlebar mustache, and wears a white bandana across his forehead. He's a freelancer here on assignment from the New York Times. You're *sure* he hasn't been by recently?"

The tent was crowded. I was speaking to a very tired-looking fellow at a reception desk. His name tag identified him as "Bernard."

"Look, Miss, I'm from the Times myself. I never heard of this guy. Maybe he was pulling your leg. A lot of kids here claim to be reporters looking for an interview, trying to get into the pants of pretty young girls like you."

"He isn't a kid and he has a Press Pass and he hasn't tried to 'get into my pants'!"

He shrugged. I tried to focus on his features. But he looked blurry, out-of-focus. Something was wrong with my eyes.

"Well, I don't know what to tell you. I suppose he could be a freelancer I just haven't met yet. But he hasn't been in here. All the outgoing calls are logged and signed for. There's no one of that name on our time sheets."

"I...well...ok..." I gulped, feeling very woozy. I started to turn away and felt myself falling face-first toward the floor...

"Stop struggling! You'll be ok. Calm down. Now, just what did you take?"

A giant WHITE RABBIT was trying to drag me into a black hole in the ground!

Strange towering creatures are reaching down from the sky, digging their claws into my naked body, trying to keep me from escaping the surface hell into the cold, beckoning depths! Say what?

Wait...was that real? No...just hallucinations.

My vision was still blurry. I felt nauseous. I was somewhere else than the press tent. I was hot. I was in another crowded tent. People lay stretched-out all around me on jammed-together mats and cots.

"What?"

"I'm Dr. Abruzzi. You're in our medical facility, at least for what it's worth. It's just a med-tent. Some of your friends brought you here when you O.D.'ed. As you're starting to breathe smoothly now, I assume you're coming down from your high. I'd like to know for my records what you've been on."

"On? Drugs? But I didn't take anything..." Uh, oh—that orange juice! It must have had something in it. "But someone *did* give me some orange juice that tasted funny...?"

"Alright then, I'll put you down as another 'accidental' LSD patient. You just rest, little lady. When you feel better you can leave on your own."

"Ok...thanks."

The "freak out tent" was nauseatingly ripe with sweat, urine, and puke. I heard a woman crying in a corner nearby my cot. On a whim I slipped off my cot and crawled over to her. She had her head buried in her arms. One hand was wrapped up in the slack big hand of a tall young black man who lay on a cot. He was a skinny guy with medium-dark skin, a short afro, and a pencil-thin mustache that drooped down to his lower lips. He wore a pair of tight-fitting blue jeans. He was shirtless. He lay motionless, staring up at the ceiling. I feared he was dead.

"Are you ok?" I asked her, somehow feeling a deep connection with the sobbing girl. I guess the LSD was still messing with my brain. She felt like an extension of me.

She looked up at me. Her scrunched-up face was buried in a mass of frizzy hair. I recognized her. She was *Janis Joplin*. And I now also recognized the young black man on the cot. It was *Jimi Hendrix*. I smelled the strong aroma of alcohol on Janis' breath. But she looked so loopy I figured she was taking something else as well. Regardless, she was clearly alive. I was also relieved to see that Hendrix was steadily breathing. His glazed expression was likely due to him coming down from a similar acid trip as I'd just been on.

"I...*love*...you guys," I choked out, knowing that in a year they'd both be dead. "And I don't want to lose your magic!"

"It's just...heroin," Janis gasped, her head lolling. "I can handle it...I'm tough."

Apparently she'd mistaken me for a nurse. Good. Maybe I could leave an impression on her!

I hauled back and *slapped* her as hard as I could across her squarish pug face.

Lucky the outside music was booming loud enough to cover the slap or I'd been tossed out on my rear.

Instead, she just looked at me, startled.

"Whenever you want to throw away your talent, your music, your genius for some stupid drug—feel *this!*" I barked into her ear.

I groped in my pocket for something to get her to recall that painful "slap." The only thing I could come up with was my *lucky marbles*. I shoved my *catseye* in front of her reddened eyes.

"Take this! Never lose it! Always keep it with you! Whenever you feel weak, just roll it around in your hand. It's a *magic marble!* It'll help you 'see' what's most important."

"It's...an *eye*," she softly replied, snuffling, taking it in her trembling hand and staring at it.

"It will help you see the Truth inside your own soul."

"I just...want to be happy," she mumbled.

I crawled off the floor and physically sat upon the chest of Jimi Hendrix. I slapped him in his face repeatedly until his eyes focused on me. Again I told him my "magic" story, placing my swirling rainbow "onion skin" marble in his dark-skinned hand.

He held it up in apparent wonderment to a shaft of sunlight falling through a torn slit in the tent above us.

All the colors of the rainbow streamed from the marble, twisting and interacting as he rotated it in his dark-skinned fingers.

"Hey, get off of him!" I heard a loud shout as a group of official-looking roadies streamed into the tent, pushing me aside. "Where you been, man? We've got to get you ready for your set. The organizers gonna have you close-out the entire festival!"

They hustled him away, apparently not seeing or caring that Janis was still huddled on the floor, her head ducked into her arms.

I embraced her again in a strong hug.

"Remember!" I grated into her ear. "Don't forget! It's *magic!*"

"I...won't," her small, childish voice, so different from her onstage screeches, answered me.

"I've got to go," I said, blinking my eyes to clear them. My un-scheduled "trip" was fast fading away. What time was it? Oh, Jesus—by the angle of the sun outside the tent flap it was late afternoon. And dark storm clouds were again gathering in the sky. I'd been "tripped out" all through Sunday!

"Where...are you...going?" Janis sniffled, now smiling up at me. It was a radiant smile. She seemed at peace.

"I need to find a man and a bomb."

"Sounds like a groovy combo," she whispered. "Good luck."

"Thanks, Janis—you too..."

I managed to get to my feet and stagger out of the evil-smelling tent. Outside I was dismayed to discover the same as inside, but even worse. The putrid smells of urine, rotting food, human sweat, and curdled mud were overwhelming. Worse yet, the sky had closed over above, dark clouds again creating an ominous gloom. Big raindrops were spattering down. Then the sky lit up as *lightning* flashed.

The music on the stage stopped as natural THUNDER took its place.

I realized then and there that *heaven* and *hell* are but two sides of the same coin.

Chapter 18

THE BOMB

__Let it burn__, let it burn, let it burn
Yellow and orange and red and blue
A clean flame without any pain or hurt
Showing who's real or fine or fake fool
Exploding all the stinky, slimy turds
Taking your heart to school

A cleansing bath of sizzling lava
From a towering, red-hot volcano
Erupting-out ash and fire into the sky
Bellowing black clouds ten thousand feet high
Shocking, killing, blasting, and healing
A slash in the earth that's fine

Clean out my soul, oh heavenly flames
Evaporating my regrets and shame
Until I arise from my own funeral pyre
Leaving behind my ugly, smoldering sin
Stretching my mighty wings to soar yet higher
Reborn as a screeching Phoenix!

The Suzette Anthology, Lyrics 18

I searched all through the rest of the day for Cleve. He was nowhere to be found. I went all through the backstage area, asking everyone. Then, in desperation, I went back out into the audience.

As the storm finally passed I continued asking and hunting into the night. All around me, *hundreds of fires* burned on the slopes.

The hippies had finally learned how to keep warm. Since this was the last night of the festival, anything not nailed down became fair game for fuel. It was surrealistic. The dancing, partying crowd became a fantastic portrait of every type of human *lit by fire!*

It was nearly 4:00 in the morning of Monday August 18th, 1969. *Crosby, Stills, and Nash* were singing the quite appropriate "Sea of Madness."

Exhausted, hungry, and sleepy I stumbled up to a campfire of buzzed-out prancing teens, slumping down close to their red flames, warming myself.

I felt a *wet nose* shoved into an armpit.

Laughing, I saw a loose dog nuzzling close to me. He was a male.

"Hey, boy," I greeted him, scratching him behind his ears. I recognized him as a Scottish Deerhound. He had a slender, long body. His head was narrow, with a pointed nose. His shaggy gray hair drooped down across his body. He was matted with mud, wet and scraggly.

"Did you lose your master?" I asked him.

Urf!—he greeted me, looking over at the closest tower. Ah, yes, a fire was there but with no one around it. Had his group moved on and left him behind? Startled, I realized that the crush of massed humanity was thinning. Many were not waiting until the official end of the festival to depart. Perhaps two thirds of the huge audience had already departed.

Tower...tower...was I forgetting something?

"Oh, Christ—the bomb!" I grated, shocked. I'd gotten so fixated on finding Cleve I'd forgotten about the bomb that was supposed to kill 200,000 people! But then I relaxed...

"It must have been just an empty threat by that 'Sanako' woman," I told the dog, "There are probably less than 50,000 people left. That's still a huge crowd, but not enough to fulfill her vicious prophecy."

Urf!

"Yep, glad you agree with me. Do you have a name? You don't have a dog collar. Did you lose it? I guess you better stick with me until we find your owner. And what shall I call you? Oh, how about 'Scotty', since you are a *Scottish* Deerhound?"

But I already had a friend with that name...

I was struck by a vision of a young, longhaired Native-American kid in the Park at Sulphur. It seemed ages ago I'd talked with Scotty Yanash. Would I ever see him again? It was doubtful, as I had no way to get back to the future. And if what Sanako claimed was even partially true, the timeline may have *shifted* such that I'd not even recognize the future. That "Scotty's" whole life may have been erased!

I shook my head. Trying to calculate "what if's" as future potential realities was getting me nowhere. And just where the hell was Cleve, anyway? Did he get "cold feet" after passionately kissing me, running away? Wouldn't that be just like a man—leading me on until he'd sparked real feelings in my heart, only to then *dump* me.

"*You're* a man, Scotty," I addressed the sweet-eyed animal with his head resting on my arm, "—so can you tell me why Cleve would run away, not even filing his second-day story? Also it seems he must have not logged in for his first story or didn't file it at all. Was everything he told me a lie? Oh, hell!" I grated, tears unexpectedly bursting from my eyes.

I didn't want the dog to see me cry, but he seemed sympathetic.

"Alright, then, Scotty," I firmly told him, standing up as I angrily wiped my tears away. "You wanted to go over to that tower. That's actually where I'd put a bomb if I wanted to do the maximum damage to the crowd. It's the last place I haven't searched. I mean, I looked up at it, but didn't actually climb up to the loudspeaker and searchlight complex. This time I'm going up to its very top."

So close to the end of the Festival, the guards were exhausted. The crewmembers and roadies were likewise glassy-eyed. I doubted anyone would stop me from climbing. Indeed, a dozen other audience members were already lounging up on its iron girders.

I walked away from the fire, Scotty trailing along obediently behind me.

It took longer than I expected to wind my way through the crowd and piled-up trash heaps to get to the tower. But I made it, carefully climbing my way up to its very top. Then I prodded and pried my way throughout all the electronics as the main speaker simultaneously blasted super-loud into my ears.

By now the sun was up. It was getting towards 11:00 in the morning. I was so weak from hunger and exhaustion I could barely keep myself from toppling off the top of the tower.

But from there I had a magnificent view of the vast Woodstock encampment. Jimi Hendrix and his band, *Gypsy Sun and Rainbows*, were on the stage, playing brilliantly. He was the last performer. He was just launching into his bone-jarring, ear-blasting, mind-twisting, totally original and dazzling guitar rendition of "*The Star-Spangled Banner.*"

I was happy to see he'd recovered from his bout in the "freak-out tent." His iconic presentation was mesmerizing. The giant speakers amplified his stunningly unique guitar vibrations all across the remnants of the Festival. His bright blue jeans contrasted dazzlingly in the morning sun with his red bandana. His white electric guitar flashed like a weapon as his fingers caressed it, seducing it with expert ease. The long blue tassels on his white shirt flopped and flowed around him as he twisted and gyrated, lost in the magic of his squealing music.

Far below I saw "Scotty" patiently waiting for me at the base of the tower. He was sitting on his haunches, his red tongue hanging out of his half-opened mouth. Now if that faithful dog could only have been Cleve, things would be great! It'd be the perfect ending to a magnificent Festival to climb down and be embraced in his strong arms.

"It's done," I sighed to myself. I marveled at all that had happened to me in my trip to Woodstock. "Maybe I stopped Phoenix, who knows. At least there's no bomb. That would have been a real 'bummer'...getting blasted into atoms. That's not how I'd want the timeline to be altered. Hah!"

As the brutally *reverberating, screeching, howling* tones from Hendrix continued blasting from the speaker beside me I paused to consider the panorama. I saw below me a sea of *mud, trash,* and human *crap.* But high above this massive garbage dump floated the most "mind-blowing" music of the entire festival: a testament to the genius of Jimi Hendrix. The contrast against the earthly refuse of humanity could not have been greater. And beside the stage *helicopters* were rising, carrying away the best musicians in the world.

It looked like a war zone.

But the "survivors" were cheering and dancing.

"*Play* it, Jimi!" I yelled out across the expanse. I knew no one would hear my feeble unamplified voice, but I joined the jumping, cheering, ecstatic people below anyway. "Play it!"

His Music capping off the previous fabulous performers was the *triumph* of Creativity versus the *devastation* of Destruction. It said we humans could rise to heights unimaginable, transcending the mud and dirt of our origins.

It was a fitting anthem for the 1960's: overcoming war, social upheaval, threat of nuclear Armageddon, and mindless drug use for a trip to the Stars!

The Woodstock performances concluded, with nothing else to do, I joined the random groups of civic-minded lingerers who were shuffling about the slopes picking up the massive amount of waste, stuffing it all into thousands of plastic garbage bags.

Scotty roamed beside me, catching up a random bit of bread or hamburger for food.

I was getting hungry myself. What I wouldn't give for a plain bean burrito with extra onion, tomatoes, and lettuce. Yum!

But the dog had no such problem, gobbling up this or that discarded morsel. He was great at finding hidden "treasures," hah!

He...*wait!* A chilling thought occurred to me. There was *one last place* to look for that mythical bomb. Cleve had crawled under the stage. I had looked underneath the platform several times from all angles, using a flashlight. But hadn't Cleve said he'd buried Sanako's body there? If so, where was the fresh mound of dirt? I didn't remember seeing anything that could have been a shallow grave. But, then again, that was why he stuck her dead body there, right? With all the deep construction necessary to hold the heavy stage, a small bit of additional disturbance would be invisible.

Invisible...

"Scotty," I addressed my new canine friend, "I think you've given me yet another idea."

Urf?—he looked at me expectantly, wagging his tail.

One more look...one more search...I *hated* not completing any task I'd set for myself. I had never actually crawled *under* the stage myself. I just trusted Cleve when he said nothing was there. And now that I knew he was a lying rat who'd walked out on me, maybe I'd better do an in-person final check. What did I have to lose? A bit more mud wouldn't hurt me.

I snagged a flashlight. Making sure no one noticed me I ducked down into the supporting maze of timbers beneath the stage.

"You scare off any rattlesnakes," I sternly instructed Scotty, who came right along with me.

Woof!

Ah, he knew about snakes. Good. If I came upon one it wouldn't be as simple as in the snake-pit in Fiji. In the clutter and confusion under the stage I might put a hand on a rattlesnake and be bit, the poor critter thinking I was attacking it. If that happened I'd likely be dead in minutes.

Christ, what was I doing crawling under there anyway? The Festival was over. I could stop worrying about a bomb!

But then in my flashlight beam in the darkness beneath the stage I saw a *hazy sphere*...

"What the heck?"

I crawled closer to that area which was nestled against a concrete slab. It looked like undisturbed dirt. But an unexplained haze hovered in the air. I poked through some sort of barrier and found myself on top of...

—a clear, plastic canopy!

"Oh, boy," I gulped.

Right beside me, Scotty *whined.*

I "thumped" the round plastic covering and it rose up, pushing me to the side. Inside I saw a seat, instruments, and Sanako's black futuristic gun...*pulsing* a deep cherry red!

Arf! Arf! Arf! Arf!—Scotty frantically barked down at it, scampering around the edges of the raised plastic canopy.

What was it that Sanako told me? She said that the bomb had the yield of a *small tactical nuclear bomb.*

This small, round craft hidden and buried beneath the stage must be her time-ship! And how had her gun gotten here? The last I saw it was in Cleve's shoulder bag...

But, no time to figure it all out—I had to take action!

"Oh, Christ, Scotty," I whispered to the dog, feeling the heat radiating from the handgun and hearing its high-pitched *whine!* "That thing's going off any second. It's been building up to an overload all this time. And if it's a nuke, then it'll take out not only the remaining crowd but *all the departing people* jammed into the roads and cars *surrounding* the immediate Woodstock area!"

A nuclear blast would easily incinerate 200,000 people.

"Beat it, pooch! Save yourself!" I said, shoving the dog away as I swung my legs over the edge and dropped down next to the glowing gun.

But the dog dived in with me.

"Oh hell," I grated, trying to figure out how to control the time-ship while roughly shoving the dog to the side. Scotty whined as he *slammed* into a panel...yelping in pain!

He was holding a hurt paw out to me, but there wasn't time to tend to his wounds.

In front of me I suddenly saw a *holographic projection* spring up. It displayed a bewildering set of intersecting colored lines. Scotty had triggered something in his bumping-about.

A *red dot* was flashing rapidly.

"Ah...that must be us," I pointed to Scotty. "You brought up a time-chart! And those lines diverging from it, the green ones, they must be destinations. Damn, this is amazing!"

Scotty growled at them, baring his teeth.

"If the thickness and brightness of the line correlates with their probability," I guessed, "—then I should choose the thickest one."

I stuck my hand into the 3-dimensional array, grasping for the brightest one...

But the squirming dog bumped me and my fingers ran through a *fainter* offshoot as the canopy flopped down hard over my head, startling me. Then I and the ship immediately *faded out...*

"*Holy Crap!*" I screamed.

I found myself upside-down *a thousand feet* above the Woodstock site! The hinged canopy fell outward. I glimpsed far below the distant stage, slopes, tents and trailers, crowded roads, and further green pastures and woods. Grabbing at a seat I just barely managed to not tumble out of the lurching vehicle.

"Hold on, dog!" I shouted, wrapping my legs around him to keep him from falling out.

But the *red-glowing gun* tumbled unhindered past me and the flopping canopy, plunging down toward the site below...

—and as we spiraled up into the sky, I saw the site of a generation's ode to *Peace and Love* instantly turned into a *fused sea of molten glass* as the bomb *DETONATED* and a blazing MUSHROOM CLOUD erupted upward. It followed us up into the sky.

The craft righted itself just as the cloud slowed its ascent, the canopy again slamming shut above me. I saw a latch and frantically synched it down. Peering through the canopy—as the craft flopped back and forth—I marveled at the mushroom cloud down below us. In its scintillating depths I spied *every color of the rainbow*. It was hideously beautiful. I had the perverse thought that it was a blazing contradiction. Actually, there was no way it could not be beautiful for it likely contained the separated, sparkling atoms of Jimi Hendrix and his mystical white electric guitar...along with 200,000 other momentarily dazzled hippies.

I guessed my "magic marble" hadn't done Hendrix much good after all.

We sped up past the atmosphere and into space. The 3D-display of possible timelines was gone. No amount of nudging or banging at the side panel could bring it back. Fortunately the small cabin stayed airtight and warm. The little time-ship must know how to provide life support to its occupant(s).

I hugged the neck of the frightened dog. His ears were plastered down against his neck, his eyes wide.

"We almost did it," I sobbed to Scotty as tears streamed from my eyes. He whimpered, holding up his hurt paw. "We almost saved Woodstock." But I had to get my grief under control, consider what an altered timeline might mean.

What were the probable repercussions? The nuking of Woodstock would surely do exactly what Sanako had stated: jump-start Phoenix. In 1969 only the U.S.A. and the Soviet Union had deployable nukes. China had the A-bomb, but not yet ready to use. A limited strike like this could only be done by U.S. or Russian agents. Both would deny responsibility. But Nixon's government had every incentive to deal a lethal blow to the anti-war, youth movement. I'd seen with my own eyes the mushroom cloud—and so had everyone else within a hundred miles. There was no denying that an atomic bomb had erased the Woodstock Festival and its rebellious participants. The already enflamed anti-war movement would erupt, shattering governments.

History as I knew it could not remain unchanged.

To the side, through the clear canopy, I saw the *round globe* of Earth: a *blue-green pearl* hanging suspended in the blackness. The thin line of its atmosphere was barely visible. And on the continent closest to us I saw a bright, flaring *spark*.

"Goodbye Peace and Love," I moaned. "I killed you. I killed all of you. If I'd just grabbed the gun before it fell out then..."

I sobbed helplessly as before us a *spinning tunnel* opened up in space. I saw a vortex of brightly sparkling *diamond patterns*.

We plunged into it. My mind was stretched to infinity and my thoughts were mercifully evaporated.

Chapter 19

NIRVANA

*It's our **Heaven-on-Earth***
Where there's no crying or dying
You're never sick or unhappy or hurt
No more cares or stress or fruitless trying

Anything we want, always sweet and fine
Food, shelter, friendship, and family forever
Except of course for forbidden pleasures
From which we must always run and hide

Their seductive beat and restless rhyme
Urging us to question, squirm, and disobey
Tempting us to test and misbehave
Stretching beyond the norms of our time

Instead of finding joy in honest work
Exercising muscles in healthy labor
Earning the sweat of our exertions
A badge of honor says we're in our place

Nestled in the arms of a loving mate
On cue popping out like-minded babies
A planned, orderly, ordained society
Missing nothing, or so it seems...
Living out our fondest dreams!
The Suzette Anthology, Lyrics 19

I awoke with Scotty's wet tongue slathering my cheek and nose.

279

"Ok, ok!" I snorted, pushing him off.

The time-ship had crashed. We were tilted precariously on a rocky slope. The canopy was smashed into a thousand pieces. The instruments of the saucer-shaped vehicle were smoking, melted. Apparently I'd only survived by Scotty pulling me underneath the seat, which had cushioned the blow of the hard landing.

I crawled out with the dog, standing upright to see an unbelievable sight. Suspended right in front of us in the air—hovering twenty feet above a golden pedestal—was the *white Sphere* I'd first seen in my Mom's subterranean laboratory!

Yep, it was the same Sphere...or a convincing duplicate thereof.

It hovered all by itself on a rocky peak that overlooked a gorgeous valley. Down the slope I saw a green meadow complete with acres of red, blue, and yellow flowers. Clouds of orange butterflies drifted on a cool breeze, descending to flutter amongst the field of flowers.

"Where are we?" I asked Scotty.

This certainly wasn't what I'd expected following the too-real nuke exploding at Woodstock.

Scotty seemed to have adjusted well, limping around me. Though his front right paw was at an odd angle, he managed to move fairly well on his remaining three feet. He loped down the hillside to the meadow, snapping at the butterflies, before hopping back to me. The bright sunlight danced across his wiry hair.

The sky above us was intensely blue, contrasting vividly with the green meadow. There wasn't even a hint of smog in the air. We must be high up in the mountains to get away from the contaminations of civilization.

"Yes, I guess we should leave," I smiled at Scotty's handicapped prancing, still fascinated by the reincarnation of the Sphere.

It rotated slowly along a tilted access. Other than its featureless white surface, it looked like a globe of Earth. Indeed, as I studied it closer I saw faint lines of continents momentarily appearing then vanishing.

Scotty was now whining, looking down the mountain slope. I followed his long-nosed gaze. There were people approaching us. They were hiking up a trail through the spectacular field of flowers.

"Where'd they come from?" I asked the dog. "Did they arrive here in time machines like us?"

That was dumb. I didn't see any other crashed time-ships. But looking further I saw that lower down the mountain there was a valley. I could just make out neatly planted rows upon rows of what were likely crops. And white smoke arose from what must be a distant village.

The line of hikers was all dressed similarly: in flowing white togas with leather sandals on their bare feet. Their heads were all shaved bald. And on their faces were bright smiles.

"Oh, great," I sighed in resignation, "*Hare Krishna* is here to greet me!"

Indeed, they were all chanting in unison:

> *"Hare Krishna Hare Krishna*
> *Krishna Krishna Hare Hare*
> *Hare Rama Hare Rama*
> *Rama Rama Hare Hare"*

And then they repeated it, on and on...

It was incredibly boring. No variation or accompaniment, not even a guitar. But despite my artistic snobbery, their still-distant voices had a peculiar effect on me. As I stood there beside Scotty, who was growling softly, I felt a *vibration* jolting through me with each of their words.

I looked up at the spinning white globe. As the approaching line of Krishna-chanters jubilantly shouted each word I saw golden *sparks* fly from the Sphere.

They were close enough now that I noticed each person wearing what looked like a *black collar* around their necks. Peculiar...

"Maybe they're not here for us," I said to the dog. "Maybe this is a religious site. Maybe they're worshipping the Sphere."

I remembered that the Krishna chant was supposed to be a form of worship to the *Supreme Godhead*. It was also supposed to induce a "transcendental vibration" that *surpassed* all forms of emotional and intellectual activity. It was also supposed to align one's spirit with all that's good and positive, pushing away evil. As such it was a simple but powerful form of purification, removing the sins of the chanters while ushering them into a state of true joy. Indeed, the Krishna-participants at Woodstock were known for their strict rejection of drugs, including pot. They claimed they didn't need the drugs.

But this was more than mere self-hypnotism. The Sphere was turning a subtle shade of *pink*. And a *stream of golden rays* was now swirling from its top up into the sky!

"Wow, this is a *real* high," I admitted, feeling waves of ecstasy sweeping through me.

Even Scotty was affected, slumping onto my feet, nursing his paw while wagging his tail.

I gently pushed him off and stumbled over to the golden platform beneath the hovering Sphere. I was drawn by its incredibly beautiful vibrations. Looking through a blue haze I saw lines carved into the golden surface. It was a map. I followed the carvings around the entire platform. It showed the flattened-out surface of Earth. Red spots dotted the map. One of them glowed brightly.

I pointed to it.

"That must be where we are now," I said to Scotty, who was again plastered loosely against my legs. "It looks like we're in the Alps, maybe Sweden."

Urf!—he happily agreed.

"Uhm, now *that's* a bit strange..." I gulped, realizing the chanters were almost upon us. The leader in front was holding out what looked like a *black plastic rectangle* toward me. And then they began exuberantly chanting something different: *"Ta kragen! Ta kragen! Ta kragen!"*

"Hey, stay off of me!" I shouted. I pulled back as they marched right up into my face.

The leader, a bald-headed old man with a long gray goatee, smiled gently. He motioned for the others to back off, which they did. Then he lowered the rectangle, which I now saw was a several-times folded-over black belt. "You speak Old English?"

"What are *you* speaking?"

Scotty whined, moving behind me. Stupid dog! Didn't he know that limping or not he was supposed to defend me?

"I usually speak our native tongue, *Swedish*. Lucky for you, young lady, I am a student of languages. We thought you were a supplicant from the wild territories, here to give yourself over to the Lords. We did not mean to force anything upon you. *Taking the Collar* is a privilege, not a requirement. But now that I see who you truly are, it is a blessing to us! We've long been expecting your arrival!"

His Followers all broke out in wild applause.

I knew I'd had a lot of fans during my successful years, but this was ridiculous. Were they "expecting" me to give them a concert?

"Taking the 'Collar'?"

He folded his liver-spotted fingers together, bowing his head to me slightly. "It is our Union with the Globes and through them unto the Lords Above. Yes, a few *wild ones* choose to live chaotic, purposeless lives. But true Unity is a beautiful thing. It joins our Earthly Music to the cosmic *Music of the Spheres!*" he concluded expansively, raising his hands to the sky.

"Uh...I kinda like being 'unfettered'..."

"That is only because you have not yet experienced Unity. Your rejection is based on ignorance, friend. Please, just touch it. It is your gift to us, after all."

"Say what?"

He held up the folded-over belt.

Tentatively I extended a fingertip...

Grrrrrrr—Scotty growled.

"Easy, boy, I'm just touching it, not putting it around my neck," I admonished him.

As my fingertip brushed the soft fabric I felt A BLINDING VISION OF THE ENTIRE EARTH, ALL OF ITS INHABITANTS, A HEAVENLY CITY IN ORBIT AROUND THE PLANET, AND THOUSANDS OF OTHER SIMILARLY CONFIGURED WORLDS SPREAD OUT ACROSS THE GALAXY...

Overwhelmed, I dropped to the rocky surface beneath me, my mind blown and my body trembling.

Scotty sprang over me, *growling* at the Leader, who hastily backed off, still holding the "collar."

"Is it not Glorious?" he smiled benignly at me.

"*Är det inte härligt?*" the Followers behind him chanted, over and over.

"You say you recognize me and were expecting me. So how did you know I'd be here?" I managed to whisper.

"It was ordained, my child," he smiled. "We've been expecting your arrival for centuries. Please, take the collar. You can remove it anytime you wish."

"Let me...see *you* take *yours* off," I challenged him, still struggling to get my muscles back under control. If just *touching* it incapacitated me what would placing it around my neck do?

"As you wish," he agreed, putting his hands up to his neck.

The Followers gasped as he undid his collar, dangled it in his hands, and laid it reverently upon the flat top of the golden platform.

"So, you see? There is nothing to fear, my child. It is but a *link* to a higher level of consciousness. And, in turn, it brings us great Power to accomplish many individual objectives. In the distant past, some religious groups eschewed it, due to engrained doctrines. But we of the *Hare Krishna* gladly welcomed its help to further our Message of true Peace and Love. Give it a try!"

It was very tempting. I looked at it, entranced, as he put his own Collar back onto his neck. The other one sat on the golden platform, *beckoning...*

"Thank you for the kind offer," I said as I struggled back to my feet. "Perhaps I'll do that later. But first I need to see more of your world. You say you've expected me for centuries? What year is this?"

He shrugged his thin shoulders.

"We've lost the Christian calendar long ago," he answered me. "I truly don't know your preferred designations. From our perspective it is 12,354 AU."

"*AU?*"

"After Unity," he nodded. All the others behind him nodded as well. "You will find out shortly what that means. After all, you are our *Prophetess*, Suzette Kingly. This wonderful Union is all because of *you!*"

Shocked to my core, I nevertheless set that disturbing revelation to the side.

"Can you take me to your village or city? I'd like to speak with the Rulers or Authorities."

"Oh, we have no Rulers. And each one of us is an Authority."

"Uh...right. Then, whoever is in charge: the people that make the decisions?"

"We each decide for our own lives."

"But...when you have disagreements you...?"

"We have no disagreements, only different talents expressed uniquely."

My head was spinning. This was surreal. *Did I really just travel over 10,000 years into the future?*

"But you mentioned the 'wild ones' and 'wild territories' that..."

"—just a few confused children willfully retreated into remote areas who..."

"So there *is* disagreement."

The wrinkles around his eyes crinkled as he grinned even more broadly.

"The few confused individuals are the 'grace' notes to a harmonious chorus. Even their defiance is part of our total contribution to the *Concert of the Lords.* When all is considered, *all* of us sing the same Song—in many parts but with one melody."

"I'd like to see for myself."

"Then do so," he nodded, stepping away from me and Scotty.

I noticed that a cloud of the orange butterflies was descending upon us, like a blessing from above.

"How?"

"Press your finger to your desired destination then step upon the Platform beneath the Globe."

"It's that simple?"

"Of course," he bowed again to me, backing off yet further.

I walked along the map on the outside of the golden platform, stopping at the American coastline beside the North Pacific Ocean. There were no national designations or names on the map, just topography. I recognized the San Francisco Bay and a red dot where the city of San Francisco should be located.

I pushed the dot, feeling it yield slightly.

Grabbing Scotty up in my arms I jumped up onto the platform. Above me, the Sphere glittered brightly. In a *flash* I was transported to who knew where.

I found myself looking out from under another rotating Sphere on an identical golden platform atop *Nob Hill*. I knew the iconic site because my *Album Three World Tour* included a concert at the Nob Hill Masonic Auditorium. I was now looking out across the bay where the Golden Gate should be spectacularly bridging the gap between the land masses.

But there was no bridge. And where the two towers at each end of the bridge should have been there were only remnants of long-eroded concrete foundations peeking out of the water.

Even more disturbing, I should have been surrounded by city streets. Instead there was nothing—just a green, lush forest.

"Oh, Christ," I said to Scotty, lowering his heavy body down onto the platform. "I guess it's true. We've gone into the distant future."

He whined, cowering on all fours.

"Here, let me help you," I said as I hopped down from the slick golden surface. I lifted him down so he wouldn't stumble on his bad paw and could stand beside me. He sniffed around suspiciously.

"But there's got to be cities. They've just moved, is all. We'll find them. And I'm sure there are Rulers. Civilization can't exist without structure. Humanity can't be just random groups of chanting Hare Krishna. That's crazy!"

I selected a new site, snatching up Scotty to transport to...

—*Athens*, Greece... *Washington, D.C....* *Guadalajara*, Mexico... *Rio de Janeiro*, Brazil... *Berlin*, Germany... *Moscow*, Russia... *Cape Town*, South Africa... *Cairo*, Egypt... and *Jerusalem*, Israel!

It was all the same. The cities were gone. In their place I found untouched nature, or neatly laid out small farms, or cozy villages. The people I talked to were all "collared" simple folks. As far as I could tell, there was no advanced technology. Yet everyone seemed healthy and happy. I transported into a few church services, of various faiths, gathered around the Spheres. They had no musical instruments, yet sang "a-capella": harmonizing their base, tenor, alto, and soprano "sans" instruments. The songs were new to me, in different languages, but by the gestures I gathered they all revolved around simple farming themes or praise of the "Lords."

I found one person particularly interesting, a seeming child with a full head of black hair. She reminded me somewhat of a young Grace Slick of the Vietnam War generation in America. This girl had an uncommon look of enthusiastic curiosity. Scotty and I were sitting on the edge of a golden platform that overlooked the lip of a high cliff. The cliff plunged 1,000 feet down to the brilliant blue Mediterranean Sea—contained within a circular, giant caldera seven miles across. It was the Greek island of Santorini. The sun was hot on my shoulders. I was getting very tired, not having slept or eaten for over 10,000 years!

"Would you like some goat milk?" the approaching young woman ventured, reverently holding out a wooden bowl to me. In it I could see creamy white fluid sloshing about. She sat it down beside me on the surface of the platform. She carried a woven bag, made of the same sturdy-but-simple woolen fabric of her clothes. From it she withdrew what looked like fresh biscuits.

Great...they still made hardtack in the distant future.

Woof!—Scotty answered her, wagging his tail.

That was a good sign. The dog had reliable instincts, warning me when encroaching dark woods seemed menacing and encouraging me when friendly natives approached.

"Yes, please," I nodded. "But first feed my dog. And what is your name?"

"I am your humble servant, Kallisti."

She put the bowl of milk at the dog's paws, which he eagerly lapped up. Also, she brought out cheese to eat with the biscuits, breaking off pieces for Scotty.

I recognized the latest spot we'd been transported to by the distinctive ring of high cliffs containing the blue ocean below us. I'd studied this island extensively while researching folksongs for my earliest two albums. The island of *Santorini* was an ancient volcano in the Mediterranean that "blew its top" around 1,500 B.C. Half the island became a vast, deep lagoon. In my time, a thriving town of white-washed stone houses existed on the high cliff's top. Now, only a few stone huts remained, apparently for local goat-ranchers.

"So you know me?" I asked.

"We have long known you would come in this time-frame, Proph-etess Kingly," the girl nodded shyly, now handing me some fried fish out of her bag. I was famished. I didn't care if the food was animal-derived or plant. I just gulped it down, along with more of her goat milk in a separate bowl from Scotty's.

"You speak English."

"Yes...I study Old English—just in case I should have the great honor of meeting and talking with you."

"People don't normally speak English? Is it a dead language?"

"Oh, it's not that," she hastened to reassure me. "We don't do much talking at all. It's so much easier to just *meld* with others."

"Meld?"

"Oh..." she caressed her black collar, "—we join our thoughts with those around us. The Lords help us when we can't understand each other. They...uhm...?"

"Translate?"

"Yes, that is true," she agreed. "If you are tired, Prophetess, you are welcome to rest with my family. Please stay with us as long as you'd like. We have plenty of room. You can have our goat-shed all to yourself if you desire privacy."

"That's very kind of you, Kallisti," I yawned, my tummy comforta-bly filled. Even Scotty looked tuckered out now, lying in the shadow of the golden platform, his tongue lolling out past his teeth. "But I'm in rather a rush. I just have a couple questions for you, if you don't mind."

"Why are you 'in a rush'?" she naively asked. "And I am of course happy to answer any questions. *I* have plenty of time."

"Oh, do you now?"

"Yes, I've completed my work for the day. I've done the milking and caught the fish for our evening meal. The rest of the time is mine to pursue however I wish. I was coming here to eat and commune at the Sphere, when I saw you materialize. I'm *so* glad I was here to meet you!"

"Well, thanks," I slipped down next to Scotty, sitting with my back to the cool metal. I scratched him behind his ears. He looked at me with grateful, big eyes. "I'm sorry to eat your meal, though."

"There's plenty more. I am happy to share."

"Ok, then...I need to ask you about 'the Lords.' I'd very much like to meet them. Where are they located?"

She pointed up at the sky.

"They're in *heaven?*"

"Yes! They abide in the *City of the Lords,* far above us."

"Have you ever been there?"

"Me? Meet the Lords in their City? Oh, no! It is not for us mere humans to meet with the Lords of Heaven. But they graciously allow us to merge our songs with theirs. The Communion is strongest when we are close to the Spheres. Sometimes we gather from across the world to make a large Celebration at a particular Sphere. But mostly we just enjoy our Union through our individual Collars."

"I...*touched* one...and saw other Worlds beyond Earth?"

"Yes!" she excitedly gestured up at the sky. "I find some of those very interesting. I visited one that is *only water,* with wonderful swimming intelligent beings. And another I particularly like has *living crystals* resonating together and..."

"You transported to them?"

"Well, in my mind—through the merging from the Lords, of course," she grinned. "I have never been physically off-planet."

"By this mental imaging, can you access all the planets inside our Galaxy?"

"Oh, no, Prophetess. That would be a waste of our time. We commune only with other worlds likewise blessed by the Presence of the Lords."

"So you know about worlds circling other stars in the Galaxy. Yet you appear to have no science or technology to...?"

"Oh, we have no need for those childish things."

I narrowed my eyes. Now I was getting somewhere. I was starting to figure out what was going on.

"*Why* do you not need them? And why are they 'childish'?"

She shrugged, putting the bowls and remnants of food back into her sack. "The Lords take care of our needs. Spending time or energy to master and make that which we do not require is stupid, like children playing with trivial toys. We focus on the most important things."

"And those are...?"

"Music, philosophy, church, and family," she replied confidently, as if reciting a mantra.

"What about scientific research, space exploration, corporate development, medical advancements, government, and business—to name just a few other types of endeavors?"

"Nope," she shrugged, "We have no need for those things."

"I still have a hard time believing you have no conflicts. Are you claiming you don't have wars?"

"Why would I fight myself? I can see inside the head of those around me, and they likewise mine. Conflicts are just misunderstandings, easily reconciled. Only a sick person would needlessly fight with a neighbor. And those with illnesses are diagnosed and cured."

"Even congenital defects?"

"Oh, certainly—but babies that have genetic or otherwise harmful faults are neither conceived nor birthed. And we have few births to start with."

"But the 'wild ones' are...?" I asked again, still not able to grasp the concept of a society without conflict, fighting, or war.

"There are only a handful of such, pursing childish objectives," she dismissed the notion.

"But wait, you're just a kid yourself, aren't you?"

She grinned. "I have chosen to remain at this particular age. It creates better harmony within my family-unit. My brother also remains at this age. We both find it agreeable to appear young."

"So just how old are you?"

"Old?"

"How many times has the Earth gone around the Sun during your lifetime?"

"Oh," she frowned, as if she were doing a mental inventory. "You ask for the number of winters I've lived through—*seven hundred and forty eight*," she brightly concluded.

I was stunned. Did I hear her correctly? Did she understand my question?

"You're saying that you are 748 years old?" I asked skeptically.

"Yes."

"But...how is that possible? Humans don't live longer than 120 years, at the very most."

"They don't? Oh," she laughed, "that was in the pre-Union days. Our Collars keep us healthy. The only deaths are from accidents, such as tripping and falling off this cliff onto the rocks below. And even then most of the newly injured can be repaired and restored to life. We don't get old or die. Occasionally one of the eldest will choose to transition further, merging with the underlying fabric of the Universe. But other than that, we live forever."

Forever? Was she really claiming a type of *immortality?*

That was incredible. Yet in all my transportations around the globe I'd seen no evidence of sickness or death. And if they really had no war or fighting, without disease or old age—why couldn't a human live forever?

Did the Lords really bring heaven to Earth?

"But when I first arrived here there was a nice old man who greeted me who had spotted skin and a gray goatee that...?"

"Oh, he was one of our Seekers. They choose to take on the appearance of advanced age as a badge of honor. But the position is rotated. Likely next year he will retreat to middle age. Or, he might return to his youth, like me."

No aging. No death. No pressure. No stress. It truly *seemed* like Paradise!

"So is that why there are so few people here?"

"There are few people here?"

"Yes, Kallisti. In my time period, just here on Santorini the population was around 16,000 people."

She put a hand over her opened mouth, staring at me incredulously. "There were *16,000 people* all jammed together on this one small island?"

"Yes. And on the planet there were close to *ten billion* people."

She was silent, shaking her head in wonderment.

"Well, it is no wonder that you had all that fighting and war. That many people all crammed together, without the Union, would be at each other's throats."

Ah, from the mouth of babes.

"And so it was," I shrugged.

"Well then *thank the Lords above* that they brought us their Wisdom: as you yourself caused to happen, dear Prophetess," she sincerely stated, now bowing her face down to the stones beneath us in abject prostration.

I gripped her shoulders and raised her up, peering intently into her adoring black eyes.

"Are you happy?" I asked.

"Yes! I am *very* happy, Prophetess."

"What do you do for fun?" I interrogated her.

"I swim in the ocean, play games with my friends, mate with my lover, do my community chores, work with my family, write new songs to sing with my brethren at church, commune with the Lords, paint pictures, and..."

"Ok, that's enough."

"It is *more* than enough. I never lack for enjoyment."

"So how many humans are there on Earth, Kallisti?" I asked, changing the subject.

"On the whole Earth?"

"Yes."

She squinted in concentration, pulling back away from me. She counted on her fingers. Then she again brightly smiled.

"At the latest Celebration there were over 5,000 people present."

"Ok," I replied slowly, trying to make my question crystal-clear: "And how many Celebrations take place across the Earth in a year?"

"One."

"And, how many of your villagers go to the Celebration?"

"Most of us—maybe 70%."

"So the entire population of Earth, including the 'wild ones' is about...?"

"Almost 7,000 individuals," she smugly answered, apparently pleased with her mental calculations.

"And off-world?"

"None."

I looked up at the bright-blue sky. No wonder there wasn't a trace of smog. Under the guidance of "the Lords above" war was abolished, disease was eradicated, death was cured, cities vanished, nature flourished, and a form of simple music was enshrined. Where ten billion humans had strained Earth's resources far beyond the breaking point, a mere 10,000 or less total population allowed Earth to revert into a paradise. Indeed, I'd read that a spaceship to another star would need a minimum of 160 people to plant a genetically viable population. But for a population of humans to effortlessly maintain its genetic diversity without active scientific intervention, the number was around *5,000 individuals.*

The population of Earth was pared down to essentials.

"Kallisti, do you know if I can return from whence I came?"

"You wish to leave us?" she whimpered, tears appearing in her big black eyes.

"I have to go back or none of this will ever exist. You understand, right?"

"Ah...that is true," she nodded reluctantly. "Well then just *think* of where you wish to go. The Sphere will take you there."

"Do I need to press a button?"

"There is no such button to press."

I stood up, hugged her tightly, swept Scotty up in my arms, and hopped up onto the platform.

I shut my eyes and began muttering softly: "There's no place like home...there's no place like home—*there's no place like home!*"

Well, it worked for Dorothy in the Wizard of Oz, didn't it?

And I fell down onto a *black* platform, looking about in confusion.

"Suzy! Oh, my God—Suzy, is it really you?"

"Hi Mom," I grinned up at her. I released Scotty who scampered away into the surrounding jumble of crushed equipment. I vaguely noticed he was chasing after a loose rabbit. "I brought a friend."

Chapter 20

HOME

Why do you cross oceans and continents
Only to return were you started
When everything you really wanted in life
Is right where you first began?

Come home, come home, come home to stay
And never again stray
Your heart and your love is anchored right here
And never will go away!

Is it terrible, nagging, painful itches
That drive you beyond far fences
Where the grass is thicker and greener it seems
If you can but leap the ditches?

Or does lustful pride drive you to more
Thinking you don't have enough
That value rests not in quality
But in sheer quantity?

Or is it simply a case of wicked boredom
Where familiar fades into obscurity
And something novel is necessary
To convince you you're having fun?

The Suzette Anthology, Lyrics 20

"How long has it been since I left?" I asked my Mom as she helped me off the raised platform.

I saw that the cavern was a wreck. One end was smashed completely down. The high ceiling was a jumble of hanging slabs. Equipment was randomly crushed by tumbled blocks of stone or standing unharmed but isolated. Above all the destruction, however, the *Sphere* loomed untouched. It radiated its *white light* throughout the surviving cavern, still spinning hypnotically.

"You've been gone for over a year."

"A year? Wow...for me it's been just five days."

"But you didn't stop Phoenix."

Sally King's voice was equal parts frustration and sympathy.

I sighed deeply, following her over to a bench where she laid out some food and water for me on a warped table. Scotty came limping up, his tail wagging happily. His muzzle was bloody. Apparently he'd caught the rabbit. My Mom put down a bowl of water for the "mighty hunter" which he eagerly lapped up.

"How'd you know I failed? What's been happening here?"

"Ah—Suzy!" a deep, guttural voice exclaimed.

I looked up from the sandwich I was gobbling down to see *Agent Anderson* wobbling up to us. He looked terrible. His right arm hung slack and useless at his side. His right leg was straight and stiff. He was minus his hair on the right half his head, which was burnt red. His right ear was completely missing. The teeth on that side of his face showed through a poorly healed wound stretching back to his missing ear. But he still wore his dark eyeglasses. For a middle aged guy who'd been shot up by terrorists then trapped in a collapsing cavern I supposed he was doing well.

And then it struck me like an axe to my heart: that *deep, rumbling voice* was familiar!

He limped over and sat down heavily in a chair facing me. If I could have seen his eyes I was sure they were welling with tears behind his dark eyeglasses. His big, mutilated head swayed back and forth as if in great pain.

"Suzy," he whispered, holding out his closed left fist to me.

Opening gnarled fingers he revealed a *bright blue marble!*

"Y-you...y-you're," I stammered, unable to get the words out.

"I'm so glad you got back safely, Suzy," he grated. "I deeply apologize for my younger self. That was the first time I encountered you—though I'd met you earlier here in your own particular timeline, later in mine. You see, I..." he tried to explain to me.

"You *monster!*" I spat at him, *slapping* the marble out of his hand.

He jerked his outstretched hand back, cowering.

"Suzy!" my Mom gasped. "Arthur saved me when the cavern collapsed and..."

"You made me *feel* for you then *ran out* on me!" I shouted at Anderson, jumping to my feet and shaking my fist at him. "And even worse than that, you knew Sanako's gun was the bomb all the time we were hunting it! You led me on—planting it yourself to finish off the entire Festival! I should *kill* you right now where you sit! You *slaughtered* hundreds of thousands of people, likely *wounding* many more, and turned our present world into *crap!*"

Sally King incredulously looked from me to him then back to me. "Are you talking about the nuke that leveled the Woodstock concert? Did you actually make it back to the Festival, Suzy? And were you there also, Arthur? If so, why am I just now hearing this?"

"Please let me explain," Anderson tried to speak to both of us, grimacing grotesquely.

"No! I want *nothing* more to do with you—'Cleve Hartley'!" I cut off his feeble response.

As I stalked angrily away, I saw him stumbling amongst the wreckage, searching for the marble. Jerk! Scotty was limping at my heels. I needed to find a place to crash. I'd been up too long already. Too many incredible things had happened. My mind was raging with a torrent of conflicting emotions. I just couldn't handle any more world-shattering surprises.

I fell onto the first cot I found and was instantly fast asleep.

"Unnnggghhh," I moaned, feeling squashed. My tongue tasted disgusting. My eyes were glued shut. And something heavy was pressing down on me...

"Scotty, get off of me!" I yelled, trying to get blood back into an arm pinned under my torso.

"Oh, sorry—but I'm not 'on' you...?"

Wow. Could dogs talk in this new timeline? That nuke at Woodstock sure changed everything!

The pooch hopped off of my back as I weakly rolled off of the cot and landed on hard flooring. Rubbing grime out of my eyes I blinked upward...

Standing over me, reaching down a hand to help me up, was a handsome young man. Long brown hair fell to his shoulders. His eyes were soulful, worried. He had high cheekbones and an angular nose. His skin was bronzed by repeated sun exposure.

"Scotty!" I gasped. "You grew up. Hey, are you a were-dog? Did you just change from a Scottish Deerhound into a...?"

"Oh, you named him Scotty like me? Well, he *does* look like a fine deerhound!"

He was scratching at the back of the dog's ears, whose eyes were closed in delight, his red tongue lolling out.

"Actually, I didn't even..."

A shy grin lit up his previously somber face. "I'm complimented, regardless. As to my age, I just turned eighteen. It's nice to see you again, Ms. Kingly. Dr. King told me you'd just returned from a scouting trip. She said you were looking for a weapon to use against the Commissioner. Did you find it?"

"What are you doing here?" I said, ignoring his strange question.

He helped me over to a nearby stool. I felt miserable. My guts were aching, rumbling and growling. I felt gas churning through my intestines, seeking an immediate exit. I itched all over from mud still caked into my every pore. I must have looked awful.

"I'm helping Dr. King and the few others who are hiding here underground. I'm able to smuggle in supplies from the town even though our Resistance movement is scattered and weak. More of us get captured every day, but we're still determined to defy the Commissioner."

"The...*Resistance*?"

"We have to walk a fine line between collaboration and passive noncooperation. Anything overt gets a person arrested, then tortured or worse. Many of us have been imprisoned or summarily executed," he softly stated, frowning.

Yes, I could see he'd grown beyond his young age in the couple years of *his* time that I'd been flitting through the past and the future. His brown eyes were sad, exhibiting the awful "thousand yard stare" of a combat veteran. He'd obviously seen terrible things.

"I'm so sorry, Scotty" I gulped, looking down at the floor. I felt unworthy of meeting his gaze. "I tried to stop all this from happening. But I only made things worse and..."

"The battle's not over."

"But if what you say is true—few resist and those that do are killed—what can we accomplish?"

"There's an old Chickasaw saying: '*The wise warrior even in defeat sees the seeds of ultimate victory.*' We Chickasaw know about being defeated but then rising again. We never give up, no matter what."

I was impressed. Yes, I knew the proud history of the Chickasaw nation: how their rightful property was stolen by the U.S. government, they were sent into exile on the "trail of tears," and then were subsumed into the general population only to fight their way back. They patiently exploited public laws to re-establish their Nation, gain gambling franchises, and accumulate wealth. It was their "revenge on the white man" to take the one thing that mattered most to their "civilized" conquerors: their money.

If anyone could "steal" the rug out from beneath the Commissioner—whoever that was—it would be the clever members of the Chickasaw Nation.

But I'd never heard that "saying."

"That's a powerful slogan," I nodded to myself, taking it to heart. "Did one of your ancient Chiefs say it?"

He ducked his head shyly. "Actually, I just made it up to give you some encouragement."

I laughed.

"It's very poetic and uplifting," I grinned. "Thanks, Scotty."

"I'm glad to help. Actually, I just stopped by to see if you need anything in particular," he smiled at me. "I came in through the secret tunnel an hour ago with a delivery. Now I'm heading back out. I can only bring what I can carry. I can't get everything, of course, but through my contacts I can acquire a lot of specialized things. I helped your Mother repair some of the damaged equipment here and..."

"*Bathroom!*" I snapped, painfully suppressing the sudden *burbling* in my belly.

I was about to explode.

"Oh, sure—right behind those smashed cabinets over there," he pointed. "Since you're getting lots of power from the Sphere with the artesian springs supplying plenty of water, you even have showers running so..."

"Thanks!" I grated, surging up off the stool and running for the hidden doorway.

I barely made it. Though the explosive fart-sounds probably impressed everyone in the complex, including Scotty (both the dog and the young man), even I was surprised by the massive amount of *evil-smelling gas* that emerged from my butt as I squatted on a toilet. My bladder wasn't too full, but my guts were twisted in knots. Successive bouts of diarrhea flushed my bowels out. Stress and strange foods across several millennia did a real job on my super-sensitive intestines.

"Are you ok, sweetie?"

It was my Mom's voice, speaking from the doorway.

"Don't come in, Mom," I replied weakly. I hoped there was a working fan to suck out the fouled air. "It's nasty in here, just like me. I'm a monster!"

"No, you're not," she firmly replied. "Whatever happened in the past you're still the daughter that I love."

"Thanks, Mom..."

"I'm putting some fresh clothes outside the door," she answered. "There's shampoo and other toiletries already at the sink. The shower is in the corner. You just take your time and get cleaned up. I've breakfast cooking. After we eat we can share our stories and make a plan for whatever comes next. Is that ok with you?"

"Yes...sure," I called back, fumbling for the toilet paper. I snapped the lever to flush the stinking contents of the bowl. "Just make sure Anderson's not there. I don't care what *his* 'story' is. He's *dead* to me, that bastard!"

"Uh...if that's what you want, but..."

"I *do!*" I yelled, still enraged at 'Cleve.'

He left me to die at Woodstock! He planted the bomb that ended up killing hundreds of thousands of people! I didn't know or cared how an older version of him managed to survive to be there in the 'bunker' with my Mom. If I needed a friend I'd get me a dog. Wait—I already had a dog, Scotty. But "Scotty" was a human boy. Uh, no...he was now a young *man*, a rather *handsome* Resistance fighter at that, and...

Jesus H. Christ. My mind was in a muddle.

"I'll be out in a bit!" I yelled as I stumbled out of the stall toward the shower. "I've gotta get cleaned up, at least my body..."

"Take your time, honey," she called back. "It's good to have you back. Don't beat yourself up too badly. I'm sure you did the best you could under the circumstances."

I ripped off my rotten clothes, throwing them into a corner. Then I fumbled my way into the shower and turned both handles as far as they'd go clockwise. A *wall of cold water* slammed down upon me. It sucked my breath away until it gradually starting warming. I slopped my way to the sink, grabbing up a plastic bottle of shampoo, and made my way back into the torrent of water. Lathering myself up lavishly I proceeded to clean away the physical (and mental) filth of Fiji cannibalism, of Woodstock overindulgence, and the disturbing future "paradise" of humanity.

Finally, slipping my wallet into fresh jeans, I felt human again.

The faint "hum" of the spinning Sphere eerily punctured the bright-white world around me as I greedily devoured pancakes, syrup, fried reconstituted eggs, hot oatmeal, and greasy rabbit meat.

It was delicious. After the "purge" that had emptied my guts of every trace of contents, I was starving.

Sally King and three disheveled, weary-looking technicians sat at the warped table with me. One was a squat oriental lady of Korean ancestry named Yee. Another was a thin, sallow-skinned, gray-haired gentleman named Fred. Yet another was a chubby, middle aged, Chickasaw-derived Native American lady named Itanale. Pointedly, Agent Anderson was missing. According to my Mom, they were all that was left of the previous hundreds who'd worked at the "Suzette

Kingly Animal Shelter" nonprofit-*slash*-military-research-base-*slash*-secret-time-travel complex.

It was a skeleton crew in the worst sense of the term. They were barely able to "keep the lights on," let alone run a cutting edge physics research program.

Of course there wasn't much left of the previously well-endowed facility. The aerial bombardment had obliterated everything on the surface while smashing flat the upper levels of the buried complex. Only the immensely hard cavern/bubble generated by the Sphere survived relatively intact deep below.

The enemy Phoenix bombers and troops were apparently convinced everything had been destroyed. Once the complex, plus any obvious entrances or exits, was reduced to a smoking crater in the ground they'd departed and not returned.

Luckily, my Mom had paid for out of my earlier, less traceable "donations" a super-secret emergency exit tunnel that led from the cavern to the nearby graveyard. It exited into an old crypt. Thus even though the survivors were trapped within the partially collapsed cavern, there was still a way to get up to the surface. Contacting Losa Yanash, Sally was able to get a regular, covert delivery service going.

The other men and women provided me with details of how they'd gotten key equipment working over the months I'd been gone.

"I still can't believe Phoenix took over so quickly," I shook my head, frowning. I was still shoveling food into my mouth, talking around a big spoonful of gooey oatmeal. On the floor at my feet, Scotty was gobbling up rabbit meat. Apparently, breeding the test rabbits was the only ready source of animal protein after the bombardment. In the rubble, a colony of them scampered about fed by greens sneaked in from above. "They had to overcome the U.S. military, didn't they?"

"Suzy, don't you remember that established governments were under Phoenix terrorism and subversion for decades before this present crisis? Once the Hollywood Bowl and other concert bombings occurred, the already simmering citizenry around the globe erupted. They blamed the 'musical liberals' for everything, flocking to Phoenix and its empty promises."

"That's not at all what I remember, Mom," I protested, setting my empty plate to the side. Finally my tummy was filled up to the brim. "People loved their freedom and creative expression. The extreme religious radicals had little power in the world's developed societies."

"Everything went downhill from the Woodstock Nuking, Suzy," my Mom stated. "The latest concert bombings, which the established governments were powerless or uninterested in preventing, were the last straw. If only you could have stopped the nuking of Woodstock, everything might have changed."

"Mom!" I half-yelled at her, "There was *no such thing* as a bombing at Woodstock when you originally sent me back in Time! All we knew was that it was the claimed origin point for Phoenix. When I went back, Woodstock was still a successful, peaceful Festival. But because I was there, I drew-in other Time Travelers. They—including Arthur Anderson—planted the bomb that I was unable to stop. We're living now in a *different* timeline than what originally happened!"

That sobered the small group at the kitchen table.

"You mean there might have been hope to stave off the Commissioner if you'd not gone back in Time?" Yee spoke up.

"Yes!" I exclaimed. "I ended up making things even worse! And a young version of your trusted aid, Arthur Anderson, *tricked* me. And just who is this damn 'Commissioner' anyway? What is life like out on the surface?"

The thin man with short gray hair, Fred, spoke up: "I've been out there with Scotty. Phoenix seems to think they're still in power. But the Commissioner's 'Peace Keepers' from an alternate Dimension are appearing in every city and town, taking control. They're moderating some of the excesses of Phoenix, but clamping down even tighter in other ways."

"Like what?" I asked.

"Mostly in areas of conflict or fighting or personal creativity," he sighed. "Punishment is quick and lethal. The 'Peace Keepers' are allowed to dispense summary 'justice.' They are judge, jury, and executioners, using their energy weapons. Any dissent is snuffed out before it even begins. There are no civil rights anymore. The State dictates everything. In their eyes, Music is the worst offender, strictly banned. Religious activities are severely restricted. Only the local faction of

Phoenix can hold sanctioned gatherings. Any other events are crushed before they begin."

Christ. My trip back in Time had made things *much* worse than before!

"Surely the people don't agree with such suppression. And how is Phoenix tolerating this invasion from another Dimension? Isn't their goal to get total control over people's lives? Won't they mount a counterrevolution?"

Fred shrugged.

"The regular folks are trading creative freedom for security. The Commissioner allows Phoenix to impose local restrictions. But, yes, they're being squeezed as well."

"How?"

"Those that defy the Commissioner's Rules are summarily executed whether they are regular citizens or High Patriarchs. It doesn't matter. The Commissioner coopted Phoenix to mute Music then control society, providing them with advanced technological tools to subvert our infrastructure. Now it's just a matter of cleaning up the last stragglers to the 'New World Order.' Phoenix and the Commissioner together have Earth by its short-hairs."

Just then Arthur Anderson shuffled around a ten-foot-tall broken electrical coil. He raised his good left hand at my budding protest, stopping me from protesting his presence.

"Now that you've gotten your food down and been caught up," he muttered around his poorly healed broken jaw, "you must hear me out, Suzy. You don't have to like or forgive me. But you need to know my story in order to move forward with your Mom and what's left of the Resistance, futile as the effort may seem."

I started to grab my plate to throw at him...

But my Mom grabbed my arm and forced me to put the plate back on the table.

"Sweetie, you have to hear him out. We talked extensively while you were recovering. I knew some of his history previously, but not what happened at Woodstock. We think that despite the dire situation facing our world, there's still hope—that is, if *we* can somehow manage to *work together*."

"Huh," I snorted, folding my arms across my chest.

"Please be reasonable, Suzy," she continued. "After all, we've still got the Sphere. That's our 'ace in the hole' that may help the dying Resistance gain some traction. Plus, our present *Arthur*—not this 'Cleve' you're so upset with—is our secret weapon against the Commissioner's Time Keepers. You've got to hear him out!" she insisted.

That tone of voice from my Mom could always jar even my most stubborn kid-fits. And I guess I was too old to be sulking like her little snotty daughter.

I still hadn't told her about my trip to the future. I already knew there was hope. A true Paradise on Earth *was* possible. But there was no clear path from the present to that distant, possible future. I needed all the information available, even if it was from a low-down, despicable traitor!

"Ok," I shrugged, "he can talk."

He stayed upright, leaning against the giant coil.

He reached up to his dark glasses. With both hands he pushed inward on the stems. I heard a sharp "click." Then the glasses came away and I saw his eyes: black pits containing *swirling diamond patterns!*

I was dumfounded.

He slapped the glasses back on his head, hiding that awful, hypnotically spinning twin spectacle.

"I admit I betrayed you at Woodstock," his deep voice rasped. "I was one of the Commissioner's Time Keepers, sent to intercept and stop you."

"I knew it!" I spat back at him. "You were in league with that 'Sanako' woman all the time. You *rat!*"

"I had no choice," he insisted. "You were my first assignment. I was sent to Woodstock to...*distract*...you from interfering with our plans to accelerate the appearance of Phoenix and so..."

"You never loved me."

He hesitated, bowing his head sadly.

My Mom looked torn between concern for me and sympathy for him.

"At first I thought you were just a silly young girl I could easily sway with my handsome imitation of Country Joe," he admitted. "But then, well, you were unlike anyone else I'd ever met. When Sanako went 'off-script' and was about to fry you I…"

"You're claiming you killed her to protect me?"

"Yes. I couldn't bear to have a world without you in it, Suzy. So I shot Sanako, my comrade-in-arms."

"Ah, but then you *didn't* bury her body as you claimed."

"Yes, that's correct. I immediately 'time-froze' her corpse, sending it back to the future in her time-Bub and…"

"Bub?"

"It's the name that the other Dimension uses for their cars, Suzy," Sally King explained.

"Ok," I waved my hand dismissively in the air, "but why did you then lead me on a wild goose chase to find the so-called 'bomb'—when you already had it ticking down to overload inside your shoulder bag?"

He scratched his half-burnt head with his good hand, apparently embarrassed.

"I…hoped to use the intervening period to build a real relationship with you and…"

"—before *blowing up* the Festival and *killing* hundreds of thousands of innocent young people?"

He bit his lower lip, displaying a hideous array of yellowed, busted teeth inside the slash on his face.

In all ways I saw him as he really was: a *monster*, just like me!

Wait, am I sympathizing with this rat?

"I was still conflicted," he continued. "Sanako didn't know who shot her. If she were repaired and revived in the future I could claim a *guard* spotted her, shot her, and I *rescued* her. You have no idea of the indoctrination forced on me by the Commissioner's ruling Empires. From a child I was raised to obey without question the dictates of the State. For me to go against direct orders was unthinkable, insane! I thought, naively, that I could somehow save you and still complete my Mission fulfilling Sanako's mandate: nuke Woodstock."

"But then…?" I forced him to proceed.

"But then I finally 'got' it," he harshly whispered, his voice barely audible to us at the table.

"And that was?" I relentlessly pressed him.

"Love trumps Power."

"So if you finally figured out the 'secret to Life'—then *why* did you run away?"

"I didn't."

"What?"

"Sanako returned, healed and resurrected, from the future. She saw what was happening. She knocked me out with a 'taser' blast when everyone was focused on you performing up on the stage. She returned me to the future for trial. She took me in her time-Bub. But before she departed she hid her still-overloading gun behind a camouflage field within my half buried Bub beneath the stage. It seems she always suspected me of being a traitor."

"So then why aren't you dead, executed for your crimes?" I asked him, skeptically.

Extenuating circumstances or not, he'd betrayed me once. I could never trust him again.

"I managed to convince my superiors that Sanako was mistaken. After all, I still had the overloading gun which I could have easily turned off. So I was reinstated."

"Why couldn't they just look through Time to see what happened?" I asked the obvious question, determined to show he was still lying.

"Fortunately, epochs where we Time Travelers operate become obscured in fuzzy quantum uncertainties, making those periods difficult to inspect distally," Anderson explained. "Anyway, many assignments and covert betrayals later, I finally broke with the Commissioner and established my own rogue group of Time Keepers. I battled her loyal Time Keepers across millennia. But she finally defeated my group. I ended up here, trying to protect your Mother, the *original* 'girl with the turtle tattoo.'"

"Original?"

Sally King laughed at me, momentarily displaying a side of her I'd never seen before.

"There have been a number of us, Dear," she shrugged "But the worst version is without a doubt facing us."

"Who?"

"The 'Commissioner'...is *me*."

"You?" I dumbly repeated.

"Well, she's me from this Dimension, perverted into the Creature that now rules the second, parallel human Dimension."

Things were getting really confusing.

"Jeez, that sucks," I gulped, impressed. "So she's just as smart as you, making her own time-travel machines, but evil. But if she's you from this Dimension, then that means *you* are...?"

This whole conversation was getting more and more weird. But then again, I'd already traveled to the past and future. Who was I to judge what was bizarre?

"I'm 'me' from the other Dimension," she half-smiled at me, her green eyes glittering alarmingly. "Your Dad 'tamed' me and I settled down to a peaceful life in the little town of Sulphur, Oklahoma. But before that, I also raised hell across Time."

"No way..."

"Yes, 'way'—and here we are with a Time Machine battling my 'evil sister' for control of the entire world across two Dimensions!"

Everyone was quiet for a moment, digesting the impact of her stupendous statement.

"Man...fate's a bitch," I said, my mind totally blown. I shook my head to clear it, getting down to business: "Ok, so what do we do now? It looks like the 'bad guys' have won. Phoenix has already banned Music and taken over the world. And now someone even crueler and cleverer has taken over Phoenix. We're royally screwed!"

"We still have the Sphere," Anderson noted.

"Can we use that to go back in Time and somehow stop the Commissioner?" I desperately asked. I still didn't buy Arthur's tearful explanation, but was now willing to work with him if necessary.

"They'll always be two steps ahead of us," Anderson sighed, "but..."

"And with the destruction of our control systems, it's doubtful I can predictably send anyone to an exact destination," Sally King interrupted Anderson. "With Scotty's stolen replacement parts I've managed to get a rudimentary control interface back in place. That may be why you returned to this exact time and place after your Woodstock adventure, Suzy. I'm so glad that the atomic blast didn't kill you along with all the rest of those poor souls. But as to mounting an attack through Time, I'm afraid we're just not in shape to go against well-supplied experts."

As if in sympathy to our predicament, the table at which we were sitting *trembled*.

"Uh...what was that?" I gulped, looking around fearfully. It felt like a small earthquake. But then *the entire cavern* trembled!

Some loose slabs dangling from the high ceiling broke loose and came CRASHING down into the equipment below.

"Everybody get into the safe room!" Sally yelled frantically. She grabbed hands and arms, rushing us away from the kitchen area to a cave carved out from the solid foundation rock surrounding the cavern.

But then another shockwave knocked us down and I saw the "safe room" collapse in a shower of dust and ricocheting stones.

"Oh hell," I groaned, grabbing onto my dog as he came scampering up to me.

But then he broke away and scuttled for the Sphere's black platform.

"Scotty!" I cried out, starting to run after him.

"It's too late," Sally said, tackling me and dragging me off to the side, "If another quake hits, then everything will come down!"

"Wait..." I said, staring at the platform.

A *hazy blue mist* was forming, congealing, and crystalizing.

With a final *SHUDDER* the Sphere above *ruptured*, showering the blue mist below with *fractured diamonds*.

Waves of earthquakes shoved the entire Cavern up and down, knocking us all off our feet.

I saw my dog limping through the swaying cavern toward the black platform...

—where the diamond shards were *reforming* beneath the Sphere into a *barefoot man in a long white toga!*

Scotty managed to hop up onto the platform and into his arms.

The man, holding the dog in his arms, *floated* away from the platform, alighting right in front of our huddled group!

He was the oldest man I'd ever seen. He had snow-white long hair and a bushy white beard. He looked like the embodiment of every kindly wizard I'd ever seen in movies. He had a benign smile on his well-wrinkled face as he stroked the head of the delighted Scotty. He wore a scabbard at his waist from which dangled a long, crystal sword with a golden handle.

"Sorry about the dramatic entrance. I hope no one was hurt. Quantum teleportation from the Galactic Core without a well-functioning target Sphere can be tricky. I just now fixed your interface. Its transportation parameters should now be precise."

My Mom just stared at him.

"I think we're all ok," I gasped.

"Ah, I see you got my present," he told me, handing me back the dog.

"You sent me Scotty?" I gulped, accepting him back.

"He helped you, did he not?"

"He sure did."

"He's quite a construction, don't you think?"

The earthquake was gone, the shudders vanished.

I dumbly nodded, not understanding his point.

He reached over and gently lifted off the top of Scotty's skull. Inside, I saw sparkling electrical circuitry.

"He's a robot?" I gulped, astonished.

"More correctly, an android—biological and mechanical elements combined," he grinned. "I made him myself. It's rather clever of me, don't you think?"

"Who the hell *are* you?" I snapped at him, finally getting my wits back. Then it dawned on me... "Wait! Don't tell me—I remember now. When I was a little kid on the playground, *you* taught me how to play marbles."

I pulled out my Taw which I still had snugly protected in my jean's pocket. I held it up in the air. It gleamed in the white light. Then a huge *ELECTRICAL ARC* suddenly leapt from it to the actual Sphere!

"Holy crap!" I yelled, almost dropping it.

"Ah, hah, hah!" the old man chortled, dancing around in a small circle, "I gotcha, Suzy!"

I slowly put the scorched marble back in my pocket, staring intently at the old prankster.

"Who...are...you...*really?*" I slowly interrogated him, emphasizing each word separately.

"It's so good to see you again, Suzy," he laughed boyishly, "Oh, you too, Mom."

Sally King's jaw sagged. She looked like she was about to melt into the floor.

I'm sure I looked the same.

"Billy?" I gasped. "But you're *old.*"

His eyes narrowed as he looked at me. I detected that same resentment from years previous. It *was* him—my estranged little brother.

"Yes, I've been with the Lords for many years, being taught in their ways. They took a shine to me and Dad when our little experiment tossed us to the Galactic Core. They helped broaden our perspectives. I'm sorry we couldn't come back except for a few times, briefly. We encouraged Suzy to hang on after the Hollywood Bowl was attacked by those Phoenix terrorists."

"I'd have given up otherwise," I gulped, remembering awakening in crippling pain. "You were both older."

"Yes, that occurred quite a while after we arrived at the Lord's planet."

"And you played with me on the school ground with the other kids."

"Yes, giving *young* Suzy her first marbles!"

"Which I still don't understand...?"

"You will," he smiled, his eyes crinkling at their corners. "I'm here now to explain their importance. Actually I dropped them off to you just a few minutes ago, my time. It was my last stop before coming here. Their 'music' helped you pursue your biggest dream, didn't they?"

I was blown-away. He'd just been with me when I was a kid. Now he was here.

"But why did you want to help jumps-start my career?" I bluntly asked him. "I thought that you were mad at me for being more successful than..."

"That's all in the distant past," he snapped, changing the subject. "It seems that you are a favorite of the Lords of the Galaxy. As such,

I—as their faithful emissary—am pleased to do their bidding: *now* helping you to succeed in a *musical contest* beyond your wildest dreams!"

"Say what?"

"All in good time," he mysteriously replied.

"So you both really *did* come to me at that motel, warning me not to interfere in the explosion that would happen at our house," my Mom gasped, grabbing onto Billy's arm apparently to make sure he was real. "You were older than your versions back at the house."

"Yes, not long after we first got to the Galactic Core we realized we'd have to come back and stop you and Suzy from interfering when the first *breach* happened. That was one those 'nexus in time' points where all sorts of possibilities were present, not just the timeline we initially experienced."

"So you and Dave accidently cracked open subspace..." my Mom shakily tried to understand.

"—and you let a piece of subspace poke through into our world," I breathlessly finished Sally's sentence, pointing at the Sphere.

"Not really," he grinned. "We *attracted* the attention of an *automatic mechanism* monitoring all planets in our galaxy."

"An 'automatic mechanism'?" Anderson's gravelly voice broke in. "Is it more powerful than the time-travel technology possessed by the Commissioner?"

"Oh, infinitely so," Billy nodded. He patted the sullen Time Keeper kindly on his good shoulder. Then he turned with us back toward the kitchen table. "The Sphere is an *alien probe*."

"An alien probe..." Anderson muttered.

"What does it want?" Fred asked.

"It's a talent scout."

"Say what?" I dumbly repeated, bewildered.

"Can we sit down?" Billy asked. "My feet aren't getting any younger and it takes too much energy to float through the air like an angel."

"Of course," Sally King said, taking him by an arm.

We all sat down together around the warped, scuffed kitchen table.

With a wave of his hand, Billy straightened the table and gave it an instant coat of dried fresh paint. He unbuckled his scabbard and put the sword on top of the table.

"That clunky thing gets in the way, hitting my old knees. But it's a part of my required uniform, hah!"

Wow, he sure knew some good tricks. And even though the sword looked ceremonial it seemed serviceable, having a sharp edge and pointed tip.

"That's better." he sighed contently. "Unfortunately, before you get too excited, let me make it clear that I'm not God and I have only limited powers to accomplish a few matter/energy conversions." For a moment he stared accusingly at me. "The most difficult part of us defeating your evil government is still before us. And there's no guarantee of success. But at least it's a chance to save humanity from its downward spiral."

"And just how are we going to do that?" I asked, as usual jumping to the most immediate priority. I definitely wanted to hear all about Billy's incredible adventures, but only after we succeeded in *stopping* the terrible disaster that had *stolen* music from humanity!

"With this," he ruefully laughed, reaching into a big pocket on the side of his toga and pulling out a small blue bag.

He slapped it down on the tabletop in front of me.

"What is it?"

"Look inside."

I tentatively unloosened a top drawstring and a torrent of *many-colored marbles* tumbled out. They bounced off the table and fell onto the floor all around us.

Scotty barked at them, hopping up and down excitedly.

"More marbles?" I asked, confused.

"They can save the world."

"Wait, please go back to the 'alien talent scout' business," Anderson insisted. He was seemingly gathering strength from the prospect of defeating the Commissioner. "Can you give us the 'take-home message' on what that signifies?"

"It keeps an eye out for advanced cultures throughout the Galaxy who crack open subspace, and..." Billy paused dramatically.

"And?" Anderson prodded him.

"—and are rich in their planet's particular version of harnessed, focused, vibrational Creativity."

"Like what?" Anderson growled at him.

"Music!" Billy gushed. "In whatever form or fashion they perceive it—*Music* that's good enough to touch and *move* the Lords of the Galaxy."

"Music..." I smiled.

"Yes!" Billy continued enthusiastically. "Across the Universe it's the most valued output of intelligent species. So the Lords of our Galaxy periodically host a Cosmic 'talent show', where the winner is granted an incredible Prize. The Contest happens only once every *million* years, at the Galactic Core. And the next one occurs just *one year* from today. That's why the Talent Scout appeared. The Galactic Lords are looking for their next slate of competitors."

"What sort of 'prize'?" I asked, afraid that I already knew the answer.

"The Lords will establish an outpost on the winning race's world: granting its inhabitants total *freedom!*"

"Freedom from what?" Sally King asked, pressing him.

"Freedom from conflicts, from illness and injury, from being dominated by others—and, in particular, freedom of expression!"

"For real?" Anderson asked, dubious. "And would it apply for...*all* of us?'

Billy stared at the mutilated man, seemingly with pity.

"It's already happened on thousands of worlds. It's very real. I've virtually visited many of those worlds and can certify that Outposts of the Lords deliver on all their promises to the blessed civilizations. All members of that species share in the benefits."

"*Exactly* what 'benefits' do the winners get?" I pressed him.

"Well, in essence the Lords grant unlimited energy, personal conversion of energy into any form of matter requested, and a type of *immortality*. But those amazing outcomes are given only to the most talented, musically endowed races. The Galactic competition for this incredible Prize is fierce."

"So...this could save us from the repressive reign of Phoenix, the Commissioner, or whatever else despotic power wants to impose its rule upon us?" Sally King asked.

"Absolutely."

"And all we have to do is win some musical talent show?" Anderson asked again, frowning. He reached up with his one good hand to adjust his dark glasses. He looked nervous, evasive.

I didn't hate him anymore. But I sure didn't trust him. I didn't trust anyone who had time-tunnels where eyeballs should be!

"Yes, if we can even qualify to enter the contest," Billy slyly winked at me.

"I knew there'd be a catch," another of the technicians at the table sighed. "I'm not good at music."

"But we've a world-class Diva in our midst," Sally King stated confidently.

All eyes turned to me.

"Gee, guys," I gulped. "I'm good, but to compete against a whole host of *other worlds?*"

"Hah!" Billy laughed, his well-wrinkled face crinkling in glee. "That's the kicker. The Sphere has already put out its 'feelers' and Suzy has *already qualified us* to enter the competition. She's not only the best in our world, but has off-world genius as well!"

"Say what?" I gulped, overwhelmed.

"It's true. You're a cosmic musical genius," Billy flatly stated.

It sounded like he was pulling teeth. This must be really hard for him to admit, that I was not just better than him musically but better than everyone else. He must be really loyal to those alien "Lords"!

"Check for yourself."

I felt an invigorating vibration spreading through my body, emanating from my pants. I yanked the Taw out of my pocket and held it up. Its glow was pulsating, resonating with the Sphere.

"These 'marbles' scattered across the floor are *emergence zones,*" Billy now laughed.

"That's...incredible," my Mom gasped.

I frowned, still not understanding.

"At the other ends of your 'wormhole', my friends,' Billy stated. "The Lords have been watching and auditioning Suzy all her life. Now all she has to do is pick out her band, backup singers, orchestra, and audience members. Then she's off to the Galactic Core!"

"So the new marbles you gave me...?"

"They're invitations," Billy matter-of-factly said. "Mom, are you prepared to gear up your spiffy 'time-machine'? I can help with fine-tuning the now fully-functional control interface. Suzy's got a lot of time-traveling yet to do."

"But, why can't *you* do it, Billy?" I asked, puzzled.

"I'm just a glorified messenger, Suze," he shrugged his shrunken, old shoulders. "*You're* the only one allowed to select 'Team Earth'. Whether you deserve it or not, you have to accept your responsibility here—just as have I."

Yep, it was definitely my snotty little brother Billy. He couldn't resist getting in a dig at me. But he was right. In my own eyes I was still a monster, hardly "deserving" anything good!

Sally King grinned wider than I'd ever seen her before. But then she sobered, putting a hand on Billy's frail arm.

"And...what about your Father?"

He sighed, tears appearing in his old, tired eyes. "Unfortunately, the Lords move at their own celestial pace. By the time they'd agreed on admitting Earth—in all its variable Dimensions and Timelines—into the upcoming million-year competition, Dad had passed onward."

Everyone around the table sobered, their elation dimmed.

"I miss him," Billy sadly continued. "But for the Lords 'passing on' doesn't mean crumbling into dust. It truly means the Spirit transcends this level of existence to something higher. I assure you that my Dad, David King—your father, husband, and beloved local school teacher—is looking down on us right now and smiling, wishing us the very best in the Contest."

He sounded strange, his voice strained. I wasn't sure if I could believe his claim. But then again, he'd been much closer to Dad than me. For Billy's only close human companion, his own father, to die on an alien world must have been devastating.

"Then let's do this for Dad," I ventured.

"Yes," all the rest agreed.

"For David King, the first human to crack open subspace and elevate his daughter to *Chief Conductor!*" Anderson gravely proclaimed.

"Amen," I seconded the motion. "I'll do my best."

Though I was outwardly positive, I was inwardly deeply conflicted. I was confident we *could* achieve the victory we wanted, for I'd already seen its fruit. Everything Billy said we'd win I'd already seen happen in the possible future timeline.

So he was telling us the truth.

But would the prize be worth the price?

Chapter 21

<u>NEGOTIATION</u>

*I want what you want, so **tell me please***
What can I do to help YOU have fun
Don't be coy or attempt to tease
How do we get to YOUR destination?

It's almost never heard, an unselfish question
Actions beyond mere loving words
How can I show my true devotion
That never would cause you to hurt

A crazy thing, an impossible theme
My giving you one hundred percent
Only feasible if you too believe
And give the same back to me

How can this be, how can it work
Let me give you a delightful hint
Not grudgingly splitting the difference
Or a fake attempt at "win-win"
But joining our separate burdens

When you see me as part of your body
And you are my actual right arm
Together we move in blessed harmony
Without any friction or harm
We both can function as one!

The Suzette Anthology, Lyrics 21

"It won't work," Arthur grated through his mangled mouth.

We all looked at him in surprise. A moment before we'd been on a real high at the kitchen table. After a break of several hours, while Billy helped Mom and her technicians make exquisite adjustments and additional repairs to her instruments, we'd returned to plan the details of our assault on the *magnificent musical history* of mankind. We were sharing an apparently rare treat in the present rationed environment: hot tea. But now Anderson was snapping our attention back to the *real* Earth: a *brutally controlled, radicalized, fearful* society resenting its loss of creative freedom while embracing the supposed safety of tyranny.

"What do you mean?" Sally King asked him, frowning.

"A founder of a dynamic, rapidly expanding church once said 'You can have *control* or you can have *growth*, but you can't have both,'" Anderson grunted.

Billy looked both amused and pensive at the same time. That was easy for him. Really old "wizards" were famous for simultaneously being both incredibly wise and childlike. He was no exception. And I'd always known him to be both sneaky and brilliant as a little brother.

I felt Scotty curl up around my feet under the table. Even though I now knew he was an artificial dog, a smart toy animal, his presence was still comforting.

I realized he wasn't limping anymore. Had Billy noticed and fixed his damaged paw? Perhaps I could give my ancient brother a little trust after all.

"An enabling structure is necessary for any advancement," I interjected. Yes, I was also now wise beyond my years. I'd seen too much to be satisfied with easy solutions. "The trick is to provide the necessary support to creative folks: in other words 'making a space' for *controlled* creativity."

"That's the essence of any world-spanning concert tour, isn't it?" my Mom added in support.

Yep, she knew the score.

"People, I assume the 'Lords' don't impose themselves upon worlds," Arthur continued, his garbled words slurring together. "This 'contest' requires the intelligent creatures of a planet to *want* the Lords to establish an 'outpost', right?"

Billy nodded in agreement: "That is correct, Agent Anderson. The Lords don't go where they are not invited. If there is significant division to the prospect of their presence, they will withdraw their offer to participate in the Contest. In fact, the live performance of a species at the Contest must be transmitted in some form to all accessible members of the participating planet."

"I know my Commissioner," Arthur grunted. "She will never accept a ruling agency greater than hers, especially one that supports and rewards 'subversive' activities."

"And what could be more disruptive than unfettered musical expression and participation?" Yee offered. "Isn't that what fueled the emergence of Phoenix in the first place?"

"Yes, and countless other disruptive movements throughout history," I agreed. "Anderson is right. It looks like we're in a real pickle of a dilemma. The Lords seem to value our musical abilities above everything else. And that's what the existing governmental bodies fear the most! You say the Lords require direct or indirect participation of the planet's population, while our regressive present governments actively *ban* music."

"I think I have a solution to your problem," we heard an approaching, older male voice.

Scotty—the young human version, not the dog—came through a tangle of collapsed slabs leading his father, Losa Yanash. The elderly man had his gray hair braided back in a thick ponytail behind his head. He was heavier built than his teenaged son, but still exuded youthful energy tempered with great experience.

He looked grim, frowning deeply.

"I'm sorry to intrude," he waved a hand at us. "But Scotty brought me the welcome news of Suzy's return plus her brother from the Galactic Core. Amazing! And I heard what you were saying as we wound our way through the debris field. It seems that my problem may be your solution."

"Oh?" I said, standing up to give him a quick hug. "Sit down and have some tea, Mr. Yanash. And please do tell us what's happening."

He sank down into a rickety chair. "Ah, my legs aren't as young as my son's. That's a long walk through the fields and tunnel. Thank you. And please call me 'Losa', Suzy. The honorific was fine when you were a child. However, you're more than a successful adult now. You're our planet's one hope for liberation! Oh, and Scotty's strong back brings more supplies for you folks."

"We are always very grateful," Sally said, taking the full sack and setting it aside as Scotty also wearily sat down.

Woof!—the dog greeted him, jumping up to offer the young man his ears to scratch.

"Well, I think one thing is settled..." I laughed.

"And what is that?" Losa asked as Sally filled his cup from a teapot.

"I'm *not* renaming my Woodstock-acquired pooch," I firmly answered. "From now your son is 'Scott' and my Scottish Deerhound is the *real* 'Scotty.'"

"Ah," Losa nodded, solemnly accepting the compliment. "Yes, my son is now also a strong adult. He deserves to be addressed without the diminutive. And I hear the dog is a robot, given to be your mechanical 'spirit' guide by your now-aged brother?"

Scotty left Scott to push his long nose into Losa's lap.

"Oh!" Losa laughed, "And a friendly robot he is, indeed."

Arf!

"Seriously, Chief—you say you have a supposed 'solution' for us?"

Losa sobered, glaring pointedly at Anderson. "I'm a tribal Elder, not a Chief."

Anderson shrugged his one good shoulder. "Whatever, I can't imagine anything you've got to offer doing us any good. We're not up against a gaming commission regulating casinos. We're up against the Ruler of a whole separate Earth! I have battled The Commissioner and her Time Keepers across the eons. They are far more formidable than you can even imagine."

"Yes, I know this."

"Their weapons are far beyond anything the armies of this world possess."

"I am aware of that as well, Agent Anderson," Losa coolly answered him, sipping delicately at his cup of tea. "But the Native-

American Nations fought against invading European armies who also had superior weapons and..."

"—lost everything!" Anderson huffed. "I don't know why we're wasting our time trying to resist the..."

"You act like you *want* the Commissioner with her pet Empires to win!" I angrily challenged Anderson. "Even if our chances are slight with the Lords, at least it's a chance to return Music to our world. Without Music we might still survive, but it'd be a sad existence. What have we to lose by accepting this *Cosmic Concert* challenge?"

Anderson shrugged. He adjusted his dark eyeglasses with his one good hand. I noticed that his fingers were trembling. I felt a momentary stab of guilt arguing with him. He'd sacrificed a lot in the service of Sally King and me. But he also vanished at Woodstock when things got tough, after *him* laying the seeds of disaster! I still didn't buy his lame explanation of being kidnapped, a prolonged disillusionment period, and finally his rebellion.

For all we knew he was a spy.

"Please, Losa, continue," my Mom invited him.

Glaring at Anderson, Losa turned to the rest of us. "I've been ordered by the local authorities to shut down our annual 'stomp-dance' celebrations. I appealed to the Commissioner. Perhaps because she originally came from this area before she went to the Second Dimension, she's granted us an audience. I'm petitioning her to recognize our tribal celebration not as a musical event but as an ancient ritual. After all, most of the white population think our 'stomping' is rather boring, anyway. Even our young people only grudging participate."

I sighed, reaching over to pat his weathered hand.

"I understand," I admitted. "When I was young I went to one of your annual celebrations at the Chickasaw Cultural Center. I found the Stomp Dance fascinating...for about five minutes. Then I left to get back to my Gospel music, blues, country-western, pop, and rock. You probably have a good chance at getting official permission to continue the Stomp as a ritual. It's definitely boring."

"And what's that got to do with us?" Anderson demanded.

"You can piggy-back on my audience," Losa stated. He stared unblinkingly, with cold dignity, into Anderson's inscrutable dark eyeglasses. "I've direct communication to her office and can add this request. You can make your case for the benefits of trying to win an *Outpost of the Lords.*"

Arthur ducked his head, looking away.

"That's...not a bad idea," Billy nodded, his long white "wizard" hair dancing about his head. "If you could get her to allow us to appear as projected holograms at a neutral site, where she couldn't just execute us all, then maybe..."

"It is already done," Losa agreed. "I was told to appear for transport to the Second Dimension at Sulphur's County Courthouse. But my lawyer got them agree to a *holographic interface* at an Earth-One site of our choosing. I haven't yet specified the place."

"Tell them the peak of Mount Everest," I immediately interjected.

"Why there?" Losa said, narrowing his eyes in deep thought. "It is difficult to reach, such that few if any other humans could observe us. I'd think we'd want witnesses to seal the deal."

"Exactly!" I answered enthusiastically. "All the participants that otherwise wouldn't dream of exposing themselves could safely make their cases. After all, we can't let either her or the government know that the Sphere is still functioning."

"But how will we have witnesses if it's so secluded?" Scott asked.

I loved how his brown eyes sparkled with intelligence in the glaring, white light. God, was I falling for him? He certainly wasn't a young high school "boy" anymore. At eighteen he was a full-fledged, handsome young man.

"I can handle our ethereal projections," Billy assured the rest of us. "There'll be no need to tap into existing broadcast systems. We'll be safely hidden here for the entire meeting. I'll explain I'm a representative of an alien race seeking mutually beneficial contact. Once she's intrigued I'll provide the terms of this 'one-time' musical event. If we win the Contest and subsequently an Outpost is established in orbit around our planet, we can all reap the benefits equally. I can, as Mr. Yanash so aptly put it, 'piggy back' on the Commissioner's signals and help 'broadcast' the proceedings globally. So the conclusion won't rest entirely just on the narrow interests of the Commissioner or Phoenix."

"Technically, it might work," Arthur mused, scratching at the scar tissue on the side of his head.

"We may value our traditions and rituals," Losa chimed in, "but we also embrace present technology. I can assure you of a solid communications platform upon which you can piggyback."

"But the Commissioner craves total control," Anderson insisted. "What do you have to offer her that would equal the increasing influence she holds over your First Dimension?"

"But what does she *really* want?" Losa asked softly. "Agent Anderson, my son says you spent many years working for her. Do you know her true, *deepest* motivations?"

All eyes turned to the mutilated, big man.

"Ah...superficially, world-domination producing an orderly, reasonable society freed from the idiocies of stupid human drives," he mused, grimacing around his mangled mouth. "As such, in my Dimension as well as this, she supported and extended the ban on all forms of Music. If we pitch this contest as a Concert she'll deny us immediately."

"But her *deepest* desires?" Losa insisted.

I was intrigued. Losa was mirroring my own intellectual cravings to *know*, to understand my own self!

"Ah...I suppose the same as any of us: to be warm, safe, fed, and free to make babies and do other creative things."

"Has she done these things?" I asked him pointedly.

"Yes and no..."

"So what does she want more than anything else, even if it should seem impossible?" I pressed him.

"Well...to extend her rule into the future, I suppose."

I nodded.

"So what if we offer her *immortality?*"

Everyone at the table looked shocked. I'd said something we all thought but wouldn't admit.

"That *is* the basis of most religions," my mother nodded thoughtfully. "Except that the doctrines only offer *hope* that life exists beyond the grave. From what Billy has told us, the Lords offer a close simulation in the here-and-now."

"It...is worth a try," Arthur answered softly. "But if it's so effective then why hasn't *your son* benefitted from it?"

All eyes turned to the white-haired, ancient "wizard."

He sighed deeply.

"Emissary though I am," he said softly, "I'm still just an 'invitee' to the contest. I can't benefit from the Prize unless my entire planet gains such. However, I've virtually visited many of the past winning planets. The benefits are real and given to all individuals of the dominating intelligent, musically endowed species."

That seemed to satisfy the rest of the people at the table.

"But to be effective, the agreement needs to also include the leaders of Phoenix," I noted. "Presumably they also share this fundamental human drive: the *survival instinct*, which normally trumps almost everything else. Is there any way to contact the Ruling Council of Phoenix?"

"I'll broadcast a pre-meeting invitation," Billy assured us. "I'll set up projecting nodules located about the Earth. In fact, we'll televise the invitation world-wide. Everyone will participate, distally. All the present Leaders of the world will certainly attend, lest they be left out of any agreement reached. Everyone will know of the stakes of the Contest: promised not just to the Commissioner, members of the ruling Phoenix Council, and us—but to every single person on the face of the planet!"

"Fantastic!" Sally King grinned at everyone. "Please set it up, Losa. Meanwhile, we'll proceed with Suzy's task: rounding up the *greatest human musical concert participants* ever assembled in one place!"

"But...if you do what you've proposed, yanking many celebrities out of history," Arthur again protested, "you risk massively changing the present Timeline into who knows what? We might not even exist, let alone be able to proceed with a virtual conference including the Commissioner and everyone else."

Again, he sounded very doubtful of the plan. What was wrong with him? He certainly wasn't the bold, decisive "Country Joe" I'd fallen in love with at Woodstock. Anderson was merely a shell of the strong, defiant Cleve. I *pitied* him.

My disgust must have shown on my face. He ducked his disfigured head, not meeting my defiant gaze.

"Well, you actually have a good point," Billy frowned. "I'd have thought we could snatch the selected, marked individuals and just return them to the same moment when their participation at the Galactic Core ended, but..." his voice trailed off.

"I don't know if I have the expertise or control to do such delicate 'surgery' of the past Timeline," Sally added. "And unless we could erase their memories, the returned 'enlightened' geniuses would surely upset their recorded histories."

"Alright then, *I* have the answer," Arthur growled, seemingly reluctantly. "I've done it many times during my trips throughout history recruiting for the Time Keepers."

"Then why did you raise the objection?" Billy asked, genuinely puzzled.

Anderson sat stone-faced, refusing to answer.

Good. The others were beginning to realize they couldn't trust the "reformed" Time Keeper.

"We appreciate your help," Losa stated for the record. "Please continue, Agent Anderson."

"I still think this whole endeavor opens us up to attack by Phoenix or the Commissioner," Anderson spat (yes, saliva actually splattered us through his half-sliced-open mouth, disgusting!) "It's unwise! However, if you're determined to proceed..."

"We are," I insisted, resisting the urge to spit back at him.

"Well, then we don't snatch the targets at significant 'tipping-points' where their alteration, however brief or mental, will change subsequent events."

"Then where do we grab them?" I asked, intrigued.

"You 'mark' them at any point in their history, but only transport them at the moment of their death. This is SOP for Time Keeper recruitment."

Everyone at the table was silent, pondering this strange proposal.

"At their death?" Scott gulped. "What good will having their dead bodies do us?"

"If we can get the cooperation of the Commissioner, she'll have a medical facility awaiting their corpses. Just as the Time Keepers did with Sanako, we'll repair their time-frozen bodies and resurrect them. This is how most of our Time Keepers were recruited, allowing us to select only the best and brightest throughout known history without altering Timelines. They'll bring their entire life-experience and wisdom while not having to return to screw up historical events. After the Concert they'll stay with us, here in their distant future."

Billy slowly nodded. "It just might work. But won't their missing corpses...?"

"In the Time Keeper recruitment process we replicated a nonliving duplicate, inserting it in their place. No one will know we've stolen the person to resume life here. Of course there is little margin for error. We have to catch them in time-freeze at the moment of death, before cellular decay sets in."

"But," Losa scowled at the misshapen man, "if this is so easy to do—snatch the newly dead, fix them, and reanimate them—then why do you not do this for yourself? You look like you are badly in need of some...'fixing.'"

Arthur looked like he was trying to hide from us, shrinking into his seat.

"I would have had to leave Sally and Suzy behind and return to the Commissioner," he sighed deeply. "I think I do some good here, protecting the 'Girls with the Turtle Tattoos.' Also, the Commissioner rightly views me as a traitor that she thoroughly hates. And, needless to say, such technology is beyond anything you have in this present Dimension."

"But if they could repair the damage done to you, then...?" I began.

"Don't pity me!" Anderson snapped at us all. "I'm not prepared to accept such a defeat, to make such a sacrifice. Despite what you might think of me, Suzy, I am loyal to my convictions—and to the both of you. For this scheme to work, we need the advanced medical facilities of the Commissioner's Second Earth's Time-Keeper Corp. I will add my voice to Losa's. Though she hates me she still respects my knowledge and skill. Together we will *intrigue* her."

"Hopefully 'intriguing' her sufficiently to acquire her agreement and support in our Mount Everest conference," Losa nodded grimly. "I am sorry, Agent Anderson. Based on stereotyping your extra-dimensional past and your present F.B.I. work, I misjudged you. As a Native-American I am naturally suspicious of governmental operatives. But just as I reject others stereotyping me, I must guard myself against projecting the same on others. Can you forgive me?"

"Gladly," Arthur said, now holding his mutilated head high.

Spontaneously, they both extended their hands which met in a strong grasp above the tabletop.

"Then I will communicate my updated request to the Commissioner," Losa stated, "backed up by Arthur's added report."

"She definitely will be interested. Even with continued treatments, our 'rejuvenation' eventually fails," Arthur added. "The last time I saw the Commissioner she was aging rapidly. A type of immortality plus unlimited control of energy transmutation will be personally tempting to all our captors, no matter their political, philosophical, or religious beliefs."

Wow. This adventure was getting beyond incredible. If I could really have *any musician in the history of the world* at my disposal—that changed everything! We could truly put on a Concert the like of which the world had never seen. And all I had to do was hop back in Time and "tag" them all...

Damn, this was getting to be *fun!*

Later, as the planning meeting was starting to break up, I put an arm around Losa's broad shoulders and handed him a gift.

"What's this?" he said, looking into my opened hand.

I held a "*mega marble lion mammoth*" glass marble. Just as when I was in kindergarten, Billy's new marbles were gorgeous. I'd carefully hunted for and gathered up all of them from where they'd rolled onto the floor. The "lion" had interlocking swirls of bright orange, yellow, and caramel imbedded a clear matrix. It was beautiful. I placed it firmly into his calloused, strong fist.

"It's me 'tagging' you for the Concert—you and your entire tribe's Stomp Dance team."

"Ah..." he now smiled. "It would be our honor."

He slipped it into his pocket and departed with Scott, *whistling* a happy Chickasaw tune.

Anderson just shook his head in apparent disgust. He was back to being a mean, irritating brute. How I'd ever had feelings for his younger self I couldn't fathom. He was disgusting!

"Your dog working ok?" he unexpectedly asked me.

"What?"

"I saw he was limping. So I asked your brother for his specs. I've always been good with mechanical things and computers. Fortunately there wasn't any damage to his vital circuitry. Some of his pseudo-bones were out of alignment because micro-gears were bent. A scalpel, needle nosed pliers, and screwdriver were all it took to fix him."

Scotty was prancing happily around both of us.

"Thanks," I reluctantly acknowledged Arthur's expertise. So it wasn't Billy who fixed the dog. That was nice of Anderson to do. But I didn't forget that Scotty was damaged in the first place because he was trying to stop Anderson's BOMB that *killed* thousands at Woodstock and almost incinerated *us* as well!

I wasn't forgiving Anderson that easily. He'd have to do a lot more than just fix my damaged robot dog.

The top of Mount Everest was a spectacular site.

I marveled that in only a few days we'd pulled off this ethereal conference.

I stood on the somewhat slanted surface looking out over a jagged mountain range filled with razor-sharp, white-black peaks. A blanket of fluffy clouds rolled past *below* the peaks. The bright sun glared down from an unnaturally deep blue sky. A rainbow tangle of smushed flags was strewn across the light coating of ice and snow at my feet, frozen in place.

Our square metallic Emitters were harpooned into the rock on all sides of the peak. They'd been delivered by jet-drones specially designed to hover in the thin air at 30,000 feet.

It was the ultimate political "summit."

There at the top of the world, projected from the holo-emitters and experienced within 3D helmets at our various actual locations, the present top Authorities of our world would soon meet for a fateful decision. They'd all accepted our invitation. We were the first to arrive. When everyone's image materialized, we'd link into satellites to broadcast the meeting world-wide. Wherever people normally received video or audio input, they'd see or hear what happened on the top of Mount Everest.

Mom, Arthur, and the technicians were checking and fine-tuning the holo-emitters. The advanced technology Arthur had smuggled with him from the 2nd Dimension, supercharged by Billy's alien tech, was working as expected, linking everything seamlessly together.

"It is an inspiring vista," Losa Yanash stated solemnly, walking up to stand next to me. The illusion of our both actually being there on Everest's peak was only broken because our feet left no footprints in the fresh snow. Fortunately we were only virtual images. The temperature that day at the "top of the world" was -25° C, a relatively "warm" day. Plus, a fierce wind was sweeping across the peak. Both Losa and I were seemingly standing there in our street clothes. If we'd truly been there in the flesh we'd be frozen solid and tossed away like twigs in a hurricane.

"It visually confirms what's at stake," I agreed, complimenting myself on my choice of venue.

"Yes, my people have always had a close connection with Nature," Losa nodded slowly. His gray braids were strangely unmoved by the hurricane blast. "Today we represent the entire Earth's biosphere, discussing its future. It is fitting we congregate on the planet's highest peak."

That was an indeed a sobering thought. Up to that moment I'd been caught up in the adventure and splendor of it all. But this "summit" was incredibly serious: *deciding the entire fate of humanity!* We could keep bumbling along on our own, poised to erupt into nuclear annihilation or societal meltdown at any moment, or seek a radically different path.

But to take that path—even if we somehow won the Concert—we'd have to cede control to a vastly older alien race.

"You don't sound optimistic," I asked, concerned with his sober tone.

"I just hope this 'peace treaty' fairs better than those previously done between a defeated native population and their technologically superior conquerors," he shrugged.

Perhaps he was overstating things a bit. But The Commissioner had already solidified her conquest of Dimension One. The various factions of Phoenix were theoretically still in charge of their different swaths of Earth, setting their restrictive rules and establishing strict oppressive governments. But with the steady increase in the number of 2nd Dimension-imported Peace Keepers, now ascending into the

'Earth One' hierarchies, the Commissioner was steadily pulling Phoenix's controlling strings tighter and tighter.

There was no defense against the technologically superior energy and cyber-weapons of the Peace Keepers. We could only proceed with our larger objective if the Commissioner agreed.

"Has subjugation of one society by another ever gone well?" I asked. I knew that though he was by trade a Park Ranger he also had a strong personal interest in all aspects of history. If he'd wanted, he could have become an acclaimed Professor of History at some prestigious University.

Losa sighed deeply, staring out across the spectacular tops of the Himalayas.

"The short answer is 'no'," he thoughtfully replied. "A forced assimilation into the victorious culture is the historical standard. In some cases the collision is cataclysmic: the 'overwritten society' is destroyed. But, more often than not, the merger results in a new equilibrium, where information is exchanged and both societies are hypothetically improved. Evolution is always brutal, Suzy, whether that of species or societies. But, from my perspective, merging two separate Dimensions is *particularly* frightening. On the Cosmic scale it's like two Galaxies colliding!" he shuddered visibly.

"—and our possible union with *The Lords of the Galaxy?*"

"Oh, that is simply beyond comprehension."

"What about the Chinese?" I asked.

His eyes narrowed as he considered my question.

"Yes, Suzy, there is a persistent myth that China excelled at 'absorbing' its foreign conquerors. They were theoretically conquered many times. But over time the imposed rulers blended into and 'became' Chinese. However, that was never really the case. The Chinese just have such a large population that it's relatively easy for them to 'absorb' its conquerors. What I said previously still held true, even for them."

"What about individuals 'going native'?"

"Sure...individuals occasionally gave up their old ways to adapt native customs...but not whole societies. Bigger guns always win, Suzy. Them's the facts. The conquerors rape, pillage, murder, and steal anything they want. The conquered just try to survive until they can gain for themselves the superior knowledge and technology of their conquerors. Only then can they hopefully negotiate a new equilibrium better than just being slaves. This is the history of my people with the European invaders."

"But what if the invaders are not conquerors but benefactors?"

"Ah, yes...*benefactors*," Losa softly replied, putting an evil twist on the word. He paused before replying.

"I'm thinking of a few people I knew in the Fiji islands," I continued while he considered what I'd asked. "Although they were hell-bent on forcing their new religion on others—in this case a Protestant Christian religion upon avowed, dedicated *cannibals*—they did so out of a sincere desire to help others."

"So they saw the natives as 'heathens' who needed to be 'saved' and 'civilized'," Losa spoke accusingly.

"Well, yes, but they didn't intend to exploit, only—from their perspective—truly help."

"Ok, then," Losa sighed. His wrinkled eyes looked weary and infinitely sad. "Take me as an example. I am no longer directly connected to Nature as an *Animist*, the historical nature-centered religion of my people. By upbringing, I'm now a Christian. I was raised in your Protestant denomination. I enthusiastically sang with you when you and your family had Gospel performances at our church. Do you think that the missionaries who initially evangelized my ancestors really did this for our good or for their own prestige, to tie another knot on their 'winning for Jesus' belts?"

That was a sobering thought.

"Ok," I admitted, "we can't see into their hearts. But suppose that true benefactors really existed, Losa—who out of the goodness of their hearts bring only gifts and ask nothing in return. What then?"

"It is not possible."

"So if they claim to be such?"

"They are liars."

"Ah..."

Billy walked up in his long, flowing toga. He radiated enthusiasm. With his long white hair, flowing beard, and flaring mustache he only lacked a gold crown to be proclaimed the snow-King at the top of the world! Hah!

I started to kid him but he cut me off... "They'll be arriving any second now," he warned us.

Beside him appeared my Mom. She was frowning, pursing her lips together.

And as if beckoned by him, with crackling "pops", others linked-in: a black-bearded, glowering-eyed Muslim man wearing a turban with an *ornamental musket* slung over his shoulder; a blue-eyed, blond haired, clean shaven right-wing Christian carrying an *assault rifle*; a steely eyed oriental Buddhist priest in an orange robe clutching a *Smith & Wesson*; a scrawny Jewish teenager with glasses, sporting a short beard and tassels hanging from under a cap, who was tightly clutching a *long knife*; and several other menacing sorts. It was the ruling council of Phoenix. Talk about caricatures.

Around them, packed tightly but extending down the slopes within easy earshout, appeared the ruling *Heads of Government* from all the major nations of the Earth.

Immediately they all began arguing among themselves.

"*Silence!*"

The virtual group cowered together as they all turned to face a newly arrived older woman: petite, gray hair pulled back in a tight bun, dressed in a sensible blue pants suit. On her feet were flat, black dress shoes. She carried in her hands an ordinary notebook and pen. She looked like an iconic computer-punching senior bureaucrat.

I'd never seen her before. But I *did* recognize her unquestioned icy Authority, which I'd seen in every historical dictator I'd ever studied. It had to be *The Commissioner*.

And ignoring her undyed gray hair—she was the exact duplicate of my mother, Sally King.

"Ah...my 'Niece,'" she smiled icily at me. It was a frightful smile, just an upward twitch of the corners of her lips accompanied by a green-eyed steady stare.

She moved toward me across the slick slope, like a ghost drifting through a nightmare.

She reached out a clawed hand and griped my arm. No...I mean she *really* grabbed my arm! I *felt* it where I stood helmeted supposedly safely hidden away in the Sphere-cavern outside Sulphur, Oklahoma. Trying to hide from her was futile. She knew where we were hidden! Her superior technology had reached beyond our subterfuge.

"I know all about your 'adventures', Suzy," she softly informed me. Her voice was like the warning hiss of a poisonous coiled snake, poised to strike. "In other circumstances you'd have made a fine addition to my Time Keepers. But now..."

Sally King lunged at her to drive her back, but with a casual wave The Commissioner *froze* my Mom in place.

"Don't be concerned, my dear 'Sister'," she coldly laughed. "You, your perky little 'pop superstar', and your other friends are not in danger. I am here for information."

She released my Mom, who staggered several steps backward.

"You promised to tell me of an *Alien Probe* offering unimaginable gifts," the Commissioner continued. "I of course knew of your late husband's experiments. He crudely cracked open subspace, giving you rudimentary time travel capabilities. But this extraterrestrial contact is a new wrinkle. You say they offer us humans an amazing Prize if we win some silly contest?"

"Yes they do!" Billy happily exclaimed. "I speak for them.'

She slowly walked around him, looking him up and down with naked distain.

"And here is my little, extremely old 'Nephew'—*Ambassador of the Invaders*—looking to help an *alien race* subjugate my little planet in all its Timelines and Dimensions. Beside me, only *you* amongst this august group weld true Power. In some ways you are my equal," she coldly acknowledged him.

He grandly bowed to her. "It is my honor to represent the *Lords of the Galaxy* who..."

"Yes, yes," she interrupted him. "I did my research after that *traitor* Arthur Anderson contacted me through Mr. Yanash. I now know all about their million-year 'contest' and the Grand Prize that..."

"You can't dismiss us so easily!" Arthur yelled at her, his pent up anger erupting. "You need to know that all the video and auditory devices of this planet are receiving the broadcast I'm sending from here to..."

With a wave of her hand he tumbled down to the frozen rocks, gasping for breath. His big hands were at his own throat, throttling himself!

"No! *Please!*" I begged her, stepping forward.

"I thought you had no love for this bug."

I had no reply.

"We n-need him," I stammered weakly.

Her glaring green eyes narrowed. She released Arthur, who convulsed, heaving and gasping, on the frozen rocks.

"You still harbor some feelings for that used-up wreck," she coldly laughed at me. "You two must have been quite an item at the Woodstock debacle. But as to his puny threat, I've blocked all retransmissions of our meeting here. The world will learn of our decision only when and if I permit such."

Everyone present looked fearful, about to cut their communications and bolt.

"But do not fear!" she ordered us all loudly. "Once we've finished our 'pre-discussion' you can transmit whatever you want to all the creatures of all Earth's Dimensions from this very Summit. Explain everything to them. But, for the moment, we need no silly political posturing. *It wastes my time!*" she snarled.

Sally stepped forward.

"Please, you clearly already know what we intended to present to you. So what questions do *you* have for us?"

The Commissioner smiled coldly, nodding appreciatively. "Yes, I should have just dealt with this world's closest analog to myself, *you!* It's so much more efficient."

"Efficient?" I asked, struggling to stay focused.

"You *all* think I'm a monster, I know." She shrugged her impeccably clad shoulders, seemingly reading my mind. "I'm not! I just want to have an *orderly* society, where people get along with each other, refraining from harming each other. Is that asking too much?" she asked, seemingly innocently.

Arthur shook his grotesque head sadly, slowly pushing himself up to his knees and then his feet: "*Yes*, if you want us to be humans who…"

"No!" she snapped at him, forcing his defiant gaze from her to the rocks at his feet. "We are not cursed to be but smart animals," she seethed at us all. "I've proven this in the 2nd Dimension. I have *one simple rule*: BE NICE! That's all. You idiotic fundamental radical 'religiosity' rulers gathered here today should already know—what with all your conflicting 'God-given' commands—my one simple Rule is *at the heart* of your true Founders' Teachings! If you didn't lust for Power for its own sake, you idiots would all see how *easy* true 'religion' can be."

The Phoenix Council members looked like they wanted to simultaneously tear her to pieces while also running away in terror. But they were frozen in place by her viciously cutting words. Also, I glimpsed behind them the ghostly figures of attending, black-clad, armed Peace Keepers. Ah yes, Phoenix was now fully under her control.

"But I'm not like you," she shrugged again. "I don't want Power. It's more a burden to me than a pleasure. I don't even want to force 'niceness' on others. I just want to have a pleasant, orderly society— by whatever means necessary! That's all..."

Did no one dare answer her?

"You *kill* that which is *most* important!" Arthur finally spat back at her.

"Oh, shut the hell up!" she snapped at him, with a wave of her hand gluing his lips together. He fell again to the ground, grasping futilely at his fused-together mouth.

"So you...approve...our entering the Aliens' Contest?" I tentatively asked, hoping she wouldn't melt my mouth shut like Anderson.

She shrugged.

"From what I've learned about these 'Lords of the Galaxy' they supply exactly what I most desire. And, somehow, they do it even better than me. Where I must *enforce* 'niceness' they *entice* their 'winners' to do so voluntarily. That would be even better than me having to post a Peace Keeper on every street corner, don't you think?"

"But...can we trust them?" I dared to whisper my doubts.

She nodded thoughtfully, walking to my side and putting a comforting arm around me.

Again, I directly *felt* the arm. And it *wasn't* comforting. Instead, it was like the rigid, spiked arm of a giant *praying mantis* drawing me closer to bite my head off.

I fought against the urge to jerk away, continuing to look her straight into her unblinking green eyes.

"My dear young girl...this pre-discussion is going so well because I've been getting reports for years about some fleeting future timeline possibilities: of an Earth where all our intractable, present problems are gone."

"I..."

"Quiet, child."

I was about to admit I'd been there, seen it for myself. But it was clear she neither needed nor required my input. For someone that didn't desire Power she definitely had the arrogance of a Dictator, Emperor, or absolute King: to whom you only speak if you're addressed.

I nodded, still matching her unblinking gaze.

"The *energy* crisis, the *overpopulation* crisis, the *food* crisis, the *resource* crisis, the *war* crisis, the *religious hatred* crisis, the *inequity* crisis, the *disease* crisis, the *climate* crisis, the *mortality* crisis, the *poverty* crisis, the *tribal politics* problem, the *space exploration* crisis, the *nuclear bomb proliferation* crisis, the *species extinction* crisis, the *empire clashing* conflicts...you name the world-wide problem and it's gone, as if by magic."

"This is what I've been telling my friends here that..." Billy tried to chime in.

She waved a hand at him and he unwillingly prostrated himself on the ground at her feet. His trembling hands involuntarily reached to his belt and drew forth his *crystal sword*, laying the symbol of his authority at her feet. It was sad to see my brother so abjectly humiliated.

"The Earth's population is voluntarily decreased to an easily maintained burden upon planet Earth," she continued her comment, "where people are healthy, live as long as they wish, have all that they desire, are in harmony with nature and each other, and they're genuinely *happy!* Who could ask for more?" she smiled coldly.

Even though everyone else heard her answering my question, I saw she was asking a new one: the very same Question that tortured me. She was beyond shrewd. I'd almost welcome her rule.

Almost...but not quite.

An uncomfortable silence extended out as we all stood there on the top of Mount Everest.

"Yes," I finally replied, clearing my throat uncomfortably: "It's Paradise for us humans—*if* we win this celestial musical talent show."

She backed off a step, withdrew her arm, and patted me on my head as if I were a prized pet show-dog.

It was humiliating. I struggled to not bite her hand.

"Well, then I certainly endorse the effort. Be a good little pop-star and do your best. Should you beat out countless other worlds with your cute songs, the Prize fits in fine with what I want," she stated.

Now she turned pointedly to the assembled members of Phoenix: "Don't you agree?"

Reluctantly, the ruling clique all nodded...except one.

He lunged forward with a previously hidden dagger held high only to be *garroted* from behind and pulled backward. His eyes bulged from his head as he was efficiently suffocated.

"So it's unanimous," she concluded. "Proceed with your preparations. My assistant will coordinate with you, providing whatever 2nd Dimension resources you may need. I only have one stipulation," she said. She glared down at the moaning Agent Anderson who was clutching feebly at his fused mouth.

"And what is your requirement?" Billy meekly asked as he still lay bowed-down to her on the ice-covered rocks.

"That *traitor* must *not* receive any of the one-time restorative procedures you will use on some of your time-recruits as you prepare them for your Concert," she ordered.

"Can we surgically fix his mouth?" I dared to ask, not wanting Anderson to starve.

"Alright then, to show you how 'merciful' I am—I'll do it for you."

She bent over to Anderson, jammed the tip of her pen into his jaw on one side of his head, and with a series of hard jerks *ripped* his fused lips apart. Blood gushed out onto her hands.

"There...all fixed," she smiled benignly, crouching to wipe her hands on the snow at her feet.

Jesus! She actually left blood on the snow! She was incredibly powerful, capable of suffusing our virtual holograms with hard reality.

I was horrified by her casual brutality but didn't have time to allow myself to feel Arthur's pain. I needed a *specific* commitment.

"And what if we need to 'resurrect' *ten thousand people* from out of Time to take with us to the Galactic Core—will that be ok?" I asked her eagerly.

She nodded. "I will instruct my Time Keepers to ramp up their processing for..."

"How about *100,000?*" I pressed her.

She looked at me darkly for a minute.

"I'm representing our entire human species, Ma'am. I need to put on a Concert that's beyond spectacular!"

"Suzy, you will only have the equivalent of *two hours* to make Earth's presentation," Billy spoke up, still prostrated. "You can't give a summary of all the musical history of the planet. The Lords have chosen you to give *your* particular perspective on Music. It has to be *focused* and..."

"So how about *a million* people?" I boldly asked. I knew I was pressing my luck, but I had to have all options possible.

Now the Commissioner wryly laughed at my audacity.

"You may gather together out of Time and take with you to the Galactic Core up to 500,000 individuals," The Commissioner relented. "If you fail, it will not be for lack of resources. Processing that many rescues will strain my capabilities, but then again—we have all the time in the world. After all, *virtual immortality* awaits us *all* if your little songs can..."

"You...*hag*," Arthur burbled around the torrent of blood still gushing from his torn mouth. "Your...*depleted* cells...will never...be again recharged to..."

She *kicked* him viciously in the head and he lay still.

"It's true I've gone beyond what is humanly possible in rejuvenating my tissues over the centuries," she sighed.

"But we're the same age, aren't we?" Sally King now gulped, look-ing at her "twin" in puzzlement.

"How long do you think it takes to conqueror a whole world?" The Commissioner growled at my Mom. "I'm me from your future, when my options are fast disappearing. I'm the ultimate Time Keeper, op-erating with my troupe out-of-time. My younger self is still pacifying the 2nd human Dimension. But I pull the ultimate "strings" balancing and directing the various Timelines and their possible permutations."

"So you've already seen what happens with our effort?" my Mom frowned, looking confused.

"Of course not! Would I be here with you time-locked peasants if I did? Around you and your daughter, Time *swirls* in strange, unpre-dictable patterns."

"We have been called 'time-twisters'," Sally admitted.

"Yes, exactly! And your daughter is *ten times* as confounding as you ever were, Sister. I should just kill the both of you. But your po-tential far outweighs your induced chaos."

"Thank you...I think," Sally sighed, smiling wanly at me.

"So I admit your proposal has strong personal appeal," this *future* Commissioner shrugged. "After all, the Prize for which you compete will bring us technology that's beyond human capabilities. Should you gain the victory I expect to rule not just a few more painfully eked-out years but for untold, glorious *eons!*"

"Fat chance!" Arthur sneered at her. He'd just recovered con-sciousness. I certainly did admire his spunk. He was a glutton for punishment.

She kicked him once again, loudly "snapping" his jaw. He moaned pitifully, lying on his broken face. Disdainfully, she now wiped the blood from her black shoe upon his quivering, broad back.

"Well, good luck then," she brightly concluded. "Win and we'll *all* benefit. Lose and I will be *very* displeased, making what remains of your inconsequential lives a living hell."

She glowered at us all.

Even Losa cringed back from her demonic stare.

"I *will* have my *permanent* orderly society," she flatly stated. "I decree that in *both* of Earth's human Dimensions you *will* be nice to each other...even if I *personally* have to make your lives *miserable!*

Obey my dictate or I will *beat* every last one of you ungrateful animals into submission. As to the Contest, you can work out the details with my trusted assistant."

I heard noises behind me and turned. Setting my VR-helmet to "see through" I saw the chilling image of dozens of heavily armed, black-clad Peace Keepers marching into the Sphere-cavern!

Oh, Christ, they'd found us.

I flipped my helmet back to virtual transmission mode and started to protest their invasion of the cavern to the Commissioner.

But she'd already vanished. In her place stood a slender, oriental woman in a stereotypic "ninja" outfit with straight black hair and equally cold black eyes.

I instantly recognized her.

It was *Sanako*.

I barely held myself back from attacking her, though I knew it'd be a futile gesture in the virtual projection zone. I wasn't the Commissioner with her solidification future technology. I saw the again-revived Arthur struggling to control his own fury at having to deal with Sanako.

"We've got work to do, people!" I yelled, stepping forward to take charge. After all, *I* was now the officially ordained "conductor" of this concert. I knew how to do it. It was just another "world tour" that happened to extend to the center of the Milky Way!

"We've only a year to pull this off," I continued. "Our first task is to explain to the populations of all the nations of all of Earth's Dimensions what the Commissioner has authorized us to attempt. Agent Anderson, despite your new injuries can you still oversee our broadcasting across all the Dimensions? Billy, are you ready with some convincing 'magic' tricks? And all the rest of you, can you please put our grand venture into terms that your particular religion or faction on Earth One will understand? And...Sanako...will you please instruct your Peace Keepers across the Dimensions to make sure everyone gets the message and will together view our Concert when it occurs? Also, order them to allow the populations to view our periodic updates on our preparations. We have to build enthusiasm. I need a *participating audience* that includes everyone!"

Yes, I didn't need just a half-million in-person, live participants. I wanted *all* the *billions* of humans presently alive on the face of the planet to actively participate through virtual connections.

I saw the individuals gathered there on the planet's highest peak reluctantly nod in agreement. It was obvious nobody wanted me in charge. Even my own mother, Sally—plus Arthur and Losa—looked irritated at my barked orders. The radical religious leaders were particularly offended that a mere "girl" was telling them what to do. But that was just too damn bad. The Lords of the Galaxy—whoever the hell *they* were—had ultimately put me in charge and I was *kicking asses* and *taking names!*

I never liked doing anything halfway. And it looked like I'd just been given permission to organize, direct, and star in the *greatest musical concert* the world had ever seen!

"Then let's get the announcement done so we can break our connections. If we're going to beat out all the rest of the Galaxy in this contest, I've got a lot of recruiting to do. Plus, I'm freezing!"

I wasn't really. I was still in my helmet in the warm Sphere-cavern. But my *soul* felt like it'd just escaped the clutches of the *Devil* herself. I sure have weird relatives.

Chapter 22

SCAVENGER HUNT

Toy elephants and cargo hats
Yellow snakes and flapping bats
Vintage cheese and newly pressed wine
Stuffed squirrels and a skeleton's spine

It's just a little game you see
A variation of "hide and seek"
Who can be the first to find them all
Peculiar "treasures" large and small

Can you find me when I'm disguised
Changed into something very funny
Making you laugh or snort or fart
Lurking somewhere easy or hard

Gregorian chants and troubadours
Italian operas and symphonies
Blues and jazz and slave traders
Thomas Edison and sound recordings

Pathos and comedy, side-by-side
Trumpets and electric guitars collide
The Grand Ole Opry versus Bing Crosby
A White Christmas in Western Countries
Find them all and you win a prize
Miss even one and YOU have to hide!
The Suzette Anthology, Lyric 22

"I can't do it tonight," Suzette whispered, looking thoroughly exhausted as she sat slumped in the makeup chair.

"Would some water help you, Ms. Kingly?" I asked, holding out a glass I'd snatched from a nearby formal crystal set awaiting use on the stage. She didn't recognize me. My hair was pulled back in a tight bun hidden beneath a big baseball hat. Plus I'd taken a trick from Anderson and was wearing dark eyeglasses. In a T-shirt and jeans I looked like any of a dozen young flunkies flitting about doing odd jobs backstage.

She was visibly trembling and nauseous. It was difficult to discern her mental state under her heavy makeup, but she was obviously suffering.

"No!" she snapped at me, batting the glass to the side.

It fell and shattered into a thousand pieces.

"You all know I only drink bottled water!" she yelled at me.

I found her "diva" sulk incredibly funny. Was this spoiled little brat really me? It felt so weird to be a couple years back in time when the awful "terrorist" assault on Music first began in my primary timeline. The Sphere had worked perfectly, inserting me at this exact, critical moment in the space-time continuum. But I was so amused by the temper-tantrum of Suzette that I almost burst out laughing, ruining my masquerade.

I barely suppressed my amusement, instead disguising it as trembling *fear*.

"Oh...I'm sorry," Suzette gulped, seemingly embarrassed by her gross rudeness.

She looked ridiculous. A *bright blond bushy wig* sat solidly on her plastered-down bald cap. Her face was painted *porcelain white*, her lips stained *ruby red*, her forehead adorned with *rubbery fake eyebrows*, and her *black eyelashes* pasted so long and low she could barely see past them.

To me she looked like a sad clown.

Her opening getup was complete. She was supposed to be a sexy, teenaged *Alice-in-Wonderland* character: with black striped leggings up to her calves, a very short blue dress down to the bottom of her butt, frilly lace white panties clearly visible at her crotch, puffy transparent sleeves, and a blue apron festooned with big sparkling jewels hanging from her neck.

This sort of silly teenaged fantasy would play no part in my up-coming Galactic Core concert. I was no longer a fluffy, superficial di-va. I was a battle-hardened woman, ready to fight for Earth's future.

"No problem, Ms. Kingly," I managed to answer without breaking out into a fit of laughter, backing off. "I'll get a dustpan to clean up the shards and find you some..."

She cut loose a long, prolonged, noisy *fart...*

"*BraaaaaaaaaaaAAApppppppt!*"

"Oh, honey, that was a bad one!" *Eun Jung* gasped, wrinkling his nose in disgust.

It was great to see Eun again. I'd never really appreciated the slender, elegant, deep-voiced man. Though he was of Korean ances-try (having grown up in South Korea as a child), he seemed to under-stand me better than anyone.

I noted the bags under his slanted eyes. The Tour was taking a toll on him. He was no longer keeping up his usual impeccable ap-pearance. I now recognized that his fashionably wavy brown-gray hair was greasy-looking, the shaved areas on the sides of his head sprouting unsightly clumps. After the bombing, I'd grieved for him more than any of the other crew or performers.

By my *not* cancelling the concert I'd doomed them all to a hideous death. Part of my terrible downward spiral after the bombing was from a pervasive sense of *guilt.*

And now I had a chance to save them all.

But he was right. That fart was epic! I could barely keep from gagging, running away in disgust.

"Sorry," She whispered, squirming. "I couldn't help it."

"Is your IBS acting up again?" Eun asked kindly, fanning at the air in front of his thin face with a hand.

"No...it's the flu or something...I'm sick."

"Oh, girl, it's your IBS. You know that your 'irritable bowel syn-drome' makes you miserable, especially when you're all agitated be-fore a performance. When that new girl gets back, drink a full bottle of water. You're dehydrated, your poor intestines all clogged up.

You'll be ok onstage if you can just hold in those awful farts. Those are *lethal!*"

I slipped back into the shadows, spying a piled-high food table. I ran over and grabbed a plastic bottle of water. Returning, I hid in the shadows until I could get Eun alone.

"No...it's more than just my IBS," Suzette muttered piteously.

I saw her slump face-first onto the table, one arm sweeping the jars and brushes off to the side onto the floor.

As they "clanked" and "cracked," Eun gasped but didn't admonish her. I admired him even more there as I stood at his side than when I'd been sitting whining in that chair. He knew me better than I knew me. Normally he would have protested at my "acting out," but not tonight. Instead he frantically phoned for my manager.

She came storming into the room, a scowl on her face.

"I've...had...it," Suzette gasped. "Honestly, Darlene...I can't do it anymore."

I stepped out of the shadows, holding out the bottle of water. Suzette grimaced, waving me away. I stood discretely in a corner, seemingly awaiting further directions.

"Sure you can, Suzette," Darlene insisted, her intense black eyes glaring. Then she fanned a dark-skinned hand in front of her nose. "Oh, God—what's that smell?"

"I farted," Suzette admitted, her voice trembling. "I'm sick. I've got a fever!"

"But the doctor gave you stronger meds, right?"

"It's just antibiotics."

"There's an old saying, kid. You know it as well as me: '*The show must go on!*'"

"Not if I'm dead," she whined.

"Look, Suzette," Darlene sighed, sitting down next to the makeup chair, "we're sold out tonight. This is the first performance of our *World Tour Six* that really counts, here in America. There are *18,000* of your fans out there. You can't let them down."

"You'll have to cancel," Suzette whispered, laying her artificial head down in the middle of the scattered makeup tins. "Tell them I'm sick. I *am* bloody well sick!"

"Come on, Suzette—you were alright the last couple days. The rehearsal this afternoon went ok, didn't it?"

"Yes..." she reluctantly admitted.

"So what's the problem? You've done this hundreds of times before."

"Ok..."

Suzette took a deep breath, tried to stand up, then collapsed back down. Her legs just wouldn't hold her up. I felt real empathy for her. She endured a fit of coughing before getting her breathing under control. Then she just *wheezed* while attempting to speak.

"Look, just get through tonight, Suzette," Darlene firmly ordered her, "...here, take this. It'll perk you up."

She put a little blue pill in Suzette's hand. I was tempted to snatch it and run off with it. Without that "pick-me-up" the concert would be canceled. Everyone would have to leave. If the bombs went off, few if any people would be hurt. But that would drastically change the Timeline, triggering who knew what terrible consequences.

I had to stick to the script, at least as much of it as I remembered.

Darlene motioned to me to hand her the bottled water. She twisted open the cap and sat it on the table in front of Suzette's white-painted nose.

"What's in it?" Suzette suspiciously asked.

"It's just a harmless stimulant...no worse than caffeine," Darlene answered. "I take them all the time myself. You know that I've a tough job also. This tour's way bigger, in every way, than anything we've attempted before. Keeping all the balls dancing in the air for the actual Concert while also organizing all the support structures is incredibly demanding. You're not the only person in the troupe hanging on by a thread. I'm just as tired as you."

"I've already drunk a ton of coffee today."

"This is much better. It'll give you strength to..."

"You know I hate pills."

"You took what the doc gave you, right? These are no different than..."

"Bull crap! This is *drugs!*"

She sighed deeply, putting a firm hand on Suzette's trembling shoulder.

"Look, if you make it through tonight we can cancel the next performance," Darlene's sharp voice insisted. "I promise you'll get a break."

"Hah...you've said that before, but..."

"You know our financial situation. This is the 'break-even' point. After tonight it's all profit. It's cost us a fortune to put on this world-class Tour. And tonight we're also paying for a *full orchestra* to back us up. Having to refund the gate tickets could throw us into bankruptcy. I won't be able to meet payroll! And that's not even to mention the IMAX filming being done tonight for a feature-length 3D film and a virtual reality game that..."

"I know! I know!"

"There's a lot on the line tonight," Arlene relentlessly continued. "To put on this giant Tour a lot of assets got leveraged—including your own personal wealth."

Suzette looked shocked by the revelation.

"And it's not just our present and future revenues," the hard-voiced woman relentlessly continued. "Like I said, your *fans* are out there waiting for you. You're onstage in twenty minutes! For God's sake, Suzette—you *can't* let them down!"

"I don't want to let anyone down," Suzette whined, "but..."

"Look, just try the pill. I swear it won't hurt you. If it doesn't perk you up in the next couple minutes, then I'll personally go onstage and announce that you collapsed. Maybe we won't get lynched or bankrupted if they think you're dying and..."

"Well..."

Darlene pointedly lifted up then thumped down the bottle of water on the tabletop.

"Look, you need some hydration whether you take more medication or not. We can't have you farting onstage! The mikes will pick it up and the family audience out there will hear it as the ultimate insult!"

"Thanks, Darlene," Suzette gasped, tearing up.

"Oh, darling, don't cry," Eun pleaded, "you'll ruin your makeup."

"Just try the pill, Suzy," Darlene again insisted, "Just this once. Look, I've got to go see about the pyros. There's some last minute problem with the local inspectors and police. I'll see you out there...or not. Whatever you decide, you know I'll handle it. I'm here for you, kid—you're number one!"

"The pyros...?"

"Don't worry about it. I'll take care of it."

"But...police? Is there some problem with the crowd?"

"It's nothing. I've got to go."

Suzette blearily watched her race out of the room.

"What do you think, Eun?" Suzette asked her faithful old friend, woozily raising her grotesquely made-up head from the table.

He shrugged.

"It's probably just Amphetamine, dearie," his deep voice soothed her, "but you never know unless it comes direct from a pharmacy. You're always taking a chance when you consume street-swag, no matter who gives it to you."

"So it's 'meth'?"

"No, honey," Eun sighed, speaking slowly as if to a little child. "If Darlene takes them they're probably just plain amphetamines. She's right. They increase focus and juice you up metabolically. They're often prescribed for ADHD or weight loss and..."

"Do you take them?"

"Huh...what haven't I taken in my younger, foolish days? Yes, I did some meth when I was a teenager. But it almost killed me. Your little blue pill is likely just a more potent form of regular amphetamine."

"Will I get addicted?"

"Just one pill, probably not, but..."

"Damn it!" Suzette grimaced, tossing it in her mouth and gulping down half the bottle of water.

She lapsed into yet another coughing fit. I felt for her. As silly and shallow was her little concert, she was fighting to deliver it to her fans.

"You ok, honey?" Eun asked, clearly concerned.

Suzette sipped studiously at the remaining water in the plastic bottle. She began to look better, more energetic.

"We've got to get you in place!" Sam Greene, my overweight stage manager nervously stated as he rushed into the dressing room. He looked very worried. It was so good to see him again! I almost lunged forward to give him a big hug but managed to hang back. He along with most of the crew had died that night, killed by the first blast.

He was frowning, one chubby hand scratching his stubbly chin while the other eased Suzette up out of her chair.

"Thanks, Sam," she gulped, staggering as he helped her along the crowded backstage.

I turned to Eun.

"You have to do something for me," I firmly stated, pulling off my baseball cap and shaking out my blond hair.

"Excuse me?" he replied, indignant that a mere "aid" was seemingly giving him orders.

I removed my dark eyeglasses.

"Uhhhh..." he frowned. Then his normally narrow eyes widened in shock as he looked closer at me. "*Suzette?* But...?"

He looked over to the retreating Suzette who Sam was helping slowly move off to the launching pad. Then he looked back at me, bewildered.

"I'm not 'Suzette'—at least not anymore. I'm just plain 'Suzy,' Eun. You were a very good friend to me in my 'superstar' years. I trusted you with my deepest secrets, just as you did me. I know that you're not gay, though you maintain an act to further your hairstyling career. You have a sweet, professional wife, Kathy, and three cute kids back in South Korea. You met her at a perfume convention in Thailand. You told no one of your secret marriage, just me. And tonight she's going to be a *widow*, your kids left *fatherless*—unless you do exactly as I direct!"

"How can you know this...just who *are* you?"

"I told you, I'm Suzy King!" I impatiently repeated, "—from over two years in the future. Look, there's no time to explain in detail. I've got a lot of other stops to make. My time-machine has limited fuel," I lied. I'd have loved to tell him everything. But being on a tight schedule that Mom had programmed into the Sphere I couldn't chit-chat endlessly.

"This is a lot for me to accept."

"You know me!" I snapped at him. Then more gently but just as urgently I continued: "All you have to do is take this *Marble* and *keep* it in your pocket! Don't stick it in a jar or a drawer. It must be on your person, in direct contact with your body, always!"

Actually, it could just be nearby. It served as a "book-mark" to quickly and easily access him, his Timeline, and all those who interacted with him. But the further it got away from him the more tenuous the time-link. Billy had taught me well.

Frowning, he reached out and took the Marble, holding it tentatively in his hand. It was a very rare antique marble: an *Akro Agate* with four red-yellow corkscrew lines set into a milky green matrix. It was gorgeous.

"I'll contact you later, after the bombs go off."

"Bombs? Should I tell the police, try to stop the concert?"

"Hah," I snorted in disgust. "The police already know of the threat and Darlene insists 'the show must go on.'"

"But...?"

"Eun, please just trust me," I said, grasping his hands in mine. "I'm going to save you. I'm going to save everyone. Just *don't lose* that marble!"

He was still shaking his head in confusion as I faded away and vanished. If he was tempted to conclude my presence was some sort of hallucination, my disappearance after solidly holding his hands should convince him something extraordinary had happened. Plus, he still had that beautiful Marble in his hand.

It was a good template for my scheduled other visits. If my Mom could place me as deftly as this into the lives of my other additional "invitees," then I was off to a running start.

I walked with head reverently bowed into the English Cathedral. The year was 2012. I could have gone far into the past to hear Gregorian Chants, even back to their origination in the Middle Ages, but I wanted modern-day Monks familiar with advanced technology.

I slipped into one of the back benches. Benedictine Monks in their iconic black habits were chanting the powerful hymn *"Dies Irae"* or "Day of Wrath." Some scholars dated the hymn back to Pope

Gregory, the initiator of the form of music known as "Gregorian Chants." *Dies Irae* was famously performed in Catholic Masses for centuries.

"DIES IRAE, DIES ILLA, SOLVET SAECLUM IN FAVILLA, TESTE DAVID CUM SIBYLLA..." the Monks chanted in Latin: *Day of wrath and doom impending; David's word with Sibyl's blending, Heaven and Earth in ashes ending...*

Though the melody was slow and simple, the voices of the Monks reverberating off the high stone pillars of the Cathedral's nave were mystical and inspiring. Indeed, Gregorian Chants are credited as the very beginning of Western music. I needed these expert practitioners! But how could I get one of them to take a marble? Although the Benedictine Monks don't take a vow of poverty, they have a radical version of communal living where everything is owned in common.

Personal gift were prohibited.

I waited until the service was over then approached one of the departing Monks. He was the leader of the group. Also, he was the Abbot of their Abbey, the one who made the decisions which the rest unquestioningly obeyed.

He was a middle aged, very fat man sporting a graying brown beard, short brown hair, and black-rimmed glasses. He wore the simple black habit of the Benedictine monks.

"Uh...hi, there! I'm Suzy King and I'm just visiting here. I heard your performance. It was magnificent! And I've got a request."

"Well, hi there yourself, Suzy. I'm Brother Frederick. Thank you for the compliment. So what can I do for you?"

"I have a question and a gift," I said.

"Ah, well I certainly love attempting to answer thoughtful questions. But I have no need for gifts, as we Benedictine Monks have no personal possessions."

"Yes, I know," I answered. "But first the question: I've read that you Benedictine Monks take three vows: of *obedience*, *stability*, and *life-conversion*. But what *really* drives you people to take such radical vows? What do you want *most* of all?"

He narrowed his eyes, looking at me intensely. I saw that he realized I wasn't just a pretty girl giving his group a superficial compliment on their performance at the church service.

"Ah, I take it you speak to our deepest motivation, not just our desire to sequester ourselves away from evil or perpetuate Truth in a world obsessed with falsehood?"

"Yes."

He fingered his beard, squinting at me.

"You seek to know why I and others of the Order of Saint Benedict choose to do such extreme things as cloistering and living by a set schedule each day—such as formally praying at least five times a day?"

"Yes, please."

"Ok, then. I guess I can't speak for everyone in the Order. But I can speak for me. Is that acceptable?"

"That would be fine."

"Well..." he paused, nodding thoughtfully, "I suppose what I want most is to *draw close to God*. Our extreme vows and rituals are just means of quieting our minds to better receive the Reality of God. In that fashion I suppose we are very similar to other cloistered religious groups throughout history."

"And just what is the 'Reality of God'?"

He sighed deeply. "I wish I had an easy answer. I conclude, as for all mystics, it's something that requires a lifetime to comprehend—which then can't be explained or taught. Each person must experience it for him-or-herself. Does that help you, Suzy?"

"What about Music?"

"You are a most interesting person, Suzy. I love your questions. Well, for us—as with other monastic traditions—we regard Music as one of our rituals that help us focus on the Divine. Also, it draws us all together as a common, inspiring activity."

"That's all, nothing more?"

He slyly grinned. "Well, some are not blessed by the Lord with musical talent or appreciation..."

"—who you don't wish to offend," I finished his sentence.

"Yes, but for me and many others...Music—in its balance, harmony, and transcendental beauty is..." he paused, considering.

"Yes?" I likewise grinned, giving him permission to state it.

"It's an attribute of God Himself."

"Ah..."

"It is the closest we come to merging with God: a *divine ecstasy* that catapults our souls beyond the constraints of earthly matters and restraints."

"So today, singing your Gregorian chants...?"

"I never felt closer to God," he quietly stated, his eyes tearing up.

I smiled at him.

"Listening in the audience, I felt exactly the same," I agreed.

"I take it you are a fellow performer."

"I do some singing. I also play the guitar, keyboards, and drums."

What a nice guy, turning the compliment back on me.

"Well you just keep it up," he grinned, patting his ample belly. "I'm afraid I must leave you as our schedule is tight. We must take our communal meal soon and..."

"Well, I was really impressed with your singing," I hurriedly continued, "—and I'd like to make a donation to your group. But I'm not sure how to go about it. That's my second question, how to give a gift to your group."

He again smiled at me: "Ah, that is most kind of you. You are welcome to write a check to the Abbey, or donate online."

"Yes, I'll look into that—but I have something else I'd like to donate other than mere money."

"Oh?"

"I hear you have a daily short period of recreation where you play various games. Do you happen to ever play *Chinese Checkers?*"

He looked intrigued. I'd done my research well.

"Actually, we do. I find it a challenging board game while still being simple and quick. It's a lot of fun for us. In fact, we've about worn out our present board."

"Well, what a coincidence!" I exclaimed. "I just happen to have a very durable antique set here that I'd like to donate to a good cause, where it won't be sold off but used and treasured. Most kids nowadays demand computer games. So orphanages and the like are out."

"That is so true," he nodded sadly. "Often the old ways are best."

I held out a box to him: "If your Abbey would like it, I'm happy to give this to you. I recently inherited it and don't have any use for it. Unfortunately I don't have time to play board games. It contains rare, beautiful marbles. It's probably worth several hundred dollars."

"That is most kind of you," he smiled, taking the box. "It will be a good addition to our communal room. Thank you very much."

"It is my pleasure," I grinned, turning away. It would be better if I could get him just to take the *celestial agate* nestled with the ordinary marbles as a personal gift. But if it was located in their communal room where they gathered like clockwork each day, I still had a shot at "snagging" the entire monastery when the time came.

"And thanks again for the great singing!" I called back as I walked away.

"Thank Pope Gregory," he cheerfully responded.

Ah, he was a Monk with a sense of humor. For Benedictines who frowned at making trivial jokes, he was certainly an enlightened Abbot. Pope Gregory, the initiator of the "Gregorian" chant, died in 604 A.D., a millennium and a half in the past. I liked Brother Frederick's easy humor. After he died and resurrected he'd be a good person to have on my team. My review of local records indicated he presently suffered from severe diabetes and would die of a massive heart attack three years hence.

Sorry to postpone your trip to heaven—I mentally apologized to him. *But your planet needs your awesome chants more.*

Likewise specifically tailoring my approach, I plowed my way onward through Time. I deposited my Sphere-marbles on, with, or nearby my carefully selected historical targets.

I visited *Mother Hildegard von Bingen*, on her deathbed in 1179, who was a German nun, scientist, philosopher, preacher, poet, and composer that founded her own Convent and spent her life seeking the "Living Light"; King Richard I, better known as *King Lionheart*, while imprisoned by his enemies in 1192, composing his most famous song "Ja Nus Hons Pris"; Jacopo Peri, better known as *Zazzerino*, an Italian composer, in 1597 as he wrote the world's first opera, "Dafne"; Wolfgang Amadeus *Mozart* during his impoverished period in 1788; the American conductor *Ureli Corelli Hill* in 1842 as he founded the New York Philharmonic symphony orchestra; *Harriet Tubman*, an African-American born into slavery, who cleverly used negro spirituals to guide rescued slaves to freedom, working as a scout for the Union Army in 1863 during the American Civil War; *Thomas Edison* in

1877 just as he invented the phonograph; the great trumpeter Louis Armstrong, affectionately known as *Satchmo*, one of the great figures of Jazz, as a young 18-year-old performing on a New Orleans riverboat in 1918; *George Beauchamp* in 1937 when he patented the electric guitar; *Roy Acuff* in 1938 when he first joined the Grand Ole Opry, placing a national spotlight on Nashville Country Western music; *Bing Crosby* when in 1942 he got the first "gold record" for his recording of "White Christmas"; and finally *Allen Toussaint* in 1982 filming the documentary "Piano players rarely ever play together," costarring Tuts Washington and Professor Longhair, whom I also tagged.

I could write separate chapters about each of those amazing time-travel adventures, but for the sake of brevity I will refrain. I've only a few days to finish telling my story, or so my state-appointed lawyer informs me. The appeals he insisted on putting forward over my objections are finished. They're making the final preparations for my execution, which will be broadcast live, world-wide. So time is short. Otherwise I'd treat you to some additional, incredible musical-history snapshots.

Anyway, trying to figure roughly the number of invitees—direct or indirect—I'd "tagged" for retrieval from the past, I reckoned I still had room to visit the near-past concerts that in addition to the Hollywood Bowl had been blown up by Phoenix. I scattered my remaining marbles amongst them to drive my potential total as near to 500,000 that I dared.

All-in-all, I spent six months being tossed across Time by the Sphere. Far from being haphazard trips, they were all under the careful direction of my Mom, Arthur, and Billy—catapulting me to key moments of musical history. A few times I almost didn't make it back. But finally the main players were all "tagged" and ripe for retrieval.

We had only our last six months left before the celestial Concert.

Now all I had to do was revive, convince, and coordinate a crowd of musical geniuses scattered across Time and Space to join together to design and participate in the *greatest concert* the world had ever seen!

Sure, we could do it. What could go wrong?

Chapter 23

RESURRECTION

Oh glorious, glorious, glorious day
When the dead shall arise *from their graves*
No shuffling zombies or lingering decay
But eternal life to stay

Sweet Aunts and Uncles and Sons and Brothers
And Mother and Father returned
Not senile or sick or confused or afraid
But healthy and fit always

And we with them in that wonderful place
Where Lions lie down with the Lambs
And everyone lives in sweet harmony
With never a gripe or complaint

No the dead are not buried or turned to dust
They live again with all their loves
Vital and helpful and cheering their fate
If it could only be that way...

Where would they go and where would they fit
And who would pay their retirement
If those who'd passed from the present scene
Came back for their encore dreams?
The Suzette Anthology, Lyrics 23

"Take it easy, Eun. Don't try to move too fast."

He blinked several times, looking up at me in confusion.

"Suzy...but...how am I still alive?" he gasped, grimacing. His expression looked like he'd just tasted something nasty.

Likely it was Eun's own blood and bile, lingering in his throat from his transformation.

"Have some water," I comforted him, raising his head up with an arm while guiding a drinking straw in a water bottle with the other.

He delicately sipped several times at the straw before pushing it aside and trying to sit up on the bed. He groaned, plastering a hand onto his forehead.

"I said not to move too fast," I admonished him, pushing him back on his pillow. I sat down on a chair at his bedside.

"What...happened?" he asked, settling back on the pillow and closing his eyes.

"That's what I wanted to ask you," I countered his question. "The medics had a hard time repairing your body. They anticipated retrieving you whole and healthy, a moment before the bomb went off. Instead, they literally had to sew your scattered pieces back together. As such, you're one of the last of the retrievals to regain consciousness."

He ruefully sighed. "I went hunting for your bomb during the entire concert. The roadies said the pyro launchers got searched by the police, who found nothing out of the ordinary. I figured that was the last place to look. However, I was dead wrong. As the concert was ending I finally discovered that the support under one of the launchers was unsteady. Moving the fireworks launcher to the side and prying open the top of the support box I found a bomb ticking down to zero. There was nothing else for me to try but yank out wires. I guess I yanked out the wrong ones. It went off in my face with a tremendous *flash*. That's the last thing I remember."

"Well, fortunately for the Timeline, having the bomb at the stage go off a couple seconds too fast didn't alter the future. Unfortunately for you, though, the blast must have caught you just as the Time Tunnel formed around you. You came through at this end in shredded chunks."

He sighed.

"Sorry to be a problem."

I stood up and hugged him tightly around his shoulders. "You're never a trouble, Eun. It was just a shock to see you fall out from beneath the Sphere as bloody pieces. But the Time Keepers have seen everything. They just scooped up all your parts, put them in 'time-freeze' to prevent any cellular decay, and then sent you to 'severe rehabilitation.' It took a week for them to repair you on the cellular level, two weeks to get the tissues reintegrated, and then another week to finally get your neural pathways reestablished. Today they woke you up. So how do you feel?"

"For a man who was blown up by a bomb, remarkably well," he admitted, impatiently pushing me away to cautiously swing his feet out over the edge of the bed. He was clad in the same clothes he'd worn that fateful day at the Hollywood Bowl. The Time Keepers were anything if not meticulous in their reconstructions. His blue silk shirt and purple pantaloons looked like they were fresh from the cleaners.

"So first tell me about my family," he said, pausing there sitting on the edge of the bed.

"They're fine," I informed him. "They're older, of course. It's been nearly three and a half years since the Hollywood Bowl attack. I let them know I'd try to tag you after we made the Mount Everest broadcast...oh, you don't know about that. Anyway, they've been waiting for you to get stitched back together. You can call them up any time you wish."

"Only call them—I can't visit?"

"Of course you can visit. It's just that we're entering a critical phase now, where I desperately need your help. I'm so glad you're back among the living, Eun! You can take 'time-off' at your discretion, but we're all going to be working around the clock for the next few months."

"So it's another World Tour, is it?"

"Nope—it's a *Galactic* Tour. We're going to represent Earth at a musical competition at the center of the Milky Way!"

"Oh, Lordy..." he sighed, shaking his head in wry appreciation, "—you never lacked for ambition, Suzette. I take it this 'Galactic' competition is going to require quite a bit of preparation and resources. I hope you have the right permissions and funding. Is Darlene here with us? She always was a good negotiator: cut right to the quick, hardball style."

I enthusiastically nodded.

"Yep, she's here. She's up to her ass trying to keep track of everything. Hah, that's good punishment for all her sneaky criminal money laundering in my earlier career."

"Say what?"

"...but that's all in the past," I continued. "Don't give it a second thought. Darlene's back on track now. But she's been neglecting *me!* That's why I need you so much, Eun—to be my personal assistant. Darlene's been pushing the Time Keepers as hard as she could to get you assembled and functioning. But they claim they can't work miracles, that they're bound by the laws of physics and biology. Haw, what do they know about laws? Anyway, she'd have been here for your revival if she could, but she's off smoothing a dispute between the Cannibals and Lionheart's royal court."

"Uh..."

"And even though mankind is in one of its most repressive periods since the Middle Ages," I continued breathlessly, "all of us Galactic Concert Invitees are being treated like royalty. We're all drawing fabulous salaries, paid for by the State. We've privileges the common people can only dream of. Anything we need we get it. Of course that's just up until the Concert. If we lose we'll probably all be hung by our necks from the closet lampposts! But until then we're top priority, getting the best of everything."

He sighed deeply, standing up unsteadily.

"There's a lot you're going to have to catch me up on."

"Nope," I replied, taking his arm to steady him, "I'll *show* you everything!"

"This is a small city," Eun marveled, looking out across the expanse.

We were at the central Guard Tower. It was 1,200 feet high, taller than the Eiffel Tower. It surveilled the entire site. Also, it was festooned with satellite communication dishes, helicopter and airplane control windows, missile defense arrays, and general security firepower. Atop the tower we could see everything above ground in the complex.

Spread out below us was, indeed, a bustling city composed of around *one million* people. Half were Galactic Core Concert (GCC) participants I'd retrieved out of Time. The rest were military guards and support staff. Buried deep below—but in a completely repaired and renovated research cavern—was the Sphere.

"Over there are the living quarters," I pointed at nice suburban-type tracts, "and the animal preserves from my 'Kingly Animal Shelter' days, the cemetery, the business district, the transportation hubs and airstrips, the military barracks, and..."

"So we're prisoners?"

"It's complicated," I admitted. "The perimeter is well guarded. We have an electrical fence plus other formidable barriers containing the GCC city. The army is here, plus Phoenix fighters, Peace Keepers from the 2nd Dimension, and Time Keepers who operate outside our present Timeline."

"So they already know what will happen to us at the Galactic Core?"

I was so glad to have Eun with me. He had a sharp, quick mind. Coming from where he'd been, it'd taken me much longer to get up to speed. He was catching up fast!

"Hah, I wish," I snorted ruefully. "They say me and my Mom are 'Time-Twisters' who throw a monkey wrench into Timelines. Beyond the Concert they tell me that the present Timeline fractures into a million equally likely shards. Apparently the fate of the world does literally hang in the balance of the outcome."

"You can do it. I have faith in you, Suzette."

"Oh, call me Suzy..."

"—no!" he snapped at me. "In order for the things you've told me about to succeed, you have to be *Suzette the Superstar!* You are #1 in the entire world, girl! Don't let anyone talk down to you. Concerts don't succeed because of the number of musicians, the pyrotechnics, the promotion, or the venue. They succeed because of the *magic* the central person or group brings. And *Suzette* has that magic! Do you understand me?"

I was beyond grateful for his affirmation. I surely doubted my ability to pull it all off. But his strong words had the opposite effect than which they were intended, placing even more pressure on me. I felt my guts roiling from the incredible stress. God, I was in for some bad diarrhea and constipation that night, both together, at the same time.

I know, it sounds disgustingly unrealistic. Believe me, my misbehaving guts could be totally divergent.

Ah, well. I had to push that all out of my mind, focus on the task at hand. That was my only hope for success: concentrate on each task as it came up, pushing all the rest out of my head.

It was my constant "mantra"—and why I needed Eun so much, to keep me correctly oriented in the overall Mission: "What's next?"

"...and over there are the minor stadiums where the various groups can practice their particular contributions," I concluded. Some of the stadiums were open-air, others covered by domes. "But the main platform is off there at a distance."

"Either that's not so far off or it's huge," Eun calmly noted, shading his eyes from the direct sunshine to see the horizon better.

"Yep, it's huge," I replied. "It's patterned after what Billy says we'll experience at the Concert Planet: a clear dome covering a hundred acres. We'll be contained within it, provided with an Earth-type gravity, atmosphere, water, and food. We can use its area however we wish for the performance. It will have extendable and easily manipulated elements throughout. It's the ultimate Stage."

"So then why not just do the performance here and send a video?"

I looked at him like he was a dummy.

"Oh, right," he agreed. "That's why there *are* such things as live performances for live people. If a video or 3D-image would do as well, then there'd be no place for the wildly popular World Tours. Nothing beats hearing and seeing your favorite performers in person, particularly when you're part of a massive, live audience. It's a completely different experience than watching a video or listening to a recording."

"And it's apparently also part of the test," I added. "They have specialized projection equipment there that will send our music to all the previous contest-winner planets."

"Why?"

"Well for one thing, the Galactic broadcast is part of the individual world-populations' 'communion' with the Spheres of the Lords on their particular planets," I shrugged. "But most importantly, from what Billy's told me, the thousands of previous winning planets will each vote on us. We will win or lose on how well we communicate our music to them. So 'long-story-short', a recording just won't cut it. Plus they say they have 'multi-sensory' mikes that transmit not just sight and sound but all the other senses as well! It's a 'virtual' reality to the nth degree!"

"Amazing....but how did you build everything here so quickly?" Eun marveled. "This facility is astonishing. It's bigger than Woodstock!"

Ah, yes, grander than Woodstock—and a lot cleaner!

"Money," I shrugged, "Lots and lots of money. For once humanity is united. Except for a few perpetual discontents, everyone wants us to win the Prize. So the world—in two Dimensions—is throwing everything at the Contest."

"So...no pressure?"

I had a laughing fit, almost tumbling over the low railing.

Eun grabbed my arm, drawing me back a safe distance.

"Thanks, my friend," I laughed again. "Yep, just a *little* bit of pressure that..."

"SUZETTE KINGLY! PLEASE REPORT TO THE EXECUTIVE CONFERENCE ROOM! YOUR PRESENCE IS REQUIRED!" a loudspeaker boomed.

"Oh, Christ," I groaned, mashing a palm into my forehead. "That was Darlene shouting over the loudspeaker. I keep 'forgetting' to carry around my cellphone and..."

"Oh, girl, you haven't changed a bit," Eun snorted. "You never did like to be at everyone's beck and call. I always had to run you down."

"Yes, but it's a thousand times more critical now," I groaned. "I really did forget all about this meeting! It's a major planning session. I was sort of foggily thinking it was tomorrow. It's the first time we're overlapping our particular performances by computer simulation. To-date everyone's been working on their individual parts. All the Principals are required to be present. I worked out a general scheme, of course—but the interfacing-details are *very* tricky, particularly improvisations."

"Improvisations?"

"I'm taking a new approach. Not everyone's onboard..."

He grunted in sympathy as we walked to the elevator to take us down from the roof.

"I take it you need me to help with your scheduling," he gently stated, "—along with everything else."

"Yep."

"Then I suppose I should put off that trip to visit my family."

"We have excellent video-conferencing facilities," I replied. "And once you help me get things under control, I'm sure you can take off a few days to fly to South Korea. Or, if you wish, you can bring them here, assuming you're willing to blow your 'gay' cover."

"Oh, I don't care about that, girl," he blithely claimed. "I'm just glad to be alive, not a pile of raw hamburger. And, yes, I'd rather they come live with me here. Then my family will be all together—which includes you and my musical colleagues."

That was heartwarming. But my stomach was already gurgling and churning. Despite Eun's comforting presence, I knew this meeting was going to be bad.

I walked with Eun into a large conference room containing over thirty arguing people. They were all yelling and screaming at each other, about to come to blows! Darlene looked like she was about to explode from frustration, her eyes wide in her dark skinned face, her lips pressed tightly together.

She was good at handling isolated superstars, but not a room filled to the brim with them.

A Phoenix "high commander" and a dozen of his goons lined the back wall, apparently uncertain if they should intervene or not. They all carried rifles and wore military camouflage outfits. I was particularly disturbed to see that the Commander was "Reverend" Grant Bedford. He was a white-skinned, right-wing official who was notorious for being a supremacist bigot. He looked like he was about to intervene, particularly against my buzz-cut African-American manager.

I had to get my Principals under control or there'd be big trouble. Phoenix tolerated our operation only because the Commissioner ordered their cooperation. They were closely monitoring all our activities. They'd be happy to see us fail.

"*Shut the hell up!*" I shouted at them all.

I strode to the head of the large conference table, *glaring* at them all!

One-by-one the warring factions sat down at chairs to the side of or behind the long table.

Fortunately for the "revenants" they'd all had their neural circuitry tweaked to understand and speak passable current English. Otherwise we'd have had even more difficulty communicating. But it was still hard to comprehend and get around epochal idioms and manners of speech, especially if everyone was arguing with everyone else all at once!

"I do not speak unless my words bring *Victory!*" King Richard the Lionheart forcefully interjected into the sudden quiet. "I will win the Prize for all those that follow me! My plan *will* defeat our foes if you have the guts to fight like devils when *I* command you!"

He had a long straight nose topped by piercing eyes. He had a short red-brown beard and mustache. His regal bearing practically demanded an accompanying suit of armor and golden crown.

"That's a great line," I mildly replied. "We should definitely include your 'Victory' chant in the concert lineup. But for now I need to..."

"*Include?*" he disdainfully shot back, rudely interrupting me. "When we arise to that heavenly heathen realm we must *take* the place! Undercover of the entertainment, my armies will..."

"Oh, pipe down, you has-been," Sanako spat at him. "What do you think swords and arrows could do against the *Lords of the Galaxy?* Even *my* weapons would be neutralized. They want your creativity, *not* cruel conquest. If we provoke them they could snuff us all out with a flick of their wrists."

"*How* dare a low-born oriental *woman* like you...!"

I bared my teeth at them both. *I* was the "alpha-dog" here!

"We have *one* objective here: to win the Contest!" I snarled at them both. "We can only accomplish that goal working *together!* If we fight each other, we lose."

Still glaring at each other, they settled back in their seats.

"The violin segments are much too short," Mozart now lamented, shaking his bushy gray-haired head sadly as I continued to stare-down Sanako and Lionheart. "And in your orchestration they are interrupted by that *vile* screech of a stringed instrument that..."

"Hey, man," Jimi Hendrix interjected, "don't you be trashing my guitar playing! Just because you don't dig it don't mean that..."

"It is not godly! It's simply is not godly!" Mother Hildegard firmly stated, shaking her habit-covered head in obvious pain. "I can see the spirituality of 'Let It Be' as a song, despite its strange accompaniment, but not..."

"Oh, Sister, *let it be!*" Janis Joplin snarled, jumping to her feet. "Music isn't all just boring church stuff. We need more *blues*, ripped straight out of people's hearts! You can't touch the rest of the Galaxy with plodding tradition that..."

"*That's enough!*" I again shouted at them. "Everyone please just simmer down! As I said, we're all on the same side. I deliberately didn't bring us together until today because I knew we'd be at each other's throats. Our forms of music are just too different to blend together easily. I apologize for being late. Fortunately, it won't happen again."

I was grateful to see Eun nodding. Darlene looked at him with relief. She knew Eun could rein in my worst excesses.

"But for now," I continued, "I'm going to lay down the rules and the rationale for *my* game plan—which we *will* all follow!"

"And if we don't?" Bing Crosby quietly but firmly spoke up.

Oh, rats. I'd counted on him being one of the reasonable participants. But it seemed he was just as pig-headed as all the other egotistical, selfish, prima-donnas present.

"No one is being forced to participate," I grated at them all. "You can't go back to your prior place in history. It would mess up the timeline. But you can walk out of this compound right now, if you wish. You'll be given a house and modest pension by the government. But remember that music is presently *banned* in all its forms worldwide. You will not be able to perform or even play music. The governments of our planet are allowing this one-time Spectacular only because of the potentially incredible payoff. The only place you can exercise your incredible talents is here, with us."

I paused to let that sink into their thick skulls.

"So...who wants to leave?"

Nobody moved. A few people glanced about furtively. But no one bolted for the exit.

"Good!" I mentally breathed a sigh of relief. I also realized that Bing had perhaps inserted the one thing that would cool the boil of the audience. As if to communicate his cooperativeness, he *winked* at me. Gratefully, I winked back at him.

"But what about my jazz band that..." Louis Armstrong spoke up in his deep, gravelly voice.

"*I want to hear each and every one of your ideas, suggestions, and concerns!*" I shouted as loud as I could, again startling them. "And I will give *each* of you a space to speak uninterrupted, for all to hear what you have to say. I will stay here and listen to each of you until you have nothing more to say, even if it takes the entire night. But that's only after you *first* listen to me. Got it? If you feel you *must* speak up then raise your hand like a civilized person and wait for me to call upon you."

I could see that with a promise to fully listen to each person, they were willing to cut me some slack. Great...I was finally making some progress.

"Ok, then, first the rationale," I began. "We only have a two-hour timeslot to capture the imagination and appreciation of the most astute music connoisseurs of the entire Galaxy. As you well know, that's barely enough time for *just you alone* to present a reprise of *some* of your greatest works. But we're not going to win this contest by any single performance or style, no matter how good. I've studied many of the past contestants from the last competition that occurred a million years ago—from recordings supplied by my brother Billy. Striking the same tone or similar style *will not* win the contest!"

Sally King politely held up her hand.

"Yes, Mom?"

"Are you saying one 'voice' is not enough?"

Wonderful! In her imminently practical way, she'd struck to the heart of the matter.

"Yes, that's exactly correct," I replied to the group. "As beautiful as a piano, a guitar, a singer's voice, a band, or even an orchestra may be—after a bit they each become *boring* because they are doing the *same* thing in the *same* way with just minor variations. A cricket might enthrall its fellow crickets with its cricketing...but then we go out of the house with bug spray to kill the damn thing."

Harriet Tubman raised her hand, a glint of deep understanding in her noble, dark face.

"Yes, Harriet?"

"In my lifetime I fought against racial bias and prejudice. Am I correct in affirmin' that you be speakin' about alien cultures judging us, even those thet may not even comprehend our words or song?"

"Exactly!" I nodded, going over and putting my hands on her shoulders. My hands rested on her simple shawl draped over a long brown woolen dress. "Folks, we've got to 'translate' our narrow human-ears frequencies and concepts into *alien* bandwidths and minds."

This caused a stir amongst those present, realizing that a seemingly brilliant concert to *our* ears might just be "cricket-noise" to the judges!

Swami Satchidananda raised his brown hand.

"Yes, Swami?"

"How do we perform this miracle? I have long espoused *Vibrations that move the Universe and Stars*—but achieving such while we operate in our own narrow frequency band now seems...difficult if not impossible. Are you, perhaps, speaking on a *spiritual* level that...?"

"No," I stopped him. "Much as I admire your teachings and those of our other spiritual leaders present here with us, we have to operate from known physical laws. To that end I propose forming a working group to explore *augmentation* of our frequency range to produce a relentlessly escalating, many-voiced presentation. Any volunteers?"

Thomas Edison, George Beauchamp, Sanako, and the Swami raised their hands.

"Excellent. Thomas, you're a genius at inventing physical instruments. George, you're likewise a genius at taking weak vibrations and augmenting and amplifying them electrically. Sanako, you know how to transcend Timelines and species. And you, Swami, are already thinking beyond our narrow human 'bandwidth.' Recruit from the support staff anyone else who can help you. This is top priority."

They nodded reluctantly at each other.

"But I don't want just a static blast into alien brains," I continued. "I want to be able to selectively apply and expand various alien 'voices' throughout the concert, in both directions. You can interface with Billy on how the Sphere and its offshoots function. Do you think you can accomplish this goal?"

They again looked at each other, shrugging.

"We can certainly try," Edison cautiously replied.

"Excellent!"

I saw they were excited at the expanded perspective, willing to work with each other to achieve the novel goal of projecting human sensibilities into alien minds.

I saw Lelea tentatively raise her hand. She was dressed in a traditional Fiji grass skirt and sash that covered her breasts. I was glad she'd kept my marble.

"Yes, Lelea?"

"I—don't know how I can help. You brought my whole tribe here. We know not of your Spheres or aliens or..."

I walked around the table to her and hugged her.

"You have what we need more than anything."

"Oh?"

"At the heart of all music—human or alien—is the *beat!* Believe me, Lelea, your wonderful drums, hitting sticks, and clapping will make all the difference. Plus I need all types of backup singing, transitions, and dancing throughout the concert. Your tribe will have plenty to keep it busy."

She smiled, nodding.

I turned back to the rest of them. "As you see from my tentative flow chart, this is *not* a 'Suzette Kingly' concert. Yes, I'm the glue that holds it together. But I'm not 'centering' the show with you-all just backing me up or adding onto my performance. No, I'm giving *each* of you a short star-turn. But neither is this a loosely themed talent showcase. No, we are giving them the best Earth has to offer as an *integrated, smooth, accelerating experience* that gets *ever more interesting!* As we work out the kinks, we'll find new and more amazing ways to use each of your particular expertise and talents. This is not 'my' concert. This is not 'your' concert. Rather, this is the *human race's* concert. And it's not going to be a set repetition, but have allotted space for free-form *improvisation*. In other words, it will be un-predictably *dynamic*, allowing for unexpected *synergism!* So how does that sound to you?"

Spontaneously they all broke into a loud round of applause.

I had them.

And yes, as I promised, I stayed long into the night listening and talking with each of them. Once they got over the stunted notion that it was a competition rather than a cooperative venture, they all had great ideas to offer. I was totally excited by their enthusiasm.

We had four months to the Concert. The last month was for di-rect setup and practice at the Galactic Core. That meant we had three months left on Earth to work out the major kinks.

"Hey, you did good," Eun smiled at me.

We were the last two in the conference room, watching through a wall-length window the sun rise across the rolling hills and peaceful ranches of Oklahoma.

"But now the really hard part starts," I sighed, suddenly over-whelmed by the task before me.

"Oh?"

"Now we've got to get really good at blending tribal music, folk, spiritual, Gospel, jazz, swing, pop, rap, blues, classical, country west-ern, rock-and-roll, and whatever other style emerges into a cohesive whole. Is that even possible?"

"If anyone can do it, it's you."

If he weren't already taken, I'd have married him right there.

Chapter 24

GALACTIC CORE

Oh take me to your **beating heart**
The very center of your being
Not the peripheral external flesh
But where your thoughts are flowing

Combining like mountain streams
Cascading over blackened rocks
Caught in a yanking gravity
We're a river roaring loud!

Plunging off a tall cliff
A long white plume that's a waterfall
Some say it's where the soul is found
Beyond mere circuitry

Where I hear your voice all crisp and loud
Saying sweetly that you love me
Sucked into your beauty
I know I'll have a lot of fun!

Caught in the glories of your face
Your mind is sweetly dazzling
It's there we truly can merge
Into a single entity

Hugging hard past our body parts
Our surging joy is ever spreading
We anticipate the ecstasy
Of exploding superstars!

The Suzette Anthology, Lyrics 24

373

I was totally discombobulated. I was falling in love with anything and anyone that gave me a halfway friendly smile. My emotions were on a rollercoaster. One moment I was miserable and the next exalted. Everything hit me too fast. My hormones were all out of whack. I couldn't remember when I last menstruated. Eggs were probably jumping out of my ovaries like popcorn from a skillet. My brain was on overdrive and my body was trying to catch up. Repeated time travel plus instantaneous quantum teleportation to the center of the Milky Way apparently scrambles one's neurons.

Even Scotty, lying on the floor at my feet, seemed agitated, alternatively sighing deeply then snuffling excitedly.

"It *won't* work!" Sally King exclaimed as she rushed into the camp's Command Tent.

Behind her came Arthur Anderson, her ever-present, loyal bodyguard. He looked particularly agitated. His dark eyeglasses were askew, almost revealing his freaky eyes.

Scotty jumped up from the floor, snarling, but settled down when he saw who was yelling.

My Mom looked awful. Her reddish hair hadn't been dyed for a while and was mostly gray. Her skin was wrinkly. She had bags under her eyes. Anderson stood by the door, his big arms crossed. I couldn't bear to look at his mutilated face, remembering the handsome fellow he'd once been when he was young. How my Mother tolerated his glowering presence I couldn't fathom.

I was there alone trying to sort out a mountain of reports, requisitions, contest score feedbacks from Billy, complaints, and raw experimental research data on the mysterious equipment that controlled the Dome and Stage. Though Eun, Darlene, Mike, and my other assistants were heroically running interference, I was the person in charge of the Concert. Only I had the authority to make final decisions. Phoenix and the Commissioner had me on a tight rein, demanding "accountability." I couldn't just be a performer, or orchestrator, or conductor, or producer. No, on top of everything else I also had to be the "CEO" *Chief Executive Officer!*

We'd been at the Galactic Core for two weeks now. We had only two more weeks left until we had to give our official contest performance. I'd barely gotten any sleep in the last two weeks. Every minute I had "free" I plugged into the central Sphere. I was 'virtually' visiting the previous million-year winners, trying to find common themes to their present societies and biology. I thought I was making headway identifying their cultural and organic key preferences. After all, they were the ones who would be judging us, awarding us points.

Meanwhile we were all observing the posted points to the continuing *Competition Performances* at the other identical, domed "stages" scattered across the surface of the Contest Planet. Totals on an elevated slab that floated beside the central Sphere were presented for us in English symbols. The "score" was a percentage of total points available. So far, the best performances were in the 90's. The present top score was 93.6875%.

We weren't allowed to actually view the other performances, least we gain a competitive advantage copying the tactics of other invited planets. All we knew of the competition was a disturbing fact: of the 1,000 total entries, we were scheduled to perform last. Wow! The increasingly *un*cooperative Billy either didn't know the reason or refused to reveal it. It might be we were "seeded" as one of the very best or thrown in at the end as fillers after the "main-eventers" did their thing. All we knew was that roughly every two hours a new percentage joined the list of completed performance statistics, alongside a 3-dimensional galactic coordinate of that race's home planet.

The competition was sequential. That allowed those that wanted to observe and vote at the already-"blessed" judging planets to always have an ongoing performance to view. In our time frame, it was taking three months to present a total of 1,000 invited competitor planets' performances in continually running, sequential two-hour chunks.

Long story short, I was being run ragged.

"*What* won't work, Mom?" I snapped back at her, extremely irritated by this unexpected confrontation.

"You're blowing off all the other Principals, Suzy!" she accused me, stomping back and forth across the tent's floor. "We haven't had a 'team' meeting now for weeks, since before we were all transported here. You continually criticize their practice performances without allowing discussion. They're going crazy! They demanded I come here to tell you that we're on the wrong track."

"We're *not* on the wrong track!" I yelled back at her. Then I caught hold of my raging emotions and replied more softly: "I know it's hard, Mom. I know they're mad at me. But we can't give anything less than our best. We've only got *one* shot at this Contest!"

"That's exactly *their* argument," Sally King retorted, red-in-the-face. I'd never seen her so angry. I supposed the relentless pressure was getting to us all. "If it were a regular concert with a central focal point and a clear theme they'd be fine with the pressure. Even if it were a series of separate performances joined together by some topic or genre they'd also be fine. But the way you're trying to blend it all together is just chaos. It's a hot mess! We're not only going to lose, we're going to be *humiliated.*"

"Mom, it's..." I patiently started to try to explain.

"It's *beyond unreasonable* to expect cannibal heathens to compliment a fine classical orchestra," she interrupted me. I got the feeling that a crowd of our people were outside the tent listening. "How can you expect Janis Joplin to blend into a Jacopo Peri opera? And for God's sake, Suzy, you're trying to get Hare Krishna chanters to join seamlessly with Harriet Tubman's Negro spirituals! And then you abruptly change things up in midstream, several times, *scrambling* us just when things are starting to halfway-gel between our performances."

"I know what I'm doing," I insisted, wearily standing up to face my mother. "Look, I'm just now starting to understand our judges. It's an eclectic blend of bizarrely different biological and chemical lifeforms. But I have found some commonalities in..."

"But that's not the worst," she brushed my explanation aside.

"Please...just sit down," I wearily motioned for her to join me at the red table. God, I hated that color. Everything here was made of the same red "stone" substance.

I groaned to myself, clutching my stomach beneath the edge of the table. I wished I could just get headaches, like a normal person. But all my stress went straight to my guts. My IBS had already provided a torrent of human wastes for the red-stone lavatories. And likely this "night" would provide a lot more.

Of course it was handy to have whatever structure you wanted sprout from the "stage" under your feet. Billy said the foundation of the presentation-Domes was a lifeform in its own right. It responded to all our demands. But it was so damn boring! Even the "tent" structures we all lived in were red stone tent-poles holding up red stone "fabric." Billy claimed it was that way so no planet's team had a competitive advantage due to unique natural resources brought with them. We'd only been permitted to bring the clothes on our backs plus essential equipment, instruments, and enough supplies for the first few days here. After that the common support structures were to provide us with whatever we needed.

Sally King slumped down in the red stone chair across the red stone table from me. I saw she had tears in her eyes. If she were anyone else getting in my face like this, I'd just have Losa Yanash's Native-American guards hustle them off. My Chickasaw personal guards weren't armed, but were tough brawlers. The accompanying Phoenix troupes, the Peace Keepers, and the Time Keepers couldn't be ordered around but thankfully were also unarmed. The "rules of the competition" proscribed any overt weapons being transported to the contest planet. But Losa and Scott still managed to maintain a tight protective net around me.

The half-million people I'd brought here to this confined space were a boiling caldron. Yes, they were very cooperative, happy to be resurrected. But they all had their own agendas and personal baggage. Already, numerous fights had broken out across the compound, some of them near riots.

I don't need any more trouble!—I groaned to myself.

But the others were correct to send Sally to confront me. Sally King was not only my mother, with unquestioned access to me, but she was also an experienced performer. In the early days of my childhood Gospel group she sang the soprano lead while I sang alto, with Billy singing tenor, and my Dad bringing up the base. I was required by "family tradition" to hear her out.

"Ok, I'm listening," I sighed, shoving the stack of red-paper "reports" to the side.

"The thing that's truly driving the performers crazy is the *improvisation.*"

"Oh?" I mildly replied as Scotty settled back down around my feet.

Anderson, by the entrance, also looked less agitated. His tensed burly arms relaxed.

"I can't imagine why you're doing this, Sally."

"Mom, the very best shows are *not* staged performances. They're spontaneous, 'framed' *Celebrations*," I insisted, staring straight into her glistening green eyes.

"That's absolutely not true. You've gone off the deep end, Sally. The authority that the Lords gave you to assemble, direct, and star in this Performance has gone to your head. This isn't the time to act out some weird theory. This is the time for putting our best feet forward!"

"Mom, I am *Suzette Kingly* who put on *six* World Tours that..."

"So let's do one of those," she rudely interrupted me. "Those were all world-class productions! In their 'pop' genre they were the very best Concerts our planet has to offer. And every one of them was *scripted* down to the *smallest* gesture and *slightest* inflection of each and every dancer or backup singer! Right?"

Wow. This was worse than I'd thought. Normally soft-spoken, nearly all her sentences had exclamation marks at their ends.

Hah...exclamation points—literary *shouting!*

Yes, I know I use too many of them in the text you're reading right now. But if you were on *death row* awaiting your *execution*, you'd also be a bit agitated!!!!!

Anyway, I tried to calm things down...less exclamation points...

"I've studied the holographic recordings that Billy confidentially provided me with for the last one hundred winners, across the last 100 million years," I quietly explained, "plus a sampling of the loser planets. Mom, our 'best' just isn't good enough. This isn't some weird theory I've suddenly come up with. I, as the 'chosen one', have privileged access to the past winners' full performances. So I've been studying their methods since even before we came to the Galactic Core and..."

"—which we all appreciate, Suzy! But you still can't be radically and unpredictably changing things in such a complex performance that..."

"—and I'm linking that with virtual visits to the presently existing voting civilizations scattered across the Galaxy, which I again have privileged access to for..."

"Why just you, Suzy?"

"How the hell should I know?" I snapped back at her. "I just have to accept what Billy tells us that it's all part of the 'test.' Regardless, now that we're actually at the Galactic Core I have direct access to the Spheres on those previous winners' worlds," I continued. "*That's* why I keep updating our performance. I get critical new insights that..."

She leaned forward and grabbed my hands in hers.

She was squeezing so tight it hurt me.

"Maybe so," she suddenly agreed. "Leaving some carefully con-scribed spontaneity in the program may be a good idea. But having *half* of the concert—adding up to a *full hour* of our precious two hours—as improvised interactions is way too much. Suzy, it's not just that the key performers and backups have to come up with new varia-tions on the fly, it's the *transitions!* Just how do I know when or *how* to come in next when the music before me radically and unpredicta-bly changes, both in content and duration?"

"It's like jazz, Mom. They do it all the time."

"These are *not* all jazz players or singers! That takes a special tal-ent. And jazz bands are typically *small* ensembles where they practi-cally know each other's thoughts!"

"That's why we have to keep working at it, Mom. That's why I'm so critical. It's a new way of thinking for large concerts. But people *do* know when to cut in and out because *I'm* the conductor! That's why they have to focus on *me* instead of just doing their own thing or reading a set music sheet. I know that's tough for us egotistic, selfish, tunnel-vision performers but..."

"That's not true."

"What?"

"First of all they're not an orchestra with set rules and lines of au-thorities. They're a *giant* ensemble of drastically different musical genres and styles! They can't be 'conducted' as if they were a super-orchestra."

"Then they have to learn!"

I frowned, under the table massaging my aching stomach. God, what I wouldn't do for a soothing *vanilla milkshake.* But all the food dispensers gave us here were the same, bland nutrient cubes. What little Earth food we were able to bring with us was quickly consumed. Lucky I still had a small stash of *dehydrated burritos.* Yum! I was eking them out, eating one only when my guts couldn't tolerate anything else. But most of the other 500,000 participants hadn't been that careful with their "stashes." All they had were the cubes. No wonder we were all at each other's throats!

"You can't ask them to do the impossible. But you're also wrong about something else, Suzy."

"I'm getting very tired of you saying I'm wrong."

"I'm your mother. I can tell you what no one else can say to you! And you're *flat wrong* that World Tours have to be scripted."

"Wait, you're *agreeing* with me now?" I laughed humorlessly. I desperately wanted this pointless discussion to end. I had too much else to do than sit there arguing with my mother.

"You're a student of musical history, Suzy," she rightly noted. "Beside jazz, is there another example of famous improvisation in *rock* concert history?"

"Hmmmm..." I pondered, now mildly intrigued. "Well, yes there is..."

"—the *Grateful Dead* concerts!" she triumphantly declared. I heard an ominous rustle outside the central tent. It was the shuffling of many feet. Though the tent was guarded by Losa's loyal forces, I sensed we were surrounded by a tightly packed crowd of key Principals, hanging on our every word. I wasn't just arguing with my Mom. This was an existential defense. The whole performance was on the line here.

I got a lot more serious, trying to focus my exhausted brain.

"That's right," I nodded. "The Grateful Dead concerts were famous for being extended jam sessions. They weren't just repetitions of the exact same words and songs. So instead of having fans come once to hear a one-time new concert featuring the latest album, the diehard 'Deadhead' fans would follow the Dead across the country. They went to every concert because each one was a unique feast of rock music. You're just making my case, Mom!"

She was unmoved by my argument.

"*But...*" she took her hands off mine and held up a warning fore-finger, "—fans said that *some* of the concerts were spectacular, mind-blowing sessions while *others* were disappointing, muddled confusion."

"Uh..."

"And the same thing is happening to us, here!"

I heard muffled voices outside agreeing with her.

"What do you mean?" I tentatively asked, frowning.

"Some of our practice 'jam' sessions have been incredible."

"Right!"

"But others have been disasters, where no one knew where to come in or how to interface—showcasing our disharmony, clashes, and even physical tumbles on the stage! We looked worse than rank amateurs. That would never happen on one of your World Tours, correct?"

"Uh..."

"Suzy, we're not giving a *series* of performances throughout the Galaxy. We're just giving *one!* We can have it *scripted to the last note* and our audience won't know the difference. It'll still sound fresh and spontaneous."

I heard a lot of agreement mumbled out beyond the tent's fabric.

"You've made a valid point," I reluctantly admitted.

"And that's not all!"

"Oh, there's more?" I laughed with sad humor. My stomach was rumbling and gurgling. I really needed some nutrient cubes, no matter how unappetizing they were. I couldn't remember when I'd last eaten.

"Suzy, we can't have the *audience* become one of the performers."

"But..."

"Sure, they can clap now and then. Sure, they can sing the chorus on some songs when we give them explicit permission. But you can't direct them like they were one of the groups up on the stage. You're trying to do too much, Suzy, once again jumbling everything up."

I stood, clutching my hands rigidly behind my back.

Scotty hopped up from the floor to pace faithfully along beside me.

"So...to summarize," I clearly enunciated for everyone listening inside and outside the tent, "you're telling me that I need to *stream-line* the concert, decide on a *set final sequence, cutout* most of the improvisation, and *strictly limit* audience participation. Is that your message?"

"Yes!"

I stared back at her, coolly and clinically.

"*No!*"

"What?"

"That's exactly what all the loser planets did," I stated firmly. I hated to do this to my dear Mother, but she had to accept that *I* was in charge. The *Lords of the Galaxy* could have invited *her* to be the "band leader" but they didn't. They'd invited *me!* And then they put our planet in the *closing, honored position* out of *a thousand planets* for a good reason: they expected us to be the best of all!

Or, we were just the filler-ins thrown in at the end.

But win or lose, I was doing it my way.

"Suzy, you've got be reasonable."

"Please go out and inform the protestors that we're doing the Concert *my* way," I stated flatly. I was giving her the task of trying to emphasize the words I already knew they were hearing from me through the tent fabric. "Yes, I know what we're attempting to do is incredibly difficult. But it's our only chance to win this thing. Those that don't like what I'm doing can literally 'take their marbles and go home'!"

"Suzy, you can't just kick out those that don't agree with..."

"Yes I can!" I snapped at her. "I repeat: literally, they can *take the Marble* I gave them that invited them to the *greatest concert ever given by humans* and run off back to planet Earth with their cowardly tails tucked between their legs—because it was just *too damn hard* for them!"

"Suzy..." Sally King pleaded with me, slowly rising to her feet.

"Yes, I've heard them muttering and complaining. They say that what we're doing 'isn't music.' They say it 'breaks all the rules.' They say we'd be 'thrown out of the first concert venue' we played at. They claim audiences would 'boo' us, kicking *us* out on our asses for mud-dling up the genres!"

"Well, yes they do."

"But let them remember what Billy told us when we first arrived, Mom. Anyone that goes back through the central Sphere can't return. This was a one-way trip, for the duration. No *one person or group* here is critical to our success! That which is going to win for our planet unimaginable rewards is our human spirit! And what I'm doing is giving us the best chance to *unleash the human spirit* upon the rest of the Galaxy!"

Despite my now-overt intestinal cramps, I stood straight with an imperial, fixed stare. I felt just like *Alexander the Great* leading his Macedonian army, or *Napoleon Bonaparte* at the Battle of Austerlitz, or *George S. Patton* at the Battle of the Bulge.

I wasn't organizing a concert. I was leading a musical *army!*

And just like any army, they needed to be inspired.

"I'll tell them," Sally nodded, reluctantly recognizing my authority. "You know I've always been behind you, Suzy. I'm just bringing the objections of others. I really hope you know what you're doing, not just trying to avenge your childhood loss at the *Nashville Teen Star* tryouts."

"That's low, Mom."

"Instead of giving them what they wanted you gave them what *you* wanted."

"Get out!"

I said nothing further as she left. I was *furious* at her for taking the side of the protestors. God damn it, she was my own mother. How dare she side with them! But, most of all, I was completely disappointed by her sinking to using my childhood agonizing failure against me.

Was I an arrogant, stupid kid? Yes! But every genius has to believe in him or herself! By definition, rising to new heights means transgressing and exceeding the prior boundaries!

Why couldn't she see this?

I loved my Mother more than anyone, but this was a betrayal I couldn't shake. I would have to marginalize her. I just couldn't trust her anymore. Perhaps after this was all over, I could bring her back into the fold. But until then she was excluded from anything critically important.

But then again, *I* sure did hope I knew what I was doing—only the *entire fate* of the human race rested on my shoulders.

My guts cramped so badly I sank down to my knees, groaning.

Scotty whimpered, licking my cheek.

"No problem," I whispered back to him. "A visit to the toilet and I'll be just fine. No one can spew out the crap like me."

Later, after a monumental dump in the tent's restroom area, I heard the outside crowd disperse. Hopefully it wasn't due to the horrendous sounds and smells I'd just produced. I stepped out of the tent and looked up at the sky.

I was disturbed to realize my Mom had left Arthur Anderson there at the Command Tent, apparently to ensure I was protected from any outraged participants. But I didn't need him. He should be with her, keeping her safe. I had my own faithful Chickasaw warrior "honor guard."

"It's awesome, isn't it?" Scott said from beside me. "We've been here two weeks and I never get tired of looking."

He was standing with his fellow Chickasaw guards around the tent entrance. Out of my peripheral vision I saw him reach down to scratch the ears of Scotty who'd emerged behind me wagging his tail.

But my main gaze was fixated on the spectacular sky.

A *giant, transparent dome* covered our huge compound. It was so clear I barely noticed it, extending up above us a thousand feet. It was visible mostly because of the small distortion it put into the celestial objects due to its curved surface.

"I still can't believe we're here," I sighed, transfixed.

Overhead I saw against the black backdrop of outer space what looked like *a solid sheet of gleaming stars*—packed at least a hundred times denser than those seen in Earth's nighttime sky. Many of the pinpoints were bright red, indicating old shrunken *red dwarfs*. Close to us were several intensely glaring larger yellow stars, which seemed to be pulsing. Billy had explained they were unstable giants on the verge of going *supernova*. This was a very dangerous part of the Milky Way.

And dominating everything else was the flat, orange "*accretion disc*" where captured stars, stellar gas, and other matter streamed into a hidden Black Hole. The disc was swirling so fast and furiously it radiated its own light. Fortunately we were far enough away from it not to be sucked into its central bottomless pit, where gravity was so intense that not even light could escape.

The Dome protected us from the intense, lethal radiation stream-ing from the Black Hole's accretion disc. That radiation had long ago stripped off the atmosphere of the Concert Planet. Inside the Dome, gravity was somehow maintained at earth-normal, the atmosphere kept fresh and pure, and what felt like gentle sunlight bathed our skin. Outside the Dome was only stark, dead rock similar to the sur-face of Earth's airless moon.

Billy had explained to us that many identical Domes were scat-tered across the Concert Planet's surface. Each Dome adapted to whatever species was presently occupying it, providing the proper environment of that critter's home planet. The living Domes could simulate an ocean for aquatic biological lifeforms, a liquid gas envi-ronment for gas-giant inorganic chemical-based life, or even solid subterranean rock for geothermic crystalline living matrices—whatever was necessary.

And we were here because "The Lords" were the surviving mem-bers of one of the first intelligent species to evolve in our Milky Way Galaxy—who had existed here at the Galactic Core for *ten billion* years!

By comparison, human-like creatures have only existed on Earth for less than ten million years. We were tottering infants in the gal-lery of Galactic lifeforms. Lucky for us the most advanced intelligent races still retained an appreciation for music. Rather than just snuff us out as irritating pests, they chose to give us a chance to join with their vastly superior minds as "chirping" artisans. And here we were, competing for that incredible recognition.

"Scott, I need to visit the Operations Tent. I've got to certify that we're on track to communicate optimally with our judges. Can you take me there?"

"No problem, Miss Suzette. I'll call a floater," he said, speaking into a cellphone.

Luckily the Dome had an intelligent electromagnetic network, which detected and accommodated our communication devices. Our cellphones brought from Earth worked fine. In fact, our phones transmitted through the Sphere to Earth with nary a pause or drop-out. We might as well be calling for a cab from Oklahoma. But after our arrival, physical teleportation from Earth stopped. We were on our own for the duration.

But the Dome had already provided us *magnetic floaters*. They were levitating platforms that coasted about the streets, transporting us many humans all around the 100-acre compound. They had inset hard seats that molded to your seated body. All you had to do was verbally instruct it where you wanted to go and it went there. Yes, it took a while to leisurely float to your destination. But it was easier and faster than walking.

Scott, me, my robot dog Scotty, Anderson, and a couple Chicka-saw guards were quickly floating along toward the central raised "stage." Luckily Scotty didn't need to pee or poop. Billy had happily explained to me how the android processed liquid and food with zero waste generated. I wish I could do that! Anyway, we didn't have any grassy areas under the Dome for pooping pets, though Billy assured us it could construct good simulations if we wanted such.

The raised-up performance-area platform at the center of the Dome was the size of an Earth stadium. It loomed above all the many low red tents, reminding us of why we were there. Next to it floated the main Sphere, drifting like a giant lightbulb atop its black plat-form.

Smaller Sphere-stations dotted the Dome's floor, around which the various tent-cities had sprung up

It was, indeed, much like a military encampment.

I was truly the General of my very own musical Army!

"You could have left the guards behind, Scott," I informed him. "I appreciate what you and your Dad are doing, but I'm not royalty that has to be protected every second."

I pointedly ignored the presence of the sullen Anderson.

Scott frowned. I admired how his smooth, coppery skin had few wrinkles. He was still a kid, but a very handsome one.

"That's actually not true, Suzette," he said as we drifted by various crowds of people who looked up at me with a mixture of anger and hope. "Since you brought along with us all those killed at Woodstock plus the Hollywood bowl, every kind of weird character is represented. Plus, I've noticed that even some of the performers don't really like you that much."

"Oh, they're just jealous!" I interjected smugly.

"Well..."

"What?"

"A lot of them think you're screwing things up," he said, slightly cringing to the side as if I were going to hit him.

"Oh, I know," I sighed. "You and half the compound probably heard me and my Mom arguing, right?"

"Yes..." he admitted reluctantly, "And in addition to a lot of your Principals, the Phoenix troops don't like you much either. They'd be happy for you to outright fail, leaving their newly won rigid religious dictatorships intact across our planet. Also, I think the Peace Keepers have orders to intervene if you endanger the Commissioner's rule. At least they can't scramble Time during our sequestration here. Billy says the Lords have placed us beyond any outside interference that..."

Arthur *grunted* in his seat, making sure we knew he was there.

"Ok, ok! I get it! Everyone hates me!" I snapped back at Scott. Then I sighed, putting a hand on his strong shoulder. "Guard me all you want, Scott. But I still don't think anyone here would attack me outright. They might think I'm a bitch, but they still need me to organize and star in the contest."

"There are a lot of people crammed into this compound," he ominously summarized. "And it doesn't help that all we've got to eat and drink is 'bread' and water."

He was right about that. Even I with my strict diet requirements due to my IBS was fidgeting and irritable. What I wouldn't give for a soothing vanilla milkshake. And many of those out in the audience had been snatched away from hamburgers, pizza, beer, and drug binges!

But this place had its compensations, for those with a mind to see them...

I again looked up in wonderment at the jam-packed sky. Without an atmosphere, space was revealed in all its intensely black glory. The crush of stars smearing the deep black was as scary as it was fascinating. And we were as smashed together in the Dome as was that

churning heavenly spectacle above. Maybe I'd gone overboard bringing along nearly half-a-million people here to the Galactic Core—but I
wanted to give a full *concert* experience to the judging alien races, not
just a simulated studio performance.

Yet Scott was also correct. I'd heedlessly brought approximately
200,000 resurrected casualties from the Woodstock Nuking, another
100,000 slaughtered audience members from the Hollywood Bowl
plus the subsequent concert bombings. A lot of crazies were mixed in
with the regular fans. Plus I'd rounded out the rest of my allotment
with my entire band and support crew for my World Tour #Six, various performers from Woodstock, an entire Opera from the 16th Century, a full symphony orchestra from the 19th century, and various
other bands and support crews accompanying my Principals.

Maybe I'd gone a wee bit overboard?

Here, at the center of the Galaxy, we were all jammed in like sar-
dines into a small tin can. Scott was right. Anything could happen.

The place was ripe for an explosion.

"We're here, Suzette," Scott announced.

I hoped off the floater and ran into the storehouse-sized *Operations Tent* and was immediately confronted by an excited Thomas
Edison.

"We've deciphered the main controls for the E.T.!" he grinned. He
snatched me up in a spontaneous bear hug. He wasn't the white
haired, wide-faced man with piercing eyes of later years. No, he'd
been resurrected as the slender, neatly black-haired, intense man he'd
been when he invented the phonograph. He was a handsome, young
genius!

I noted Scott almost imperceptibly grimacing at the hug by Edison, but he kept his cool. Arthur just glared at me. Both men stepped
back against a red-rock tent wall, politely letting me have a small
space with Edison.

"Uhm...the 'E.T.'?" I asked, gently pushing Edison off of me. I
hadn't heard that acronym before, except in a famous movie of the
20th Century. Surely he wasn't saying he'd caught an alien "extraterrestrial" lurking amongst the many instruments we'd found waiting for us?

"It's the 'emotional translator' matrix," he breathlessly explained, leading me over to where George Beauchamp was strumming various chords on my red electric guitar. "Listen!"

A "baby" sphere was floating beside him, centered on its own small black platform. I sat in a chair beside it.

He hit a D-minor and it felt like my soul had dropped out of my body. I'd never felt so sad. Then he hit a C-major-7 and I saw a herd of ghostly wild horses come thundering past me. It was glorious!

"We're plugged into the E.T.," Edison explained. "It's not only translating the emotional impact of the vibrating strings, but piggybacking on the musician's actual thoughts as he plays the chords."

"That's fantastic!" I gasped. "That's just what I hoped you'd achieve. But for *alien* minds...?"

"That's the rub," Sanako said from another high bank of switches where she was methodically flicking inputs while watching wavering dials. "We think we've a matrix here that we can proactively adjust for the different types of alien minds. But like everything else, we have to guess at the settings."

"Ideally, I'd like to translate not only hearing but also the sensations of touch, taste, smell, and sight," I added, "—all five of our senses!"

"You are asking a lot, Miss Kingly," Swami Satchidananda noted. "Intelligent organisms that evolved in a completely different environment may not even have analogues to our five senses—or may have *additional* means of sensory input."

"I've studied many of the past winning performances plus virtually visited their present home worlds," I told him. "Though many are radically different from us, I could still comprehend what they were doing. I'm certain the means to translating our full range of senses exists here. We've just got to discover the right controls and settings. Then we can not only transfer a crude representation but actually *amplify* our presentation into terms the alien brains can scvor!"

It was true. We'd discovered the operational control banks for the Stage once we arrived at the Dome. Walls of complex instruments had arisen out of the flat floor that initially greeted us, along with the many tents and support housings. Billy, however, unexpectedly refused to guide us in their usage. He claimed our discovery process was part of the "test" to which the Lords subjected all contestants. I didn't know what was going on with him. The ancient gentleman was getting increasingly moody and short tempered.

But regardless of his problems, Billy definitely left us adrift concerning the critical "stage" controls. Supposedly "universal" symbols adorned the control banks, buttons, switches, and sliders to explain their operation and purpose. However it was only through trial and error that we could link them up to the connection ports that rose from the Stage on command.

Many of their functions were unknown. Despite the complex symbols, most of the instrument banks were still baffling mysteries.

"Well, that's great progress," I complimented them. "Keep up the tests. We need as wide a slate of options as possible for the actual Concert. If you can give me the ability to command escalating levels of alien amplification, we'll have a fighting chance. Otherwise we're dead in the water."

"It is, indeed, a fascinating 'test'," Sanako confirmed.

"Yes, you're helping to calm my anxiety," I complimented her. "If we can't impact minds beyond fellow humans we might as well quit right now. Believe me the Galaxy is filled with intelligent lifeforms that are beyond our comprehension. Is there any way to accelerate your progress?"

"Well, we could use your dog," Sanako said, pointing to Scotty.

"For what?"

"He's the closest analog we've got here to an alien mind," she observed coldly. "After all, the Lords constructed him. If we monitor his reactions to..."

Arf?—he responded, looking at me quizzically.

"Absolutely not, Sanako," I replied. "Surely the Lords left mechanisms beyond the symbols for puzzling out the more complex interfaces."

"Yes, but it would be quicker to..."

"So show us just how smart you are. Figure it out!"

She glared at me, her black eyes smoldering. She was really pissed at me for not turning over my alien-tech inspired mechanical dog for her probing. Well, that was just too bad. Sanako, who'd tried to kill me at Woodstock, was now my ally only out of necessity. I had no doubt she'd happily slit my throat if she felt it would please her Commissioner.

"I think I've found suitable gauges," the Swami interjected cheerfully. "Let us try those before experimenting with nonhuman minds. I think they will allow us to link to alien inhabitants on specific worlds through our little test Sphere. Then we can acquire feedback pulses."

"See?" I snapped at Sanako. "You've got to work together. Use each other's talents. We've only two weeks until we give our final performance. We can't just 'wing it' and hope it works."

"I hear that is exactly what you're doing with the concert," Sanako shot back at me. "It won't matter if we have the best alien brain 'amplifiers', 'resonators', and 'translators'—if the original performance is pure *crap!*"

She was simultaneously defying and insulting me. *I* was the General of this army, not her! It was *my* job to give orders and her duty to carry them out. I *lurched forward* to stick a *fist* into her sneering face when Scott abruptly stepped between us.

He caught my shoulders in his strong hands, physically pushing me back.

I struggled to get my emotions under control.

"Uh, no problem here, Scott," I sighed, twisting away. What the hell was happening to me? I almost got into a fist fight with Sanako! Other than the fact she'd probably wipe the red rock floor with me, it'd be a terrible sign to all the rest. News of my "instability" would sweep through the entire encampment.

"We are all on edge here," Satchidananda observed, his swarthy bearded face radiating wise counsel. "I suggest taking a break, getting some rest—especially you, Suzette. If you can't dispassionately steer the 'ship of state' then we will all surely slam into the rocks."

Ah. Now I was the Captain. Just what I needed: yet another position of impossible, crippling authority.

"Yes..." I shakily agreed, finally getting my surging emotions back under control. "I want to...thank you all, plus your assistants. I know you're all doing a fabulous job figuring out this giant puzzle in just a few short weeks. Normally it would take years of scientific research to decipher this maze. And you are absolutely correct, Sanako. On 'Earth One' we have a computer-programming saying: 'garbage in, garbage out.' I swear I will do my best to not provide you with garbage."

Her intense expression of distain softened slightly.

"And I...will be less confrontational with my accurate conclusions," she reluctantly agreed. "I am not used to working as part of a team. I prefer being a lone operative."

"Thank you for making the effort," I managed to conclude the discussion.

I was still shaking with pent-up anger as I stumbled from the Operations Tent with Scott's strong hand supporting my arm.

Outside, I looked up again at the awesome cosmic display above me.

"Will we ever get through this?" I whispered. "Two more weeks sounds like an eternity."

"Sure we will, Suzette," Scott gently smiled. His brown eyes were gentle and soothing. His wavy brown hair was glorious. His broad shoulders were like pillars. "I have faith in you."

I grabbed him and hugged him close.

Giving into my feelings, I *kissed* him full on his mouth. My lips lingered warmly on his. He tasted like nutrient cubes. He must have recently eaten. I should have been repulsed. But I was strangely aroused.

"You're a good friend, Scott," I sighed, closing my eyes and hugging him tighter.

"Whatever you need, I'm here for you," he assured me. His strong arms encircled my trembling back, holding my body firmly and confidently against his.

Out of the corner of my eye I saw Anderson visibly snarling. The grimace certainly didn't accentuate his positives. He looked like a ripped-up wolverine after a losing fight.

To hell with him! He had his chance with me back at Woodstock, but let himself be abducted away. Now he was a broken-down, middle aged, wreck. *Scott* was my new love!

—or, maybe young Edison, or the resurrected Maurice... *How the hell am I going to make it to the Performance this emotionally screwed up?*

But then I pulled away from Scott, a *cold chill* going through me.

What if something was sabotaging this Concert by scrambling my emotions?

Above all else, I had to focus on the true priorities. At least I *thought* they were the true priorities...

It was only hours from the Final Performance when a last-minute meeting of just the Principles at the Command Tent was disrupted. A *bloody, battered* Arthur Anderson stumbled in.

He collapsed onto the floor as Scott ran in behind him with a dozen of his Guards.

"I'm sorry, Suzette, he ran past us and..."

"No...please hear me out," Anderson moaned. His face was almost unrecognizable. It was a bloody mess. Even his ever-present dark eyeglasses were damaged, cracks running through both lenses.

Jarred out of my momentary shock I leapt over to him and held up his profusely bleeding head.

"I'm here, Arthur," I said, bending over him, "What happened?"

He whispered to me, so faint that only I could hear: "It's your mother..."

"*What?*"

"She's been kidnapped..." he barely managed to sputter in my ear. "Her captors say that you have to...throw the competition...go overtime, anything to disqualify us...or they'll kill her. Don't try to find her...just *lose* the competition and she'll be fine."

His eyes fully closed and he was unconscious.

"What did he say?" Janis Joplin said, knelling down beside me.

"He wants us to stop the Production."

"Well, to hell with that!" Mozart snapped grandly. "My new symphony must be performed! To do less would be an affront against God!"

Yes, a bit of hyperbolae there. True, he'd written a fresh symphony, part of which we were performing, but it wasn't any better than his most famous works... What was I thinking? My mind was going in a million directions at once. Supposedly my mother was going to be *killed* if we even tried to search for her!

"Some of the malcontents must have ambushed him," Scott growled, more upset than I'd ever seen him. "I'll get the Guards out in full force. Did I hear him say something about Dr. King?"

I struggled to get my panic under control.

"Oh...he said she's fine, resting in her tent after the attack," I lied to them all. If I told them the true situation, the news would surely get to the kidnappers that their game was up. They might then cut their liabilities, killing my Mom. "Don't disturb the crowds. We need them to perform on cue. It's too late to do a major investigation for the trouble makers and send them back to Earth. Just keep a keen eye out for any additional trouble, Scott."

"We can't control a crowd this big if they turn on us," he mused, nervously biting his upper lip. "After all, we've got no weapons. I've got to inform the Phoenix troops and Peace Keepers that..."

I had no idea who'd taken my Mother. It could be anyone, including elements of Phoenix or the 2nd Dimension Keepers. And the kidnappers would surely know what was happening if extra security began interrogating everyone.

"No," I replied. "Just do the best you can without informing them. The crowd's sure to get agitated if they see their 'jailors' searching everyone."

Arthur was barely breathing, blood bubbling from his gaping, now-toothless mouth.

"But...?"

"Take him to the med tent," I ordered, gently lowering Arthur's battered head to the floor. "The show must go on!" I smiled at them all, trying not to obsess on the fresh blood smearing my arms. "We won't let a few thugs stop us. You know Arthur's short temper. He got into a fight with a gang. It's nothing to worry about."

As the others left I pulled Scott to the side, whispering to him. "They took my Mom. If I don't throw the competition, they're going to kill her. Arthur said she's done for if they think anyone's searching for her. You've got to quietly rescue her before the Concert ends. Otherwise...well...I don't know what I'm going to do."

His deeply tanned face blanched with anger. "I'll find her. You can count on it."

"I'll have Sam maintain a direct link between you and me."

"Regardless, you *must* do your best to win this contest," he said, steel shining from his normally placid brown eyes. "Your mother would want you to give it your all, for the good of the human race. You know that, right?"

"Yes," I reluctantly agreed. "The 'Girl with the Turtle Tattoo' always puts the welfare of others before herself."

"What?"

"Just some sort of flashback," I mumbled, turning away.

I was too tired to think straight. And in mere minutes I had to give the performance of my life. This whole affair was fast turning out just like my last concert at the Hollywood Bowl, or when I searched for the bomb at Woodstock—struggling against all odds while lethal villains lurked in the shadows.

Where before they'd failed, would they now succeed? After all, "three times the charm."

Christ, what a depressing thought...

I only wished the last couple weeks I hadn't shunned my Mother. I'd barely spoken to her, making up some excuse whenever she wanted us to get together.

And now it might be too late.

Chapter 25

<u>ROCK THE STARS</u>

Why do we love Music
That throbbing flowing vibration
Be it adorned with flowery words
Or naked notes resonating
Could it be our beating hearts
Amplified strong and hard
Convincing us we're still alive
In a cold, uncaring Universe
We're not just a meaningless curse
Doomed to experience everything
That's in an instance snatched away
Leaving us dying, empty, and lonely
But knowing the soaring heights of love
And the bitter taste of rancid hate
The awful expanse of outer space
The terrible letdown of failure
In the nestling breast of mother earth
In an instant we bloom from seed to tree
And reach up to the distant sky
Sprouting enticing, lovely fruit
Hoping that somewhere far up above
Is something reaching down for us
And humming a happy tune...

The Suzette Anthology, Lyrics 25

The present highest percentage on the scoreboard was a whopping 95.3892%. We were up next, the last competitor planet. Billy told us he had no idea exactly how the points were awarded from which the percentage was derived. It was some sort of complex formula that differed from judging planet to judging planet. It accounted for the number of individuals voting, their relevant senses, and what they valued in the performances. But across thousands of judging planets the voting boiled down to one final number.

Regardless, we had to beat that leader percentage to win the competition.

And we had to do it now. Sam was counting down in my earbud... [four...two...one...*go!*]

I hung suspended in a white mist, a rocker angel. My feathery wings were flapping grandly. It was my "homage" to the terrible end of the *Suzette Kingly Album Six World Tour:* a new beginning of something far grander!

Then the substance of the Stage transformed on command: OUT OF THE WHITE SWIRLING MISTS OF LOW FLYING CLOUDS BELOW ME, MOUNTAIN PEAKS BEGAN TO EMERGE...

These were not stage effects or projections or even 3D simulations. The "red stone" substance of the stage beneath us was actually transforming into the desired scenes. It was beyond real. It was mesmerizing!

A cold wind on my skin got warmer.

And a distant, constant, slow "drumming" drew ever closer and louder...

Sam's stage direction, which I and other key participants heard over our earbuds, was unorthodox but compelling. A small army of assistants was controlling the lighting, the special stage effects, and complex two-way transmissions. Edison, Sanako, Beauchamp, and the Swami had finally figured out how to communicate in both directions with our immediate human audience, with Earth's broadcast-linked population, with thousands of alien previous winner-worlds, and most importantly with the observing Lords.

Plus I had at my fingertips the *uber-controls* to enhance our human sensations: translating from our special multi-spectral microphones and cameras not just human *sound* and *sight*, but also *touch*, *smell*, and *taste* into a spectrum of alien analogs.

I was orchestrating it all over my throat micro-mikes and augmented-reality "AR" contact lenses. All participants whether onstage or in the audience had transmitters at their throats and on their various instruments. Teams of technicians were controlling various specific components. This was a mammoth concert production, beyond anything ever attempted in our world's history.

My contact lenses on each eye provided me with an overall feed of what was transmitting to the various audiences, plus a variety of prioritized options.

My angel wings folded into my back as I alighted on the top of Mount Everest. Then my white robe transmuted into my "official" uniform: unbuttoned plaid blue-brown long-sleeved shirt, white tank-top showing only a hint of cleavage, tattered blue jeans, and white tennis shoes. A broach of orange-yellow-white agate stones was pinned above my left shirt pocket. I wore only a small amount of makeup, my lips slightly reddened with lipstick. My natural blond hair (not a wig) was curly, long, fluffy, and gorgeous.

With my signature red electric guitar slung across my shoulder, I was ready to conduct the grand-symphony.

"Are you READY to ROCK THE STARS?" I screamed out as loud as I could

I was indeed the grand "orchestra director" simultaneously participating in the production while floating above it all exercising ultimate control. Blinks and twitches of my eyes controlled a battery of virtual buttons and sliders that seemed to hang in the air before me. I could sing for everyone or speak discretely to any individual component.

It was glorious. I'd never had such control over my previous concerts. But I had no time to wallow in self-congratulation or admiration. After our previous six months of tumultuous preparation, it was finally the real thing.

There'd be no "second takes." This was it, our one and only chance to win the Prize. We just had to "go with the flow" and hope for the best.

And I still didn't know what to do about Mother. Scott was linked-in, covertly searching for her with his people. Everything hung in the balance of his efforts.

The concert proceeded in a series of loosely scripted scenes:
AS I FADED FROM VIEW, OUT OF THE MISTS BELOW ME A BLACK-SKINNED WARRIOR BEAT WITH TWO THICK STICKS ON A SIX-FOOT HOLLOWED OUT LALI...
—*supplanted by a ring of Lalis in a jungle village's central-square now pounding out a thunderous chorus...*
LED BY LELEA, HALF-NAKED NATIVE DANCERS POURED FROM THE HUTS, ME AMONGST THEM NOW CLAD ONLY IN A SINGLE-PIECE, GLARINGLY WHITE DRESS, RACING FOR A LONE LALI IN THE CENTER...
I was reprising the incredible spectacle and emotions of my primitive Fijian "concert"...
—*a battery of small Lalis joining with a high "clatter", then deeper bamboo Derua pounded into the ground, then the sharp "clacks" of stones slapped together, and sticks "slapped" sharply...*
Warriors streamed into the village square, "whooping" and shouting while waving blunted stage-weapons: *clubs, spears,* and *battleaxes* brandished high above their heads!
[Cue audience clapping...now entire Earth clapping...]
And pounding-away with a modern-drumming pattern I also mentally received the picture of overlapping millions and billions of people all connecting beyond the visuals in a triumphant, thunderous BEAT...
OUT OF THE SWIRLING MISTS AND JUNGLE A LINE OF NATIVE-AMERICANS EMERGING...LOSA YANASH AND HIS STOMP DANCERS ENCIRCLING A NOW-TOWERING CENTRAL BONFIRE...
[Cue audience circling...]
THREE HUNDRED THOUSAND AUDIENCE MEMBERS NOW STOMPING AND CIRCLING IN OPPOSITELY MOVING RINGS ARROUND THE STADIUM PLATFORM HOLDING THE JUNGLE DRUMMERS...
[Cue Earth audience...]

CLAPPING *BILLIONS* BACK ON EARTH NOW STOMPING IN-PLACE TO THE RIVETTING, THUNDEROUS BEAT...

Suddenly added to the mind-rupturing overlapping beats the PIERCING BLASTS from Jimi Hendrix's white electric guitar splitting the air as he levitated out of the flames of the central bonfire, his band simultaneously emerging from the surrounding jungle foliage...

"You got my pride!" he screamed over his wailing guitar and the pounding beat... "You got my soul! You messin' around with my life! You got my heart!"

[Cue chorus...]

As he improvised brilliantly on "Freedom" I stood on top of my Lali—blazing white in my dress—and led the entire still-circling rings of the audience singing back to him: "YOU GOT MY PRIDE! YOU GOT MY SOUL! YOU MESSIN' AROUND WITH MY LIFE! YOU GOT MY HEART!"

He finished a squealing, reverberating blast on the high notes of the guitar and yelled back: "*Freedom*, give it to me!"

[Add in Earth audience...]

"*FREEDOM*, GIVE IT TO ME!" billions sang back as they continued clapping and dancing around their broadcast devices to Jimi's earth-shattering overlapping notes.

"That's what I want now!" Hendrix shouted.

"THAT'S WHAT I WANT *NOW!*"

"Freedom, that's what I need now!"

"FREEDOM, THAT'S WHAT I *NEED* NOW!"

"Freedom to live and give!"

"FREEDOM TO LIVE AND GIVE!"

And he launched into an even more hectic and incredible sequence on his *reverberating, squealing guitar* as his band danced with the Fijian and American natives with everyone playing their own instruments...

MISTS ROLLING BACK IN AS THE MUSIC AND NOISE FADES...

[Cue Mother Hildegard]

Sudden silence...the mists clear out...again back on the windswept peak of *Mount Everest* an elegant, black-hooded nun appears.

She looks up at the sky: in all its glory the Galactic Center with its millions of packed stars glares down...

She slowly raises her long-sleeved arms to the sky.

—as a *SPHERE* EMERGES FROM THE STAR FIELD AND REGALLY DESCENDS, GROWING BRIGHTER AND BRIGHTER...

Yes, it's a naked appeal to our sponsor. I'm not proud of it. But all the winners had an element of "suck-up" built into their performance. This was mine...

"Behold the Living Light!" she smiles in rapture up at the white-glowing, descending Sphere.

I stride up next to her, strumming softly on a wooden acoustical guitar.

—as she recites a loose English translation of a passage from her work *"Ave Generosa"* concerning the Blessed Virgin Mary:

> *"And your womb held joy*
> *Heaven's harmonies ringing*
> *From you Celestial Music*
> *Heralding your child by God*
> *Your flesh bearing joy*
> *Sparkling with the dew*
> *Heaven freshens the earth*
> *Oh Mother of springtime..."*

And the two of us together launched into the Beatle's "Let it Be"— she singing sweet soprano and me harmonizing at alto. Our original plan was that Sally King would join us at alto and I'd slide down to tenor. But my mother wasn't available. She was kidnapped and facing death if I didn't somehow sabotage our performance. I still didn't know what I'd do. But the final production was in progress. We had to go with whatever happened.

And as the stars seemingly descended around us to spin in hypnotic, intersecting circles the Earth and concert audience all joined in on each chorus: *"Let it be, let it be, let it be, let it be...whisper words of wisdom, Let it be!"*

[Slowly fade to black.]

{Scott! Anything to report? Please answer me! We're in the first brief interlude.}

{Yes, I hear you. I've a lead. It's in the *underbelly*.}

{What do you mean?}

{It's not just a few malcontents. There's a *dark subculture* embedded within our people here...more than just a scattering of trouble makers. I had no idea it ran this deep...but I'm making progress.}

{Thirty minutes of the concert are gone, Scott. There's only an hour and half left. *Please*, Scott...}

{I won't fail you. But the plot's wider than just your Mother, Suzette. Be on your guard! I, *unggghhh*...(incoherent shouts)}

{Scott! Scott!}

[Cue the prison.]

EVERYTHING WAS SHROUDED IN A DEEP, MOLDERING BLACKNESS EXCEPT FOR ONE LONE CANDLE LIGHTING A SMALL STONE CELL...

King Richard I peers upward with an angry scowl. He is furious. His short beard and mustache are grimy and unkempt. He wears a tattered one-piece tunic. Then he looks down at a wooden bench before which he sits cross-legged on the cold floor. He is hunched over a paper, scrawling on it with a vengeance.

"No man in prison can tell his true story," he mutters. "No one can know what the prisoner experiences least he endure the same torture. Before I was captured, I had many friends. Now my so-called 'friends' are long gone. For two whole years I've languished as they 'forget' to pay my ransom. It's only in writing and singing my songs I find some comfort."

He grinned evilly and *sang* what he just wrote.

[Cue the plantation field.]

The blackness swallows him as the periphery of the stage lightens, revealing a line of black-skinned slaves working their way through a cotton field. Some have baskets on their heads, carrying loaded raw cotton to a mule-drawn cart.

They're singing as they work: "*Swing low, sweet chariot...*"

[Cue Suzette and Lionheart...]

I was revealed standing next to King Richard. Now he is in his full, regal clothes. He has on a fine, blue garment with a yellow collar. On his head is a regal golden crown encrusted with flashing jewels. His disdainful, unblinking stare are every inch that of a King. Behind us both appears my full band, *Strinjet*.

We all begin clapping to the verses of "Swing low, sweet chariot," a slow, plodding beat.

[Cue concert audience...cue Earth broadcast recipients...cue Galactic viewers' feedback...]

A monstrous BEAT was slowly accompanying the singing slaves toiling at their backbreaking labor in the field.

Then *Harriet Tubman* steps forward into the fields, holding up her hands to the sky.

"Everyone join in!" she ordered.

And on each chorus, accompanied by my wailing electric guitar and blasting full band, we all sing in unison:

> *"Swing low, sweet chariot,*
> *Coming for to carry me home,*
> *Swing low, sweet chariot,*
> *Coming for to carry my home."*

"It's not enough!"

Everything comes to a screeching halt. The people toiling in the fields stop singing. Harriet frowns. I turn to look at King Richard. He is laughing, his previous dour expression turned to amusement.

This was completely "off script." Was he taking me at my word that inspired improvisation was welcome during the performance? Was he carried away with the spirit of the occasion? Or did he have a darker agenda?

Is he somehow involved with the abduction of my mother and the threat to kill her if I don't throw the contest?

"You can be your *own* 'chariot'!" he shouted out across the stage. "*Take* your 'freedom'! *Don't* let your body, heart, or soul be imprisoned! *Fight* for your freedom! Suzette isn't in this for you! She's got her own agenda! She's just using you! This whole 'concert' is a sham!"

His admonition was totally unexpected but totally inspirational. Close-ups of the toiling slaves revealed new determination, fierce rebellious grimaces.

I could feel the hundreds of thousands of audience members also drinking in King Richard's outrage. I realized they were primed and ready to riot. If they stormed the stage, turning on the performers, the entire concert would come to a grinding halt.

"Wade in the water! Wade in the water, children!" Harriet Tubman shouted back at King Richard, seemingly in agreement but from a totally different perspective.

She was continuing the script as planned.

And as one, the plantation slaves fiercely sang out:

> *"Who are those children all dressed in Red?*
> *God's gonna trouble the water.*
> *Must be the ones that Moses led.*
> *God's gonna trouble the water!"*

The audience surrounding the stadium-stage all shouted and screamed out their approval, lustily taking on the banner of blood-drenched warriors.

I struck up my band and motioned for everyone to sing with me when the chorus came up: *"Wade in the water! Wade in the water, children. Wade in the water. God's gonna trouble the water!"*

And after each verse sung by the slaves, I and all our audiences chimed in lustily...

We were back on track. King Richard's concert-busting subversion was overwritten, at least for the moment.

[Cue in Armstrong and his jazz band...]

Matching the lead melody, Louis Armstrong blasted out his warbling, piercing *trumpet...*

—joined by *King Oliver's Creole Jazz Band*...horns and drums and fiddle and base pumping out a snappy, dancing tune!

It was the perfect counterpoint to the self-righteous "Lionheart."

And suddenly the plantation was gone...leaving a wide dance floor as the folks onstage began jitterbugging with each other, the vast audience around us joining in spontaneously.

Whew! A near riot had transmogrified into dance! It was glorious! I and my band joined in the writhing and twisting...

And then Armstrong broke out into "Summertime"...an incredible trumpet solo masterpiece causing the audience to stop in its tracks and listen, mesmerized.

And Louis briefly paused his trumpeting at various points to sing a phrase in his gravelly voice, grinning widely as he motioned for everyone else to repeat it back to him...

"Summertime, and the livin' is easy..."

[Cue in lakes and streams...]

BLUE LAKES AND MOUNTAIN STREAMS; PASTURES AND GRAZING COWS; FIELDS THAT LOOKED LIKE THEY WENT ON FOREVER; SHADE TREES WITH PEOPLE LOUNGING UNDER THEM; PORCHES WITH ROCKING CHAIRS AND PITCHERS OF ICE TEA; A LAZY RIVER WITH KIDS SKINNY DIPPING WHILE ELDERS FISHED LEISURELY FROM THE BANKS...

"Fish are jumpin' and the cotton is high..."

And so the song continued, Armstrong adding the words and the massive human audience echoing his phrases between his incredible trumpet riffs and improvisations...

"—so hush, little baby, don't you cry," he finished.

[Cue in Acuff and the Grand Old Opry.]

A magnificent high-pitched "squealing" sounded as Roy Acuff joined in. He was playing "Turkey Buzzard" on his fiddle, backed up by his band. He joined Armstrong and the Jazz band that seamlessly switched from jazz to Country Western.

Suddenly everyone was stomping and swirling around on wooden flooring. Losa Yanash and his stomp dancers came prancing onto the stage, joining the freed slaves. It was a country "ho-down" square-dance!

LARGE TIERS OF BLEACHERS REACHING UP INTO THE SKY; THOUSANDS OF THE SURROUNDING AUDIENCE MARCHING UP ONTO THE STAGE AND OCCUPYING THE SEATS; SWARMS OF PEOPLE GYRATING IN EACH OTHER'S ARMS TO THE SEDUCTIVE COUNTRY WESTERN BEAT...

"What a beautiful thought I am thinking concerning a great speckled bird," Acuff sang in his twangy voice accompanied by a fellow in blue coveralls tweaking a seductively sliding steel guitar.

And the seated audience chimed in, swaying to the gentle tones...

"She is spreading her wings for a journey
She's going to leave by and by
When the trumpet shall sound in the morning
She'll rise and go up in the sky..."

Armstrong let loose a soul-jarring blast on his trumpet, improvising a long sequence as he joined with Acuff's soaring fiddle.

And as the Grand Old Opry faded from view, a single light shone down from the darkness, illuminating...

—A BLACK GRAND PIANO WITH TOP RAISED; A GRAY-WHITE FLUFFY-HAIRED AFRICAN-AMERICAN MAN IN A WHITE SUIT SITTING SILENTLY AT THE KEYBOARD; HIS FACE TO A SILVER MICROPHONE; HIS WISE OLD FACE HIGHLIGHTED: A BROWN MUSTACHE, A WIDE FACE, A HIGH FOREHEAD AND KNOWING EYES.

Then a tinkling, flowing melody reminiscent of a bubbling stream on a hot summer day...prancing along like a kid out skipping down a one-lane country road...

Allen Toussaint proceeded to captivate the vast audience with his flowing piano solo, unaccompanied by any other instrument, playing "Southern Nights"...

SURROUNDING FIELDS, TREES, LEAVES WAVING LEISURELY IN A WARM EVENING BREEZE; SHIMMERING FLOWERS OF EVERY COLOR; BOUNCING KITTENS CHASING HOPPING CHICKENS; FIREFLIES TWINKLING IN THE FADING EVENING LIGHT; OLD MEN SITTING IN CHAIRS WITH LAZY DOGS SNORING AT THEIR FEET; FRUIT TREES HEAVY WITH RIPE FRUIT; OLD WOODEN PORCHES UNDER SAGGING ROOFS.

The approaching night swooshed like a tide coming in. The moonlight was crisp. Bugs chirped and buzzed in vast choruses. Harmonicas and banjos dueled. Homemade hooch was slurped

*gustily. Rockers squeaked and cracked. Ghost stories drew breath-
less gasps.*

Jesus Christ—I suddenly realized we were *all* ghosts! All of us
there at the Galactic Core were previously dead but now resurrected,
either literally or figuratively. And now I was trapped in the seductive
snare of a dead Allen Toussaint, as was the rest of the music-
appreciating Galaxy.

{Suzy...can you hear me?}

I was broken out of my revere, struggling to divide my attention
from the mesmerizing "Southern Nights" back to the search for my
mother.

{Scott! Is that you, Scott? Are you alright?}

{I'm alive, just barely. No, I'm better than that, since...}

{What happened?}

{We were ambushed. But we fought them off. One of my guards
is dead. Two others are wounded. Then had *guns*, Suzette! They're
not just fanatics. I don't think they're Phoenix. They're cold-blood
killers. We captured one of them and got him to talk some before he
cracked open a cyanide pill hidden inside a tooth, killing himself.
They're planning something big, before the end of the concert.}

{But how'd they get guns? Weapons of all types were strictly
banned from transport to the Galactic Core. For God's sake, even
harmless kitchen knives failed to reappear on this side. Even the
Peace Keepers had to leave their 2nd-Dimension energy weapons behind.}

{Yes, I know. But the guy we caught had a bullet-firing, regular
gun. We took it apart. The saboteurs must have smuggled them
through the transporter in small pieces brought by an array of individuals, assembling them on this side.}

{Oh, Christ! That's a real conspiracy—from before we all transported to the Galactic Core! How can we stop guns?}

{Now that we know they're armed, we can overwhelm them with
stealth or numbers, or maybe...}

Toussaint began singing to his continued piano playing, entrancing the entire Galactic Audience. He ended with:

"Feel so good

Feel so good
It's frightening
Wish I could
Stop this world from fighting
La dee Da, La dee Da..."

That was a very timely notion. Why were there traitors trying to stop the contest? It was a conspiracy, obviously planned from before we transported to the Galaxy Core. Who would reject immortality and all the other incredible gifts that the Lords had for the winner of this contest?

And joining Toussaint onstage in the spotlight now were *two other pianos:* one manned by the slender, black-hat-wearing Jazz piano player *Tuts Washington* and the other by the New Orleans blues singer and pianist *Professor Longhair*, his dark eyeglasses and pencil-thin mustached head turned up to the sky in ecstasy. They played wild counterpoints as Toussaint began a final reprise of the "Southern Nights" melody.

It was magical.

Then the spotlight narrowed back to only Allen. He continued the magnificent piano playing as the light softly faded away until only his smiling face was illuminated, eyes closed in sad contemplation.

And then there was darkness.

The second "interlude" was finished. There was only one hour left to save my Mom, Sally King.

The second half of the concert started innocently enough...

A line of bald-headed, robed *Hare Krishna* came swaying up a mountain path, chanting:

"Hare Krishna Hare Krishna
Krishna Krishna Hare Hare
Hare Rama Hare Rama
Rama Rama Hare Hare"

A MOUNTAIN GLADE, COMPLETE WITH A CASCADING WA-TERFALL FALLING INTO A PEACEFUL POND; WARM SUNLIGHT

SPILLING THROUGH GREEN LEAVES; FLAPPING BIRDS AND JUMPING FISH; MOSS AND VINES COVERING EVERYTHING; SWARMS OF ORANGE AND BLUE BUTTERFLIES FLUTTERING THROUGH THE AIR...

And then the Krishna began chanting faster. The scene opened up and Fijian natives again were drumming on small Lalis. Then from a nearby mountain peak I joined in with my rock band, adding in my twinkling electric guitar riffs...

[Cue concert audience...]

The 200,000 surrounding participants took up the chant as the still-marching Krishna and I fell silent, a *thundering* sound that swept us all up:

> "HARE KRISHNA HARE KRISHNA
> KRISHNA KRISHNA HARE HARE
> HARE RAMA HARE RAMA
> RAMA RAMA HARE HARE"

[Cue clapping...concert audience...Earth audience...]

A steady "CLAP, CLAP, CLAP..." punctuated the continued massive chanting.

[Cue dancing...]

In the hypnotic words and BEAT a spontaneous jerking-back-and forth and hopping up-and-down spread through the crowd...

[Cue Mozart and the New York symphony...]

The full orchestra appeared on a transparent disc floating in the sky, descending to hover above the Krishna.

Mozart stood on a dais at its front, conducting them with full sweeps of his arm: leads from *strings, horns, drums,* then *organ* amplifying and spreading the Krishna chant in a new composition written by the Master just for this performance.

[Cue Hill...]

Ureli Corelli Hill stepped up to the front of the orchestra. Unlike the rapturous performers and audience he looked solemn. He had on a vested full suit with a bowtie at his neck. His eyes were wide and staring, the corners of his mouth downturned. His short beard and brown hair were trim and neat. He put his violin to his shoulder and added a piercing, entrancing *violin solo* on top of everything else...

[Cue Galactic audience...]

And I felt at one with the Galaxy as thousands of alien races joined in with their aligned emotions, motions, and vibrations...

[Cue the Swami...]

Satchidananda stepped up beside me as I continued riffing on my electric guitar. He held a large multi-sensory microphone. He had a beatific smile on his swarthy face. His gray-white long straight beard, mustache, and wavy hair swayed in the breeze. His high forehead was turned to the sky. On top of the chanting, clapping, dancing, rock band, and symphony orchestra he loudly proclaimed in a monotone:

"Change yourself to change the entire world!
Truth is always the same:
Doing good gives you true happiness...
Doing wrong brings you suffering...
Find meaning in what you do!
Purify your minds, removing misery and pain...
Discover wisdom, not in many words
But in thoughtful silence!"

He held his orange-robed arms up high before sharply *clapping* together his hands.

Instantly, everyone and every instrument fell silent.

It was a moment of transcendental beauty...until *King Richard* stepped up behind Hill and *snatched* his violin bow away. In a daring leap he fell from the disc down to where I stood, *plunging* the sharp violin bow into the Swami's back!

"Don't buy that bull-crap!" Lionheart shouted, jerking cut the bloody bow and holding it high over his head, *"Attack! Attack! Attack!"*

Grimacing in pain, the Swami crumpled into my arms.

Stunned at this grotesque departure from our script, I caught the wounded man and dragged him off to the side.

King Richard "the Lionheart" was charging my band, savagely scattering their instruments! And behind me I heard an ominous rumbling as many in the surrounding mass of humanity converted from ecstatic chanters to a mindless, rioting mob!

{Suzette! They co-opted the food dispensers, making them produce pizza and beer. And they put some sort of time-release, mind-altering chemicals into the beer. Those that drank it are now out of their minds!}

{They're throwing away heaven on earth for comfort food?}

{Yes, it's just like the story in the Bible, Suzette—giving up their birthright for a bowl of stew.}

{I see the crazed leaders out there in the audience—don't let them get onstage...keep them away by all means necessary!}

{We'll try.}

A huge fight was erupting around the stage as those suddenly under attack from vicious, drooling "druggies" tried to defend themselves. Blood was being spilled. Images of brutal kicking and punching dominated my feeds.

I "conked" King Richard on his noggin with my heavy electric guitar, knocking him flat to the ground.

Instantly, my band members pinned him down.

I shouted out on full-broadcast, loudspeaker-mode to all present and onward to the entire Galaxy: "WE HAVE A CHOICE! WE ALWAYS HAVE A CHOICE! WE CAN MAKE WAR OR WE CAN MAKE PEACE! WE CAN SEEK TO TEAR DOWN OR STRIVE TO BUILD UP! WE CAN SURRENDER OUR MINDS TO SIMPLE SOLUTIONS OR STRUGGLE WITH DIFFICULT CONCEPTS AND DECISIONS! WE CAN EMBRACE MIND-ALTERING DRUGS OR WE CAN VALUE HEALTHY PAIN! WE CAN SELFISHLY GUARD OUR GAINS OR SEEK TO SPREAD WHAT WE'VE BEEN BLESSED WITH TO OTHERS! WE CAN LOOK TO THE NEXT MOMENT OR ON INTO THE LIMITLESS FUTURE! CHOOSE! *CHOOSE THIS MOMENT* WHO YOU WILL FOLLOW—A DERANGED KING SEEKING TO ENSLAVE YOU UNDER HIS TWISTED EDICTS, OR THE BEST URGINGS OF YOUR VERY OWN HEART!"

Wow. It was a great speech, spontaneously ripped from my own soul at our moment of greatest peril. I was proud of myself. Apparently others were also.

"Even when the whole world is engulfed in war, we can still call up our best angels," a warm baritone voice sounded from behind me. "Let's listen to our favorite angel, Suzette Kingly!"

Bing Crosby gently took hold of my arm and guided me aside.

"You lived through a terrible Word War," I spoke in my normal voice.

"Yes, I did, Suzette. It was awful. But we did not fight to conquer or destroy. We fought to stop evil dictators, for peace!"

His soothing tones plus the new change of set had a dramatic effect on the audience. The roiling fights slowed then stopped.

[Cue the grand piano and fireplace...]

"Let me tell you about a wonderful holiday that's the opposite of stupid conflict," he gently smiled, settling down at the keyboard. Everything else faded to background. A few groups in the audience were still fighting and struggling. But they became a black-and-white backdrop to his calming presence.

I sat on a chair behind him, listening intently.

Again, we were back on script.

"I'm dreaming of a white Christmas..." he began slowly singing as the orchestra in the darkness chimed in behind his simple piano playing.

A SMALL TOWN COVERED IN A FRESH BLANKET OF SNOW MATERIALIZED; KIDS LAUGHING AND PLAYING ON SMALL SLEDS; A HORSE-DRAWN LARGE SLED WITH A HAPPY COUPLE KISSING BEHIND A DRIVER; SLEIGH BELLS TINKLING MERRILY; FLUFFY WHITE SNOWFLAKES FALLING ON GRINNING CHRISTMAS SHOPPERS; AN INDOOR CHRISTMAS TREE ADORNED WITH SHINING ORNAMENTS AND CANDLES...

And as Bing completed the first verse, I took the part of Marjorie Reynolds in the famous movie Holliday Inn, singing harmony with him on the second verse. Bells chimed from the orchestra. Bing Crosby then started his famous whistling harmony as I took up the melody. And finally, together, we sang the last words, me taking the lead melody with Bing on harmony: "*And may all your Christmases be white!*"

—fade away leaving only the fireplace, which then goes dark also.

There wasn't a dry eye in the house. All the fights in the audience had been quelled. Even King Richard seemed chagrined at his actions, ducking his head as he was led away by security.

The production hadn't stopped. We were still going. Hell, the new "script" was even better than the old!

—but what about my mother?

{Have you found the conspirators, Scott? There's only thirty minutes remaining! Are you certain King Richard wasn't subverted by Phoenix operatives?}

{We're deep into the extras' tent city, Suzette. And, no, I still don't think Phoenix is behind this. From what I've found in the historical archives about Richard he wasn't really motivated by religion. Even his extensive role in the Crusades was driven by pride and greed. History says he was a good commander, but cruel and immoral. The far-right radical Christians presently ruling America with their strict religious rules wouldn't appeal to him; or him to them.}

{Then how was he turned?}

{Maybe he didn't need any conversion. Perhaps he's just a mean, spiteful ruler who wants to regain his prior glory.}

{Maybe, but...}

{We're close, Suzette. I've got to go. Remember, they've still got guns at the concert venue. Don't get complacent!}

{I won't. Thanks, Scott. Let me know the moment you know anything!}

[Cue the Cathedral...]

Rising up out of the mists were the towering inner stone walls of a magnificent, tall Cathedral. Trudging down the central isle was a line of Benedictine monks, led by the rotund Brother Frederick. They were singing a Gregorian chant, "Dies Irae." It was an English version of the original Latin hymn, the Gregorian Chant for the Dead. Their sonorous voices echoed and reverberated off the stone walls:

"Day of wrath and doom impending,
Heaven and earth in ashes ending,
When Death is struck and nature quakes
All Creation is awakening"

As they continued to chant, *Jacopo Peri* walked out on one of the Cathedral's inner balconies and spread his arms. He was a thick-lipped, round-eyed, long-haired young man. Yes, he'd been resurrected as yet another contender for my tender heart.

Hah...if only there'd been time for actual romance.

"Love is a cruel mistress!" he shouted.

Taking my cue, I strode out on another balcony: "Are you my true suitor?"

"I am but one of many," he sadly intoned. "Would that you might swoon, stricken by my manly charms! For you I would be a god. I would take upon myself the powers of Apollo to find favor in your beautiful eyes!"

Playing in time with the continuing Chant for the Dead, Mozart struck up his orchestra, building to a crescendo of sweet harmonies.

"Why are we slaves to our passions?" Jacopo sang lustily, in full "opera" mode.

"We *are* our passions!" I sang back from my balcony.

I heard distant "pops." Oh, Christ—guns were being fired! I ducked to the side as *bullets* slammed into my balcony. The post I'd hidden behind protected me, though chunks were knocked out, spraying me with fragments. Jacopo wasn't so lucky. Hit by a bullet, he staggered backward But he righted himself, clutching a shoulder. Blood was spreading on his arm. But he continued his song.

"Then what of reason, my dear Suzette?" he warbled.

I saw in the distance clots of the audience members swarming onto the shooters. They wouldn't threaten us again.

"Our minds are prisoners of our hearts," I bravely sung back to him. For all anyone knew, the drama that'd just occurred was a planned part of our performance.

"So must we embrace the moment or turn to dust?" he grimaced, clutching his bleeding shoulder.

"In but a moment my beautiful hair turns to rust, my perky bosom to hanging bags, my smooth skin to wrinkles, and my ripe body to rotting decay..."

"—and likewise my manhood withered and dry, my strong muscles to feeble clay, my blazing blue eyes to white cataracts," he frowned, clamping down on his shoulder to slow the loss of blood.

"But we are renewed and reinvigorated!" I loudly proclaimed.

"And how, thusly, do we live yet again to repeat the same—over and over?" he laughed his question past his obvious pain.

"It is the miracle of our embrace, a merging of our bodies: the rebirth of youth itself!"

"It is renewal! Long live the eternal Spring!" he shouted...

—as Louis Armstrong stepped onto another inner balcony in the Cathedral and began to sing in his gravelly voice *"What a wonderful world!"*

The spotlight focused on him as the cathedral faded and accompanying, fresh vistas surrounded him:

AN OLD GROWTH FOREST TOWERING UP HUNDREDS OF FEET INTO THE AIR; FIELDS OF RED ROSES; A MOUNTAIN LAKE UNDER A DEEP BLUE SKY; A RAINBOW ARCHING GRANDLY FROM HORIZON TO HORIZON; A BUSY CITY STREET WITH A PANOPLY OF DIFFERENT FACES; FRIENDS AND FAMILY EMBRACING; BABIES CRYING, GURGLING, FEEDING, TOTTERING THEIR FIRST FEW STEPS...

"—and I think to myself: *'What a wonderful world!'*" Louis smiled, rolling his eyes up in joy. Then, more quietly and thoughtfully, he repeated: "I think to myself: 'What a wonderful world'!"

"God damn it, you're *wrong!*" Janis Joplin shouted, pushing him aside. "It's just one insult after another."

"No, my young friend, there's beauty and love and..."

"Love?" Janis snorted. "Love *stinks!* Your joyful 'jazz' always gets smothered by the *blues!*"

The audience roared its approval.

She began gyrating and twisting, hands up in the air, as Armstrong took out his trumpet.

"Take another little piece of my heart!" she screamed as her backup band struck up behind her.

Armstrong let loose a harmonizing blast from his trumpet.

And together they *rocked the platform* as she invited the audience to join her every time she hit the chorus, concluding: "You know you've got it if it makes you feel good!"

I smiled as my old flame *Maurice* pranced out to join her onstage while the audience "rocked and rolled" all around us. He sang counterpoint to Janice's verbal eruptions. Yes, he was the perfect foil for her iconic blues. He knew all about casually ripping out the hearts of his conquests.

Then she seamlessly launched into "Cry Baby!"

It was slow and mournful, sung with utter sincerity. Her intense vocals cut into the hearts (or functional analogs thereof) of all those linked into the Galactic presentation.

"Honey, nobody ain't ever gonna love you the way I tried to do," she continued mournfully.

{We've got the tent surrounded where Sally King is being held. We're negotiating with her captors.}

{Tell them we've blocked their disruptions at the concert. Richard and the shooters are captured. Their rebellion is over. Tell them they've lost but I'll grant clemency. If they release Mom unharmed, they'll not be punished. Once this is all over they'll be given a forum to make their twisted case back on Earth, whatever their stupid reasoning may be.}

{I've demanded unconditional surrender. But we can't just storm the tent. They've already fired shots at us. They're threatening to execute Dr. King.}

{No! Tell them what I just said!}

There was a pause...

{They still insist you have to throw the competition. If you lose, then there's no problem. If you don't comply, then she's dead.}

{Get her out of there!}

{I'm massing my fighters. We may take casualties. But we'll have her out before the concert ends.}

{It's just fifteen minutes from now!}

{I know, Suzette. We won't let you down. Trust me.}

"Cry, cry, baby!" Joplin shouted as a billion humans chimed in with her on the chorus. "CRY, CRY, BABY!"

Then she fell silent for a moment, looking like she was about to crumble into dust. Her frizzled mass of hair drooped forward, hiding her squarish, pug face.

"You know the grass always looks greener when you're lookin' at someone else's yard..." she plaintively sang, "—but honey you have the real thing waitin' for you at home...you don't have to go away to find yourself...don't you realize your life is waiting like a God-damned fool right *here?*"

That was my cue...

THE DOME APPEARED ABOVE US, THE REAL STARS OF THE GALACTIC CORE BLAZING DOWN FROM ABOVE.

I joined her, harmonizing at alto as she and the entire human audience at the Galactic Core and back on Earth yelled out: "*Cry, cry, cry, cry baby!*" over and over again...

"No!" Jacopo shouted, stopping everything in its tracks.

All eyes were fixed on him as he strode defiantly up to me.

"Tell them, Suzette! Tell them!"

I strummed a few plaintive chords on my electric guitar...then launched into a joyful, *happy* riff.

[Time check: 7 minutes and counting down...]

We were only allowed two hours. One second longer and we'd be disqualified. If I wanted to throw the competition, that would be the easiest and least obvious way to do so. All I had to do was to let the final sequence slide just a tiny bit too long. Caught up in the massive exuberance of the "grand finale", no one would think I'd done it on purpose.

{Scott! Any word?}

{We're launching our assault...}

"*There's an Eagle on the wind...*" I began.

A GIANT EAGLE APPEARED ABOVE US LEISURELY FLOATING THROUGH THE SKY BETWEEN SNOWY PEAKS...

A cascade of other guitars, drums, base, violins, and flutes swirled around us as all our bands fused together with Mozart's full orchestra.

"EAGLE ON THE WIND..." Maurice echoed, swirling his luxuriously long brown hair with one hand as he strode up next to me.

"*Looking for his love...*"

"LOOKING FOR HIS LOVE..." Maurice answered loudly, looking longingly at me.

"As high as the sky and as deep as the sea..."

"DEEP AS THE SEA..."

"Could he find...me?"

"Me...me...me...me..." his voice trailed off, moving at each word up higher from deep base into tenor.

"Sing me a wind-song, calling to me..."

He was silent. Then he joined on the repeat, harmonizing in falsetto at alto:

"Sing me a wind-song, calling to me!"

"Up into the blue, always being true, never departing, always together, flying in formation, wingtip-to-wingtip we sing..."

"—dream a Wind-song!" I belted out the concluding words of the first verse.

"—dream a Wind-song!" he echoed in tenor.

"—dream a Wind-song!" we finished together, he an octave lower and me at soprano.

"Everyone, all together!"

The entire human audience plus the alien equivalents all across the Galaxy all belted out together: "DREAM A WIND-SONG!"

[Time check, *sixty seconds...*]

[Clue clapping by all, dancing...]

As the orchestra and bands surged their instrumentations. I took the lead with my guitar: hammering out a magnificent improvisation as I belted out the other verses with Maurice singing counterpoint and harmony...

—ending the lyrics but riffing violently on my guitar as Jimi Hendrix joined me on his, then Roy Acuff on his fiddle, then Louis Armstrong on his trumpet...

And all the performers came onstage, dancing and clapping with glee!

{Clue subspace celestial interfaces!} I ordered the control teams. Amazingly, I'd not had to redirect or alter any of their manipulations to this point. They'd done a fantastic job. But this final, induced subspace cosmic vibration was incredibly dangerous. I needed to take full responsibility for its implementation...

In the actual sky above the dome: RED-GIANT STARS SHOT OFF BRILLIANT YELLOW FLARES; NEUTRON STARS COLLIDED IN ROILING BLUE PLASMA CLOUDS; AND SUPERNOVAS EXPLODED!

Actually, those were just simulations. The actual events were taking place lightyears away and would take years or decades to locally observe. But the superimposed replications on the Dome above were completely believable and breathtaking.

I was deeply conflicted. I desperately wanted to save my mother. But humanity needed their Prize. And *I* hated to lose at anything...

[Ten seconds...*nine...eight...seven...six...*]

"Thank you!" I shouted.

Everyone fell silent, those with instruments laying them at their feet.

With tears in my eyes, and sweat dripping from my brow, I shakily set my guitar down, totally exhausted. I couldn't do it. I couldn't throw the contest. I'd come too far, endured too much. And the Prize for all humanity was just too great.

And *I*...totally selfishly, truth-to-tell...didn't want to die. I wanted to live forever, free of pain and disease, healthy and happy, with total creativity at my fingertips, able to manipulate energy and matter.

I *wanted* the collar!

[*Three...two...one...*that's a wrap, everyone! Well done! We're off-broadcast.]

Everyone stood silently in place, all our eyes fixed on the giant score screen that floated beside the Sphere there alongside the mammoth Stage. I knew that the score was still being accumulated. The alien races had the next five minutes to log in with their votes. Our score was already at 91% and climbing. As the final contestant, to win we "only" had to beat 95.3892%. At the four minute mark our total climbed past 94%. At twenty seconds remaining, we crept past 95%. Everyone stood totally still, riveted in place, staring at the scoreboard. Then with five seconds left we hit 95.3893%, the score still climbing.

The whole place exploded in applause.

"WE WON! WE WON! WE WON!" we all screamed, jumping up and down, hugging each other. It was pandemonium! Despite all the glitches and terrorist attacks, we'd soldiered through and won the Prize! The greatest Reward in the Galaxy was Earth's!

And then it hit me.

I slinked off to the side of my wildly celebrating group and sat down on the now-naked red stone floor of the stadium.

{Scott?}

No answer.

{Scott! What happened?}

{I...we...} came his faint reply.

{Tell me!}

{The assault was successful. We overwhelmed them before they could get a bead on us. But they all pulled the same trick as the one we captured earlier. They killed themselves with poison pills hidden in hollowed-out teeth...}

{—and my Mom?}

There was a lingering silence...

{She's dead, Suzette. I'm so sorry. The instant we moved on them they shot her through her heart.}

{But...but...there's time-freeze! We can grab her the same way we snatched all the others here. We can transport her to the Time Keepers, repair her body, and...}

{We're still under the dampening Dome, Suzette} he listlessly replied in my earbud. {Neither we nor the Time Keepers can intervene. She's gone.}

I felt numb. It was like being in a bad dream. You know it's a nightmare and want to wake up, but you can't. You're trapped in an awful limbo, unable to go forward or backward.

"Please! Everyone! Your attention, please!" I heard a familiar voice.

Looking up, I saw a translucent projection of Billy looming over us. He looked very sad but determined. Did he know what had just happened to our Mom? Surely he knew, but his words were completely different than what I expected.

"You've won, yes. But you haven't won the Prize—at least not yet. The top three scoring planets out of the 1,000 entries now have the option to go on, into the Final Round. Not informing the contestants before this moment of this requirement is yet another part of the Test. Otherwise you might have held back from giving the Lords your complete best effort, leaving something in reserve."

People were looking at each other in confusion and consternation. What did he mean, a "final round"? What the hell was this? We'd just put out a supreme effort, "won", and now there was *more?*

"Your time here at the Contest Planet is extended seven more days. Those who wish to return to Earth may do so. The Final Round consists of a 20-minute performance by each of the three finalist planets' chief advocates. That means Suzette Kingly will give another show, upon which will be determined the final vote. She is not allowed to have any other human on the Stage with her. It has to be a solo performance. And it must be new material not previously presented in your group concert."

Jesus H. Christ—this was totally unbelievable! I'd just let my own mother be killed for *nothing!* Even though I was definitely good, I knew I wasn't a world-class solo performer. During my early career in bars and nightclubs my solos were ok, but nothing world-shaking. I'd always depended on a backup group, band, and/or special effects team for spectacular sets.

"Fortunately..." Billy's white-haired image continued after a long pause, "—since you scored highest overall, you'll again be going last. You are allowed to see the first two performances. All the hard-won knowledge you've gained in your initial concert is still intact. I expect another spectacular effort. Good luck!"

His image winked out.

Upon completing our monumental effort, then apparently winning, I'd felt my knotted guts finally relax. Now they wrenched together into a burning, throbbing *bomb* threatening to rupture my intestines!

The flaring pain from my abdomen almost made me fall vomiting to my knees.

But everyone was looking at me, expecting me to do the impossible.

I managed a feeble grin.

Truthfully, I didn't know if I could make it another seven days at the Galactic Core, let alone give a winning solo performance.

Chapter 26

FINAL ROUND

Set 'em up again, Mick,
We'll drink till we're sick
It's obvious we'll never win again
We'll guzzle until we forget all the pain
The day we were brought down in shame

We could 'a been champions as brutal as Tyson
Making those other poor bastards whimper
While we pranced and danced and dodged like Ali
Knockin' their brains to the sky

Ropin' them dopes and stingin' like bees
It would 'a been others droppin' like fleas
We'd be swattin' and bashin' and bobbin' away
While our foe swung back just a little too late

But something strange happened that very last fight
When our opponents turned out our lights
One moment we were the "King of the World"
And the next we lay prone in the dirt...

So it's ok if we slobber and cry in our beer
As long as the alcohol's not thinned by our tears
Sure we might get up and learn to do better
But it's easier to stay down and hurt.

The Suzette Anthology, Lyrics 26

Scotty whimpered at my feet, sensing I was upset.

Well, I was entitled to be distraught. My *mother's dead body* lay beneath a red-rock sheet. She wasn't even on a bed or stretcher. She lay limply on a table, a mere examination slab. Presumably her body was there in the med tent either so that the attending physician could perform an official autopsy or for preparation to be sent home through the Sphere.

"Get *out!*" I yelled at all the doctors, nurses, attendants, and patients.

Those spontaneous words cut through my heart like a knife, throwing me back to when I'd last confronted my Mom in a similar tent...

I also felt momentarily guilty at ordering the medical personnel to evacuate their base of operations. But there were five other nearby med tents. A lot of people had been injured during the riots and shootings. The folks I kicked out could readily move to those other tents.

They hastily withdrew, leaving me alone with the corpse.

I went over to the table, drew back the sheet, and looked down at her.

"Hi Mom," I whispered, taking her cold hand in mine. "We won the Contest, at least for the moment. What comes next I don't know. I'm sure you'd tell me to forge on ahead, regardless of consequences. But now with you gone it hardly seems worth the effort."

Her face looked strange. It wasn't the face of the mother I remembered. My mother's face was always full of deep emotions: love, sympathy, anger, thoughtfulness, or determination. This face was slack and frozen. The lips were slightly parted, revealing dirty looking teeth. My Mom kept her teeth impeccably clean and white. The eyelids were shut but bulging, as if the hidden eyes were trying to escape. Doubtless they were just swollen. And her hair was limp, gray, and dry—like desiccated seaweed. Yep, they were trying to foist some *fish* thrown up on a shoreline for my vibrant, healthy mother!

But the bloody hole in her chest said differently. That was clearly a smashed human heart I glimpsed behind broken bones. The organ wasn't beating. No blood was pumping to the brain. Ergo, there was no neural activity. Without oxygen, cells in the body die. Even if we could time-freeze the corpse, there was nothing left to later resurrect, just an empty shell.

Sally King was truly gone.

"I'm...so...sorry," Scott said as he shuffled in, refusing to look at the dead body on the table. Losa was right behind him, hanging back a respectful distance.

I pulled the sheet back over her, sitting down wearily on a chair at the side of the table.

"I'm sure that you and your men did all you could to save her," I stated flatly without emotion. "It's not your fault, Scott. I really appreciate what you, your Dad, and the Chickasaw warriors did to stop the evil people who did this. Without your diligence they would have also crippled or stopped our performance."

"T-thanks..." he stammered, tears dripping from his eyes.

"We interrogated the shooters at the concert," Losa said, his normally guttural voice even more muffled than usual. "They don't know anything. They're just stooges, hyped up on that spiked beer thinking you were the devil or some such nonsense. The ringleaders who put the assembled guns in their hands are all dead. When captured they killed themselves with their cyanide pills, just like the crew that took your Mother."

"And what about King Richard?"

"He's an idiot. He still thinks he's back in the 12th Century when a tyrant could gin up an army of ignorant peasants. The organizers of the rebellion fed his ego sufficiently to insure he'd add to the disruptions during your concert. Other than wanting to be a dictator again, he's clueless."

"Scott doesn't think the leaders were Phoenix religious fanatics. What do you think, Losa?"

He shrugged. "I suppose either Phoenix or the Keepers—or elements thereof—might want to sabotage the concert. Neither of them would like to have their authority upended by the Lords."

"But you don't think that's likely?"

"Naw...I agree with Scott. It's more likely the instigators were from any number of subversive or criminal organizations back on Earth. The Phoenix religious rules are onerous. The Peace Keepers are even tougher. All our 'rights' have been thrown out the window, including the covert ones previously enjoyed by criminals. Lots of groups that flourished under the loose laws of normal governance are now getting squeezed. They don't want yet another 'super'-authority imposed from above. They're hurting enough as it is."

"I haven't been out on the streets for a long time. You're saying the regular folks don't see the 'Lords' as potential saviors from the repressive authorities who have banned music?"

"Hah—that's a laugh. This whole expedition to the center of the Galaxy is broadly regarded as a wild goose chase," he shrugged, chuckling. Then he visibly remembered where he was. "Uh, no disrespect to..."

"I'm not concerned with politeness or propriety," I snapped. "There will be time for grieving later. Right now I'm still running this operation. I'd hoped one way or other we'd be headed back to Earth by now. Unfortunately, this new 'wrinkle' of a final solo performance means I can't yet relinquish command. I have to 'keep my act together.' And I expect you both to do the same! I suspect that after experiencing the magnificence of our broadcasted Concert the public sentiment on Earth is now firmly on our side?"

"Of course," he nodded. He was now all-business. "What do you need done?"

I saw that Scott was unhappy at his Dad assuming command. After all, Scott had been assigned by the Chickasaw Nation to oversee my security. That made sense because he was young, spry, and obviously had my favor. But he was still just a young man, barely eighteen. The older, wiser Losa was always the one truly in charge.

"First, make sure there aren't any covert cells left of these conspirators. Second, find and get rid of all that LSD-contaminated beer. Third, put guards on the food dispensers so they can't be further tampered with or altered. Fourth, ration uncontaminated beer so we don't have more drunken riots seven days from now. Fifth, make sure there's pizza for everyone, as much as they want. Those food cubes are nasty. I don't blame anyone eating only the cubes for wanting to riot! Finally, recruit from the crowds we brought with us those you can trust enough to be deputized. I want our security seeded throughout the crowds and backstage in sufficient force to control any discontent at my final performance. Your Chickasaw warriors were only meant as a token guard for me. Now, since we can't trust Phoenix or the Keepers, we've got to form our own police force, even if it's just for the remaining week."

"You're expecting more trouble?"

"What do you think will happen if we lose the final round?"

He frowned, considering. Many scenarios were possible, most of them frightening.

"But Suzette, I'm sure you can..." Scott began, trying to reassure me that I'd win, not lose.

"Shut up, Scott," I curtly ordered him.

Yes, he was a loyal friend. Yes he was still gorgeous. But he'd assured me he was going to rescue my mother. I trusted him. Instead, he brought me her corpse. Although I intellectually understood he'd done all he could, emotionally I could never forgive him for not keeping his promise to me.

"But if we *do* win?" Losa tentatively asked

"Well, then I suppose that will solve all of our problems," I shrugged. "The Lords of the Galaxy will establish an outpost in orbit around Earth. They'll grant us many baby Spheres. Through the Spheres we'll have intimate communication with the Lords and all their other 'blessed' planets. Music will be restored to our civilization, better than ever."

"And there's more?" Scott asked, eager to be vindicated.

"Sure...freedom from illness and injury, a type of immortality," I mused. "Plus we'll be granted the personal means to manipulate energy and matter, sort of like what happens here with the red clay this place is built from. We'll all have anything we want, instantly at our fingertips, that is—those that accept the 'collar'."

"Collar?" Losa asked, frowning.

"You can put it on or take it off whenever you want. It's like a magic wristwatch I suppose. It provides a personal energy shield, the ability to materialize things out of pure energy, instant telepathy with other users, and other good stuff."

Losa paused, considering.

"So...that means there won't be any money or crime or governments?"

"I guess not."

"Can this really be true?" Scott gasped. "Suzette, it sounds like heaven on Earth!"

"From what I've seen on the 'blessed' planets I've virtually visited through our Mother Sphere here in the Dome, the Lords are true to their word," I shrugged. "The winning species is granted all that and more. Their planets—though sometimes bizarre to our tastes and needs—are all paradises."

"So there'd be no more need for guns, conflicts, or even tragedies like your mother...?"

"No need for any of that. Anyone injured will be instantly fixed, a mere matter of exquisite cellular repair. We'll all be wealthy beyond our wildest dreams. It's why even our repressive governments have allowed us to enter this competition. The personal benefits of winning are so huge it's obvious they trump any other consideration."

We looked at each other in silence. They still seemed uncertain, scared even. But I knew better. Over the last four weeks I'd visited many of the past winners. The miracles promised by the Lords were absolutely real.

And now, finally, I realize what I have to do for Earth.

"Any other questions?" I glared at them both.

Losa shrugged. "Can we conference with you daily?"

"I have to spend most of my time working on my new set," I sighed, "but I'm at your disposal. Interrupt me whenever you need. Scott, I still expect you and your men to keep my body well-protected. Though the criminals are put down, the crazies will likely be out in force."

He perked up at my show of confidence.

"Again, thanks to you both. That's all. Please don't allow anyone else in this tent for the next hour."

"Sure...no problem."

When they were gone I reached down and scratched Scotty's ears. I heard his tail "thumping" on the floor. The tent "walls" were so thin I'm sure those outside could hear his tail wagging also.

Sticking my face down into my folded arms I silently bawled my eyes out.

I'd lied to them earlier. I couldn't put off my grieving until later. I had to do it now, get it out of system. I needed my full attention and resolve for what lay ahead. What I was planning for my "Final Round" performance would be the *most difficult act* I'd ever done in my entire life!

A burning, seething FURY was consuming my brain. I couldn't see straight. Everything around me was turning a deep, bloody red...

The *bastards!* The God-damned, slimy, putrid *cowards!* How dare they kill the one person I truly loved in order to force me to do their bidding? So they didn't want immortality if it meant losing their fleeting, temporary power over other people? Well they *didn't deserve* the Prize of eternal life. *Every single one* of those short-sighted little slugs that turned my vibrant mother into a dead corpse would *pay* in full!

"So how are you doing, Suzy? Do you need something for your IBS?"

I grimaced, massaging my aching, swollen tummy.

"Is it that obvious?" I half-grinned at the white-stubbly face of the overweight Dr. Spencer. "I don't mean to stink you out of the tent."

"You're under a lot of stress, Suzy. We all understand and appreciate what you're attempting."

"Well, my guts have a mind of their own. I tell them to behave and they just ignore me," I shrugged. "But none of your medications help, Doc. I just have to avoid trigger foods and let my diarrhea flow freely, avoiding induced constipation. Whenever I get clogged up and the pressure builds in my guts...well, that's not only painful, it's debilitating."

"Can you hang on until we get back to Earth?"

"Well, those fibrous 'nutrient cubes' are particularly bad for me. Thankfully I've a few of my dehydrated, plain bean burritos left. Softened up with water in a microwave they're tolerable."

"Have you tried the pizza?"

"Yep—but it's got too much sauce, too spicy for my sensitive guts. Plus as a vegetarian I have to pick out the meat products. And the thick bread is *way* too fibrous for me, constipating my intestines. It's delicious on my lips, but in my present stressed-out state my guts just can't tolerate it."

"Well, I wish I could mix you up a nice vanilla milkshake, Suzy. I know that since you were a little kid those are soothing to your intestines. But I don't know how to program that damn food dispenser."

"Neither does anyone else," I sighed. "How the subversives did it is still a mystery. Regardless, I think the pizza and carefully rationed beer are helping restore order among those who remained and..."

"*You see what these animals do?*" a loud voice proclaimed to all within earshout.

I was about to leave the med tent, having just been assured that my Mom would be shipped in a refrigerated casket to Earth within the hour. Anderson had recovered enough to accompany her body. He would see about getting her back to Sulphur for a proper burial. Dr. Spencer had kindly changed that awful subject to something else: my ongoing chronic medical problem.

And there—standing beside Dr. Spencer—was Billy.

I hadn't heard him enter the tent. But then again, my mind was fuzzed-out. Too much had happened too fast. I just wanted to get back to my tent and crash for twelve hours.

"Couldn't *you* have prevented this?" I angrily accused him. "Or at least, couldn't you have the Lords preserve her body in a viable state until it could be repaired?"

He sighed deeply, now avoiding my fierce gaze.

"As I told you before, the Lords only grant those privileges to winners. We're still mere contestants. There was nothing I could do, Suzy."

His eyes were red, apparently from crying. His long, flowing white hair was twisted and wild. The scabbard holding his ceremonial crystalline sword was askew on his white robe. His face was ashen. He looked ill.

"I thought you were our 'intermediate' who spoke for the Lords?"

"I'll let you two speak in private," Dr. Spencer gulped, hastily departing.

Together with my dead mother I was confronting a person I'd thought was a strong ally.

But he'd been less than honest with all of us since we arrived at the Galactic Core. What was he hiding?

"I am their Advocate," he stated. "But as I've told you before, I'm not God. In many ways the Commissioner and her Time Keepers' technology is already far beyond my capabilities. The Lords gave me a few tricks to convince my fellow humans I'm an official emissary. But other than that, I'm as helpless as anyone."

He staggered, almost collapsing.

I grabbed his thin arm and led him to a chair. He was trembling. It was easy for me to forget how old he was. I still saw him as my snotty younger brother.

"You're sick. Let me call back Dr. Spencer."

"No!" he grimaced, his wrinkled face twisted in pain. "It'd be a waste of time. I'm dying, Suzy. There's nothing Spencer or anyone else can do. In human years I'm well past one hundred. My organs are shutting down. This was my last assignment from the Lords."

I was stunned. I slowly sat down next to him.

First Mom and then him? Was I losing everyone I held dear?

"But you're still alive. Surely they can place you in time-freeze until we can...?"

"Hah!" he laughed ruefully. "I begged them to do the same for Dad. But they gave me the same answer I gave you. To them we're on the level that *ants* are to us! Only if our planet can win the 'occupied' status can we receive their privileges. Otherwise, we're just clever curiosities."

"But...there's this eons-long Competition, their pursuit of our beautiful star-spanning Music, their willingness to put Outposts in orbit around our planets, and then give us incredible Gifts through the Spheres! How could they possibly regard us as mere ants? That makes no sense to me, Billy."

"Sure it does, Suzy. Even as humanity relentlessly destroys its own birthplace, don't a few of us still try to preserve dying species? We pave over a pristine forest with parking lots but still give a token nod to 'bio-diversification', especially to helpful insects like honey bees. Or we can appreciate the potential extinction loss of a beautiful bird and its unique songs, while still acknowledging it is far beneath our own level of achievement and intelligence."

"So we're part of a Galactic preservation project?"

"I don't know exactly, Suzy," he admitted, feebly reaching out to clutch my hand with a scrawny fist. "Maybe so...finding and preserving the best Music that's evolved throughout the Galaxy. It's truly 'above my pay grade.' From my perspective—what I've managed to pick up on their home planet—we're just one of many of their initiatives that reach out across our Galaxy. We're lucky we happened to grab their attention when we accidently broke into subspace. Otherwise they'd not even have noticed us overrunning and destroying our planet."

"I suppose..."

"If you can bring home the Prize, though, it'll save our planet—and me!"

"What? I'm just not that important to..."

"Just look at the latest stupidity of our species!" he continued his rant. "For God's sake, Suzy, our rulers have *banned music!* Music is one of the few existential achievements of humanity. But the repressive governments we've created in both of our human Dimensions are trying to kill our greatest achievement. And it's all in the name of 'security': to force *other* people to 'dance to *their* tune'. Hah! Even that incredibly idiotic policy is self-inconsistent."

He was breathing shallowly, clearly over-exerting himself. But facing the fact of our murdered mother's corpse lying on the table behind us, he was finally letting down his guard. At last I was getting the truth out of him.

"I'm not arguing with your observations, Billy. But I'm not convinced we need an outside agent to force us to tamp down our excesses."

He laughed bitterly.

"We're *not* going to save ourselves," he grimaced. "Humanity is fatally flawed. Face it, Suzy. All the major religions predict an agent of God returning to Earth to save us, knowing we can't save ourselves. Frankly, we just haven't evolved beyond our animal motivations. We're stuck at the evolutionary level of being just smart monkeys. We destroy our planet while our little tribes war with each other over shrinking territories. If we don't win this Galactic contest, our civilization is doomed."

"That's a rather stark assessment."

"We'll go the way of the dinosaurs, Suzy. Maybe it won't happen overnight. After all, it took millions of years for the dinosaurs to finally go extinct. But in the end all that will remain of us will be fossilized bones. *Homo sapiens* will keep fighting and squabbling into the future, with remnants lingering on for maybe thousands of years. But in the end we'll destroy ourselves: either through exhausting the resources of our home planet, or clogging it with our mountains of waste, or in a self-conflagration from atomic weapons or worse. Admit it, Suzy. *You're our only* hope!"

"Well, I agree things will be grim back home if we lose, but..."

"And you're *my* only hope," he desperately concluded.

I was struck silent, not knowing what to say.

"It'll happen quickly, Suzy," he whispered to me. "If we win, those of us here at the Galactic Core will be the first to be blessed. That includes *me!* We'll finally be worthy of 'preservation'. For those who voluntarily take the Collar, tissue regeneration will become the norm. I *won't* have to be an old, dying man anymore! You'll *save* me, Suzy, along with everyone else."

I still wasn't buying into this "messiah" stuff. That was too much hype. He'd already admitted he wasn't God and the Lords were just an ancient, higher-evolved biological species. And surely his "regeneration" couldn't be instant immortality. There had to be more to the puzzle than what he was admitting...

—and yet I was convinced I already knew the whole truth. He was just confirming my worst fears.

"So this is what you've been hiding?" I accused him. "This entire exercise was just to keep you alive?"

He groaned, his wrinkled face twisted in pain. He leaned in close to me and whispered so only I could hear: "Yes, I've been selfish," he admitted. "Even to not warning you and the world of the dangers..."

"Dangers?" I snapped at him. "What are you talking about, Billy?"

"I'm so sorry," he sobbed, tears dripping from his reddened eyes. "You didn't think this fabulous contest was free, did you?"

I grabbed him by his thin shoulders and shook him hard.

"Tell me!"

"It's already happened," he again whispered so that no one else could hear, evading my intense gaze.

"*What's* happened?"

"Before this, no one outside our solar system even knew that Earth and its riches existed."

"Riches?"

"Earth's vast mineral and water resources, but mostly its incredible biological diversity that..."

"Oh my God!" I cut him off. The awful truth hit me. I whispered back to him, also careful not to let any of those outside the tent hear me. "Are you saying that *not* only the Lords and their peaceful past winners can tap into the Sphere broadcasts?"

He nodded, not meeting my eyes.

"There are...many other ancient races out there," he whispered back to me, "who are not as benevolent as the Lords."

"And we've just advertised our presence and riches across the Galaxy!" I gasped.

"The winners are protected. But the losers..."

"*I'll do my best to get Earth what it fully deserves!*" I loudly proclaimed, standing up.

I knew that all those listening outside could hear that shout, just as they'd heard what Billy had previously loudly described.

"I knew I could trust you, Suzy...I always could," he whispered to me. "I should have told you earlier. We *have* to win or we're ripe for plundering by predatory, technologically superior alien races. You're my older sister and I love you...uh..."

He slumped off the chair onto the floor, his eyes closed.

I felt at a protruding blood vessel on his leathery neck. He wasn't dead. But his heartbeat was erratic.

"Dr. Spencer!" I called out. "I need your help!"

He and his assistants rushed back in, clustering around Billy. They lifted his frail body onto an examination table.

"Can you do anything for him?" I anxiously asked.

"I heard what he said about his condition," he sighed, pushing his sliding black glasses up onto his nose. His double chins quivered. He looked as ragged as I felt. "I can stabilize him temporarily, but it's clear he's dying. He doesn't have much time left."

"How much time?"

"If he makes it through your final performance, I'll be surprised."

"Please do your best, Doctor," I softly instructed him. "He's my brother."

Dr. Spencer was inserting i.v. lines into Billy's shrunken veins as I left the tent. I knew he'd do everything within the capabilities of modern human medicine. But death knows no limits. Those criminals who fired a bullet through my mother's heart proved that axiom. Eventually, everything dies.

This was our greatest fear: the certainty of death. The Galactic Lord's offer of *cheating death* was what fueled the hysteria over this competition. If the world leaders had known the danger of exposing us to a hostile Galaxy they'd likely still have insist we proceed. Even Billy had succumbed to the Lords' siren song. But I knew it was a *false* hope, though I had to keep up appearances. My desperate *plan* was crystalizing.

Unlike the preliminary continuously sequential performances, the final three contestants were spaced out, one per day. Also, all three races got to view each other's concerts simultaneously with the judging planets.

So on the fifth day of our extra week we got to see a solo performance from the race that'd scored third-place in the overall competition. Tomorrow would be the second-place team. Then we'd finish things up the last day.

I was with the remaining Principals in the Operations Tent viewing the performance via its baby Sphere, as were other tent communities across our Dome. Fully half of our people had already returned to Earth, assured they'd still get the limited planetary broadcasts. Half remained to see the contest through to the end and assist me in any way possible. I was immensely grateful for their loyalty, but terrified by what would happen if I lost.

Likely, despite their present fawning encouragement, they'd tear me to pieces on the spot!

"It's starting," I gulped as my mind was taken over by a startling Vision (playing out for my concert-director mind as a grotesquely scripted sequence):

A SINGLE, BLUE-GLOWING CRYSTAL IN THE DARK

Its pulsations <u>penetrating through our eyes</u> into our brains
All around us the Universe **throbbing and vibrating** in tune
<u>Shaking our bodies</u> like leaves in a hurricane
BRIGHT YELLOW SPARKS ERUPTING AS A STREAM
EACH FLASH OF LIGHT EXPANDING INTO A SUPERNOVA
The burning smoke <u>searing our nostrils</u>
The **concussion blasts** of their explosions slamming together
COMPRESSING THE ONE CRYSTAL INTO A TINY PINPOINT
Provoking one single note splitting the cosmos in half
A MIRROR IN WHICH WE NOW SEE OURSELF
REFLECTED BACK AS AN ELDERLY MAN OR WOMAN
Feeling "flippity, hoppity," **vibrant youth** slipping back on us
A LITTLE BABY JOYFULLY SUCKLING AT A NIPPLE
Warm milk <u>gurgling in our eager mouths</u>, rich and sweet
WE SPROUT INTO A MAN OR WOMAN AND SEE OURSELVES
Holding hands we laugh and twirl around our sister/brother
<u>*Hearing ourselves*</u> *singing to the Universe and each other*
TWO CRYSTALS HOVERING SIDE-BY-SIDE IN THE DARK...

And then it was over.

"What the *hell* was that?" Sanako gasped, slapping her hands to her head and pressing hard. She had a dazed look in her squinted black eyes.

Exactly 20 minutes had passed while we were totally entranced. The temperature in the Operations Tent had risen by ten degrees from the intensity of the received performance.

"Whatever it was..." Swami Satchidananda marveled, fingering shakily at his long gray beard, "—it was beautiful!"

Bing Crosby just shook his head, smiling wryly.

"That ain't music," he pronounced. "But maybe it's even *better* than music!"

"I think it was simple reproduction," Allen Toussaint mildly observed, "pure and clean. It translates for any living creature. Anything that's alive has to reproduce."

"Whatever it was, let's see their score," I directed them, getting my team focused back on our task.

As the blazing mental image of the *crystalline concert* faded, our main scoreboard took its place.

As before, the judging races had five minutes to award their points.

The percentage summation was already at 94.3887%. As we watched, it quickly climbed past 95%. Then as the clock ticked down, it went past our previous high score of 95.3893%. The *crystalline race* that had previously been in third place was now in first place, ahead of us! As the full five minutes passed by the score stopped at 96.1362%.

For a moment we all sat in silence, shocked.

"Maybe you should just have sex for your final performance," Edison grinned, breaking the silence. In his young, resurrected body the man was certainly not the scholarly, dour man of science depicted in history. "I volunteer to be your partner."

For the first time in weeks I smiled, feeling genuinely amused.

"Well, unfortunately for you, Sir," I primly replied, "no additional human performers are allowed on the stage. Otherwise, you'd be high on my list of possible fornicators!"

He shrugged good-naturedly.

"Masturbation?" Janis Joplin leered, getting into the giddy mood of the group. She tossed her mop of hair provocatively. "I'd be glad to give you some personal tips!"

"I think we'll stick to my present plan," I mock-coldly replied.

Everyone laughed. Good, the tension from our being blown out of the water was relieved. Now we could get back to work...

"Ok, folks, let's analyze what we saw. Clearly, I've got to do as well if not better. What were the main elements?"

"It was a universal experience," Mother Hildegard solemnly stated, "not even lewd or sinful—almost spiritual."

"Yes," I nodded. "Any other living creature could understand the need to reproduce—whether they are made out of rock, flesh, or pure energy."

"There were no pauses," Jacopo ventured. "For having only one participant, it was brilliantly staged and sequenced. One element moved directly to the next without allowing time for anything to drag."

"Yes, no boring repetition," I agreed.

"The scope was cosmic," Louis Armstrong sighed in his husky voice. "It showed one little rock, then the whole universe, then back to individual sparks, then exploding stars, and finally back to each of us. That's what I've always tried to do with my trumpet solos, induce that sensation."

"Hey, I wish you were out there instead of me, Satchmo," I smiled. "But you've got to help me achieve the same effect."

"Oh, most certainly," he nodded, wiping sweat from his broad brow with his iconic white handkerchief, "We all behind you, Miss Suzette."

"Did you see how that transmission acutely impacted all of our senses?" I pointed out. "This is the first time you've been on the receiving end of all this alien equipment. I've seen a lot of these in my privileged sampling of past winners. You need to *tweak every circuit here* to make sure that my performance is *equally* provocative! I want those crystals out there vibrating to *my* music! I want them— and every other connected alien lifeform—to intensely 'hear', 'feel', 'smell', 'taste', and 'see' within their sensory frameworks *everything* that I do on the stage. Replay and analyze that transmission in every detail."

"With pleasure," young Edison laughed.

"Well, not *too* closely," I admonished him wryly.

"Hey, I dig it," Jimi Hendrix frowned, one of his elegant dark-skinned hands scratching thoughtfully at his towering afro. From all my Principals I least expected the drugged-out master of the "flower child" psychedelic electric guitar to be the most serious of my eclectic group. But then again, he'd done things with his guitar strings, amps, and reverberations that no one else of his time-period could duplicate. "To win, we've got to not only 'rock' our nearby stars, but the whole Galaxy! It's groovy, man."

"I always preached that musical vibrations can alter the Cosmos," Satchidananda smugly summarized. "We've just now *seen* and *felt* it done. It is beyond amazing!"

"Yes, I *heard*, *tasted*, and *smelled* it as well," Bing Crosby nodded in admiration. "My ears are still ringing, my tongue feels like it was dipped in acid, and my nose is scorched from those supernova blasts. It was the bee's knees!"

"It wasn't insects, Bing—crystals!" Janice laughed.

"Sorry, old slang," Bing smiled. "It was, what do you young people say today...cool?"

"More like smokin' hot!" Armstrong grinned.

"Well, whatever the superlative, that's *exactly* what we have to do to them!" I emphatically agreed with them all.

"So we'll have to ramp up and expand the output range of..." Edison began to discuss the details with Sanako.

"Just see that we likewise overload *their* senses!" I snapped at them, now back to my stressed-out Commander mode.

"I wish we could get your brother to help us to..."

"Even if he weren't in a coma, you know he's constrained from giving us details," I cut off that line of thought. "Let's just hope that tomorrow's second 'final round' performance doesn't set an even higher bar for us. Honestly, I don't even know how we're going to beat that bloody crystal, let alone a performance that's even better."

That sobered them. They knew my practice sessions were coming along well. But "well" wouldn't cut it. I had to be *spectacular!*

And I would be. I'd stun them all. Of that, I had no doubt. My plan was proceeding just as I expected. But there was one more critical element I still had to put into place...

As the others went off to their tasks I pulled Edison to the side.

"Tom, I've got a favor to ask of you."

"Name it."

"I need you to figure out a way to give me, during my performance, *total control* of all the Concert parameters."

He frowned, puzzled.

"But can't you already...?"

"Yes, I can make unilateral on-the-spot changes. But what I need is an 'over-ride' capability that *locks out* you and everyone else here at the Operations Tent."

"But, why do you...?"

"I'm probably not going to use it, Tom. But I need the psychological edge of being in *complete* control: such that, say, if I sense a need to ramp up the 'touch' parameters while my fingers are rippling over my acoustical guitar strings then I can instantly make it happen with no second-guessing or modulation back here. Remember we've only one shot at this. Can you do this for me?"

"Well, I can certainly check with Sanako and George on..."

"No! This is just between you and me. They can't know."

"But...?"

"Look, Tom," I smiled shyly at him, tucking my arm around his, "I trust you. George is brilliant, but a showman himself. He might tweak anything under the pressure of the moment. Sanako...well let's just say I don't trust her at all. Anyone else messing around with the controls—among your many technicians and assistants—one little accident or miscue and we lose the competition!"

"I can see what you're saying, but still..."

"Like I said," I soothed him, "I'll probably not need it. After all, in our full two-hour performance I had overt over-ride authority but only used it once at the end, right? In spite of the severe disruptions, we'd practiced so well the entire team responded flawlessly."

"Yes..."

"It would mean *so* much to me," I smiled sweetly, putting my hand lightly on his.

"I'll see what I can do," he gulped.

The next day we were all gathered back in the Operations Tent around its baby Sphere. We were eagerly awaiting our last competitor's performance, while simultaneously dreading how good it might be.

I grimaced, clutching at my churning guts.

"Are you ok?" Scott asked, clearly worried.

No, I wasn't "ok." I wasn't ok at all! But I didn't want my bodyguards or anyone else knowing I was suffering big-time from my IBS.

"Want some more pizza?" Scott asked, handing me a slice. Clearly he was mistaking the grumblings of my stomach for hunger.

I waved him off. I was eating nothing but pizza. My mouth found it incredibly delicious. But it had far too much fiber for my delicate guts. My intestines were loaded to near exploding. I was constipated worse than anything I'd ever previously endured, even during my oxycontin days.

I only had one single plain bean burrito left. Though I found those soothing, I couldn't eat the last one. It had a big job left to accomplish.

"It's starting," Bing pointed.

My mind slipped again into script-mode, highlighting each and every scene and conversion...

One little round blue seed falling from a purple sky

A "swishing" and "zinging" as it plummets

BRIGHT ORANGE MUD SWALLOWING THE SEED

Sputtering and spitting as green tendrils slashed through the mud

ERUPTING OUTWARD AS A LAWN OF **SILVER BELLS**

Flower-like structures gleaming and glittering

Tinkling and jarring and clanging in an ear-splitting cacophony

GREAT **RED TRUNKS** REACHING UPWARD TO THE SKY

Clouds of white spores bursting from the chiming bells

COATING THE TRUNKS IN SNOW AS THEY DANCE IN UNISON

The bells settling down into a racing harmony of glee

The trunks intertwining into a Palace towering up to a Sphere

ELECTRICAL DISCHARGES RACING UP AND DOWN

Lightning crackling and arcing down onto the forest

A furious horde of stampeding thunder blasts exploding

Dissolving and melting; falling and thudding; merging...

THE **ORANGE MUD** ABSORBING IT ALL, EXPANDING

Changing into one giant clanging Bell announcing Armageddon

PULSATING WAVES OF **RAINBOWS** INTERTWINING

And slowly combining, resolving, and metamorphosing...

LEAVING BEHIND ONE LITTLE BLUE SEED

Singing plaintively to an empty Universe...

And then it was over.

"God, what was *that?*" Sanako gasped.

Exactly 20 minutes had passed since we'd first fallen with the seed into the mud.

"I think it was a similar theme as the last one," Roy Acuff shakily observed.

"There was a theme?" Brother Frederick frowned, stroking his short beard nervously.

Lelea, sitting beside me, shuddered: "It reminded me of when I was a little scared kid being trained to become a fanatical cannibal."

"Yes, the theme was death and renewal," Harriet Tubman nodded thoughtfully. "That one seed we saw became a whole symphony, then a civilization, then a kernel for energy and creativity, and finally the means to start it all over again. Yes, it was life summed up in twenty minutes."

"It was like an alien farm scene," Roy Acuff agreed. "It didn't have the depth of the last performance, but was wider in scope."

"Let's see the score," I said as the scoreboard image came up.

It started at 92.3467%. By the time the five-minute cutoff came up, it had only arisen to 94.8631%. It was far below the blue crystal's high of 96.1362%.

"So what does that tell us?" I asked the assembled Principals.

"We can't go with the same theme," Allen Toussaint said, pursing his lips. "*Renewal* is worn out."

"Then I think our present performance is right on track," I firmly stated.

Sanako looked doubtful.

"The whole future of humanity rides on your decision," she coldly replied. "Our original 2-hr performance was joyful and hopeful. I think a smaller version of that would compete well with what we've seen in the final round."

"You mean to celebrate life?" Mozart asked.

"Exactly," she stated firmly. "Don't give the Lords and the voting planets more weird vibrations that..."

The Swami glared at her.

"—puzzle them. Instead, give them rock and roll!" she finished triumphantly.

I grinned at her: "Sanako, I never knew you were a rocker."

"Well..." she ruefully replied. "I'm a loyal citizen of the State and agent of the Commissioner. I don't listen to illegal noise. But during my travels through Time I admit I've gone undercover to a few concerts in addition to Woodstock."

"Is that right, girl? Am I your favorite rocker?" Jimi Hendrix grinned good-naturedly at Sanako.

"You are...very good, indeed," she slowly stated, "—but my favorite rock group of all time is the Beatles."

"Ah, old school," Hendrix snorted cheerfully. "Yep, outside of me they're my favorites too."

"Then I'll try to put more of an uplifting, rock-beat into my performance," I concluded. "But I still think the theme I've selected is our best shot."

"What, 'remembering'?" Sanako replied snidely. She was back to her aloof, arrogant persona.

"*You* 'forget', Sanako, I've seen hundreds of winners already," I reminded them all. "You've only seen a couple finalists. As the Advocate for our world, I've had privileged access to the recorded winners. It's not one single theme that wins. The thrust of the winning performance varies across the eons. But my 'cincher' was seeing the present 'blessed' societies. I've had privileged access to virtually visit many of them via their planetary Spheres."

"And what is it you see there that they lack the most and would likely appreciate more than anything else?" the Swami sincerely asked.

"Their pleasant, peaceful societies need to be *reminded* from whence they came," I informed them. "By forcing the voting planets to recall their racial histories they'll be struck with not only gratitude but nostalgia. That's what all the winning performances had in common: an ability to *strike to the common heart* of all living creatures, no matter their present form or origin. After all, that's the essence of Music, isn't it, the emotional resonance?"

The others in the tent were silent. Either they approved of what I'd said or were intrigued.

"So, shall we go do the dress rehearsal? Afterward you can each give me your critique. We have until tomorrow to incorporate any last-minute tweaks."

They nodded and turned to depart. Outside, floaters were waiting to take us to the central Stage.

I caught Edison by his elbow, holding him back.

"Well?" I asked him.

"It's all set," he whispered conspiratorially. "You'll see a new icon on your contact-lens virtual display. It's a *lock*. Click on it and it'll snap closed, preventing anyone external to the presentation-dome having access to you or altering the settings. Click it again and it opens."

"Thanks, Tom. You're a peach!"

He grinned shyly. "Maybe afterward...?"

"Maybe!" I brightly answered, speeding up to catch the others.

Yes, I liked him. But romance was out of the question. If I'd wanted a 'relationship' with him, Scott, Maurice, or anyone else I should have done it previously. Now, I was out of time.

[*Nine...eight...seven...six...*]

I was in the center of the elevated, orange-rock, stadium-sized stage. It was just me, a lower multi-sensory microphone for my acoustical guitar, a similar standup mike for my singing, my synthesizer keyboard, and its attached singing mike.

No other person would be allowed onstage at the Final Round performance, by order of the Lords. So the stadium-sized Stage's small Dome was activated, its force field excluding anyone but me from entering. But that didn't mean I didn't have an army of support personnel back at the control tent. They would produce all the special effects commandeered from the pliable orange stone, modulate and transmit the sounds and images, and steer the filtered two-way feedbacks from the audience onsite, back on Earth, and from the voting "blessed" planets throughout the Galaxy.

So I wasn't all alone. It just felt like it.

Even my non-human companion Scotty, sitting there attentively at my feet, didn't relieve my isolation.

It was a full dress rehearsal. I was uneasy because it was being fully recorded for subsequent detailed analysis. There'd be no interruptions. I was dressed in my "iconic" Suzette Kingly outfit: natural orange-blond hair, minimal makeup, blue-brown plaid long-sleeved shirt, white tank top, old blue jeans, and white tennis shoes. On a stand beside me sat upright my bright red electric guitar, ready for my closing sequence.

[Three...two...one...*now!*]

I was sitting on a stool holding my vintage acoustic Gibson "hummingbird" guitar. It was a beautiful classic guitar with a cherry sunburst motif. I'd had it since I was a kid. Its sound was both mellow and resonate.

I slowly strummed the opening chords then launched into a nostalgic rendering of "*Try to Remember*," written by Tom Jones for the 1960's musical comedy "The Fantasticks." The whole intent of the show was to help people mentally go back in time and remember the *emotions* that set them on their path in life...

A FARM ON A BEAUTIFUL SEPTEMBER DAY BATHED IN GENTLE SUNLIGHT; RIPPLING FIELDS OF YELLOW GRAIN; CATTLE GRAZING IN GRASSY MEADOWS; WITH STRAPPING YOUNG MEN AND WOMEN TENDING TO CHORES...

"...when life was so tender..."

THE YOUNG MEN AND WOMEN EMBRACING, KISSING; RUNNING HAND-IN-HAND ACROSS MEADOWS TO BUBBLING CREEKS; GIGGLING AND LAUGHING AS THEY PEALED DOWN TO SKINNY-DIP IN THE COOL WATER...

"...try to remember, and if you remember—then follow!"

A *guitar riff* as a brief interlude... switching to the internal mike, I got up and danced with Scotty in circles.

Yes, I couldn't have any other humans present. It was still a solo performance. But everybody loves a fluffy, friendly dog!

SNOW FALLING AS THE LEAVES DROP FROM THE TREES; THE GRASS GOES BROWN, THE CATTLE MOVING TO THE BARN...

"...deep in December it's nice to remember..."

I moved from the stool over to the synthesizer as I finished the words, pounding out the melody in full-piano mode; then launching into a wild upbeat improvisation. Scotty did his part prancing about the full keyboard, barking excitedly. Simultaneously I clicked through a random selection of keyed-up programs that brought in surprising combinations of beats and other instruments.

Then settling back to the melody of "Try to Remember" I invited all the audiences to join in on the final verse (now, only the studio audience; next day everyone would be linked in)...

[Clue all audiences to sing along...]

Then, without a pause, locking in an adaptive program to the synthesizer that was the near equivalent of an accompanying band, I moved back to the standup mike, this time with my "iconic" red electric guitar.

A launched into a spirited rendition of my own song that I'd written especially for this occasion: "Rock the Stars!"

It wasn't just a random theme. Much as "Try to Remember" was written especially for a particular musical, my song was an *anthem* I'd written for this whole Galaxy-wide, eons-long contest.

I shouted as loudly as I could as Scotty barked furiously:

<u>"ROCK THE STARS"</u>

Why do we love Music?

ETHEREAL, GHOSTLY SCENES OF FIJIAN NATIVES
DANCING AROUND LALI DRUMS; MISSIONARIES IN
CHURCH SINGING BELOVED GOSPEL HYMNS; GREGORIAN
MONKS CHANTING IN A CATHEDRAL; JANIS JOPLIN WAIL-
ING TO A CROWD OF THOUSANDS; MUSICIANS IN A SYM-
PHONY ORCHSTRA RAPT AT THEIR INSTRUMENTS; A
COUNTRY WESTERN BAND IN A SEEDY BAR;

That throbbing flowing vibration
Be it adorned with flowery words
Or naked notes resonating

LOVERS HOLDING HANDS STARING UP AT THE STARS;
LITTLE KIDS FROLICKING ON A PLAYGROUND; A FOOTBALL
TEAM PLAYING A CHAMPIONSHIP GAME IN A STADIUM;

Could it be our beating hearts
Amplified strong and hard
Convincing us we're still alive

A VIEW OF THE MAGIC MARBLE OF BLUE-WHITE-GREEN EARTH AS SEEN FROM THE SURFACE OF THE MOON; GLIMPSES OF THE OTHER PLANETS OF THE SOLAR SYSTEM; MOVING ON OUTWARD TO VIEW OUR ENTIRE SPIRAL ARM IN THE MILKY WAY;

In a cold, uncaring Universe
We're not just a meaningless curse
Doomed to experience everything
That's in an instant snatched away

A FRESHLY DUG EMPTY GRAVE, CASKET AT THE SIDE; GRIEVING RELATIVES CRYING; A COMFORTING MINISTER HOLDING A BLACK BIBLE;

Leaving us dying, empty, and lonely
But knowing the soaring heights of love
And the bitter taste of rancid hate
The awful expanse of outer space
And the nestling breast of Mother Earth

A DIZZYING VIEW OF MAGNIFICENT FORESTS, JUNGLES, AND WILDLIFE OF MOTHER EARTH; ZEROING IN ON AN ELDERLY WOMAN SEEDING A GARDEN; SEEDLINGS SROUTING UP INTO FRUITS AND GORGEOUS FLOWERS;

In a flash we bloom from a seed to a tree
And reach up to the distant sky
Sprouting enticing, lovely fruit

DESCENDING FROM THE BLUE SKY, A GLOWING WHITE SPHERE;

Hoping that somewhere up above
Is something reaching down for us
Humming a happy tune...

[Clue all audiences to join in...]

And together with the studio audience (and next day everyone else on planet Earth and elsewhere, speaking in English or their equivalent language translations) we again sang the final words: "HOPING THAT SOMEWHERE UP ABOVE...IS SOMETHING REACHING DOWN FOR US...HUMMING A HAPPY TUNE."

Scotty, right on cue, stopped barking and lifted his pointed snout up expectantly at the sky.

I flicked my virtual "lock" and saw all the other indicators on my augmented reality screen turn red. Above me, the transparent protective Stage Dome turned milky. Great, all external manipulation was frozen. But before anyone else noticed what I'd done, I flipped the lock back to "open." The flicker of the Dome would hopefully be disregarded as some momentary glitch.

[Countdown to end: *nine, eight, seven...*]

And my last, escalating guitar riff up to the highest notes, accompanying my highest register voice: **"Singing a happy tune!"**

[*Two...one...*]

I dropped my head in humble acknowledgment of the anticipated vast audience, one hand stilling my guitar and the other landing on Scotty's cutely panting head.

Uproarious clapping swept over me from the "studio" audience.

It was a good dress rehearsal. Now, would it be enough?

From the enthusiastic praise I received afterward with only minor criticisms, I saw I'd achieved my goal. The dress rehearsal audience—the Principals, crew, stadium audience, Earth audience, Phoenix, and The Commissioner—were all placated.

They wouldn't expect it until it was over.

Tom had done his job well. I'd better at least hold hands with him that evening, keep him happy so he didn't tell anyone of our subterfuge. I would beg off anything more romantic, rightly claiming I needed to be fully rested for my final performance the next morning.

But he'd be anticipating a great reward after the last performance ended.

Too bad he'd be disappointed.

I'd turn in early to my tent so they couldn't see me trembling in fear. And meantime, I'd stuff my gurgling guts with as much as of that nasty pizza as I could tolerate.

Chapter 27

<u>BETRAYAL</u>

***Reach on over** to the other side*
Don't be slow and don't be shy
Take what you need without regret
Or you'll end up saying "what the heck?"

I know it doesn't sound so very nice
Your Momma says it isn't polite
But if you don't jump you'll be too late
For a very, very important date

A lot of people fear to try
They say that thing is much too high
If you stretch your muscles out that far
You're liable to trip and fall down hard

But sometimes you must say: "Is it worth
The trouble and risk of making us hurt?"
When it'd be so much easier to stay
From that danger far away

But in the end you've got to be true
If not to others then to you
So "grab-the-bull-by-the-horns" without delay
And you'll be proud of what you did that day
Whether you live or die, it's your last goodbye...
The Suzette Anthology, Lyrics 27

[Nine...eight...seven...six...]

I was again in the center of the elevated, orange-rock, stadium-sized stage. As in my dress rehearsal, it was just me, a lowered multi-sensory microphone for my acoustical guitar, a similar standup mike for my singing, my synthesizer keyboard, and its voice mike.

We'd done the rehearsal so many times now all I had to do was just relax and let it flow. I'd never before been so well prepared to do a solo performance.

Yes, no other person was allowed onstage at the Final Round, by order of the Lords. The stadium-sized Stage's small energy-Dome was in place, actively excluding anyone else from entering. But yet again I knew I had an army of support personnel back in the control tent. They were primed and ready to produce all the special effects commandeered from the pliable orange stone, modulate and transmit the sounds and images, and steer the filtered feedbacks from the audiences. It was my faithful control crew which connected me to the thousands onsite, the billions back on Earth, and the thousands of voting "blessed" planets scattered throughout the Galaxy.

So I wasn't all by myself. It just felt like it.

Ever eager to do his part, Scotty, my allowed non-human companion, sat attentively at my feet.

It was the Final Performance upon which the fate of the Earth hung. I was yet again dressed in my "iconic" Suzette Kingly outfit: natural orange-blond hair, minimal makeup, blue-brown plaid long sleeved shirt, white tank top, old blue jeans, and white tennis shoes. On a stand beside me sat my bright red electric guitar, ready for my closing sequence.

Everything was just as it should be, supposedly...

[Three...two...one...*now!*]

All of my staged *visuals, sounds, smells, tastes,* and *tactile interactions* were now broadcasting live via the Sphere to my studio audience, all those watching on Earth, the Galactic audience of thousands of voting planets, and the Lords of the Galaxy.

In that instant I realized this would be the worst time ever for any human being to have *stage fright...*

Just as in my dress rehearsal, I was sitting on a stool holding my vintage acoustic Gibson hummingbird guitar. Again, I noted its beautiful cherry sunburst motif. It would be a shame to damage the magnificent instrument. But what had to be had to be.

I stood up, carefully placed the guitar flat on the stool, and crossed my arms, staring straight ahead.

[Uh...Suzette? Your new improvisation is costing you overall time. You'll have to compensate later for pausing now. Are you trying to build up the drama?]

Sam sounded concerned but not worried. He knew I was a consummate professional. He knew I didn't do things onstage that weren't carefully planned or appropriate to the moment.

But then a *full minute* went by as I stood there seemingly frozen in place: doing a fine imitation of the bronze statue of me beside the artesian fountain in Sulphur, Oklahoma.

Now there was real panic sounding in my earbud communications...

[Suzette! Snap out of it! This is no time for stage fright!]

Yep, they thought I'd lost it.

Urging me to "snap out of it" was Darlene. Sam had wisely patched her into my control feed.

Yet another minute went by as I stood there frozen in place. There was now only eighteen minutes left for the rest of my performance.

Even Scotty looked worried. Still sitting faithfully at my feet he looked up at me, whining softly.

[Uh, hey girl. I dig it. You're all alone out there in front of the biggest audience in human history. Look, if you need a break, come on out of the stage Dome. I'm waiting right outside the barrier. It's cool, really. I can take your place. I can do your numbers easily, maybe not as well as you but still groovy. Sam says I can take your place until you're ready to continue. Ok? But if you're sick or something, I'll just come on in anyway. But that'll be embarrassing if the guards gotta pull you off the stage, so...]

That was sweet of them. They were asking my permission for Jimi Hendrix to run in and grab my electric guitar. Yep, the Lords might even allow a "pinch-hitter" for a frozen solo performer. Who knew? But to get in, they'd have to breach the energy barrier...

—and I wasn't allowing any such thing! With a flick of my eyes, I activated the LOCK icon.

Instantly, the stage Dome went from clear to milky white. On my virtual control panel, all the previously green indicators went to red. I could still control everything. But those outside were powerless.

I continued to stand impassively, arms crossed.

[Kingly! What the hell are you doing? How did you lock us out? Whatever you did, reverse it. We can't help you if you've frozen all our controls!]

It was Sanako, the sneaky bitch. I don't think I'd ever before heard such desperation in her normally steely voice. I took momentary pleasure in her bewilderment and anger. Her dearly beloved Commissioner must really want her Lord-allotted dose of immortality.

I dispassionately viewed a scurrying group of crewmembers gathering beyond the now-milky energy barrier. They were bringing up Stadium-supplied construction equipment, desperate to bull their way through. The surrounding audience of thousands looked agitated, uncertain of what was happening.

They were getting the idea that I wasn't exactly fighting to get them their tremendous Prize.

If not the bulldozers, that increasingly agitated mass of humanity might launch itself at the barrier.

Let them try. They'd fail. Even if they could breach the barrier, which I doubted, it'd take them too long. Keenly watching my virtual chronometer, I patiently stood frozen in place until the countdown hit *seventeen minutes remaining.*

[S-Suzy...it's me, B-Billy...they woke me up to t-talk to you and...]

I ignored their desperation-fueled attempt to reach me through my dying brother. I discounted his scratchy, feeble voice in my ear. Against the Dome, the agitated audience had become a mob, now surging futilely against the energy barrier.

I noted on my display that only *sixteen minutes* remained.

Suddenly I dramatically reached into an inner shirt pocket, plucked out a plastic-wrapped item, and held it high above my head for all to see.

I knew that my vast audience was shocked by my sudden and peculiar movement. The mob outside the Dome stopped moving. An entire Galaxy was transfixed.

Clearly visible on the wrapping were the words: *bean burrito*.

Still clutching the packaged burrito, I grinned widely, hunched down, stuck my elbows out at my sides, and did a cartoonish jig (Scotty hopping up and down excitedly at my side) as I loudly launched into a well-known kids' song:

"BEANS, BEANS, THE MUSICAL FRUIT...
THE MORE YOU EAT, THE MORE YOU TOOT ..
THE MORE YOU TOOT THE BETTER YOU FEEL...
SO LET'S HAVE BEANS AT EVERY MEAL!"

I ripped open the package, took a big bite out of the burrito, and chewed grotesquely with my eyes stretched wide and a huge stage-grin plastered on my face. Simultaneously I tossed the rest of the burrito to Scotty who happily gobbled it up.

I threw the wrapper up into the air where it fluttered briefly before falling back to the red stone flooring. Then I perkily and cutely *bent way forward*, placed my hands on my knees, and stuck my butt up against the multi-sensory mike meant for my acoustic guitar.

Unfortunately for the studio audience, Earth, and the rest of the Galaxy, the fabric of my worn out blue jeans was thinned and frayed.

I relaxed my tortured, packed guts and *cut loose*...

"*BRRRRuuuuppppttttt...fffiiiiirrrrrrttttttt...ptptptptpt...FFRRRA AAPPPT...bbbbbllllllaaarrrrrrrttttt....whup, whup, whup....*"

Ah...sweet music to my cramping, clogged guts!

I swear a *green, noxious cloud* momentarily enveloped the guitar multi-sensory mike...

Even *I* was taken aback by the horrendous, foul stench. I'd been holding it in for such a long time the accumulated blast was near-lethal!

[Oh, God! (hack, cough, gag)... *What the bloody hell?*]

Great, the full sensory effect had transmitted to all the viewers!

Even Scotty looked shocked, cringing away from me with his long ears plastered down to the sides of his narrow head.

I slowly stood back up, put a *fierce glare* on my face, and again stood with arms folded in front of the two microphones.

[*Fifteen minutes* remaining, Suzette!   Quit clowning around! *You've just disgusted the entire Galaxy!* Whatever you're planning to turn this debacle around, do it!]

[Everybody stand back. I'll get through to her.]

Ah. It was Billy again. He sounded much stronger. Dr. Spencer must have injected him with a stimulant of some sort. I dispassionately watched my brother from several hundred yards away SMASHING his crystalline sword again and again against the energy barrier. It made a marvelous "ringing" sound.

"BLANG! BLANG! BLANG! BLANG! BLANG!"

A cloud of *brilliant sparks* blazed and glowed from each of his mighty blows. It was quite spectacular. He must be drawing on all his Lords-endowed special powers to make this last heroic attempt to subvert my overt betrayal of humanity. He looked just like the Greek God Zeus what with his angry face, white hair and beard, white robe, and mighty sword calling forth lightning bolts.

It was truly high drama...

—as he *split open* a slit into the Dome and leapt through. Even worse, the ragged tear remained behind him, alternately widening then shrinking. Oh, hell! The breach was stabilizing! I might outtalk Billy, but the enraged audience would overwhelm me with their sheer numbers.

"We can get in! We can stop her!" the thousands massed around the stadium screamed, surging as one for the gap...

—reached first by Lelea and her people: warriors, Chiefs, priests, and fierce tribal women.   They were poised to come flooding through...

Oh, Christ, I'm royally screwed!—I groaned to myself. *Lelea and her fighters will be here in moments, sweeping me off the stage so Hendrix can take over the performance...*

But Lelea stopped dead in the middle of the wavering gap—and in a stage-gesture WINKED at me!

She turned and faced the raging crowd, her tribespeople poised in rows in front of her, now facing the onrushing thousands. The Fijians' blunted but still functional stage weapons—war clubs, spears, and battleaxes—were held at-ready.

"Stay back!" she yelled. "Soozee knows what she's doing!"

But the enraged crowd did not obey. They SLAMMED into the lines of Fijian warriors, engaging them in fierce hand-to-hand battle.

[*Ten minutes* remaining, Suzette...]

As Billy stalked toward me across the stadium floor, Scotty ran to meet him.

I was sad, thinking that my faithful robot dog was deserting me. But then again, Scotty *was* a gift from "super-Billy," a product of the advanced technology of the Lords. I didn't blame him for abandoning a sinking ship...

But Scotty skidded to a stop before the relentlessly advancing white-robed man and began snarling and barking at him!

With a disdainful kick, the white-robed man sent the robot dog spinning off to the side.

Urf!—the dog yelped before lying still.

Oh, Christ! Did he kill Scotty? I needed him alive for later! And there wasn't time for Anderson to come onstage and try to repair him and get him working again, even if he'd be allowed, which he wouldn't. Wait, he'd already transported out with Mom's body and...

My mind's wandering! I've got to stay focused till the end.

[*Nine minutes* remaining, Suzette...]

"I don't want to hurt you, Suzy!" Billy shouted as he advanced on me, his sword held high, "But either you turn off that app you secretly constructed locking the rest of us out or I'll *rip* the contact lenses out of your eyes and do it myself!"

"Don't even think of it!" I warned him, slowly reaching down to pick up my acoustical guitar by its neck.

"You always thought you knew better than the rest of us, Suzy," he growled as he bent into a crouch, his razor-sharp sword swinging menacingly before him. Who knew that the "ceremonial" blade could be an actual weapon? "You never cared what others thought. You just went head-on with whatever weird scheme popped into your head. Well, your 'fart-joke' won't stop the human race from putting its best foot forward. There's still time for Hendrix to take your place and..."

"The only way you'll take me offstage is hauling away my corpse!"

"Then *so be it!*" he screamed at me as he lunged forward.

I danced to the side, *smashing* my guitar down on his head. *CLANG!*

He staggered back, angrily swatting away the broken slabs of my busted wooden instrument.

"You stupid child," he snarled. Then, unexpectedly, he *swirled* his lower robe at me—wrapping it about my legs, pulling my feet out from under me, and *slamming* me down onto the hard stone floor.

Momentarily stunned, I looked up helplessly as with both hands he lifted the sword high over my head, about to fling it down into my skull!

Arf! Arf! Arf!—Scotty barked as he leapt into the air catching Billy by his long white beard, spinning him around.

Billy sliced at the dog, knocking him off.

"Not me! Attack Suzy!" he yelled. "Priority over-ride!"

I hopped up, grabbed my *solid* electric guitar by *its* neck, and swung it like a baseball bat into Billy's ribs.

I heard his bones "snap" as he crumpled to the floor. Another swing of my "bat" knocked the sword out of his hands...*DING!*

And a third swing aimed at his head left him in a heap at my feet...*THUNK!*

Blood was gushing from a gaping head wound.

[*Eight minutes* remaining, Suzette...]

I slumped to the floor beside him, cradling his bloody head in my arms.

Scotty again lay crumpled off to the side, motionless.

"Billy..." I gulped, looking down into his now ancient, crinkled eyes. His surge of adrenalin-fueled super-strength was gone. His Lord-powers were likewise drained.

All that was left of what once had been my snotty little brother was a dry husk.

"Hey, Suzy," he half-smiled around swollen, mashed lips, "I love you..."

Sobbing loudly, I bent over him, wrapping my arms around his shriveled upper body. His head lolled against my own as *he whispered his last words* into my ear. I nodded, reluctantly agreeing with him. What he told me in those last few words, inaudible to anyone else, was awful. I didn't want to do it. But even with him there dying in my arms, I couldn't take the chance. It had to be done!

[*Seven minutes* remaining, Suzette...]

I lifted him up to stand wobbling on his feet.

Bending I snatched up his sword and *plunged* it into his chest. He *gasped* as the bloody tip emerged out his back.

Seemingly in slow motion he fell backward as I still tightly clutched the haft of the sword, feeling the blade slip out of his body as he dropped.

Scotty slinked forward, whimpering. He tentatively sniffed at Billy's dead body. Then he looked at me, growling. The fur stood up on the back of his neck as he barred his teeth at me.

"Stay back!" I ordered him. But he'd transformed into a different dog than my sweet Scotty. Apparently Billy's last order succeeded in changing his programming. I saw that his previously mellow-brown, sweet eyes now glared a BRIGHT RED!

Arf! Arf! Arf!—he barked at me as he circled menacingly.

I held the sword high, tip pointed down. Then as the new "devil-dog" Scotty lunged at me I *jammed* it through his back. He "yelped" piteously, tried to crawl away, and then lay still in a pool of spreading red blood.

I guess even androids can bleed...

Oh no, not the dog! Sure, kill millions in a brutal war, decapitate your captured enemy soldiers, rape the women and drown the children—but *don't kill the dog!*

In the eyes of my vast audience I knew I was now irredeemable. I even saw Lelea in the distance gasp. She moved away from the gap in the barrier, leaving it undefended to the rabid crowd. The viewing audience hadn't seen Scotty's red eyes. What I'd done seemed to them but another deranged, evil act. If anyone had felt even the slightest twinge of pity for me after I'd stunk up the stage, Earth, and the Blessed Planets, that sympathy was gone. I was instantly the most *reviled* and *hated* person in the entire Galaxy!

I grabbed the sword and SLAMMED it time-and-again into the hard stone beneath my feet. After five blows the sword SHATTERED into a thousand pieces...the *glass-splintering* "CRACK" echoing like an explosion within the Presentation Dome.

[*Six minutes* remaining...] Sam's dejected voice sounded in my earbud.

Lelea and her disillusioned warriors had now completely abandoned the gap. But that didn't matter. Now that the sword was destroyed, the gap it had created sealed itself, just averting the onstage mob riot.

"Ok!" I shouted to the rest of the Galaxy. "Let's have a *real* rock concert! Watch how we Earthlings *love* to behave!"

I picked up my still-intact solid electric guitar. Holding it by its neck I advanced on my synthesizer. In vicious swings I savagely attacked the piano-sized instrument...

CLANG! CRUNCH! CRASH! BANG! BRONG!

I methodically *SMASHED* the synthesizer into a pile of rubble.

Panting heavily, I returned to Billy and the dog. To make sure the message was clear I did exactly the same to them...

BASH! SMASH! SMUSH! CRACK! BLASH!

In the process of beating the two corpses into shapeless heaps of twisted body parts, I drenched myself in a rain of blood and gore. Exhausted, I looked down triumphantly on the bloody piles of broken bones, raw flesh, wires, transistors, and circuit boards.

"*That's* who I am!" I shouted into the still-intact, standup microphone. "That's who we *all* are! We humans are freaking *animals!*"

AWWWWRRROOOOO!—I howled up at the Dome like a raging wolf!

I grabbed a meaty femur bone out of my victor's pile of destruction. By its length I knew it'd come from Billy. Standing tall, I held it up defiantly—*screaming* at the star-filled Galactic Core sky like a brutish cave-woman: "LET US ROCK *YOUR* WORLD, YOU BITCH-ES!"

[*Two...one...*we're off...] Sam whispered dully in my earbud.

I blinked at the *Lock* icon, flipping it back to "open."

I saw a torrent of angry humanity come spilling into the now-accessible stadium as all my virtual indicators switched from red to green.

Lelea and her surviving tribespeople were at the head of the mob, surrounding me and insisting I be tried for my hideous crimes, not lynched on the spot. I wished she hadn't saved me. I deserved to be immediately *torn to shreds* by my abused fans. But I was too weak and exhausted to protest.

Surprisingly—despite my grotesque betrayal of humanity—we still almost won the competition! Apparently our racial advocate, Billy, didn't count as an additional banned human up there on the stage.

Our final score was just short of the winning 96.1362%. The peaceful, beautiful judging races preferred crystal replication to bloody annihilation, but just barely. Though I hadn't intended to do so, the drama of my last performance captivated their attention. But a final message in English was tacked on after our score, there for all the rest of the Galaxy to see: "Suzette is hereby cursed."

Well, *duh*...

It was kind of fun to sit in a red-rock jail cell there at the Galactic Core right across from King Richard. He took grim satisfaction seeing me imprisoned for the very crimes I'd previously accused him. I alternatively grinned or stuck my tongue out at him. I just wished I still had my Taw to *throw* at his smug regal face! But they'd taken away all my personal possessions, especially my Sphere-contacting wormhole exit.

Phoenix and the Commissioner didn't want to take any chance that I might find a way to escape. After all, an enraged population of Earth—blatantly denied the greatest personal prizes imaginable—needed a scapegoat to direct their rage upon: me. The still-repressive religious radicals couldn't have the music-starved, frustrated billions rising up against them. The Commissioner's Peace Keepers were likewise still vastly outnumbered by the seething billions of the First Dimension. It would be decades if not centuries until they finally "domesticated" our Dimension.

So even though the authorities tried to slam down a lid on the world's population, their anger at me blowing our chance to gain true Immortality erupted across the planet. Yep, there ain't no anger like that of a person offered a yummy cookie, then having it snatched away at the last moment.

Millions were injured or killed in the resultant riots.

Well, I won't go into the Trial. You all saw it. It was broadcast throughout both human Dimensions.

I sat silently throughout, bored stiff. After all, I didn't need to hear the details of everything that led up to my betrayal of the human race. I'd lived it all already. Through the court-appointed lawyers I tried to plead guilty. But the court insisted on a full trial, my lawyers attempting (unsuccessfully) to argue I'd gone temporarily insane. Whatever...I just wanted to be judged and sentenced. I waved all appeals, though some were required by law. I wanted the execution to happen as soon as possible, without any delay.

Unfortunately, the trial was held at The Hague, in the Netherlands, in the International Court of Justice. Capital punishment had long been banned at The Hague. Due to the unprecedented nature of my crimes, the United Nations had to pass a special exemption allowing a one-time firing squad if I were deemed guilty (which everyone assumed would happen). It took a while for that resolution to wind its way through the bureaucratic halls. That accounts for my still sitting here in my prison cell in the "Peace Palace" at The Hague with time to write my autobiography.

It's a maximum security solitary confinement cell, so I guess I'm lucky, having the time and the means to tell my story. There's nothing else to do. And the government is obviously eager for me to certify that it was all my doing, with no blame on either the "protecting" Phoenix or the "benevolent" Commissioner.

Ok, then. I hereby totally certify it wasn't their fault! I'm the only one to blame. Just as Billy said in his final desperate attack on me, I'm prone to get crazy ideas and act on them without regard to what others think. Maybe that's how I became a pop superstar. It's certainly how I became the most reviled criminal in the history of Earth.

But that's not really why you read my lengthy book, is it? You already knew I was guilty. I admitted upfront to my "foul" deed, didn't I? What you want to know is *why* I betrayed Earth.

Well, let me satisfy your perverted curiosity.

Before that, however, allow me to *apologize*—not for denying you wealth beyond your imagination, freedom from all illness and injury, or blissful happiness. No, I'm apologizing for the necessary delay in publication of this manuscript following my execution. You see, I encrypted it with three layers of cyphers, only known to me. Yes, any good governmental agency can eventually crack my cryptic code, but it'll take a while. I wanted to make sure there'd be time for any last minute appeals or delays to be exhausted. This confession must *only* be made public after my death!

I'm dead, right? Ok, then, here's the real deal...

You may not agree with or accept my rationale for doing what I did, but here it is: winning the Prize offered by the Lords would *doom* humanity!

No, they weren't lying. Yes, they did provide all the magnificent promised benefits to their "outpost" planets. But in world after alien world that I virtually visited while studying their "blessed" societies I saw the same exact thing: *stagnant remnants* of previously dynamic, incredibly talented races. Beyond accessing the Spheres or exercising their Collars they had no technology. They had no space programs. They had no science institutions. Their populations had shrunk to the lowest viable number. Sure, the "immortal" individuals left behind were deliriously happy, but their civilizations were cold, stone *dead!*

But, you say, this wouldn't happen to us! No, we'd use our freedom from want, from sickness, from death to fuel a new Renaissance in human development. It would be a "quantum leap" in mankind's evolution. Freed from physical wants and woes we'd have massive gains in all areas of philosophy, art, scientific research, and space exploration. Right?

Huh. That's the exact *opposite* of what would really happen. I already showed you what I saw in that possible future timeline of a Sphere-worshipping Earth. Humanity had shrunk to a mere 7,000 individuals, who spent most of their time "communing" through the Sphere with each other and like-occupied worlds.

They were blissfully contemplating their own belly-buttons, lost in their leisure and freedoms.

So here's the "bottom-line": I'm convinced that the "Lords of the Galaxy" are *psychic creativity vampires*. For whatever reasons— likely their vast age having depleted their own artistic impulses—they drain the "life-blood" of the most talented, younger Galactic races.

We provide them with the stimulation they can't get on their own. But like ticks sucking blood, they carry *deadly diseases* that steadily weaken their hosts: addiction, lack of initiative, and stagnation. Thus their need to periodically reach out and drag others into their web of "blessed" planets.

Even poor Billy didn't know much about his "benefactors." But he did observe that the Lords were cool and distant, viewing us as mere ants. We were theirs to be used as they wished for their own purposes. They had no compassion for my brother or father. Again, humans were mere pawns in the Lords' eons-long game. Well, I *wasn't* going to let that happen to Earth!

I know it's hard to accept. But we owe our existence on Earth's surface to the laws of evolution: where *death and renewal* allow for *mutation and advancement,* where *struggle and fighting* winnow out the weak and reward the better-abled, and where creation is always preceded by *destruction!*

What holds true for individuals and species also holds true for civilizations.

Dear Lelea and her people, plus Losa and the Chickasaw warriors, defended me until I killed the dog because they instinctively knew I was doing the right thing: as certified by their own peoples' sad experience with colonization.

If we are ever to truly *Rock the Stars* we must accept and continually *struggle* against our own problems. Fighting forward despite our limitations, stupidities, and evil is, after all, at the heart of the best Music.

Taking a short-cut to Heaven will only guarantee us Hell.

Ok, I realize it's an academic argument. I know it won't sway most people, let alone my guards. They—and you—hate me with good reason. I neither blame them nor you. In a snap of the fingers your loved ones will wither and die. You yourself will be elderly, shriveled, and then crumble into dust. If I hadn't betrayed mankind you'd have another option: the Collar. Instead, because of my hubris—thinking I alone could dictate the fate of humanity—you're doomed.

Yes, I've killed you. By my betrayal I've murdered all of you. You doing the same back to me is only fair. Don't be ashamed that what you want more than anything else is sweet *revenge*. After all, it's only human.

And, maybe, that's truly the deepest "want" of us humans. We're tossed into a cold, uncaring Universe that births brilliant brains only to casually squash them. We're like magnificently constructed bugs splashed onto a speeding windshield. We just want to "get back" however futilely. We want to *shout out* across the Cosmos: "WE WERE HERE! THE *UNHOLY TRINITY* OF MOTHER NATURE, LADY LUCK, AND HUMAN FRAILTY WON'T RULE ME! SCREW YOU, UNIVERSE! I KNOW I'M NOTHING IN THE GRAND SCHEME OF THINGS, BUT I'M STILL *KICKING* TILL THE LAST SECOND!"

I wish we could be nobler, higher-minded. I wish we could "want" beyond our short-term selfish desires. I wish our deepest motivations could transcend and inspire. But what do you expect of us cosmic "ants" struggling to survive our own little ant-hill wars?

So I don't begrudge your revenge upon me. I screwed all of you. It's only fair you "drill" me back. Bring on the firing squad!

So that's it...oh, I almost forgot. Why did I have to fight so savagely against Billy and that lovely, faithful robot dog?

Ok, I promised to answer all your questions, so here's the scoop. As I mentioned previously, Billy told me that the losing planets would be left exposed to predatory alien races. Having advertised our riches across the Galaxy during the Contest, superior aliens would flock to us to steal our resources. I couldn't let that happen. When I threw the contest I knew we'd lose the protection of the Lords. If I was opening us up to exploitation then I had to also tamp down alien enthusiasm for raping our precious little planet. The final battle between me and Billy demonstrated to everyone watching that we humans would be tough nuts to crack.

So perhaps you agree with me that a final battle demonstrating the fierce fighting skills of humans was necessary. But perhaps you're still curious as to why I would actually *murder* the old man? Well, it's what he whispered to me in my ear, too soft for anyone else to hear:

"Your final performance can be contested as long as you, the Conductor, are alive. Even a prior recording can be submitted, such as

your excellent dress rehearsal. And I'm *required* by the Lords to announce this after the losing score appears. You *have* to kill me to stop
this from happening, Suzy. I'm already dead anyway. *Do* it!"

"I can't," I whispered back.

"You *can* do it! Do it for me. I don't agree with what you're attempting, but...I trust you, Suzy. You always thought you knew better
than me because you really *did* know better than me. Finish the job—
and make sure my corpse can't be revived."

So I killed my own brother.

Oh, and why the dog?

Killing faithful Scotty, devil-dog or not, was necessary to ensure
no leniency like "life imprisonment" was given to me. To be certain I
was executed and couldn't be used to appeal the contest's result, I had
to ensure I wasn't just hated but *reviled*. The Earth would never be
safe from the Lords as long as I lived. If anyone discovered the final
rule of the Lords for the loser planets, a new submission could theoretically be done as long as I lived. Yes, it wasn't likely since the
Spheres were withdrawn from Earth after we all transported back
from the Galactic Core. But what if another subspace-communicating
alien race visited us, or subspace again got cracked open?

The only solution was my *permanent* death.

If I could have, I'd have killed myself during the final performance. But my suicide would have *emboldened* the plundering alien
races, not scared them from risking clashing with vicious humans.

I did what I felt I had to do. And, given the same choices, I'd do it
all again, changing nothing.

But if you somehow feel a sliver of pity for me, don't bother. I had
a great life. I traveled all throughout Time. I made friends with some
of the world's greatest musicians, both living and dead. For God's
sake, I performed at Woodstock! I even went to the Galactic Core and
sang my songs for the largest audience ever assembled in the history
of humanity. What musician or performer could ask for more?

At least they took Billy and Scotty's mangled corpses back to Sulphur, Oklahoma for dignified burials. That was comforting to know.
They both become heroes for trying to stop me from betraying Earth.
I'm told their memorial services were fitting tributes, to which the
most powerful world leaders journeyed. I wish Agent Anderson

hadn't been allowed to organize the funerals and other tributes. I'm still mad at him. But Billy and my dead robot dog did deserve only the best. After all, their hideous deaths served to warn off the aliens that would have flocked to plunder our rich Earth.

Now Billy has a crypt of honor in the Oaklawn Cemetery, not far from where my mother is buried. An even bigger crypt right outside the human Cemetery contains the remains of Scotty, who captured the hearts of humans across both Dimensions. As for me, I've heard they're going to cremate my body and stuff my ashes into an unmarked grave somewhere on the grounds. There will be no turning me into a martyr. Hah!

But...it's not all negative. No, someone in the government had a twinge of pity for me. I'm sitting here on my plain, hard bunk sipping a big, thick, cold, *vanilla milkshake!* Ahhhh...it's *so* delicious! My sincere thanks to whoever provided my last meal.

I thought it might be a parting gift from my family physician, Dr. Spencer. But I've had zero problems with my IBS since being transported back to Earth. Yep, no more world-shaking farts! I'm entirely at peace. My future is clear. Even as I sit here awaiting my imminent execution, I feel no stress at all.

Hah! Those damned "Lords" were totally *wrong* about me being "cursed"!

Well, I just finished the milkshake, sucking out every last drop. That was incredibly delicious. I'm filled to the brim with liquid fat and sugar.

Life is good.

And it looks like I finished this document just in time. I hear the heavy footsteps of that "sad, old Padre" tromping down the hallway outside my cell, accompanying my executioners. I asked for Brother Frederick. He's still quite heavyset! But seriously, it's nice to have one friendly face by my side as I'm marched to the firing squad. He never did buy into the Lords' "heaven on Earth" crap. I see he's got a big black Bible in his hands. My jailors are to each side of him, carrying cuffs and chains...not necessary.

I won't put up a struggle. As I've repeatedly stated, I deserve this. One person can't be allowed to decide the fate of humanity. Such hubris alone merits execution. And, indeed, I've *got* to do this or humanity will remain in potential, existential danger!

Yes, things may look dark now. I unilaterally stopped you from winning incredible prizes that would have magically taken away all your problems and pain. But have faith, my friend. *Music* will endure and eventually reemerge. That's something wonderfully positive to anticipate! Without Music we have nothing. It's what truly connects us to God. And it will take us into a future far more glorious than anything those alien leaches offered us!

Ah...they're kindly giving me a couple minutes to finish up typing. I was right about the Authorities wanting my full confession.

So here's my final "take home" message: I know that you *don't* only want to be happy in the moment. I was just venting when I harangued you on that point earlier. As you saw, I myself went down that enticing rabbit hole. I totally agree with my good friends Alice, Janis Joplin, and Jimi Hendrix: pursuit of happiness sucks! Find and *do* the things that bring you *lasting* joy. Pursue your Passion with a single-minded focus and the emotions will take care of themselves. Do so whether society approves or not, whether nasty individuals say your stuff sucks, or even if *not one single person* ever appreciates what you do! Screw them! Know that the *true reward* is not in getting to "heaven" but in overcoming hard knocks *fighting forward* on the good path, step by grueling step.

Like Jesus said, the easy path—whether downward *or* stagnation—leads to hell. The truly rewarding path is the upward journey!

God smiles upon *these* people. Be one of them!

Smell the flowers. Admire the scenery. Marvel that you're still here in this moment, alive, and still capable of trying to make your dreams come true (whether they do or not). Hug those that you love. Laugh with those who give you the energy to "keep-on-keeping-on." Politely shrug off those that try to hold you back. Enjoy whatever you've got while you've got it. Grab life by its horns and hang on tight for the entire amazing ride. *Savor* the ever-present sweet Positives. Learn and grow from the bitter Negatives. *Thank* your critics for bringing insights that make you a better performer. It's all an incredibly exciting Cosmic Concert done for the *true* Lord of the Universe.

Rock on!

Chapter 28

EULOGY

She was a pistol

Hot, hard, compact, and lethal

A challenge to love or to hold

She went to the top

Then fell to the bottom

But never boring, always fun

You welcomed her warm hug

Until, that is, she squeezed too tight

And you just had to put up a fight

When you extinguished her light

And discovered the darkness inside

Poor little girl longing for approval

She gave it all up for integrity

Above applause of the crowd

The supposed purity of her soul

Shown in a higher form of Music

Far beyond question or doubt...

The Suzette Anthology, Lyrics 28

<u>Updated Declaration of Execution, International Court of Justice</u>:

"Six months prior to the publication of her official memoir, Susan H. King (a.k.a. "Suzette Kingly") was executed by military firing squad in the inner court of the Peace Palace in The Hague, Netherlands. Penalty of death was decreed following her "guilty" judgment of unprecedented crimes against humanity. The event was televised live, broadcast throughout all the United Earth Empires and Nations, across both human dimensions. The event occurred beneath and

469

within a Time Keeper-authorized energy barrier precluding any tampering with the remains. Death was certified by three examining physicians, from numerous projectiles puncturing vital organs including heart and brain. Cellular death was confirmed by relevant onsite laboratory tests. The corpse was remanded to relatives in the town of Sulphur, Oklahoma for cremation. Her posthumously published autobiography further substantiates her egregious guilt."

Obituary, published in the Sulphur Times-Democrat:
    "The ashes of disgraced favorite daughter 'Suzette Kingly' were interred at the Oaklawn Cemetery in a private ceremony last Monday. The gravesite was unmarked. An official memoir will soon be published: *The Girl Who Rocked Stars.*' When available, the local Phoenix Council recommends purchasing a copy. Her confession is said to be a cautionary tale about immoral excesses gone wild. Her undisciplined life resulted in disaster for both herself and the human race. Despite reputed claims in the autobiography to the contrary, her riveting story illustrates the pernicious effect of unfettered music upon the fabric of society and why such filth must forever remain banned."

False Urban Legend, attributed to subversive "Jiggers":
    I woke up inside a cramped, cold, steel box. It was totally dark. I was naked. I was shivering uncontrollably. Every inch of my body ached. I felt like I'd been run over by a truck.
    "Where the hell am I?" I whispered, feeling tentatively around.
    As my eyes adjusted, I saw faint glimmers of light down at my feet. They were coming through a tiny break in the steel container...a doorway?
    "Ah...ok," I grunted. I felt behind my head, noting a depression.
    I was in some sort of metal drawer. And if I just pushed hard enough behind my head while jiggling my legs up and down...ah yes! I felt a latch pop open outside and dim light flood in as the drawer jerked outward.
    "Let's get out of here," I ordered myself. I squirmed downward, over a high lip, and *flopped* painfully out onto a hard cement floor.
    Exhausted from my efforts I took a minute to get my bearings. Only a dim red nightlight illuminated the room. I saw two steel tables

on wheels. Three other closed drawers were set into the wall behind me. My opened drawer protruded above my head. I saw what looked like laboratory equipment hanging by hooks on the walls. In the corner was a furnace...sporting a heavy iron door coated with black ash.

"What is this place?" I gasped, trying to get my mind working.

My head hurt like it'd been rapped several times with a hammer.

The last thing I remembered was going down a long corridor in chains, walking out into a sunlit courtyard. On one side a line of uniformed military types stood with rifles. On balconies above the court were many people, a lot of them jeering and shouting at me. Mass-media video cameras were rolling and...

Oh, Jesus Christ, I was executed! This was a mortuary! Even more, it was a crematorium. They were preparing to incinerate my corpse!

"Oh...no, *no,*" I moaned. "How can I be alive?"

I staggered to my feet and looked into a full-length mirror. Yes, I could see numerous round bruises on my chest and head. I'd been hit by a barrage of bullets! But the wounds were almost all completely healed...?

And then I remembered the pronouncement of the Lords on the scoreboard: "Suzette is hereby cursed."

"As long as I'm alive...the future of humanity is uncertain."

I lurched over to one of the steel tables, grabbed a loose scalpel, and in one ragged jerk *sliced* my own throat!

As the blood gushed out and I choked on my own life fluid, I dropped to the cold floor and writhed in agony.

Everything went black.

I opened my eyes to the same dimly lit room. It must still be night. I felt at my neck. Although it was coated in clotted blood, the ragged wound was completely gone.

"What would happen if I was cremated?" I wondered, wearily dragging myself back up to my feet. Actually, I didn't want to know. Just cutting my own throat had hurt like hell. I didn't want to find out what it felt like to be burned alive.

Instead, I hurriedly scooped out old ashes from inside the furnace, piling them up into my half-opened drawer, hoping the funeral director would get the hint: the government wanted ashes and he could just hand them over. Unexpectedly, my hand grabbed onto something hard. Holding it up, I saw a blue marble. Hah! Maybe my luck was turning. Grabbing a hanging lab coat I slid the marble into its pocket and staggered out of the crematorium, looking for an exit.

The place was locked down like a vault, but to keep people out rather than prevent someone inside from escaping. However, I had to make it look like a robbery. After searching for a few more things, I deliberately broke some doors as I exited.

The Lords exacted a terrible punishment on me. I couldn't reveal myself least I imperil my entire species. But granted a second chance at life, an all-consuming *rage* now infused me. First of all I wanted to find out who killed my mother. And then there were those damned alien "Lords." I *lusted* to teach them they couldn't toy with *Homo sapiens.* Soon those alien bastards would sing and dance for *me!*

Right or wrong, more than anything else, I wanted *revenge!*

I guess my final, noble "sermon" fell on deaf, dead ears...

Sulphur, Oklahoma Police Report: Williams Funeral Home break-in:
(*Published in the Sulphur Times-Democrat*)

"John Williams reported last Saturday morning that his Funeral Home was broken into Friday night. Several locked doors were smashed open. Blood was found, indicating the intruder was injured. Janitor clothes and the petty cash drawer were stolen. Investigators suspect a connection to local Jigger unrest due to the recent arrival of Suzette Kingly's body. Williams, however, reports that Kingly's corpse had already been cremated. The Funeral Home's security cameras were disabled, but a nearby fast food establishment's external cameras caught a single shadowy figure emerging about 4:00 A.M., joined by a stray canine. Fingerprint and blood analyses were inconclusive. The specimens were smeared or badly corrupted. Unless further developments occur, the vandalism is tentatively attributed to a clever vagrant and his dog. Citizens are directed to report any similar or possibly related incidences. Be nice!"

THE END

[continued in: *The Girl Who Could Not Die*]

Thank you for reading!

Dear reader,

I hope you enjoyed **The Girl Who Rocked Stars**. It was great fun to apply my own musical background to Galactic concerts. And plucking my favorite singers and musicians out of history was fabulous. The sequel to this book, **The Girl Who Could Not Die**, finds Suzy deep in the criminal subculture of a dystopian Earth, seeking sweet bloody revenge.

I hope you are intrigued by the sequel's central question: 'How do you continue to live when you want to die?" One answer is you find the courage to establish a brand new set of compelling priorities.

Finally, I need to ask you for a favor. If you enjoyed this book and would like to encourage others to read it, **a review written by you** on the Amazon.com page for this book would be greatly helpful. It's hard to get reviews nowadays and your support will be very important to both me and other readers. If you'd like to do this, I sincerely thank you in advance for your time. It can be as long or short as you wish.

Thanks again for reading my **Girl with the Turtle Tattoo** books and experiencing with me the awe of "driving imagination to new extremes."

Sincerely,

About the Author:

Daniel Basil Lyle holds a Ph.D. in Biology, is a lifelong amateur herpetologist, taught medical immunology at a University, completed a career in cell biology research, lectures on how to apply theological and psychological principles in practical ways, and has a strong interest in all aspects of cosmology and physics. From a small kid he was fascinated with dinosaurs. As such, he has always lived with exotic creatures, including harmless snakes, all housed in his own homemade habitats. Some of his tame pet pythons and anacondas ranged up to twelve feet in length. He is the author of over thirty books, many of which are religious in nature. His writings go beyond the ordinary, exposing deeper aspects of life. His books are meant to be fun, conversational, and helpful. His various works are available at LylePublishing.com and Amazon.com. The "Girl with the Turtle Tattoo" science fiction series was inspired by paintings done by his mother, movies adapting Stieg Larsson's crime novels, and various men and women sporting spectacular body-art tattoos. The author hopes that you, the reader, find his characters spontaneous, quirky, surprising, and even thought-provoking—just as did he!

www.ingramcontent.com/pod-product-compliance
Lightning Source LLC
Chambersburg PA
CBHW071632260626
47170CB00001B/62